$\mathcal{P}$REY

THOMAS EMSON

snowbooks

Proudly Published by Snowbooks in 2009

Copyright © 2009 Thomas Emson

Thomas Emson asserts the moral right to
be identified as the author of this work.
All rights reserved.

Snowbooks Ltd.
120 Pentonville Road
London
N1 9JN
Tel: 0207 837 6482
Fax: 0207 837 6348
email: info@snowbooks.com
www.snowbooks.com

British Library Cataloguing in Publication Data
A catalogue record for this book is available from the British Library.

Hardcover 978-1-906727-28-4
Paperback 978-1-906727-36-9

Printed and bound in the UK by J F Print Ltd., Sparkford

PREY

THOMAS EMSON

PART ONE.

LAURA GREENACRE MUST DIE.

CHAPTER 1.
RUN FOR YOUR LIFE.

BLACK MOUNTAINS, SOUTH-EAST WALES – 3.30 P.M., MARCH 7, 2008

SOPHIE Thorn, fifteen and not knowing if she wanted to live or die, watched the creature tear up the mountain towards her.

She squinted, trying to make out the animal and see what it was.

The gloom crawling across the mountains made it difficult to see. The monster had white-gold fur. It looked like a horse to start with. Then it looked like a bear. Then a very large dog.

And then it looked like what it was.

And Sophie knew she should've started running a while ago.

Drizzle made the grass slippery. It was difficult to run in wellington boots. Lactic acid quickly filled her thighs, and they grew tired.

The slope seemed to stretch, to angle upwards. Her lungs burned, and she could feel the tobacco swirling about in her chest, choking her of air.

She glanced over her shoulder.

Bad mistake. Her belly turned icy. The creature was forty yards away. She saw its long teeth and her mind scattered and she started babbling.

She was going to die.

Death didn't scare her, but the way of it did.

This would be painful.

Fear tightened her chest. She panted for air. She was almost at the top of the slope. Gasped with relief when she reached the crest.

Her legs felt like paper. She kept running, but she was swerving from side to side. Downhill made it harder to keep her balance. She was crying, and the tears blurred her vision. She yelled out for her home, for her dad.

Her dad, who'd already saved her life four months previously.

Her mind filled with what had happened. The betrayal hurt the most. She'd been in love. Knowing she wasn't loved back damaged her more than anything the men did to her after they bundled her into the van.

She looked over her shoulder.

Twilight brushed the ridge.

She gasped with relief.

The creature wasn't coming.

Had it been real? Had it been conjured by her broken mind?

Sophie started to slow and looked behind her to make sure the monster wasn't coming. Sweat coated her skin. Her clothes were stuck to her body. She wanted to stop. To collapse in the damp grass and gasp for breath. Her chest was so tight, and if she didn't stop soon, she'd drown; she was sure of it.

She tripped and lunged forward. She reached out her hand, and it slammed into the ground. Pain jolted her shoulder. She yelped, did a forward roll, skidded on her backside. Her foot plugged a divot. Her body carried on going, and she screamed when her ankle twisted. She gritted her teeth, tried to get up. Her ankle buckled, and the pain made pins and needles explode in her head, and she cried out.

She threw a glance towards the ridge.

Nothing. Just the darkening sky.

The werewolf had been in her mind.

She sat in the wet grass for a moment to catch her breath and listen to her heart.

It sounded like it was grunting in her chest.

Grunting?

She furrowed her brow.

Strange noise, she thought.

She narrowed her eyes, listened. Her heart grunted and beat at the same time.

The back of her neck grew cold. The grunts lost time with the beats. Sophie shivered and whimpered.

She turned her head, knowing what she'd see.

The white-gold werewolf appeared on the crest of the hill. The creature hunched down and glared at her. The blonde fur bristled. The animal's rhythmic grunts became louder, building into a roar.

Sophie shrieked till her throat charred.

And the werewolf hurtled towards her.

CHAPTER 2.
MY YARD.

RASHAD Drewitt named himself "Shed" after he'd killed a man for the first time when he was twelve.

"I have shed my old skin, my childhood skin, and today I am a man – I am Shed," he said.

That skin had stretched over the years to become full and heavy, and now it leaned into Porous's face and said, "This is my yard. Any bitch coming into my yard should bring a bone with which to appease me. I see no bone from you, bitch."

Shed's breath reeked of cigars and garlic. Porous screwed up his face. The odour made him sick.

He couldn't go anywhere. Shed towered over him and the other thugs horseshoed them in the alley. Moonlight showed the thugs' faces, creased with hate. Porous's guts squirmed with fear.

He said, "I tell you, Shed, I had appeasement for you, but I got mugged."

Shed scowled. "Mugged? Who mugged you? You tell me who mugged you, I'll have them castrated. You go ahead and say, Porous."

"Shed, I don't know who it was mugged me. It was dark, man. He was Asian, I guess."

9

"Asian, huh. I send my sniffer dogs out, they bring me back a suspicious-looking Asian, you have a look at him. Yeah?"

Porous shrugged, thinking his plan wasn't working that well but going with it. "I guess," he said.

Shed shoved him against the wall. Porous's head cracked the brickwork. Stars burst in front of his eyes. His legs gave out, but Shed held him up by the collar.

"You know why we call you 'Porous', Porous?" said Shed.

He shook his head. Shed's fingers pressed into his throat. Choking him. He gargled, trying to say no, he didn't know why they called him Porous.

"Because" – Shed gave him a shake – "you're so full of holes, Porous. Everything you say. Full of holes. Bullshit. That's why no one trusts you. But I, I gave you an opportunity. I have, you see, the milk of human kindness coursing through my veins."

"I – I appreciate – appreciate what you did, Shed. I – I was – coming to pay homage."

"Homage my ass. I'm six-four, three hundred pounds of bullshit radar, Porous. You're so full of holes, the shit is leaking out of you, boy. Now you know you're unwelcome in these parts. You know that pain of death is the pain upon which you return. So why you back? And this time, give me some truth."

Shed let him go and Porous gasped. He sucked in air, and his throat hurt. He made a face.

Shed said, "Throat hurts?"

"Yeah, man."

Shed drew out a .44 from inside his long, leather coat. Porous grew cold. He threw his hands up and pressed himself against the brick wall.

Shed said, "Want me to blow a hole in it, let the pain out?"

"That's – that's OK, Rashad. I'll – I'll be cool."

"Good." Shed tucked the .44 in his belt. The gun moulded into his massive belly. He said, "Share with me your reasons for being here."

Porous's throat was dry. He coughed, clearing away the nerves. "I – I got family, Shed. You know – my girl. The kids."

"The kids? You ain't got offspring, Porous. You ain't got a girlfriend or a boyfriend, neither. You're one of God's creatures that breeds with itself. Parthenogenesis, I believe they call it. Means you fuck yourself, Porous."

10

Shed laughed, and his pack laughed. Porous scanned their faces. The laughter didn't come from their eyes. Those were cold and dark.

They were all big guys. He didn't stand a chance. Porous was no tough man, anyway. He was small fry. A runner who ferried dope from street corner to street corner. That was until he got greedy and pocketed the goods.

Rashad Drewitt's goods.

"Your ass is exiled forthwith, you fucking blowjob," Shed had told him two months previously, casting Porous out from the comfort of his Brooklyn square mile. "I see your ass here, I slice it off. Cheek by cheek. And then I gonna make you eat them, Porous. Is that clear as day to you?"

Porous had no choice at the time but to say that it was as clear as day.

Shed's thugs had tossed him in the trunk of a car, and for a long time he thought exile meant a bullet in the back of the head.

But they dropped him off – turned out to be somewhere in Queens – gave him a beating and left him there, bleeding and thanking Christ he was alive.

He'd come home two days later. Slept rough and ate from trashcans. He had nowhere else to go. This was where he'd always been.

"I know it's hard when a lower mammal is taken out of its habitat," said Shed now. "I know the urge is to return. Come back to what it knows. You watch National Geographic, Porous?"

"Ain't got a TV, Shed."

"Shame. Well, you can learn a lot about life and how life came to be from slime like you and how slime became – I guess, me – while other slime just stayed" – he flicked a hand at Porous – "slime. So what I'm saying is, I tell you you're exiled, that's what I mean. It's not a metaphor, Porous."

Porous made a face. Shed's talking scared him. The man was dangerous and clever. Porous had no words to match the ones Shed gave him, so he opened and closed his mouth like a fish.

A clanking sound came from the trash tub down the alley.

Shed said, "What the hell was that? Go take a look, Snow."

Snow, hair bleached-blond, swaggered down into the alley. Porous narrowed his eyes, trying to watch Snow back there in the darkness. Snow stood on tiptoe now and looked into the trash tub. He flinched and flapped a hand in front of his face.

"Stinks, man," he said.

"That's you, Snow," said Shed and he laughed, and then his guys laughed.

"Nothing in here, boss."

"Nothing?" said Shed.

"Garbage, is all."

Shed seemed to lose interest. He turned back to Porous, and Porous again felt the weight of attention fall on his shoulders. He cowered, trying to make himself look small.

"Garbage, huh," said Shed.

Porous's legs grew weak. He felt his bladder swell. He said, "Oh, man – I'll – Shed, man – I'll get lost – go back to – shit, man – please don't – "

"If you lot don't fuck off, I'm coming down there, and you don't want me to come down there, I promise you."

Porous stopped jabbering. Shed's brow furrowed. He turned and looked up. Standing on the fire escape, three storeys up, was a woman. Looked blonde to Porous. Shoulder-length hair. Nice shape to her. But he couldn't appreciate it properly at this distance, in this light.

"What you say to me, bitch?" Shed asked the woman.

Porous's nerves twinged. He wanted to run. He scanned the alley. Shed and his pack glared up at the woman. He could dart past them. Be away before they reacted.

"I'm sorry," said the woman, not sounding to Porous like she was at all, "I didn't realize the fat around your waist had filled your ears and made you deaf."

Porous gasped. He got gooseflesh. He'd never heard anyone speak to Rashad Drewitt like that. He'd known Shed since they were both fifteen – that was twenty years ago. Shed had always been top dog around here, man and boy.

But the woman didn't know this. She didn't have a New York accent. What was it? She said, "I told you to fuck off. People are trying to sleep. Did you hear me?"

"Who the fuck you talking to, English bitch?"

That was it – English.

He liked the English. James Bond.

The woman said, "What kind of question is that? I don't know who I'm talking to, other than a noisy, fat twat who should be at home with his mother."

"Don't you say nothing about my mother, bitch." Shed's voice was high-pitched. Porous had rarely heard Shed's voice getting high-pitched. Once or twice, maybe, when he was really stressed, really pissed. But usually Shed was cool and cruel. His large frame heaved. Then he seemed to cool down. His voice grew calmer. "You get your white titties back indoors, and we forget about this indiscretion."

Porous swallowed.

The woman leaned her forearms on the rail.

Porous thought, *Go indoors, lady.*

But the lady wasn't moving.

Shed rubbed the back of his neck. He said, "Did you not hear me?"

"We've concluded that my hearing is fine. If it weren't, I'd be asleep, now. I'd not have been disturbed by a bunch of overgrown kids playing gangs."

Shed got high-pitched again. "Jesus, bitch, you asking for me to come up there and put you on all fours."

There was a pause.

Then the woman said in a voice that made Porous think she was serious, "I'd like to see you try."

Shed's guys gasped and cursed. They looked at each other.

Porous went for it.

He shot through a gap.

Shed said, "Get him."

Porous made the mistake of looking back.

He tripped over a garbage bag yards from the salvation of the sidewalk. From streetlights and cars.

He screeched when a hand clasped his ankle. Someone dragged him face down along the ground.

He got a kick in the ribs that knocked the air out of him.

Shed said, "When I'm talking to a bitch, I expect you to show some patience, Porous. Stay where you are till I'm done."

"If you don't leave" – it was the woman again – "I'm going to have to come down there and bare my teeth."

"Who is this bitch?" said one of Shed's guys. "Want me to go up, Shed? Slap her?"

"No need. We deal with Porous here, then I go visit the fucking queen of England up there and show her some American hospitality." He looked up. The woman still stood there. "You hear me, bitch? After I'm done with this basic life form here," – he gestured at Porous – "I'm coming to pin you down. You hear me?"

"I think your bark's worse than your bite," she said.

Porous, experiencing pity for another human being for the first time in his life, thought, *Please stop, lady. You'll get hurt.* Shed and the guys turned back to Porous.

The woman said, "But I can assure you, mine isn't."

Shed ignored her. He said, "Get him to his feet."

Two of Shed's thugs hoisted Porous off the ground. They roughed him up, pushing their hands into his face, slamming him against the wall. They moved aside, Shed stepping in. His wide chest level with Porous's face.

"You're lucky tonight, Porous. Lucky we had an intervention."

Porous glanced up beyond Shed's shoulder. The woman stood on the fire escape. She pulled her tanktop over her head. Porous shuddered and blinked. Shed went on, Porous's eyes coming back to him:

"I was going to dispose of you because I had the urge, but now I have another urge, and a lady up there –"

Porous looked up again. The woman was perched on the railings. She looked naked.

" – is going to help me deal with it. Meantime –"

But she wasn't naked, though. Not quite. Seemed she had... Fur...

And she was changing shape...

Porous moaned. His legs gave way. He saw the woman leap, but she wasn't a woman any more.

"What the hell–?" said Shed, twisting, seeing. "Jesus Christ!"

Porous watched the huge, black animal with yellow eyes and fangs spring down off the fire escape, through the darkness, and plough into Shed and his pack.

Porous crawled down the alley towards the street. Tears rolled down his cheeks. His teeth chattered. And as he went he wished he didn't have to hear the screams and the tearing noises that came from behind him.

* * * *

Safia, eight years old and used to wandering the streets late at night, knew her dad was dead.

She'd *heard* him die. Heard his voice scream for mercy. Him and his gang. But not *just* die, though. Shed and his pack had been butchered.

Now Safia tucked herself into the corner of the trash container. She snuggled in among the garbage. It stank, but she didn't care. She was used to squalor. Her apartment was filled with beer cans, pizza boxes, rats, and cokeheads. Her mom screamed at the rats and the cokeheads, but they never left. The cokeheads said, "Shed says we stay here, Phelia," and the rats said nothing. Just chewed through Safia's clothes and ate the food.

She called up the image on her phone.

There it was. A black blur on the screen. A swish of darkness. A haze of white and red as the jaws opened. The smudge of streetlights could be seen in the background. A passing car smeared across the shot as it swept past the mouth of the alley.

What Safia had seen here was the animal.

The animal.

The one she'd read about on the internet. The werewolf from England. The internet was her friend, her only one in a world of grown-ups who shouted and screamed at each other, who sometimes killed each other. Safia had found forums where they talked about this fantastical creature. She'd been drawn by the stories, and for a year now she'd followed the topics.

She didn't expect to see it here in Brooklyn.

Safia's father had turned up at the apartment earlier that evening to pick up Snow, his right-hand man. Snow was sleeping with Safia's mom, now. Safia's father didn't seem to care. He didn't really care about any of the women he'd given babies to.

Her sister Neela, who was fourteen and went out working the streets every night, said Rashad Drewitt had hundreds of kids.

"He's been making them since *he* was a kid," Neela had said.

Safia got to her feet. The garbage spilled off her. She peeked over the edge of the dumpster. Her eyes widened at what she saw in the alley.

Chunks of men were strewn around. A cat sniffed at the meat. Steam rose from the flesh. Blood glistened in the moonlight and smeared the walls and pooled on the ground.

Safia had heard her dad talk to a woman. He'd called her a bitch, like he called Safia's mom a bitch.

Then something happened. The men had screamed. The creature must've come from nowhere. Safia didn't know – wasn't looking at the time. Had already been hidden away in the trash by the time Snow peered into the container after Safia kicked the bottle.

Now she played the video on her phone. She'd only poked her hand out of the sea of garbage, over the edge of the trash container. She'd not dared look. Hoped she was focused on what was happening.

The footage played on her mobile phone. The lights flared. The car in the background swept by. Screams and growls came from her phone. The sound tinny, high-pitched. Her eyes couldn't take it all in. Everything was so quick. The black blur shot in and out of the image. Shed's men were being tossed around.

One body had clanked against the dumpster, making Safia flinch.

Then something else had hit the dumpster. Something large. The whole tub had shuddered, Safia being rocked about.

Silence fell. Safia had stayed still, the only sound her heart thumping against her chest.

She'd peered out. The man her dad called Porous stumbled out of the alley. He slipped on the meat and the blood a couple of times before he got away. It was then that she'd buried herself back in the trash to study her footage.

When Snow and her dad had left the apartment, Safia snuck after them like she did most days. She knew they were bad people, and she wanted her dad to get caught. Her mom didn't care that Safia wasn't there. Wasn't aware her daughter spent most of her time tracking Shed, collecting evidence, maybe.

Her friends around the world, the ones she spoke to on the internet, always said she deserved better. And when they'd said it, she started to believe it. She'd tell them about what she'd seen here. She couldn't wait. They'd been waiting years for this.

CHAPTER 3.
REMAINS.

MAJOR Lev Dasaev, thirty-nine, in a suede jacket he'd bought the previous day, put the phone back in his pocket and closed his eyes. He leaned his head against the wall.

Galina wasn't answering. She never answered. Out all night again, making him look a fool. Why didn't their marriage mean anything to her?

Dasaev opened his eyes. He tried to shake the thought of her from his head, but an imprint remained. She was always there, that was the problem.

He looked up and down the corridor. A *militsioner* spoke to one of the residents. More militsiya officers filed in. They lined the passageway. They spoke in whispers. They glanced in Dasaev's direction. He felt himself blush.

Were they talking about the incident, one of the most brutal attacks he'd ever seen? Or were they talking about his wife and the picture of her in yesterday's paper, on the arm of another playboy?

Dasaev turned away and entered the apartment. It was situated in the Leninsky Prospect Area. The Stalin-period building had been renovated in the Western style a few years previously. The development was in a decent area, a well-to-do neighbourhood.

Dasaev scanned the apartment.

Vasili Kolodenko's remains were scattered around the living room. Blood covered the walls. Lumps of meat steamed on the carpet. A leg hung off the chandelier.

Kolodenko had been torn apart.

Dasaev watched as his colleagues from the Ministry of Internal Affairs – or the Ministerstvo vnutrennykh del, the MVD – scoured for evidence. A toilet flushed. A dog barked.

"Parts of him have been eaten," said a voice next to Dasaev.

He glanced round and saw Viktor Staparov's shiny bald head. Staparov was UBOP, Directorate for Combating Organized Crime. He adjusted the belt around his belly and blew air from his cheeks.

Dasaev said, "Have you been testing out the facilities, Viktor?" The flush trailed off.

"I made a bad smell in the bathroom, Lev."

"You make a pretty bad smell wherever you go."

"Indian food. Can't get enough of it."

"I can see that," said Dasaev, patting Staparov's belly. He turned his attention back to the slaughterhouse. It looked like art – the cream-coloured apartment with modern furnishings sprayed in blood and meat. "Tell me about Kolodenko."

Staparov burped. "Trafficking and drugs. He ran girls into the UK and the US. He had delusions of grandeur. Thought he was one of the big boys. But he was just a common thug, really. Flirted with extreme right-wing politics. Funded small, one-man-band Nazi groups. He had a good start in life. Didn't have to drag himself up out of the shit like most of us. His father, Alexander Kolodenko, was a top dog in the Moscow Communist Party during the halcyon days. Your dad might have come across him."

Dasaev narrowed his eyes. "I've never seen anything like this, Viktor."

"No. Me either. It's a mess."

"What do you think?"

"Hey. I'm UBOP. I deal with organized crime. This doesn't look organized to me. It looks like a fucking mess."

"Were you after Kolodenko?"

"No. Like I say, small fry. His name crops up on our lists, so I'm dispatched. I wouldn't have hung around if he'd been shot or knifed or burned." He gestured at the bloody scene. "Just wondered what you lot at the detective division made of it, that's all."

Dasaev scanned the walls. The blood had sprayed from Kolodenko's body. Dasaev tried to visualize the gangster's death. Kolodenko was wearing chinos and a white shirt. They'd been shredded in the attack. His remains showed evidence of teeth marks – big teeth.

"Someone's brought a wild animal in here," said Dasaev, thinking out loud. "A big one, like a lion or a bear. We should check the circuses and the zoos."

Staparov said, "What happened to a good old-fashioned gun to the head? Even slitting his throat would've been more traditional."

A uniformed *militsioner* entered the apartment. He had a quick glance at the damage and turned his pale face to Dasaev. "Major, we've got the bodyguard outside."

Five minutes later, out in the building's parking lot, Dasaev smoked a cigarette in the bracing wind.

Yuri Tomich leaned on a wall, his arms folded. He wore a scowl. He was built like a T-90 tank. He was unshaven. Wore a leather coat, black Levis. Hair sprouted from his gnarled knuckles. They'd been broken a few times, Dasaev guessed. Probably on someone's face. Three *militsioner* lingered nearby.

Dasaev tossed the cigarette away into the snow.

He said, "How long you been with him, Tomich?"

Tomich glared. "Do I get to go up, *musor*?" he said, using the slang for *militsioner* that meant "trash".

"You get to go up when I say, Tomich."

"Fucking *musor. Eb' tvoyu babushky.*"

"You tell me to go fuck my grandmother again," said Dasaev, "I'll have you pissing blood and confessing to this and every other unsolved murder in Moscow by the end of the day."

"You threatening me?"

"Yes, I'm threatening you. When did you leave Kolodenko last night?"

Tomich's shoulders sagged. The fight had gone out of him. "I left at ten. He had guests. His English doctor."

"English doctor?"

"Yeah. Kolodenko's into living forever." Tomich guffawed. "This doctor, he gets paid to find the elixir of life."

"Didn't manage it, then," said Dasaev. "You know this doctor's name?"

Tomich shrugged. "We call him 'Doc', that's all. Kolodenko called him 'Doc', too. Early seventies, mean-looking, likes to fondle girls."

"You said 'guests'. Who else?"

Tomich said, "A woman. She'd been coming along for the past few weeks when the doctor visited. Might have been his wife, don't know."

"Describe."

"English. Sixties. Glamorous. Elegant. I'd fuck her, and I like them young."

CHAPTER 4.
MEET THE SMITHS.

BARCELONA, SPAIN – 4 P.M., NOVEMBER 10, 2007

RUTH Templeton said into the phone, "Laura Greenacre must die. John Thorn must die. There is no question. There is no debate. There are to be no excuses. I will murder excuses."

She dabbed her brow with a handkerchief. She bristled and then allowed her heart to slow. The rage faded, and she relaxed her shoulders.

She said to the caller, "We are Mr and Mrs William Smith, if you're trying to get a hold of us," and then told him where they were staying.

Ruth sat on the couch. She'd finished her second gin and tonic. The glass stood empty on the coffee table. She stared through the window at the bruised sky. There would be rain later. It would wash away the blood she'd spill.

A groan drew her out of her thoughts. Lawrence Procter dragged a suitcase towards the bedroom. He strained and heaved. The tendons on his neck stood out. His face reddened and he grimaced.

Ruth clicked her fingers. He looked her way and she made a drinking motion with her hand. He dropped the suitcase and sighed.

"There's nothing the matter," she said into the phone. "Lawrence complaining, that's all. Has there been anything in the papers regarding Moscow?"

"Nothing here," said Ellis Cole. "Not in the papers. It's all government this, government that."

"Naturally," said Ruth. She imagined Cole, the office-bound werewolf hunter on her payroll, sitting in his bedsit in Newcastle, surrounded by piles of newspapers, books, pornography, printouts, video tapes, computer discs. He used to be a lawyer, initially representing Laura Greenacre. But then he turned on his client and abandoned his career, becoming obsessed with finding Greenacre after she'd disappeared in 1999.

Procter brought the drink. Ruth made a face and waved him away, mouthing "lime" to him.

Cole said, "It gets a mention on some websites. Not much detail. But the forums, of course, are crawling with it."

"Crawling," said Ruth, motioning for Procter to put the drink on the table. He grunted and went back to the task of dragging the suitcase through to the bedroom.

Ruth said to Cole, "Tell me about these forums."

"For eight years the internet speculation about Laura Greenacre has intensified. She disappeared after Trafalgar Square, after Michael's – sorry, Ruth."

"That's all right. Vengeance makes me strong. I lost my son, my nephews, and my brother because of that girl. My hate for her gives me power. I shed very few tears these days."

"I'm glad. So anyway... the forums. They've always focused on her. There've been sightings, or alleged sightings. Nothing concrete. There are a lot of Laura admirers out there. I think they like the rebel in her. The fact that she clearly showed courage at Trafalgar Square, saving people from – I'm sorry."

"Yes. All right, Ellis. There's only so much forgiveness that I'm capable of."

"I – I understand."

"Anything on that bastard John Thorn?"

"Nothing. He went off the map. I keep in touch with his ex, a girl called Julia, but the court order makes it difficult these days."

"You shouldn't have enjoyed your work so much. You should have kept your hands off her."

"She's pretty. Couldn't help myself. Lawrence has had his hands on her, too. She was the first one to report him."

23

Ruth sighed, glancing at Procter. *Men*, she thought, *weak*.

"You're still married?" she said.

"Technically, yes, but Karen left me last year."

Ruth didn't really care. It was only habit that caused her to ask after people. She was well bred.

"I'm coming to England in the next few days," she said.

"Really?"

"Yes, but we might not meet. Far too stupid a thing to do. Unless you have remarkable news for me. And" – she glared at Procter as he hauled the case into the bedroom – "I'm travelling with a fugitive."

"All right," he said. "It would be good to meet – "

She cut him off. "You keep me abreast," she said. "I'm sending you this month's cheque."

"That's good news, Ruth. Bills, you know."

"Yes. All rather mundane."

She paused. Night approached. Time to hunt.

"Find them for me, Ellis. Find them so they can die. Find them so that I can avenge my family."

CHAPTER 5.
PHOTOGRAPHS.

IT had gone badly.

His first words to her were: "Very fitting that we meet in a shopping arcade, Galina."

Her green eyes blazed. The fake eyelashes flickered. "This isn't a very exclusive mall, you know. More practical. Hoped I could exchange you. They'd be more likely to take you back here than somewhere in Petrovsky. I still have the receipt." She flashed her wedding ring.

Dasaev said, "I thought you'd exchanged me already."

He slapped a copy of *Komsomolskaya Pravda* on the table. The paper nudged his cup, and coffee spilled into the saucer. Galina picked up her own cup and turned away from him. Her gaze washed over the shoppers in the arcade. Some of the patrons in the coffee shop glanced towards them, perhaps recognizing her from today's paper.

The headline on the tabloid blared out in red that a Second World War veteran had been robbed of his medals. A headshot of the hero looking glum stared out at readers.

But the blurb across the bottom of the page showed a photo of Galina on the arm of Sergey Kirovski, a footballer eight years younger than her.

25

Dasaev felt himself blush.

"I can't bear to look at it," he said and swiped the paper away.

"No one is forcing you to."

"You're forcing me, Galina. Every time you're photographed. Did you sleep with this one, too? Should I beat him up, is that what you want?"

"A real man would."

The rage flared in his chest. He lit a cigarette. Drew the nicotine into his lungs.

He said, "When I beat that clown of an actor up for sleeping with you, it almost cost me my rank. You loved it. Adored being in the bloody papers, the magazines. I won't beat them up any more. It's not their fault. You snare them, tell them your marriage is a sham. I know you do – that's what the actor said. Why?"

"A model's career is short. I need to be looking at other ventures, other possibilities. I got a presenting audition off that little fling."

"You make a mockery of your wedding vows."

"Marriage is a contract, a deal like any other." She leaned across the table. "You were a high-flyer once. They said you'd be a general."

"I still might be."

"You've been a major for eight years, now. Time you got another promotion. What's wrong? Why haven't you been promoted?"

"It takes time. Is that all that matters, my rank?"

"I want to be the wife of a general – before I'm too old to enjoy it."

She looked at her watch.

"Am I boring you?" he said.

She stared at him, her eyes glittering. "Yes, you are. I have an appointment with my plastic surgeon."

"Jesus, Galina," he said, and crossed himself.

"I'm thirty-five. Thirty-six in three months' time. I want to be this beautiful forever, Lev. Do you want me beautiful, or are you OK for me to be ugly?"

He frowned at her. "I want you to be my wife."

"Divorce me if you want. The publicity would be wonderful."

His anger grew again. "Our marriage is nothing to you."

"It is what everything is to me, darling Lev – a photo opportunity."

She rose and threw her coffee over his shirt. He sprang to his feet, his chair crashing to the ground. The liquid scalded his chest. He glared at her. Shouted her name.

A camera flashed.

Dasaev winced and looked towards the flare. A photographer waved and then scuttled away down the escalator.

Galina, striding away, said, "Buy the paper tomorrow, Lev."

* * * *

Two hours later, at the Criminal Militsia's offices in the MVD headquarters, Dasaev watched Dominika Burgasova hook a strand of auburn hair behind her ear.

She bit her lip as she read the computer screen.

Burgasova was a sergeant, thirty years old. She was single and pursued, but never caught. She'd been married to a cop once. Bank robbers had shot him dead four years previously. They never found his killers.

Dasaev would ask her out if he were single. Not that marriage made any difference to his wife. His heart felt heavy. The pain pulsed through him. He touched his chest, still smarting from Galina's attack.

He said, "What does it say?"

Burgasova leaned back in the chair and read. Her screen showed the website of a local Spanish newspaper in Barcelona. Burgasova spoke Spanish. Dasaev thought he might like to hear her speak it one day. He shook his head, scolding himself for thinking about her that way. Thinking about another woman.

Burgasova turned to face him, and her grape-coloured eyes widened, the pupils dilating. She bit her lip again and Dasaev's belly twinged. He flustered and blushed.

Burgasova crossed her legs. Dasaev gritted his teeth, forcing himself not to look down as her skirt rode up over her knee. She twisted her chair from side to side and said, "Five days ago, a man was killed in a Barcelona suburb. Torn apart. Along with last night's attack in Paris, and Kolodenko – three in just over a fortnight, all similar, victims dismembered."

"Have you been in touch with local forces?"

She nodded. "They all say the same thing. Unofficially."

"Animal?" said Dasaev.

"Animal," she repeated. She licked her lips and looked Dasaev in the eye. His skin goosefleshed, and heat rose up from his belly and into his chest. She spun her chair round to face the screen. Dasaev snapped out of his trance.

Burgasova continued:

"There was a major incident in Trafalgar Square, London, in 1999. You might recall."

"I probably don't," he said.

"Here," she said, gesturing that he move his chair closer.

Dasaev glanced around. The room bustled with detectives. Voices crisscrossing, officers on the phone, chattering in the aisles. Dasaev's team, looking into Kolodenko's murder, was holed up in a corner, corralled by desks. He shuffled closer to the sergeant.

Dasaev had tasked Burgasova to find similar murders to the Kolodenko killing. She'd done well.

Three years previously, six men had been slaughtered in New York. They were drug dealers. Police claimed they were victims of a rival gang. The alley where a resident had found them had been sealed off. "Serious injuries," was how the New York Police Department described the men's wounds. "Torn to pieces, blood and guts everywhere," was how the resident described the scene to reporters.

Now, as Burgasova had said, there had been three killings in two weeks – Moscow, Barcelona, and Paris.

Were they linked to the London incident Burgasova was about to show him?

"It was astonishing," she said. "Wild animals rampaging through central London." She carried out a search on her computer. A video-sharing website came up. She typed in a name into the search window. "Look at this."

Dasaev leaned in. The scent of her perfume drifted up his nose. Her odour quickened his pulse.

He focused on the screen and shoved thoughts of Burgasova

aside. Their legs brushed. She didn't budge. He drew his leg away, saying, "Sorry, sergeant," in a quiet voice.

"Here," she said, pointing to the screen, ignoring him.

Dasaev watched grainy images showing a man standing in front of Nelson's Column in Trafalgar Square. The man laughed. He spoke German. He gestured with his hand towards the square, and the camera panned.

Views of London. Old buildings. Tourists milling around. Red buses. Black cabs. Werewolves attacking people.

"Jesus," said Dasaev. He crossed himself.

Screams filtered from the computer screen. The footage jerked. The crowds scattered. The man who was being filmed shouted in German:

"Durchlauf! Es kommt! Es kommt, Hans!"

Run!, he was saying to his friend, *It's coming! It's coming, Hans!*

The footage showed the speaker running, beckoning to Hans the cameraman to follow.

A dark streak whipped across the screen.

The camera juddered.

Hans – it must've been – screamed.

A monstrous creature, bear-like, savaged the fleeing German as Hans screeched and filmed the killing.

The footage cut. Another filmmaker this time. From another corner of the square.

"See there?" said Burgasova. She tapped the screen with a long, red-painted nail.

Dasaev saw – another bear-like creature, or an enormous wolf, red-furred, attacking the screaming tourists.

The camera panned. A group of children and a woman sheltered in a fountain. A monster stalked them. A black-furred creature intercepted the stalker, crashing into the monster. The two animals fought. They were a smear of black on the screen before it went blank.

Dasaev sat back. The footage lacked quality, and he thought it might be a hoax. "Like that Bigfoot film, you know?" he said.

Burgasova said, "The Patterson-Gimlin film, 1967. I know. But don't you remember this London business?"

"I was in Siberia in 1999. You don't hear much out there."

"The authorities in the UK covered it up."

"How can you cover this up? What were they?"

"They said it was wild animals – just wild animals."

"Isn't that what they are?"

"I don't think so." Burgasova guided the cursor across the screen. She flicked to another window. The blurred image filled the screen and it made Dasaev shiver. It showed a head that looked like a wolf's head. The bared teeth were longer and sharper than any creature Dasaev knew of. Pieces of flesh, pink and raw, draped from the incisors. Blood stained the gums. The creature's eyes were yellow, the pupils black diamonds.

"What is it?" he said.

"Some say they were werewolves."

"Sergeant Burgasova, werewolves don't exist."

She said, "After they were killed, the ones in Trafalgar Square, they turned back into men. It's the biggest mystery of the 20th Century. The biggest conspiracy. Bigger than JFK, bigger than the moon landings – "

"The moon landings? They weren't a conspiracy."

"Yes they were. American conspiracy."

"They happened, Dominika."

"You're only saying that because you lived there. You were brainwashed, poor darling." She raised an eyebrow, and the side of her mouth flickered.

Dasaev's nape grew hot. She was playing with him, and he wasn't programmed for it. Galina had stolen his code for flirting. Or deleted it all together.

He said, "You said these animals were killed. What killed them?"

Burgasova turned back to the screen. She opened a third tab on her computer and it showed Google. She chose the "images" option and typed a name into the search box. A selection of photographs appeared. Burgasova clicked on one of them.

Dasaev's mouth dropped open. He squinted, leaning in to take a closer look.

The photo showed one of the plinths in Trafalgar Square, the so-called Fourth Plinth that had nothing on it. But there was something perched there in this photo:

A girl – long, dark hair. She was naked, her skin muddy,

glistening with sweat and blood. She sat with her arms wrapped around her legs, her knees tucked into her chest. Her eyes stared at the camera. They were yellow and their pupils black.

CHAPTER 6.
ROSE BLYTHE.

ZAK Weaver said, "Why won't you go out with me?" He sat in a booth, and she had her back to him, clearing dishes from a table. He raised his Nikon. The camera chirped as he took her photo.

She spun round. Her autumn-coloured eyes blazed. She wore a black vest top, which showed the pale skin of her shoulders and arms, and a short, black skirt. A cloth draped over her left shoulder. She had plates and cups on a tray.

He looked straight at her and smiled.

"Come, on, Rosie," he said, "I'm a lot of fun."

"I'm not," she said. She dumped the dishes on his table, and they clattered. Patrons glimpsed. From behind the counter, a tall man with glasses scowled at them. He was the manager and always glowered at Zak when he chatted to Rose. Now she turned her back and wiped the table she'd been clearing. Zak looked at her legs.

"I'm sure I can bring out your fun side," he said.

"I haven't got a fun side." She faced him again. "I've got a side, but it's not fun."

Zak sighed. He glanced around the restaurant. It was a gloomy little place in Greenpoint. Set on a residential street and clamped between redbrick apartment buildings, the place offered breakfast, lunch, dinners, coffee, and liquor.

It also offered Rose Blythe.

He sipped his coffee and then took another picture of her.

She wheeled, blonde hair flicking across her face. Anger flashed in her eyes. Zak flinched and put the camera down.

She said, "You can stop, now."

"I like taking your picture."

"I might not like having my picture taken, Zak, have you thought of that?"

He did think about it now but said no, he hadn't.

"What do you do with them?"

"I'm building up a portfolio. See if I can get an internship on a newspaper or magazine here."

He was hoping she'd come to see a movie with him after work, but she'd said no. She'd been saying no for weeks. Ever since they met.

"No dates," she'd said.

She was in her early thirties. He'd opted for thirty-two, since she wouldn't tell him. That made her eight years older than he was. He played the innocent abroad when they met, and it seemed to work. Not as well as he'd hoped it would, but it got her talking.

He looked her in the eye. He loved her eyes. They were brimming with anger and passion.

She said, "Photos of me won't get you a job, Zak. You need to think of something else to take pictures of."

She turned her back. Went back to wiping the table.

He looked at her shoulders. Her skin was beautiful. Unblemished, except for the –

"Are you going to sit there all day?" she said.

"Only until you're done. Thought we'd go watch a film – or 'catch a movie' as they say."

"I'm not catching anything with you, Zak."

"You sure you haven't got a boyfriend, husband? What's wrong with going out with me? I don't bite, you know."

"You've been asking the same questions since we met."

"And I don't get answers, so I keep asking."

"Can't you take a hint?"

"I'm not good at hints."

"I've been quite straightforward with you."

He shrugged. "What's a boy to do? He doesn't know anyone in New York. Meets a lovely English girl. Thinks they can be friends."

She didn't say anything.

Zak said, "This is the bit where you say, 'We can be friends, Zak, but nothing else.' Isn't it?"

"It's not. We can be nothing. I'm just being slightly affable, that's all. I'll have a coffee with you, like I've done. You can talk to me, but nothing else."

"You're really friendly, you are. I don't know why I bother."

"Why do you?"

He looked at her. She was beautiful. "No idea," he said.

She picked up the dishes from his table and strode towards the kitchens. He looked at the camera, at the pictures he'd taken of her. The one of her with her back to him. Her bare shoulder. He smiled.

CHAPTER 7.
REVEALING THE IMAGE.

SAFIA browsed the computer for the image she'd uploaded from her camera. Her eyes flitted around the classroom. Mrs De Souza was busy with another pupil, helping the girl with her PC.

Safia had to be careful. Phones were banned in class. Kids had to leave them outside the principal's office and collect them at the end of the day. But she'd snuck hers in so she could download the video.

Three years ago, when the werewolf killed her dad and his crew, Safia wanted to share the pictures she'd taken with her friends around the world.

But a girl calling herself Wolfwatcher wrote a message to Safia that said, "Keep the pictures safe, Little Queen" – that was Safia's username – "and never tell anyone. People want to kill this beautiful animal, but this animal saved my life and saved many other lives. It's our duty to protect her."

But in the last two weeks, the forums had buzzed.

There had been killings in Moscow, Barcelona, Paris, and last night in Calais.

Safia got a message that morning from someone with the username Wolfwatcher's Mate.

The message said that forces were rising up against their werewolf: "Email me the footage, then destroy it. We can't let them find her. They will annihilate her."

Safia didn't know who these "they" were, but she trusted Wolfwatcher and Wolfwatcher's Mate. They sounded like good people, nice people.

The werewolf had killed Safia's father, but that wasn't a bad thing. Now he wasn't there to keep them trapped in that horrible life they led. He wasn't there to make her mom and Neela sleep with men for money. It meant she and her mom had escaped their squalid apartment. Her mom got help to get off the crack and found work in a store and was now an assistant manager. Neela had gone to school and then to college. Safia lived in a decent neighbourhood, with nice people, and she'd made friends.

Her father's death had saved her life.

She checked the file had downloaded onto the computer. Her gaze flickered around the classroom. Mrs De Souza busied herself with the other kids. Safia held her breath. The icon appeared on her screen.

She signed into her email account. Typed in Wolfwatcher's Mate's address. She attached the video to the email and sent it. She puffed air from her cheeks and sat back in her chair.

Mrs De Souza's voice came from behind her, saying, "What's that email you're sending, Safia? This is not an email session. Would you like to show me and perhaps share with your classmates?"

Safia gulped.

* * * *

Rose Blythe's shift ended at 8 p.m. She walked down Franklin Street, turning into Huron Street. She passed the derelict Public Baths. The building's Roman pillars made it stand out here, on this modern, residential street of red bricks and grey concrete. Graffiti decked the front of the baths.

Rose strolled on, head down. Cars swept by. Raised voices came from an apartment. Music blared down the street. But she barely noticed any of it. Her mind spiralled. Something gnawed at her stomach.

She got to her apartment building. The lobby smelled musty. The copper-painted walls peeled. She checked her mailbox.

Empty. Tears welled. She felt lonely here, always felt lonely. But now fear trailed her as well.

She took the stairs, third floor. Mrs Januszowski popped her head around her door and said, "Good evening, Rose, are you well tonight?"

"I'm very well, Mrs Januszowski. How are you?"

"My back, you know."

"I know. You take care of yourself. Ask if you need anything."

"You're kind. A kind English lady."

They said goodnight and Rose Blythe entered her apartment. It had one bedroom, with the kitchen and living space combined. The walls were cream. No pictures, no photos hung on the walls. The mantelpiece above the fireplace was bare. Two suitcases lay on the floor – one for clean clothes, the other for dirty clothes.

She looked at them, and her chest felt heavy.

This was how she lived.

What kind of life is it? she thought.

She sat at the table. Took the netbook out of her shoulder bag. Fired it up and logged on.

She found the BBC News website. She saw the headline, and the hairs on her nape bristled. A chill ran through her. She clicked on the link. The story said, "The remains of three asylum seekers were found on the outskirts of Calais last night. The men had been dismembered, according to French police. They were returning to the Sangatte refugee camp when they were attacked. The killings bear resemblance to recent incidents in Moscow, Barcelona, and Paris... "

Rose Blythe shut her eyes and turned her head away.

Her enemies had re-surfaced. They were still alive.

She let out a cry. *How could that happen?*

She'd seen them all die.

She went to lie on the bed. Weariness washed over her, and she closed her eyes. The face of a man flashed into her mind. It was always there, but she kept it hidden. Seeing it made her hurt. But here it was, smiling at her.

She started to weep, her body shaking, and then the man in her mind said her name:

Laura, he said, a breath in her ear, *Laura*.

And that made her anguish grow.

* * * *

Midnight, and Laura sat on the floor in the phone booth in the lobby. She had a sack of coins on her lap. She fed the coins into the slot when the tone indicated her time was running out.

She said, "Have you heard anything?" and Elena McIntyre told her she'd heard nothing.

"You can't ask me that, Laura. I've got no good news for you. I'm here, now. The other side of the world."

"What's the weather like there?"

"It's early evening, five o'clock. It's sunny and warm."

"It's the middle of the night here, Elena."

Laura rubbed her eyes. Sadness stabbed at her heart.

Elena said, "Are you all right?"

"No, I'm not. I'd found myself all those years ago, and now I'm lost again. I don't know how long I can do this. I miss him so much."

"I know, darling. I'm sure he misses you, too."

"How do you know? He might be married. He might be happy."

"Last I heard, he wasn't any of those things."

"But you've heard nothing since."

"It's best not to," said Elena. "The Templetons, they're powerful. He's certain they were responsible for killing his ex-wife. I saw him at the funeral. He knew it was dangerous. He knew they were still a threat. That's why he told me to leave. 'Go as far away as possible,' he told me."

Laura remembered her days dancing at Bliss, the club Elena ran in Newcastle. Elena was Laura's aunt, once married to Richard Greenacre. But she wasn't clan. She wasn't lycanthrope. And the close-knit Greenacres never went outside their kind to find mates. Richard finally divorced Elena, family pressure too much for him. But Elena never stopped loving him. And when she'd found Laura in Manchester in June 1999, she'd taken the last Greenacre under her wing.

The last Greenacre, thought Laura now. She pondered her family and how she'd lost them. All of them murdered by Sir Adam Templeton. Laura left alone in the world – and still alone now.

She said, "I want to be with him, Elena."

"You can't. It's too dangerous. Either the Templetons will kill you, or the authorities will take you away. They're still looking for you, you know. They've not forgotten Trafalgar Square."

"Sometimes I wish you hadn't found me. I wish you never saw me in that bloody club. I knew nothing, then. Didn't know who I was. Nothing."

"So you're blaming me?" Elena's voice didn't sound like she thought that. But Laura said she wasn't, anyway.

"I'm just saying... " she said, and trailed off.

"Are you keeping a low profile, now? No more butchering gangs in dark alleys," said Elena.

"I am. But someone isn't."

They discussed the killings in Russia, Spain, and France.

"Do you think it's a werewolf?" said Elena.

"I don't know."

But she did know. She could feel danger like others could feel cold or warmth. She relaxed her body, finding the "now". That's what her animal side gave her: no shame about the past, no fear about the future.

Only the now.

Her heartbeat was under thirty beats per minute. Blood drummed slowly through her veins. The animal in her was content.

But then the human in her reared its head.

"Do you think he's safe, Elena?"

Elena paused.

And she said, "I don't know."

CHAPTER 8.
PRISON VISIT.

ENGLISH weather, she thought, staring at the lead-coloured sky.

She turned up the radio. Beethoven's Ninth blared from the BMW's speakers. She sat back, let it wash over her. The music faded.

She leaned forward over the seat and said, "What are you doing?"

"It's too loud, Ruth," said Lawrence Procter from the driver's seat.

Ruth turned the knob attached to the console in the back of the car, and the Ninth blared again. She rested her head on the seat. Allowed the music to sweep over her for a few minutes and then switched off the radio.

"Thank you," said Procter.

"Shut up, Lawrence."

He sighed and picked up a Russian newspaper. *A Soviet Sun*, thought Ruth, seeing the paper over his shoulder. Red headlines garlanded its front page. A photo of a glamorous, fur-clad woman tossing coffee at a man plastered the right-hand side of the cover. Ruth tutted.

"Are you going in?" said Procter, studying the front page.

"Why do you get those papers?"

"Practise my Russian. Never know when I'll need it."

Ruth shook her head. She looked towards the prison. A grey block cresting the black perimeter wall. Redhill was set in the Cumbrian countryside. It housed more than 600 prisoners, some of them Category A – the most dangerous kind.

Not as dangerous as me, she thought, and recalled the early hours of the morning.

The kill.

They'd stayed in Carlisle, fifteen miles west of the prison.

Ruth had left the hotel at 3.00 a.m. to hunt.

She'd left the ruins of her victim near Carlisle Castle.

While driving to Redhill that morning, they'd listened on the car radio to the local BBC news report the grim discovery. Ruth had basked in the terror she'd triggered in the community.

Now she said, "I'll give it another ten minutes."

"Why?" said Procter. "Can't you just get this over with so we can go?"

"Have patience, Lawrence. And anyway, I'm savouring the taste of meat in my mouth. That girl tasted fresh this morning. Her blood matched the dawn. It warned of rain."

"Now you read entrails. Like a Roman witchdoctor."

"The animal in me sees no future, Lawrence. I only see the moment."

"Can't you foresee the death of John Thorn, then? The doom of Laura Greenacre?"

"The human in me does." She sighed. "While I'm inside, I want you to get on the phone to Ellis Cole. We're going to pay him a visit."

"Why do we have to see that creep?"

"Pot calling the kettle black, I think, Lawrence."

"I'll let that go, Ruth."

"That would be best. And we're seeing Ellis because he has something for us. Something quite dramatic, he says."

She opened the door and stepped out. The chill bit into her. She grimaced.

"Why won't you let me drive you inside the perimeter?" said Procter.

"They'll sympathize with me, Lawrence. A woman of my age, walking in this weather. They'll let me through without asking too many questions. And anyway, they might recognize you and not let you leave."

CHAPTER 9.
PROTECT THE WEREWOLF.

JÄRFÄLLA, NEAR STOCKHOLM, SWEDEN – 12.36 P.M., NOVEMBER 19, 2007

GALA Larsson gasped as the image opened on her computer screen.

She played the video. The footage was blurred. The noise was tinny, but you could make out growls and screams, someone shouting, "Jesus, Shed, what the fuck is it?" and then shrieking. A smear of black whipped across the screen now and again. And then white teeth and yellow eyes flashed, and Gala flinched, rolling her chair away from the desk.

She put her hand to her chest and felt her heart knock.

The footage paused.

The video had been uploaded recently to a website called Find The Beast. It claimed to be footage shot three years before, in New York. Was it the video mentioned by Little Queen, the Brooklyn girl who'd been making contact with Gala over the past few years? Gala had told her back then to keep the pictures to herself. Gala was desperate to see them but knew that secrecy was vital in keeping this animal safe from those who wanted it dead. Those who would strap it to a table in a laboratory and experiment on it.

She squinted, moved back to the desk.

Was it her?

Was it Laura Greenacre?

Was it the creature that had saved Gala and her friends eight years previously in London?

Gala thought she was going to die that day. She and her church friends had watched one of their teachers killed. Torn apart by a beast she couldn't name.

And then the creature had turned on Gala and her companions.

But another animal came. Black-furred and wolf-like. The creature fought with the other monsters. Killed them. Allowed Gala to lead her friends out of the fountain.

Gala wrote an instant message to Little Queen. She didn't know what time it would be in the States, but she had to try. She asked why Little Queen had posted the video. Gala chewed her nails. Her skin prickled. Her mind reeled back eight years, Trafalgar Square, a visit to London with Mr and Mrs Heg, who ran the church group. Gala's mum and the rest of the mothers and fathers weren't keen on their kids going to London. Stockholm was Sodom to them. London was hell itself. But Mr Heg had said, "We should show them the city before the devil takes it."

The devil took it when they were there.

Gala got up, made coffee. She stared at the walls of her flat. They were covered in newspaper cuttings and photos. They were all related to werewolves. She read the latest cutting she'd pinned to her corkboard.

She'd only printed off the BBC's website that morning. A girl had been butchered in the city of Carlisle in the north of England.

Gala furrowed her brow. What was going on? So many incidents in the past few weeks. And now this video being made public.

Was Laura Greenacre responsible for these murders?

Gala couldn't believe that.

No, Laura was surely good.

The computer pinged.

Gala gasped when she saw the time. She'd been daydreaming for two hours.

She sat at the computer. She rubbed her hands together and felt her heart speed up.

Little Queen had messaged her saying, "Your friend, Wolfwatcher's Mate, told me it was time to show the video because Laura is in danger. Wolfwatcher's Mate said, 'Email me the image, then destroy it. We can't let them find her. They will annihilate her.'"

Gala grew cold.

She wrote: "There is no Wolfwatcher's Mate. I am alone."

Little Queen messaged back: "You have friends. We are all friends."

Gala again, her arms shaking: "I don't know Wolfwatcher's Mate. He is a liar. He deceived you. He is an enemy."

Gala's heart raced. She sweated and her head hurt.

She continued: "Wolfwatcher's Mate is not a member or a supporter of Protect The Werewolf. The video will be used against her."

Little Queen wrote: "I'm sorry. I'm sad. I've done something terrible."

Gala bit her lip. Sweat layered her palms. She told Little Queen that it was all right and it wasn't her fault. Panic coursed through her, and she thought she was going to hyperventilate. She tried to steady her breathing.

She logged on to the forum and posted:

"The enemy has tricked us. Laura is threatened. The time has come. Does anyone know Wolfwatcher's Mate and findthebeast.com?"

She waited.

CHAPTER 10.
FIND THE BEAST.

N<small>EWCASTLE</small>, E<small>NGLAND</small> – 5.03 P.M., N<small>OVEMBER</small> 19, 2007

RUTH said, "Where did you get this?"

Ellis Cole said, "I'm a member of Protect The Werewolf."

"What?"

"This bunch of fruit loops. People who say Laura Greenacre saved them that day at Trafalgar Square."

Ruth bristled. She said, "Protect The Werewolf."

"Internet group. Nutters. Lonely people. Inadequates."

"Like you, Ellis."

"Now. No need for that. I do this for you."

Ruth glared at him and he flinched. She said, "You do this for money," and then turned her attention to the image on Cole's computer screen. She'd watched the video already and felt her inner beast awaken. Watching a kill ignited her instincts. Brought out the animal in her.

Being a werewolf was a sensual experience. She cursed her family for dousing this part of their nature for centuries. "Why didn't we know about this at the time?" she said. "This says it happened three years ago."

Cole blushed. He coughed. He said, "Well, we did know, but we weren't sure. We couldn't get much detail, you see. And you... you were in prison at the time. We sat on it. Treated it like any of the other so-called sightings. There are so many, Ruth. People have sent images of a cat to these forums claiming it's the Trafalgar Square werewolf. I've even seen a man dress up in a fur coat claiming a reward."

"How did you get this video?"

Cole chortled. "Well, I was pretty clever – "

"How did you get it, Ellis?"

"I – well – I joined this forum, made contact with someone called Little Queen in New York. The forum's moderator, someone called Wolfwatcher – "

Ruth tutted.

Cole went on:

"Anyway, this Wolfwatcher said the video had come to light, but it would not be shown. Too dangerous, a threat to Greenacre."

Ruth bridled. Cole went on:

"I got in touch with Little Queen. Called myself Wolfwatcher's Mate and said I was part of the forum, told her to send me the video so I could view it, keep it safe."

"And you posted it on your website."

"I did."

"Now everyone knows."

He flushed and Ruth could smell the sweat coming off him. She could smell other things too. Ellis Cole's bedsit-cum-office was piled high with yellowing newspapers and books. Damp stained the walls. The paint peeled in places. Dust and hair covered the carpet. The place stank of rot.

"Never mind," she said. "We still can't be certain. It's not tremendous footage, is it. Might be anything. However, Ellis, it is the best we've seen. And we must take it seriously."

Cole's shoulders sagged and he sighed.

Ruth got out her phone and dialled Procter's number.

She told him about the footage and then said, "You know someone in New York, don't you? Through this Kolodenko fellow I ate."

Procter, the sound of traffic making him difficult to hear outside in the car, said he did: "He's a Nazi pimp. He handles Kolodenko's traffic Stateside. I spoke to him a few times. He has a medical problem he wanted me to address."

"What would that be?"

"He's been married five times, and his wives haven't borne him children. He wants me to find out what's wrong with the latest one."

"Don't you think that it might be him and not the women?"

"It *is* him. But the last doctor who told him that died of rather unnatural causes."

Ruth smiled. "I think we should go visit your friend," she said.

"He's... he's not a very nice man, Ruth."

"I'm not a very nice woman, Lawrence. What was his name again?"

* * * *

LUBYANSKAYA PLOSHCHAD, MOSCOW – 8.25 P.M., NOVEMBER 19, 2007

"Wheeler Burns," said Dominika Burgasova, dabbing her mouth with a napkin.

Dasaev nodded, studied the sheet of paper Burgasova had passed to him across the table. The sheet showed a photo of Burns. He was heavy, in his fifties. Grey streaked his ginger hair. He had a rifle slung over his shoulder. He wore a camouflage jacket and jeans with cowboy boots.

Dasaev stared at the boots. He liked them. They were tan with figures of horses weaved into the hide.

In the photo, Burns stood with two other men. One of them was tall and muscled. A bodybuilder who also carried a lot of fat. He had a beard à la Souvaroff – the moustache joined to the sideburns. His bicep sported a tattoo of the *Parteiadler*, the Nazi eagle grasping a Swastika medallion in its talons. The other man with Burns was lean. He had dark, spiky hair. Black-rimmed glasses rested low on his nose as he read a newspaper.

"A good friend of Kolodenko's," said Burgasova. She sipped her beer and glanced around the bar. She eyed the customers, making sure no one was taking too much notice.

Dasaev grinned at her paranoia. Maybe it was the building that made her suspicious.

GlavPivTorg was styled after the Stalin era. Sturdy leather furniture, grand chandeliers, red and green carpets and heavy curtains. The former Ministry of Foreign Affairs once had its offices in the building. The KGB used to be based not far from here.

"Did you know that the Molotov-Ribbentrop pact was signed in this place?" he said.

She turned to look at him, and her eyes flashed as if she were seeing him for the first time.

He said, "Nazis and Communists making a deal on how to rule the world. But you can't trust a Nazi or a Commie. One was bound to betray the other."

Burgasova tilted her head to one side. "Perhaps we should make a pact?" She bit her lip.

His belly fluttered. "What kind of pact did you have in mind, sergeant?"

"I don't know. A happiness pact, maybe?"

"Happiness?"

"After this is done... perhaps we could... "

The heat rose in him. He looked away, and his shoulders sagged. Shame had swept the passion out of him.

"Why won't you divorce her, Lev?"

He looked up. She was leaning forward. Her eyes blazed. He smelled her perfume. His throat burned, so he drank some beer. He jabbed his finger at Burns's photo and said, "Tell me about this man, sergeant."

She leaned back, folded her arms. "This is not a date, then."

"Date?"

"A Monday-evening meal, drinks." She shrugged. "Has the makings of a date."

"This... this is business, sergeant, of course. It was convenient, that's all."

He was blushing, he knew it. He hoped the dimly lit bar would hide the redness in his cheeks and the jabbering clientele and the music might disguise the tremble in his voice. Maybe it was convenient, getting away from the office. But in his heart Dasaev knew why he was here – he was here to be with her.

He said, "Kolodenko and Burns. Please."

Burgasova sighed. The fire left her eyes. She began:

"Kolodenko had an English doctor. Lawrence Procter. Procter was engaged in making sure Kolodenko lived forever."

"Was he an expert in longevity?"

"No. He was an accident and emergency doctor in England. He fled the UK a few years ago. He was about to face trial for sexually molesting nurses."

Dasaev raised his eyebrows.

"You have incredible eyes, Lev, do you know that? They should set her on fire. They're black."

"Obsidian," he said.

"There's something wrong with her."

Burgasova's voice left fiery trails in his loins. He squirmed and took another drink.

"And this man?" he said, gesturing at the picture of Burns.

"Burns is Kolodenko's US contact. Burns has Russian ancestry."

"Tell me."

She said, "His great-grandparents fled the revolution in 1917. They were White Russians. Their daughter, Ludmilla, was twelve. Eight years later she married William Burns, a butcher of Scottish descent. Their first son, Wallace, was born in 1926. Wallace made money in meat distribution. And not always dead meat. Wheeler is Wallace Burns's second child, born in 1950. He took over the meat distribution business. Both legal and illegal."

"And the illegal he gets delivered from Russia?"

"From anywhere he can source it," said Burgasova.

"American authorities know anything about this?"

"The curse of democracy, Major Dasaev: the requirement for evidence."

"Ah yes, the heady days of accusing anyone you fancy. Of sending innocent people to prison camps. Of rewarding the guilty."

She grinned. "Burns has been investigated, but he's a powerful man. Very rich, now. On the back of a legitimate family business, of course."

"How does Procter know Burns?"

Burgasova produced another sheet. It showed a list of phone calls made from Procter's apartment. "See here? American numbers. New York."

"Burns?"

Burgasova shrugged. "We don't know. We assume so."

Dasaev furrowed his brow. "You think this Burns and Procter plotted to kill Kolodenko? Take over the business?"

"What do you think, major?"

He didn't give a view. He said, "What about this doctor? Have we found him?"

"No sign of him. His apartment's empty."

"Left the country?"

"There is no Lawrence Procter known to have left Moscow. But a day after Kolodenko's death, a Mr and Mrs William Smith took an Aeroflot flight from Domodedovo airport to Barcelona."

"Barcelona?"

She nodded and smiled.

"The killings – in Spain, in France, in England today," he said.

She nodded again.

"So it was Procter," he said.

"We're guessing that Procter is Smith. We're awaiting CCTV images from the airport. But the woman, we don't know. There's a photo here. Passport quality."

Dasaev studied the photo. The woman was in her sixties, according to the date of birth, but she looked younger. She had white-gold hair and blue eyes. "Mrs Smith," he said. He raised his gaze to Burgasova. "We need to find them, sergeant."

"They're gone, major."

"We need to bring them back."

She looked at him. "Why are you so concerned? Kolodenko was a crook, a human trafficker."

He narrowed his eyes and thought for a moment. And then he said, "Everyone deserves justice, sergeant. Doesn't matter who it is. If it's Jesus Christ or the devil himself, everyone deserves justice."

"Does everyone deserve happiness, Lev?"

He looked into her eyes. He could do that for a long time and never grow tired, never see mockery or disdain. He got the feeling her eyes would always shine for him.

"Why won't you divorce her?" she asked again, leaning forward.

"I believe in marriage, Dominika. I believe in fighting for it, in the vows I took."

"She doesn't."

She touched his hand. Her skin was warm, and he quivered under her touch. A fire lit in his belly.

She said, "My heart breaks when I see the photos, Lev. She mocks you. She uses you. I have to say this. You're so dignified, but dignity won't get you through this. She uses your name. She uses your reputation. Then shreds it with her" – she glanced away, looking for the word – "vulgarity."

The energy drained out of him. He put his hand to his brow. She raised her other hand to his face, touching his cheek.

She said, "After Yuri died, I never thought I could love again. But you came, and I knew it could happen."

"Dominika... "

"I know, you're married. But it's not a marriage. It's a showcase for Galina. She loves the scandal. She loves being the scarlet woman. It brings her fame. But you let it happen. You allow her to make a fool out of you."

He drew away and called for the bill.

Burgasova's face showed grief, and her eyes grew damp. She shook her head and apologized in a wispy voice. She tried to reach for him again.

"Sergeant, there might be press here, you know." He rose and dropped roubles on the table before the waiter arrived. "I don't think I need to be photographed intimately with a woman who is not my wife."

She looked up at him. "I think you do, Lev. I think you do very much."

CHAPTER 11.
THRILL KILL.

WHEELER Burns, rifle in the crook of his arm, said, "It was more fun hunting my wives than these pieces of human debris."

The Toyota Land Cruiser 70 Pickup trundled through the pine and spruce forest that carpeted the slopes north of Sorrow Hill, Burns's out-of-town estate. The vehicle's headlights sliced through the darkness. The prey stumbled through the trees.

Burns held on to the guardrail behind the driver's cab. He always stood in the back. Made him feel like a king in a chariot. The Toyota bounced along the track, jolting Burns about in the back, but he didn't worry about it.

"He's up ahead," said Cleaver.

Cleaver drove the pickup. Leonard Longman, a TV producer, one of Burns's hunting buddies, filled the passenger seat.

"I know, I see him," said Burns.

The growl of engines made him look over his shoulder. They appeared through the cloud of dust coughed up along the trail by the Land Cruiser. Allen Hurst, a New York doctor, scooted along first on his quad bike, his crossbow strapped across his back. He wore goggles and a red-patterned neckerchief over his mouth and nose.

Burns slapped the roof of the pickup. "Pull up – we'll trail him on foot from here."

Cleaver halted the vehicle. Hurst on his quad bike pulled up next to the Toyota. He pushed his goggles up and tugged down the neckerchief.

"See him?" said the doctor.

Burns gestured into the trees behind Hurst, and the doctor turned to look over his shoulder. "Can't see a thing," he said.

Burns sighed.

The buzz of another quad bike's engine drew his attention away from the trees. He looked down the trail.

"Here comes Lomax," said Hurst. "He owes me another hundred bucks. I'm always first up that hill. Twenty years younger than me, twenty years slower." He was off the bike, his crossbow bolted.

Lomax Delaney, a local councilman, drew up beside the pickup and took off his helmet. His cheeks were red and he puffed. "Is it here?"

"It's here," said Hurst. "We're going in on foot."

"Excellent." Delaney swung his leg over the quad bike and slid his rifle off his shoulder.

"Waiting for... " Burns trailed off, the cough of an engine stopping him. "Here they come, Laurel and fucking Hardy."

The motorbike and sidecar appeared through the dust cloud. James Wellington and Harris Schumann. Bankers grown fat on their bonuses. Wellington heaved himself out of the sidecar.

"Where's the animal, gentlemen?" he said.

"Can't you smell him, Jim?" said Hurst.

"Yeah," said Delaney, "because I'm sure he can smell you."

Hurst and Delaney fanned the air in front of their faces and wrinkled their noses.

Schumann said, "Imagine what it's like travelling with him."

"I had a particularly excellent Chinese meal at lunch," said Wellington. "That I fart is a natural, perfectly normal by-product of that meal."

"Don't shit in the woods, Jim," said Longman, out of the pickup, "or you'll kill the wildlife."

"Hey, maybe if I did fart, I could kill this prey?" said the banker.

"Be the first time you made first blood," said Hurst.

The men laughed.

Burns jumped down from the pickup. "Come on, you bastards. Fan out. Ten thousand for first blood."

Five minutes later, he and Cleaver had the prey in their torch beams.

"This is too fucking easy, Cleaver," said Burns.

He picked up his pace. The prey was a hundred yards ahead. It weaved and stumbled through the trees. The green jumpsuit they forced it to wear did nothing to obscure it in the dark forest.

Burns strode through the woods. His belly shook under his camouflage jacket, but he liked that. Made him feel full. Made him feel meaty. His ancestors had starved when they came to America, both Scottish and Russian. But he was never allowed to. His father dragged the family from the gutters. Instilled in Burns a love of primal things: food, women, hunting, and being a man.

Food was good. Women were fine. The hunt was OK, but too easy these days. But being a man was toughest.

Stella, his fifth wife, wasn't pregnant despite the missed period.

She was thirty. Breeding material. Fifth daughter of a tenth son. A fertile family.

"So how can you not be pregnant?" he'd said to her the previous day before leaving their Manhattan apartment.

"Wheeler, I don't know."

"You missed your period. That means you're either pregnant – "

"Or I'm not."

"Or you've been playing me. You've been screwing around."

"It doesn't mean that. How does it mean that?"

"It means that because you're a bitch." He'd grabbed her hair. She'd screamed. He'd slapped her face like he slapped them all when they did this to him. "There's nothing wrong with me. It's you, Stella. It's you who can't give me a son."

She'd screamed until he stopped. Until he'd left her beaten and bleeding in their bedroom. He let the memory trail away and turned to Cleaver.

"Where did you find this one?"

Cleaver said, "In the troughs and the sewers of society, sir. As usual."

The prey stumbled on. Burn's flashlight beam framed the quarry, and it stopped and turned, and Burns saw the terror in the man's grey face. Burns smiled and a jolt of adrenaline pulsed into his heart.

"Come on, let's finish it," he said, and quickened his pace.

Sweat coated his body and his lungs burned, but the prospect of a kill gave him energy.

He looked for the prey. His eyes raked the darkness. Where had the man gone? He'd lost him. He swept the torch from side to side, and anger slowly filled him. But then he saw the man and cooled again. *Found you*, he thought. The terrified fool had veered left, trying to head back to the trail.

Burns smiled.

Losing sight of the prey had made the hunt interesting for a moment. It was the green-coloured coverall that did it. Made them blend into the background.

At least I give them a chance, thought Burns.

That made him feel good. He was being fair. Giving them camouflage against the pines and spruces.

The estate lay a two-hour drive from Burns's Manhattan home, where Stella was probably nursing her wounds.

Maybe I'll make her *prey*, he thought. *Maybe I should've done that with all the bitches who betrayed me, all the bitches who didn't give me a son.*

They moved through the trees. Burns swatted branches aside. They snared his jacket. He stomped through the undergrowth. He drew the rifle off his shoulder. Grasped it under his armpit.

"We should've brought the dogs, Mr Burns," said Cleaver.

"Too easy. Too easy with the dogs," said Burns.

"There he is," said Cleaver, swiping the flashlight to the left, spraying light over a cowering figure thirty yards away.

"Run, you bastard," said Burns. "Run, make a game of it."

"Please... " came the reply.

"Come on, Cleaver," said Burns.

The hunters forged ahead.

Burns felt energy spurt through him. The kill always

excited him. Murder made him hard. *Nothing wrong with me*, he thought. *It's these women. I choose barren whores.*

They cornered the prey.

Cleaver shone the light into its face.

It squinted, held up a hand as if trying to hold back the beam.

Burns raised the rifle to his shoulder, aimed at the man.

"Is this it, you piece of shit, is this all you have?"

"Jesus Christ," said the prey. He was in his early twenties. Crew cut. Mud and tears streaked his face. His face was moon-pale in the flashlight's beam. "Jesus Christ."

"I'm not Jesus, but if you're saved, you will meet him tonight. Are you saved?"

The prey shuddered and cried. He lay against the stump of a pine. "What – what have I done? Why are you doing this?"

"Because I can, son," said Burns. "Now, are you saved?"

"Christ – "

"Don't blaspheme, you son of a bitch."

The prey screamed. The smell of piss filled the air.

Burns locked the rifle into his shoulder. He fixed on the prey's head. He said, "I take no pleasure in this. You're making it too easy. Too damn easy."

The prey sprang from the tree.

He scuttled through the undergrowth, shrieking.

"Don't show me your arse," said Burns.

The prey crabbed away.

Burns fired.

The prey howled as the bullet tore into his buttock.

Voices filtered through the pines. The others, alerted by the gunshot.

The idiots couldn't track a pig in a sty, thought Burns.

The prey writhed and screeched. His face contorted in pain. He started to choke. Burns stood over the victim as he panted for breath, his eyes wide and glazed and his mouth agape. He twitched now, as if someone was jolting him with electricity.

Burns stared at the convulsing creature. "Do you think I killed him with a shot to the ass, Cleaver?"

"Bullet must've travelled up through his body, sir. Good shot."

The prey trembled and moaned. He croaked. Blood came from his mouth. He reached out a hand and said something. It sounded like: "Hurts... hurts so much... kill... "

Cleaver said, "You should put him out of his misery, sir."

"No, I want to see how long it takes," said Burns.

Burns tilted his head, studied the dying thing.

He wondered how painful it was for him. Wondered about the bullet's trajectory.

"He's shitting himself," said Cleaver.

Burns noticed the smell.

Delaney, who'd arrived first out of the group, said, "Hell, stinks worse than Jim."

Burns watched mesmerized by the prey's fight for life.

Take as long as you like, he thought.

"Sir, he's suffering," said Cleaver.

"Yes, I know. I want him to. He was no good, was he. Not worthy prey. Not a challenge. He doesn't deserve respect."

The prey's back arched. He sagged and gasped out a final breath and became still, his eyes open.

Dead from being shot in the arse.

Burns shook his head. "It's no fun any more, Cleaver. There's nothing left to hunt."

CHAPTER 12.
THINGS TO HIDE.

WHEN he said that, she turned away.

Rose Blythe's gaze drifted over the other customers in the City Bakery on 18th Street. Steam rose from her hot chocolate. Her cookie sat half-eaten on the plate. She wore a hoodie that was a size too big. She looked cute, despite the shadows cradling her eyes and her grey complexion.

Zak smiled to himself.

Then he drew a serious expression on his face and said, "But you lived in the UK eight years ago, you told me. How could you not have heard of what happened at Trafalgar Square? How could anyone in the world not have heard?"

Rose turned her attention back to the food, nibbling on the cookie. "Not all of us are interested in other people's lives. Not all of us care."

"You don't have to care. It's like knowing about stuff. It's not about caring."

He noticed how her jaw tightened. Her knuckles whitened as she made fists.

She'd been swigging her hot chocolate when he raised the subject:

59

There are rumours on the internet that the animals that killed all those people in Trafalgar Square in 1999 are back.

That's when she looked away.

"I was there that day," he said.

"Were you?" She picked at her cookie, not interested.

"Yeah. Fifteen and on my first visit to London. A kid from the sticks. Up from Dorset to the big city. And what a first visit."

"Yes, what a first visit," she said, but didn't sound like she meant it.

"It's incredible. The government has tried to cover it up. Making up all kinds of excuses. Wild animals, they're sticking with. A private collector losing all his stock. Bollocks. You can't hide wild animals in your back garden these days. It's been like a plague on the internet. For eight years. And now it's starting again. Rose? Rose, what do you think?"

She looked him in the eye and he flinched. She said, "Why are you talking to me about this?"

He shrugged. "Thought you'd be interested."

"I'm not."

"Why not?"

"Zak, I'm being friendly with you."

"OK."

"And it's not something I do often."

"I noticed."

"But you know, I was glad of the" – she looked about for the word – "companionship. You were sweet enough."

He grimaced. "Sweet. Nice."

"I know you fancy me."

"I won't pretend I don't."

"I don't fancy back, Zak. Never will."

"You might." He raised an eyebrow. "People change."

Rose glared at him, and he sensed a threat in her eyes. His throat became dry, and fear tickled his bowels.

She said, "You don't know anything about me, do you."

He looked straight at her. Her pupils flared and narrowed, flared and narrowed, narrowed to a slit. And then he thought her eyes had changed colour, just for a second, the reddish-brown fading to yellow, then back again. His guts were cold, and the hairs on the back of his neck itched.

"I might do," he said.

She scowled and leaned across the table.

He could smell her muskiness. It was like...

His mind went looking for a description and found it:

Dog.

Rose, her voice low, said, "If you do know anything, you know that it's for the best that you keep away from me."

Zak flashed her a smile. "What do you mean? I like you, that's all. I'm not ashamed to say it."

She sat back and looked through the window. Zak followed her gaze. The pavement was packed. He thought about Trafalgar Square when he saw the crowds. He thought about the excitement he felt when those animals attacked.

It was like being in the middle of a hunt. Lions tracking zebras. Cheetahs chasing gazelle. Werewolves hunting humans. Like the Battle at Kruger you saw on YouTube: lions vs. crocodile vs. buffalo.

He remembered being shoved around, people screaming. Crowds poured out of the square. Police tried to control the exodus. Panic took hold. The crowd stampeded. Hundreds stayed to watch, unable, despite the dangers, to look away.

How could they miss such a fabulous sight?

How could they miss werewolves in London?

And in the middle of the day.

No need for the night. No need for a full moon. Here they were in daylight. Rampaging through the capital.

Zak had dreamed of being a photographer at the time. He'd come to London with his mates, Russ and Jazz. They got separated in the chaos. Later he discovered they'd been killed. He would also discover that he didn't care. Didn't feel grief. Wasn't sad that they were gone.

The crowd had pinned him. He managed to lift his arms. Aimed his camera at the creatures and got some shots.

People screamed and scattered. They stumbled. Some were crushed. Fights broke out. They barged into Zak, but he stood his ground and kept his finger on the shoot button.

He scanned the square through the lens. He saw monsters attacking men, women, and children.

Teeth and claws tore flesh. Blood sprayed. Guts spilled. Death was everywhere.

A helicopter crashed, sending a ball of fire across the square.

He felt the heat but kept taking pictures as the fire engulfed those who were too close, who couldn't get away in time.

Zak recalled the smells: petrol, smoke, blood, meat... fear.

The image finder swept over the Fourth Plinth, the empty plinth.

But it wasn't empty.

Zak gasped. Steadied his camera. Zoomed in and focused.

A figure sat on the plinth. Blood coated her naked body. Matted her long, dark hair that hung in tendrils over her face.

He photographed her. She stood up. He took more photos. She leaped from the plinth. Zak blinked. The woman changed in mid-air. It was like CGI, like watching a movie through his camera. She just melted from human to werewolf.

Zak followed the werewolf through his camera, shooting all the while. The animal bounded away. The crowd parted. The creature shot down into the underground. Zak drew the camera down and stared. He stood among the carnage, eyes fixed on the entrance of the Tube station.

A howl came from the bowels of London that made Zak quiver.

He looked at Rose now, staring out of the window of the City Bakery, and the howl echoed in his mind.

He drew an envelope out of his rucksack.

"Look at this," he said. He slid an 8x10 photo from the envelope. Her gaze fell on the picture. He tried to see if her pupils flared. Tried to spot any sign of fear, panic, or anger.

She showed nothing.

Her eyes stayed on the photograph of the werewolf Laura Greenacre crouched on the Fourth Plinth.

"Ring any bells?" he said.

CHAPTER 13.
FATHER AND SON.

DASAEV'S father said, "Most of the folk in these graves were smokers. They wouldn't begrudge you a cigarette. Now, it's maybe *because* they were smokers that they are in these graves, but that's only an assumption on my part. I have no evidence."

Dasaev lit a cigarette. The nicotine raced through his blood. He blew out a plume of smoke.

"Better now?" said his father.

"Always better after a cigarette."

His father poured coffee from the flask and took a drink. He smacked his lips. "Warms you up on a cold day." He looked up at Dasaev. "Are you standing there all day, or will you be sitting with me?"

Dasaev sat next to his father on the bench. He looked out at gravestones. Grids of them spread across the landscape. Grey and cold, markers of death. Chekhov lay in the cemetery. Gogol and Eisenstein too. Nadezhda Alliluyeva, Stalin's second wife was here. Reinforced glass protected her tombstone from vandals. Buried here also was Raisa Gorbachev, elegant wife of Mikhail Gorbachev, the man who unlocked the chains that choked Russia and her neighbours.

Elegant wives, he thought. *How lucky men are, they say, to have elegant wives*.

His father said, "I like to be among them, you know."

"I know."

"I mourn for some of them, like Madam Gorbachev. I have nothing but scorn for others. Khrushchev. Alliluyeva. Molotov." He drank his coffee. "So they've asked you to go to the States."

Dasaev smoked, scanned the graveyard. He said, "Gromeko has."

"Gromeko. My old friend, Gromeko. We hounded anti-Communists together, you know. Hassled students. Harried journalists. I mean we were just cops, ordinary cops, but we had to do the dirty work, didn't we. Made me sick."

"What about Gromeko?"

"He just followed orders. But he had a conscience. Never went in too hard. A good man, really. But like many, he had a wife and kids to support."

"So did you."

His father shrugged. "Look where it got me."

"You kept your dignity."

"I lost my family."

"Not me, Dad – you've not lost me."

"I know, I know, but you know what I mean... "

They said nothing for a while. Dasaev thought about his mother. She died when they were fleeing Moscow in 1977. Died somewhere in Finland, the cold too much for her weakened body. She was pregnant, seven months gone.

They had to leave the Soviet Union because the authorities were on to Dasaev's dad. They knew he was a Christian, a member of the Russian Orthodox Church.

They got to the States and found their way to Detroit. Dasaev, his dad, and his sister. Two years later she was killed. Hit and run. They never found the driver.

"It was Gromeko who told me, you know," said his father now. "He said, 'They're coming for you tomorrow,' whispered it to me in the showers. He came close, you know, and at first I thought he was coming on to me. But then he said it: 'They're coming for you tomorrow.' He stuck around, reaped the rewards. He always wanted to be a general."

"He sends his regards."

"I hope you sent him mine."

"I did."

"Why are you going to the States? Anything to do with this Kolodenko character?"

Dasaev said yes it was and told his father what was going on. Told him about the links between Kolodenko and Wheeler Burns. About the English doctor and the woman.

"Who do you think killed Kolodenko?" said his father.

"I don't know. He was diced. Scraps of him everywhere. I've seen nothing like it."

"You think this English doctor had anything to do with it?"

Dasaev said he didn't know. "But he's our prime suspect. And there's an opportunity to investigate Kolodenko's links with this Burns character."

"What about these animal stories, tales of monsters?"

"I don't know."

"There have been murders across Europe."

"And an English couple, the Smiths, have been present in each city at the time of the killings."

"The doctor and this woman?"

Dasaev said, "My instinct says yes."

"Are you going to the States officially?"

Dasaev said no, he wasn't.

"Are you going as you, on your American passport?"

"I'm not, Dad. I'm going as someone else."

"Who are you going as?"

"I don't know, some dubious character running from Russian justice, I expect."

"Does Galina know?"

"She doesn't."

"She'd want to come with you, get herself photographed. Bitch."

Dasaev said nothing. He dropped his cigarette and stamped it out.

"You made a bad choice, Lev."

"I know."

"I told you at the time. Empty eyes, I said. Cold."

"You did say that, but I was twenty-five; my brains were in my balls."

His father bristled. "Men's brains are always in their balls, whether they're twenty-five or seventy-five. We've got an old priest, in his seventies. Arrested yesterday for trying to pick up a prostitute. And not just any prostitute, a male one. A fourteen-year-old male one."

Dasaev said nothing. Closed his eyes and listened. The wind hissed through the trees. In the distance he could hear the hum of traffic. He wished it could always be like this. He opened his eyes again. "People say I should divorce her."

His father sucked air through his teeth. "Dogma is such a dreadful thing."

"Do you think I should divorce her?"

"As a priest I say no, as a father I say yes. I don't know if you believe in God any more. Do you?"

"I don't know. I leave it at that and don't think about it too much. I only try to do what's right. I believed in my wedding vows, and I'm trying to keep them. For better or worse, you know?"

"And it's mostly worse these days, son. She was in the paper again yesterday. With some pop star."

Dasaev looked away and shivered. The betrayal scored his heart. The wounds would never heal, he knew that. And if he didn't do something about it, they'd worsen. He thought of Burgasova, their evening at GlavPivTorg. Shame rose up in him at the way he'd behaved towards her, the way he'd reacted when she'd craved him.

"I'll see how things stand when I get back from the States," he said. But he'd already made his decision.

CHAPTER 14.
BUYING AND SELLING.

ZAK slideshowed through the images on his laptop.

She was beautiful. He stared at her face as her pictures slid across the screen. *You never smile*, he thought. He didn't have a single photo of her happy. But it didn't matter. He was still drawn to her. She was like a magnet; there was something about her that pulled you in.

He'd thought about her since Trafalgar Square. She was in his head all the time. She'd cost him relationships and jobs. She'd cost him his life. Wasted all these years on her.

So he deserved some payback.

He owed her nothing. She'd not saved him that day in London. And since people were offering £100,000 to find her, he'd decided years ago that he deserved a slice of that. Or all of it, perhaps. He'd spent eight years thinking about Laura Greenacre, six of those hunting her down.

He'd known her for three months, now. He knew it was her. He'd stared at that picture of her perched on the Fourth Plinth every day. So when he saw the woman in Central Park, his heart quickened.

It couldn't be.

Zak guessed she was in New York years ago. Rumours buzzed on the internet. Suspected sightings of large animals. Nothing concrete, but enough for him to pack his bags and jump on a flight. He got this apartment in Midtown, not far from Central Park.

He'd trawled the city for a couple of years and was ready to come home. But then the man who'd hired him, the man who was paying his rent, got in touch. It was three years ago. The man asked about some gang being killed in an alley in Brooklyn. Zak had said what did that have to do with her? The man said, *It might have something to do with her. It's a lead.*

So Zak decided to stay. He kept looking and kept finding nothing.

But then, three months previously, he was meandering through Central Park. He saw her sitting on a bench, eyes closed, head back, letting the sun wash her face.

He stood and gawped. He thought it was impossible. Too much like luck. He photographed her. She opened her eyes and glared at him.

"What are you doing?" She rose from the bench, strode towards him.

Fear squeezed his balls. He retreated.

"Nothing, just taking a picture. You're – you're beautiful – I'm a photographer. No harm done."

She stopped coming towards him and stood there and tilted her head to one side. Her nostrils flared as if she were sniffing. She said, "You're English?"

"Well deduced, Sherlock," he said, gave her a smile. He went to move towards her, knowing the smile was an ice-breaker, a heart-melter.

She didn't budge. Glared and sniffed. He halted again. His back was damp with sweat. He swallowed, trying to wet his throat.

"OK," she said.

He was sure it was her. The hair was different – shorter, blonde. But he was sure.

He hung around with her that day, asked to take her picture. She said no, "and if you do, I'll smash your camera."

"Deal," he said, smiling again, but he took photos anyway, despite her warnings.

She said her name was Rose Blythe, and he told her it was a lovely name, but inside he mocked her:

Rose because of that Thorn character, the disappearing cop who helped her all those years ago. Blythe... Zak had been told Thorn had once stayed at a cottage called "Bwthyn y Blaidd" in Wales. The words were Welsh. The sound "blaidd" made was "blithe". In English the word meant "wolf".

He nearly belted out a laugh in her face. Scorned her for being sentimental.

The more time he spent with her, the more he knew it was she.

Laura Greenacre.

And the more time he spent with her, the more he yearned.

She burned in his heart. She was in his head all the time. Shame he had to betray her, because there were times – weak moments – when he thought he could save her:

"Be with me, and you won't have to die. John Thorn won't have to die," he imagined himself telling her.

But he never did. His heart quickened at the thought of the money. His belly fizzed at the thought of her murder. He'd not be weakened by sentimentality like she'd been. He'd be strong. Strong, that is, until he finally told her he fancied her. And she spurned him.

OK, bitch, he thought, *the time's come.*

He had the photo, now: the proof.

He studied it on the laptop. The one he photographed a few days ago. An image of her back. Her bare shoulders and the mark on her skin.

His mind made pound signs swirl on the computer screen. He stared at the churning images. His memory re-wound.

* * * *

NEWCASTLE, ENGLAND – 10.30 P.M., JANUARY 3, 2001

"Is this money for real?" he asked the man, and the man said, "For real."

Zak Weaver, seventeen and with a hunger for cash, licked his lips. He said, "And how do I get this money, once I've found her?"

69

The man chuckled. "You find her first, sonny."

"I will. But how do I get the money?"

The man sighed. "You give us a bank account, we'll wire it. What makes you so sure you can find her?"

"I haven't got a life."

"Haven't got a girlfriend?"

"No." He looked round the office. A girlie calendar stared down from the wall. Miss January was dressed for cold weather: woolly hat, scarf, and mittens – nothing else. Files cluttered the desk. Mounds of newspapers were stacked along the wall. Shelves heaved with books and box files. A damp smell hung in the air. Dust coated the windowsill. The window showed a grey, terraced road, the houses across the street boarded up. Streetlight glowed orange outside.

The man was called Ellis Cole, and he used to be a lawyer, but now he searched for Laura Greenacre.

"The money comes from Ms Ruth Templeton. Formerly Mrs Ruth Andersson. Sister of the late Sir Adam Templeton," said Cole.

"But she's in prison."

Cole grimaced, showed yellow teeth. "Not for long. You saw Laura, did you? Saw her as a – werewolf?"

"I did," said Zak, and told Cole about Trafalgar Square.

Cole shook his head. "The authorities still deny they were werewolves. They try to put it down to mass hysteria. Do you know I had footage? My wife – she wasn't my wife then – but we filmed the Greenacre werewolf killing a policeman here in Newcastle."

"Ken Travis. He was a rapist, yeah?"

"That's right, lad."

Cole reddened and humphed. He put his hands behind his head. The stink of sweat came from his armpits. His navy shirt was stained.

Cole was fat. His brown hair thinned. He looked mid-forties to Zak. He smelled late eighties. Just like Zak's granddad in the home. Zak shut his eyes for a moment, saw the old man twitching in his chair, drool stringing from his mouth.

"Listen, lad," said Cole, "if you think you can find her – "

"I can, I will."

70

"Good – if you think you can find her, go find her – "

"I need money. I'm a student."

Cole sighed. "You come to my office, make claims, beg for money – "

"How many people do you get coming here, saying they can find her?"

Cole scowled and said nothing.

"I guessed as much," said Zak. "People think you're a loon. Or people don't want to talk about it. It only exists online, now. It's alive there, isn't it? A world of believers. A world of hunters. But only in that netherworld, Ellis. Do you mind if I call you Ellis?"

Cole opened his mouth to say something, but Zak ignored him and went on:

"The mainstream won't touch this. Sometimes you get experts denying it, showing how it could've happened scientifically – just like they do with UFOs, like they do with ghosts, with... with God. It's the same. You're a nutter to them. No one walks through your door, Ellis. But I did. I'm serious. I can find Laura Greenacre. It might take time, but I'll do it twenty-four-seven – if you pay me."

* * * *

MANHATTAN, NEW YORK – 12.38 A.M., NOVEMBER 21, 2007

Zak dialled and listened to the ringtone. A voice, gravelly with sleep, said, "Who the fuck is this?"

"It's me, Ellis."

"Fucking hell, Zak, it's five-forty in the morning."

"So? You busy?"

"Busy?"

"Yeah, busy. You doing anything?"

"Uh, no... "

"There you go then."

"Jesus!"

"She's got my scent."

"What?"

71

"Rose Blythe. Laura Greenacre. She's got my scent."

Silence for a moment.

Cole said, "What do you mean?"

"I've found her, Ellis. I have found your girl."

Cole rasped. Zak guessed he was sitting up in bed. He told him everything and then said, "Do you have your laptop handy?"

"Yes," said Cole, "right here."

"Watching porn in bed?"

"That's right," said Cole.

Zak emailed Cole a few of the photos he'd taken of Laura Greenacre. He heard a ping on the other end of the phone, his messages landing in Cole's inbox.

He waited for Cole's astonishment, and it came after a few seconds.

"It's her, it *is* her," said Cole.

"It is, isn't it."

"Yes, for certain. The birthmark. The sign of the Greenacre clan. They all had that. Like a mark of Cain. A stain on them. She looks good."

"She looks great."

"Blonde, eh. That's nice. Few roots coming through. She'd still be a black-fur, wouldn't she. Their natural hair colour comes out when they change, you know."

"Really. How fucking interesting."

"Preferred her dark, myself."

"Did you, Ellis?"

"Yes. There was a wildness about her when she was dark."

"There's quite a wildness about her now, too."

Cole said, "You shagged her?"

"No. She's not up for anything. She's like a nun."

"She mentioned John Thorn?"

"No John Thorn. Nothing at all."

"What d'you talk about then?"

"Me," said Zak. "Me and... asking her for dates."

"Yeah, I tried that, too. She wasn't up for it."

"Well, she wouldn't be, would she, Ellis."

"Why's that?"

"You're fat, sweaty, and ugly."

"Hundreds of women wouldn't agree with you, lad. I'm lying next to one now."

Zak smiled. "Yeah, like fuck."

"You're lucky you've got these photos, lad," said Cole, "or Ruth Templeton wouldn't be too pleased with you, talking to me like that."

"Whatever, Ellis."

"Anyway, this photo confirms what we suspected." Cole told him about a video he'd recently acquired. "Of the killing in Brooklyn those years ago. Remember?"

Zak remembered: the lead that made him stay in New York.

"So they're going to kill her?" he said to Cole.

"Yes. Shame, really. Nice bit of flesh." Cole yawned. "But Laura Greenacre's being put down."

CHAPTER 15.
IT'S ALL COMING TOGETHER.

LAURA Greenacre was doomed, and now this.

Ellis Cole couldn't be having a better day.

He said to the youth on the phone, "You've done great. I had your dad in here a few days ago telling me all about it. Tell me, have you, um, had your oats with the lass yet?" and the youth told him no. "Ah, well," said Cole. "Not to worry."

Cole felt light-headed. The grey morning light streamed into his bedsit. He'd not slept since Zak's phone call woke him at 5.40 a.m. Ten minutes later a visitor arrived and Cole took him upstairs then came back down and went to his desk. Cleared away the debris and set up the laptop. He'd trawled through the photos of Laura Greenacre that Zak had sent, groaning at her beauty, craving her.

Shame she has to die, he thought, and then: *If you'd've only been nice to me, Laura, I could've protected you.*

But she'd spurned him and turned to John Thorn, the policeman who should've been hunting her, not screwing her.

I don't care, he thought, *I've seen you naked too.*

Cole had been a regular at Bliss, the club where Laura pole-danced.

74

She still looked fit. But Cole maintained she looked better dark than blonde.

He'd waited until 8.00 a.m., then called Ruth Templeton.

She was saying, "Are you sure, Ellis, are you absolutely sure?" She sounded tired.

"I am sure, Ruth. These photos add to the video evidence. It's her. She's *definitely* in New York, now."

The excitement gave him gooseflesh. It made him hard. He'd have to visit Kelly at the massage parlour when it opened in three hours.

Ruth told him to email over the images and he did.

She called back and said, "It is her," and Cole said, "I know, isn't it great."

Ruth, her voice shaking, said, "It's perfect. Procter's got in touch with that Nazi of his in New York. We can be sheltered there, get this done."

"How... how will you kill her?"

"I don't know. Quickly. Cleanly. I want to wash my hands of her, of all of this. I want to come back to England and move back into Templeton Hall. Make it the family home again, the centre of everything. A tribute to my brother, my nephews, and my son."

"Will *you* kill her, Ruth?"

"Are you fantasizing about a catfight, Ellis?"

"More of a werewolf fight, really."

"I'll see. She's strong, remember. She's been this creature all her life. I'm new to it. Like Michael and the others were new to it. I want it done effectively."

Cole was still shaking when he put the phone down, and when it rang immediately, he jumped.

He looked at the clock on the phone: 8.43 a.m. He answered the call and it was the youth. The one who's dad had been in a few days before. The one who'd found John Thorn. The one who hadn't had his oats.

And after speaking to him, Cole rang Ruth again and said, "We've found Thorn, too. For sure. One hundred per cent."

Ruth gasped.

"Are you OK, Ruth?"

"This is perfect," she said.

She asked where Thorn had been found, and Cole told her.

"Hiding in the hills, is he?" said Ruth.

"Coward," said Cole, and cackled.

"Is our assassin there with you yet?"

"Arrived about ten to six this morning. Looked like a grumpy bear. He's in a bedsit upstairs. Warmed up a pizza for him and gave him some beers. He didn't say thank you, though."

"He never does," she said.

"There's not been anything about it on the news."

"There wouldn't be. How do you explain it? Such a prison break has never been heard of before. I have wounds. They had dogs. They had men. But I killed many, Ellis. Took them between my teeth and opened them with my claws. The walls were covered in blood, and gore swam down the corridors."

Cole broke out in a sweat. She loved describing her kills. He listened to her breathing. Ruth planted fear in him, but it made him excited.

She said, "You can let him loose today, Ellis. Take the leash off that big dog. But tell him to wait for my word. Wait until we have Laura too. Then he can murder Thorn in the place we said. Thorn and his bitch cub."

CHAPTER 16.
ONCE A KILLER.

Newcastle, England – 8.54 a.m., November 21, 2007

THE brute lay on the mattress.

He stared at the ceiling. The paint was cracked. Cobwebs draped from the single bulb that illuminated the room. Dust and rat droppings covered the floorboards.

An empty pizza box sat by the mattress. His breakfast. The four cans of Special Brew he'd finished off after the meal were strewn about the room. First beers he'd had in eight years. His stomach grumbled. His muscles had used up the pizza for fuel, and he was hungry again.

He listened to his heart. It bumped at twenty beats per minute. If he'd learned one thing in prison, he'd learned how to relax. How to lower his heartrate, slow his breathing. He'd learned fuck all else – only that he'd never change.

He'd always be a killer.

She'd come to see him in prison a couple of days previously and said she wanted him to kill Thorn.

"I've been wanting to kill Thorn for eight years," he said.

"Now you can do it right."

"How do I do it in here?"

"You won't be in here too much longer."

He cocked his head and looked at her. He'd fucked her more than 25 years ago, and he'd fucked her again eight years ago. But she was still cold. Still treated him like scum.

He said, "You've got me. I'm confused."

She rose and said, "Be ready – don't sleep."

"I never sleep," he said.

He did wait. He was ready. And it came.

A tempest tearing through the prison.

He was given an address and told to go there. He stole a car and headed west. Ditched the car and then nicked another one. Ditched that and walked the last seven miles. Got here about three hours ago.

The wimp who greeted Craig at the address hurried him into this room. Gave him clothes and food. Told him he was waiting for a call and that he'd have to be patient.

"I can do patience," he'd told the wimp.

Now he heard footsteps on the stairs.

His host, the wimp.

What was his name? He'd said it this morning, offering a hand.

The brute closed his eyes.

Cole. That's right. Ellis Cole.

He'd glanced at Cole's hand, then looked him in the eye. Cole withdrew his hand and shuddered.

He opened his eyes now and someone rapped on the door.

The brute sat up and said, "Yeah?"

The door inched open. Cole's pudgy face peered into the room. He wore a grin, the sides of his mouth quivering.

"Come in and close the fucking door – it's cold enough as it is."

Cole did as he was told.

"I – I've been on the phone," said Cole.

"Get to the fucking point."

Cole flinched. He swallowed. He said, "We – we've found John Thorn."

The brute tensed. His nerves caught fire. He leapt to his feet.

"Where is he?"

Cole said, "I've spoken to Ms Templeton."

"Where is he? The bastard broke my back; now I'm going to break his."

Cole told him and then said, "Don't rush into this. Meet with Nick Sears. He's waiting for you. You'll have to brief them. They're not professionals. And Ms Templeton says to kill Thorn in the house. She's, you know, superstitious. Thinks that by spilling his blood there, it'll make things better. Lift the curse. Purify the place."

The brute picked up his jacket. "She's right – spilling his blood will make things a whole lot better."

"And Ray?"

He glowered at Cole. "It's Mr Craig."

Cole trembled. He tried to say something, but it came out as a rasp. Then he found his voice: "His daughter, too."

Ray Craig smiled.

CHAPTER 17.
FIGHTER.

"SO, tell me your name," said Wheeler Burns, peeling the apple with a hunting knife. He sat at the kitchen table. The headless carcass of a white-tailed deer lay in front of him. Blood dripped from the neck. The smell of meat filled the air.

"My name's Oleg Arkov," said Dasaev.

"Oleg Arkov, huh?"

Dasaev nodded.

Burns cut off a chunk of the apple and tossed the slice into his mouth. He said, "You knew Kolodenko?"

"Not well. Of him. I had a friend. Yuri Tomich. He worked for Kolodenko. Tomich said I should see you about a job."

"You here legally?"

Dasaev shook his head.

Burns looked him up and down. "How tall are you, son?"

"Six-one."

"You weigh what?"

"Just under two-hundred pounds."

Burns looked down at Dasaev's cowboy boots and said, "Nice," and then looked straight at him and said, "You done security work, bodyguard stuff?"

Dasaev nodded. Burns ate the apple, core and all.

"Do any fighting?" said Burns.

"I boxed."

"Pro?"

"Amateur."

Burns stood, gestured for Dasaev to follow. He opened a door and disappeared down a staircase. Dasaev hesitated. He looked into the gloom. Burns's voice came from the darkness saying, "Come on, Arkov. You scared of the dark? No good to me, if you are."

Dasaev took a breath and stepped through the doorway. Burns stood at the bottom of the stone steps. The room was dimly lit. Shadows sliced across the pool of weak light. Red dust covered the ground. Dasaev's nose tickled and he sneezed.

"Bless you," came a voice from the cellar.

Dasaev stiffened.

"That was Cleaver. You're OK," said Burns.

Dasaev entered the cellar. A strip light hummed overhead. A rope formed a circle in the rust-coloured dirt. A ring of some kind. Dog-fighting, perhaps.

Two chairs sat next to a fold-up table in the corner. A man in glasses with black spiky hair sat in one of the chairs. Dasaev recognized him. He was pictured with Burns in the photo Burgasova had showed him. The thought of her made his heart twinge.

"Mr Cleaver," said Burns, "this is Arkov. Russian. Knows Kolodenko."

"Uh, no I don't. I knew Tomich."

"Yeah, whatever," said Burns. He went to sit with Cleaver.

Dasaev looked at them, wrinkled his brow. He shrugged.

The light dimmed. A shadow fell across the room. Dasaev turned, looked up the stairs. He retreated a couple of steps and gawped.

A Goliath with close-cropped blond hair trundled down the stairs. Dasaev was conscious of the room trembling as the giant descended.

"Arkov, this is Mr Stokes," said Burns.

Stokes stood six-ten, weighed four hundred pounds, maybe.

"Take your jacket off, Arkov," said Burns.

Dasaev took no notice. He stared as Stokes lumbered into the roped-off ring. The giant scowled at Dasaev.

"Arkov," said Burns. "Your jacket. Take it off. You'll get blood on it."

"Is this necessary?" said Dasaev, watching Stokes. The colossus cracked his knuckles. His fists were nearly as big as Dasaev's head.

Burns furrowed his brow. "It's a test, Arkov. Very necessary. I don't want unqualified men working for me. I need tough men. You were a boxer, weren't you? Box."

The blond growled. Dasaev slipped off his jacket. The blond took off his T-shirt. He carried a lot of fat, but there were big muscles under the flab.

"Don't kill him too much, Stokes," said Burns. "Just a little."

Stokes snarled. His pale blue eyes glittered.

Dasaev curled his lip. How the hell had he got himself into this?

Stokes charged, the slab of fat around his waist quaking as he rumbled forward. He clawed his hands and yelled as he came. Dust kicked up. The cellar shuddered.

Dasaev whipped his jacket like a sling. It scooped up dust. Sprayed it into Stokes's eyes. The giant threw his hands up. He yelped and screwed up his face.

Dasaev lunged forward and dropped to his knee. He hooked his right arm behind Stokes's right ankle and rammed his body into the giant's kneecap.

With his foot anchored to the ground, the big man was off balance. He toppled backwards, yowling as he went.

Dasaev kept rolling, bringing his left elbow around hard into Stokes's groin.

The giant hit the ground. Dust coughed up around him. He grunted.

Dasaev leaped to his feet. Stokes tried to sit up. Dust masked his face. His eyes were watering. He coughed out red powder.

Dasaev smashed the heel of his hand downwards into the man's nose. The nose cracked. Blood spurted. Stokes yelled.

Dasaev kneed Stokes's damaged nose. Stokes screeched, fell back.

He rolled over, blood pulsing from his nose.

Dasaev kicked him in the thigh with the point of his cowboy boot, dead-legging him. Stokes crawled out of the ring.

Dust misted the cellar now.

The giant curled up in the corner. He groaned and trembled. Dasaev looked over at Burns and said, "He's had enough."

"No he hasn't."

"He has. I'm not going to kill him."

"Just a little, Arkov," said Burns. "He was going to kill you a little."

Dasaev strode over to Stokes. The floored giant's bloodshot eyes were wide with fear. He grimaced and raised an arm over his broken face. Dasaev leaned forward. Stokes whimpered, expecting to be hit. Dasaev hooked his hand under the man's elbow and said, "I'll help you," and he struggled to assist the giant.

Stokes staggered, blood streaming from his nose. He moaned. Dasaev took a handkerchief from his pocket and gave it to the big man. Stokes snatched the cloth and dabbed his nose with it. His knees buckled, and he almost fell, Dasaev supporting him. When the man got his balance, Dasaev crossed the ring. Stood facing Burns and Cleaver.

Burns sighed. He said, "I like men with killer instincts, Arkov. You should've finished him."

Dasaev said nothing.

Burns narrowed his eyes. "Do you hunt?"

Dasaev hesitated trying to imagine what other tests Burns had for him. "Yes, I hunt."

Burns nodded. "Do you drive?"

CHAPTER 18.
NEW ARRIVALS.

MANHATTAN, NEW YORK – 3 P.M., NOVEMBER 25, 2007

RUTH held up the photograph that showed Laura Greenacre in a hooded top and combat trousers, leaning on a bus stop, surrounded by commuters.

She looked different from the last time Ruth saw her. She was blonde in this picture, her hair shorter. She looked older and appeared sullen, but there was nothing special here.

It was an ordinary photo of an ordinary woman.

"Dead soon," said Ruth and tossed the photo on the bed with the others.

She rose from the chair and went to the window. The Le Parker Meridien Hotel offered a view of Central Park. Lakes glittered in the grey light. The woods covering the park were thick, and Ruth thought it would be a good place to hunt. She gazed over Manhattan. *A nice place to live*, she thought. She'd been here once before, years ago. When she was married. When everything was normal.

She and Procter had arrived the previous evening, a flight from Heathrow. They travelled as Mr and Mrs Smith again. The fake passports and IDs were holding up well. She liked being Mrs Smith, being anonymous. Didn't like the way the hotel receptionist looked at her when she said she and "Mr Smith" would require separate rooms, though.

Ruth glared at the woman and said, "He has a disease."

Procter was herding a couple of luggage carriers towards the elevators.

The receptionist said, "Oh, I am so sorry."

"Don't worry too much," said Ruth. "He's only contagious if you sleep with him. Just wash the sheets thoroughly after we've left, and there will be no infection."

Now Ruth sighed, turned away from the view and made herself a gin and tonic with a slice of lime in it. She sat down at the desk and let her thoughts drift. Her mind played out John Thorn's death.

Craig, her brute, would do the job.

Craig wanted revenge. Thorn had broken his back in London eight years previously. The policeman getting the better of the mercenary in a fight. Craig hated that. And he ended up in jail, his past as a killer-for-hire catching up with him.

But now set loose by Ruth, he could take his wrath out on Thorn.

And then the authorities, no doubt, would scoop him up again and make sure he never again saw the light of day.

Two bastards with one stone, thought Ruth, *and no need for me to get my claws dirty.*

She swigged the G&T and wondered how Thorn would die. She glanced at her watch. It wouldn't be long. The next day or two. Once she'd got Greenacre trapped. And then they could die together, at the same time. Knowing they'd never see each other again.

She saw the photos of Laura on the bed. The anger rose in Ruth. Her hate for the woman, for the Greenacres, simmered. It scalded her insides. But it would be fine. She'd quench the rage with blood – Greenacre blood.

But how would she do it without risking her own life?

Someone rapped on the door.

She said to come in, and Procter entered. Ruth blew air out of her cheeks.

He said, "No need to get so excited to see me, Ruth." He threw a glance around the room. "Nice, aren't they? Grand hotel. The staff look at me strangely, though. Steer clear of me. Like I've got a disease or something."

"Really?" said Ruth, and then: "Have you been in touch with this Nazi?"

Procter reddened. "Wheeler Burns. Yes."

"And?"

"He's sending a car."

"Where does he live?"

"He has a place here in the city, but he's in his mansion up north, in the Hudson Valley."

"How far?"

"Couple of hours' drive."

"Mansion," said Ruth. "What does he do up there?"

"I don't know. Hunts."

"Hunts. Good." She finished her drink. "This man, he's a pimp, isn't he?"

Procter said he was, that Burns "helped" girls from the former Soviet Union get work in the US. "The girls came through Kolodenko," Procter added.

"Helped, what does that mean?"

Procter shrugged. "I imagine it means securing them a green card, or pretending to, at least. Then he has them holed up somewhere before distributing them around the New York area, New Jersey, Florida."

"How delightful. You have such lovely friends, Lawrence."

He looked her in the eye and said, "Yes, I do."

Ruth guffawed. "Don't regard me as your friend, Lawrence, I'm not your friend."

"Neither is Burns." He saw the photo on the bed. "She's changed."

Ruth said nothing.

"How are you going to kill her?" said Procter.

She went to the window and looked at the trees blanketing Central Park.

"I have a few ideas," she said.

The phone rang. They both looked at it. They looked at each other. Ruth said, "Well answer it, then."

* * * *

Dasaev waited in the lobby. Pillars stretched up to the high ceilings. The tiled floor shone. The receptionist smiled at him again, and he smiled back.

The smell of cooking wafted from Norma's, a burger joint situated in the lobby. His stomach grumbled. He thought perhaps food might calm his nerves. He checked his watch. He'd been waiting 45 minutes. He glanced towards the elevators.

The drive took him two and a half hours. Burns had given him a black Mercedes. GPS brought him to the Le Parker's garage, where a valet parked the car: "Eight dollars for 30 minutes, sir, $16 for an hour."

It would be an hour, Dasaev guessed, looking at his watch again.

He had arrived in the States three days ago, travelling as Oleg Arkov. The MVD arranged everything. "All you need to do is turn up," said Colonel Gromeko. "You speak the language. Find Burns, and you'll find this doctor."

They were convinced that Procter and Burns had collaborated in Kolodenko's murder. They had no idea how the criminal had been murdered – the pathology report suggested a large animal. Kolodenko had been torn to scraps. Dasaev figured that Mr and Mrs Smith, who'd left Moscow the day after Kolodenko's death, were making their way across Europe with the intention of travelling to the US.

A trail of corpses led him to regard the Smiths as his prime suspects.

"Circumstantial evidence," Gromeko had said. "Not good enough for an international warrant. That's why you're going undercover."

"And what happens when I get there?"

"You're an experienced officer, Lev, make it up as you go along."

"Do you want me to bring them back?"

"That would be ideal, yes. The doctor particularly. He has something. A substance that he was injecting Kolodenko with. It's blood, but we don't know what kind. Or why he was using it on Kolodenko."

Dasaev thought of the monsters he'd seen on Burgasova's computer in the office.

87

Gromeko said, "This doctor's up to something. We need him in Moscow, Lev. We need what he's got. We need this substance. This blood."

"Why?"

Gromeko's jaw tightened. "We just do."

A concierge came over and said, "Mr and Mrs Smith will be with you in two minutes, sir. I'm sorry you had to wait."

Dasaev said it was no problem.

What did Procter have? Why had he been injecting Kolodenko with blood? The Russian criminal had always been obsessed with eternal life, finding its source. But blood? What kind of blood would defeat death?

The elevators opened and the man Dasaev recognized as Procter came out. He matched the CCTV images from Domodedovo airport.

He rose and went to greet them.

The woman fixed on him. She wore a blue dress. Her arms were bare. Light splintered off her white-gold hair. Her mouth, painted scarlet, turned up slightly at the sides when she saw Dasaev, and she tilted her head to the side.

He felt something move down his spine and he shuddered.

He introduced himself, telling them Mr Burns had sent him, asking if he could take their luggage.

Procter furrowed his brow and stared at him saying, "Have we met?"

Dasaev tensed. "I don't think we have, sir."

"Mr Burns tells me you knew Kolodenko?"

"Of him. Yuri Tomich was a friend. So I did not know Mr Kolodenko directly."

They took the elevator to the garage. Dasaev could feel Procter's eyes on him. He'd never met the Englishman. There was no way the doctor knew who he was.

"I didn't know Russians had blond hair," said Mrs Smith.

"We have all colour hair, Mrs Smith," said Dasaev.

He loaded the luggage. Two small cases. They wouldn't be staying long. The woman pouted at him.

They drove away, Dasaev's passengers in the back seat. He glanced in the rear-view mirror. Procter glared at him.

CHAPTER 19.
TRYING TO REMEMBER.

WHERE have I seen you? thought Procter, eyeing the Russian. He watched the man hoist the baggage from the trunk of the car.

Wheeler Burns said, "And it's wonderful to meet the sixth Mrs Wheeler Burns."

Ruth scowled. "I don't flirt, Mr Burns," and strode past him towards the house.

The Russian followed her. A man with spectacles bowed a greeting at the door, and Ruth entered the house.

"What do you think of my home, Dr Procter?"

Procter gazed at the house. "Very English."

"I had it built just so. I wanted it to echo the days when America was young. When Americans ruled America. Do you know, we might have a black president next time, doctor? Doctor? Are you listening to me?"

"Who is that man, the driver?" said Procter.

"I told you on the phone. Arkov. Russian. He knew this Tomich fellow. Why's that?"

"I thought I'd seen him somewhere."

"Maybe that's where you saw him. With Tomich."

"Maybe."

Burns ushered Procter towards the house.

"You know, Lawrence – may I call you Lawrence? – you know, it's good to meet face to face after all this time. Tragic circumstances, yes, but still good to meet. And this lady of yours, well – "

"She's not mine, Wheeler – may I call you Wheeler?"

"Whose is she?"

"No one's."

"No man in her life? Not you, Lawrence?"

"Not me, Wheeler."

"Why's that? You're a" – Burns looked him up and down – "a fine looking fellow."

"I like my women servile and timid."

Burns laughed.

Procter said, "Ruth's a bit of a... a maneater, I fear."

* * * *

THE HUDSON VALLEY, NEW YORK STATE – 8.22 A.M., NOVEMBER 26, 2007

"This is good hunting land here at Sorrow Hill," said Burns, waving a hand to indicate the landscape on show from the floor-to-ceiling window.

Procter drew his eyes from the Russian, who was standing near the door, and gazed out. Horses galloped in a corral. Dogs barked in the kennels. Two pickups stood on a patch of asphalt. The country sloped upwards to a carpet of pine and spruce. A road sliced up from the rear of the mansion towards the forest and then branched out into narrower trails that fed into the trees.

A piano tinkled somewhere in the house.

After arriving the previous evening, they'd eaten dinner and drunk brandy. Procter had stared at the Russian. The Russian stared back. Ruth had gone to bed early. Procter stayed up with Burns, discussing the American's lack of an heir.

"These women, they're all barren," he said to Procter. "Is

there anything you can do to help, doctor?"

And Procter said he was sure he could help.

Now Burns said, "I've got 10,000 acres. The nearest community is Pawling. We're two hours from New York City, 70 miles from Midtown Manhattan."

Burns, Ruth, and Procter stood at the window in the lounge. They'd eaten breakfast and were now enjoying coffee. Procter dwelled on the Russian through breakfast, trying to remember where he'd seen him. He was convinced it wasn't with Tomich and Kolodenko. He mostly saw Tomich in nightclubs when the bodyguard accompanied his boss. There had never been anyone else with them. He was sure of it.

Ruth asked Burns, "Do you live in the city?"

"I have a couple of apartments in Manhattan. Mainly for my wife. She works out there."

"What does she do?"

"Shops. Here... " He burrowed in his pocket. Brought out a key and tossed it on the table. "Keys to my – ha! – crib, as the young and the black say. Use it when you want. Feel free. Make yourselves at home. You're my guests."

Ruth scooped up the keys and thanked him. Then she said, "What do you hunt out here?"

Burns looked her in the eye. Procter flinched: *Don't challenge her, Burns*, he thought. But Burns was no pushover. He was a murderer, a remorseless killer who'd once shot dead a doctor for merely diagnosing a possible ailment. The medic suggested Burns might have a low sperm count, which was why none of his wives could get pregnant. Burns didn't want to hear that, so he'd blown the MD's brains out. And he got away with it. "How?" Procter had asked Kolodenko after the Russian had told him the story.

Kolodenko had grinned. "Because my friend Wheeler, he has knives at many throats and guns in many backs."

Now Burns answered Ruth: "I hunt whatever I can, Ms Templeton."

"Do you have many thrilling animals here?"

"Thrilling? What might you mean by that, ma'am?"

"I mean animals that provide you with a challenge, Mr Burns. I imagine a huntsman such as yourself enjoys a challenge."

"I do enjoy a challenge."

Burns and Ruth stared at each other.

After a few seconds Burns said, "I have trophies."

"I'm sure you do," she said.

"Would you like to see?"

"I'd like to see very much."

Burns looked over at the Russian and the other man, the one with glasses. He said, "Cleaver, we're going downstairs. Will you get the keys?"

They followed Cleaver. The Russian made to follow them but Burns told him, "We won't need you, Arkov. Go wash the car. It's probably dirty after being in Manhattan. Stinks of blacks, I guess."

CHAPTER 20.
NEW PREY.

PROCTER shivered. Cleaver handed him another brandy. His hand shook as he tried to drink. He slurped at the booze, and it dribbled down his chin.

"Pull yourself together, Lawrence," said Ruth.

They were back in the lounge. Procter sat on the couch. Burns stood with his back to the room, gazing out of the window.

Procter said, "I – I – I can't believe what we – we – just saw down there – "

"What did you expect?"

"Not that, Ruth, not that. I expected, I don't know... deer, bear, mountain lions – tigers, perhaps, elephants – "

Ruth tutted.

Procter went on:

" – but I – I didn't – didn't expect *that*, Ruth, I didn't expect – "

Burns came over. "Ms Templeton has saved your life, doctor. If she'd been like you, I would've killed you both. I didn't expect such a reaction. You must've known I was a hunter. Kolodenko knew."

Procter screwed up his face. "I never thought. I never thought you – and to – to keep trophies. Good God, man, what if someone found out?"

"If anyone found out, they'd make good prey," said Burns. "Maybe you'd make good prey, doctor?"

"That's enough," said Ruth.

"Excuse me?"

"I said that's enough, Mr Burns."

"This is my home, Ms Templeton."

"And we are guests," said Ruth.

Procter started to feel better. What he'd seen downstairs in Burns's trophy room had shocked him. He'd been sick, but three brandies settled his nerves. He looked towards the Russian. The man had black eyes. He'd never seen anyone with black eyes before.

Never seen anyone with black eyes before.

But where have I seen you?

"You're right," said Burns. "I apologize, Ms Templeton. I don't apologize to Procter. This has put me in an awkward situation. I imagined you both knew. You'd spoken of hunting in our discussions, doctor."

"There was a reason for that," said Procter.

"I guessed there would be. I thought you wanted in," said Burns.

"How do you mean 'in', Mr Burns?" asked Ruth.

"I thought Procter here wanted to join our hunt."

"The hunt that provides you with those trophies downstairs?" said Ruth.

"Sure, that hunt. I guess I was wrong."

"You were, Mr Burns," said Ruth. "Dr Procter does not have the stomach for such things, as you noted today. He is a wisp of a man who prefers to paw young women."

"Now hang on a – "

"Shut up, Lawrence," she said.

"OK, so it's you who wants in, Ms Templeton. I'm afraid we don't permit women."

"You would if you saw me hunt, Mr Burns, but no," said Ruth, "I'm not here to request an 'in', as you call it."

"Then what the hell's going on?"

"We have prey for you," said Ruth. She held out her hand to Procter. He rose. His head swam, and he nearly had to sit down again. But he made it to the briefcase sitting under the coffee table. He placed it on the oak table near the window. Burns and Ruth came to the table, and Burns gestured for the Russian and the man called Cleaver to gather round.

Procter opened the briefcase. Removed the laptop and photographs.

He handed the images to Ruth, who flicked through them and laid them on the table.

"Laura Greenacre," said Ruth. "Taken recently in New York."

One image showed Greenacre at a bus stop. Another was taken from the rear, showing her a back in a vest top. Showing a birthmark on her shoulder.

Procter watched Burns tilt his head back and forth as he studied the images.

Burns scowled. "I don't get this. How can this woman be any better than the others I've hunted over the years?"

Ruth said, "This woman can offer you the ultimate hunting experience."

"This is bullshit," said the American.

"Show him, Lawrence."

Procter fired up the laptop. They huddled behind him, watching over his shoulder. He sourced the video he was looking for and played it using Windows Media Player.

"What're we watching?" said Burns. And then he gasped.

Footage, poor quality, from the Trafalgar Square incident played on the computer.

"Jeez," said Burns. "What the hell is that? What the hell are those – fucking – things? Jeez." He reeled away. "Is this some kind of bullshit?"

Procter paused the footage. He noticed the Russian studying the photograph.

Ruth told Burns about Trafalgar Square, what had happened. Saying it had been in all the newspapers, all over the TV.

Procter watched the Russian. A memory flared. Procter felt cold. His guts turned queasy. The Russian caught him staring and stared back: a hard, cruel stare through obsidian eyes that shrivelled Procter's balls.

Burns said, "And you're saying that this animal, this creature, is her?"

"Yes, it's her. And she's here in New York," said Ruth.

Burns scratched his chin. "You know, I kind of remember this."

"I remember it, sir," said Cleaver.

"OK," said Burns.

"Would you like to hunt her, Mr Burns?"

"I'd like to hunt her as *this*, Ms Templeton," he said, pointing at the paused image on Procter's laptop.

Procter glared at the Russian. His flesh itched with excitement.

Burns said, "What do you want for bringing me this – this animal?"

"I only want her skin," said Ruth. "You can have her head. To add to your collection."

Procter thought, *I know who you are – major.*

CHAPTER 21.
COVER BLOWN.

"YOU'RE bullshitting me," said Burns, his cheeks red with fury. "I don't like to be bullshitted."

"It's true," said Procter, his voice a whine. "He's a policeman, a Russian policeman. I saw him in the paper." He looked at Ruth. "When we were outside the prison."

"Prison?" said Burns.

"Are you sure, Lawrence?" said Ruth.

"I remember him. His wife, she's a TV presenter or model. She was pictured throwing a drink over him. It was him. It said he was a major in the MVD."

"MV-what?"

"The Ministry of Internal Affairs, Wheeler. Their police force. The man's a detective."

Burns fumed. He was shaking. He turned away, stared at the floor. "Why's he here in my home?"

Procter said, "He must be investigating Kolodenko's death. He knows there's a link between the two of you."

Burns turned and glowered at Procter. "Yes, doctor, and you're the link."

Procter had told them who Arkov was after the Russian and Cleaver were dismissed by Burns, the American saying, "Cleaver, contact the hunting party. Tell them we've got something special. Take Mr Arkov with you. Show him the ropes."

"He might have followed us," said Ruth. "Tracked us from Moscow. They knew you were Kolodenko's doctor, Lawrence. They must have done. And then, after his death, you disappear. They then linked the both of you."

"How?" said Burns. "What link? Me and the doctor, we've only communicated by – " He trailed off and gawped. Then he said, "By phone. You rang me from Kolodenko's phone."

"Not always," said Procter, flustered now. "Occasionally from my flat."

"Which they probably raided after you left," said Ruth. "And your phone records, they've trawled through those."

"You dickhead, Procter," said Burns. "I should make *you* prey."

"Hey, now hang on a second – "

Ruth raised her hand. "It doesn't matter. He's here, now. Let's make sure that here is where he stays."

She sipped her coffee. Procter's loins fluttered. She did that to him. Untouchable slut that she was. He was terrified of her.

"What d'you mean?" said Burns.

"How long has he been here?" said Ruth.

Burns shrugged. "Couple of days."

Procter felt anger grow in him. "Didn't you suspect anything?"

Burns craned his neck and scowled at Procter. "He was a Russki. I like Russkis. I liked Kolodenko. And this guy, he's tough. He beat the crap out of Stokes, and Stokes doesn't get beaten. I made a call, OK? I was careless. I don't worry about Russian cops, Procter, because I'm not in Russia. They have no jurisdiction here. The guy definitely doesn't have jurisdiction."

"You don't think it's a US–Russian investigation?" said Ruth.

"No way," said Burns. "I'd know, because I know people. I am untouchable here. Ma'am, I have photographs of prominent US citizens proudly displaying the heads of the animals they've just killed in a hunt – and those animals, ma'am, were less prominent US citizens. There's no way that the authorities would come at me without me knowing about it – and knowing about it before they did."

They were quiet for a half a minute.

98

"Then this man's here without proper authority," said Ruth.

"We can have him arrested," said Procter.

"No," said Burns. "Then he'll start spilling his guts. And then they *might* come at me. I don't want that. I won't have it."

"You won't need to. We'll kill him," said Ruth.

The men gawped at her.

"A policeman?" said Procter.

"I like that," said Burns.

"Let me do it, Mr Burns," she said.

Burns smiled and nodded. "Call me Wheeler, honey."

Procter jarred.

Ruth said, "Call me ma'am, Mr Burns."

Procter said, "Wait a minute, we can't – "

"We can," said Burns.

"It'll give you an opportunity to see what you're up against when you hunt Laura Greenacre," said Ruth. "It'll give you time to prepare. Time we won't be giving this Russian police officer."

CHAPTER 22.
THE NAMES OF THE PREY,
THE NAMES OF THE
HUNTERS.

THEY hunted humans here. They planned it for the woman in the photo. They'd stalk her through that forest.

This is good hunting land.

Dasaev leaned on the gate. The horses grazed in the corral. His heart pounded and dread seeped through him.

They hunted humans here.

He rested his head on his arms.

Cleaver took him to see the trophies. A room of varnished wood and antique furniture housed a murderous exhibition.

Cleaver said, "What do you think, tough guy?" and Dasaev had to steel himself, tighten every nerve, every muscle to stop himself from buckling.

Cleaver said, "Tell you the truth, it's sick, but the boss, he's into it."

Cleaver opened the drawer of a Welsh dresser. He drew out a leather-bound ledger. He opened it and showed Dasaev. The pages were split into two columns.

"The names of the prey," he said, running a finger down the left-hand column of page one, "and the names of the hunters," he added, pointing to the names in the right-hand column.

"There's a group of them. Rich guys. Powerful guys. All Mr Burns's pals."

Dasaev said nothing. He tried to stay relaxed. Inside he was shaking with dread and revulsion. The odour of decay and varnish seeped into his nostrils. He felt dizzy.

Cleaver turned to the back page of the ledger. He said, "Here are the hunters' names. Contact is by phone. Landline. We ring these guys and tell them, 'It's a lovely day out here in the valley, sir, and Mr Burns wondered if you'd enjoy a stroll through the pines,' and they'll say if they can or can't." Cleaver chuckled. "It's so stupid."

Dasaev didn't know if he could go through with it.

Hunting humans?

He looked at his watch. It was 10.30 a.m., 6.30 p.m. back home. He got his phone out and dialled.

Galina answered.

"It's me," he said.

"Baby," she said, her voice like silk.

"You sound tired. What're you up to?" It wasn't an innocent question. It was loaded with jealousy, with mistrust, with fear.

"Me? Nothing. This and that." She groaned.

Anger stirred in Dasaev's belly.

He said, "Who is it tonight?"

"Oh, Lev. Don't start. You know how I live. This is how we both live."

"Not how I live. I want our marriage to work."

"It won't unless you make more of an effort."

"What more can I do?"

"Become a colonel," she said. There was an edge to her voice. "I've got a reputation to maintain. I can't do this as a major's wife. Get promoted. Make a name for yourself. Catch this killer of Kolodenko's and we might stand a chance. Marriage is a contract, Lev. I agreed to marry you on the grounds that you would be a great policeman, a high-flying young officer."

"I married you because I loved you, Galina."

She huffed. "You are sweet."

"What if I divorced you?"

"You? You divorce me? You are too wracked by your father's religion, darling Lev. It would be shameful for you. The guilt, the guilt would tear you apart. That's what I love about you, you see: you are weak inside."

"Why don't you divorce me?"

She sighed. "Because I still hold out some hope for our marriage. I still believe you can get your arse up that ladder, sweep up the ranks. Kiss a few backsides, Lev. Cut a few corners. Just... " She trailed off.

Lev said her name.

Galina said, "Wait a minute."

"What is it?"

"Where... where the hell are you?"

"I can't say."

"You can't say?" she said, her voice silky again.

"No, it's confidential."

Galina hummed and the sound she made ignited something in his loins.

"Do you know I love you, Galina?"

"Oh, you sweet, darling fool. Anyway, confidential. Sounds thrilling. This is exciting. You're not lying to me are you, darling? You're not having an affair are you?" She laughed. "Not with your fancy woman? Oh, how delirious. You breaking you marriage vows. It would be like me becoming a nun." She laughed again. "Confidential. You must tell me when this 'confidential' investigation comes to an end and I can buy a new dress. I'm sure we'll be on TV. If you catch Kolodenko's killer – it is to do with him, isn't it? – but when you catch him, I'll orchestrate *our* PR, darling: '*Captain* Dasaev and his beautiful wife rekindle their love.' How does that sound?"

"Galina – "

"My husband," she said, her hand over the phone, telling someone.

A jolt of rage flashed in Dasaev's chest.

She came back on the line: "Now, Lev, where were we? Tell me again about this – "

He cut her off.

He ran his hands through his hair. He needed a cigarette. Burns, killer of innocents, hater of women, was a non-smoker and would not allow the whiff of tobacco anywhere – not even outside the house.

Dasaev lit one anyway. He dragged on the smoke. The hit brought on a memory of being a kid at school here in the US. Sam, Kimo, and he would sneak off from class and smoke Marlboros till they couldn't breathe, till their throats burned. And they'd swagger back to school, feeling cool, stinking of tobacco, Mr Han saying, "If you think you've come up smelling of roses, fellas, you've got it all wrong," and they'd get detention.

Dasaev thought about his childhood, now. The days spent in Detroit. His father an exile because of his faith, because he was an honest cop.

The communists hated his honesty and his Christianity.

Dasaev acquired his father's candour, but he couldn't embrace his faith. He accepted some of its doctrines: treat others as you would expect to be treated yourself, even if they betray you, shit on you, lie to you, sleep around on you. But he didn't approve of the brutality that was also contained in the religion.

"You can't pick and choose," he told his father once. "You have to live by the good things, and you have to live by the bad things, also. You live by the love, you live by the hate, too. You must. That's why I can't have your faith, Dad."

"Typical of you, Lev," his dad had said. "All or nothing."

He blew cigarette smoke out of his lungs and with it the pain of Galina's betrayal. He had a job to do.

Mr and Mrs Smith: Procter and... who was the woman?

She'd been introduced as Ruth Templeton. He'd texted the name to Dominika. She'd texted back asking if he was OK and looking after himself. She'd said they all missed him at the office. He hadn't texted back.

What the hell am I doing here? he thought. *Why couldn't we have done this officially?* He wondered about this substance Procter had. The blood Gromeko was interested in. A myth, probably. Just like werewolves.

He put his head in his hands.

His phone rang. He jerked, thinking it might be Galina. Burns's name flashed up on the Nokia's screen.

Dasaev answered.

Wheeler Burns said, "There'll be a hunt tomorrow. Get yourself ready, son."

CHAPTER 23.
NOWHERE TO RUN.

LAURA shovelled her clothes into the suitcase. Her nerves jangled. Something smelled bad about this Zak situation. He hinted at things, and Laura didn't like it. She could do one of two things: kill him or run.

Run, she thought. *Killing's just messy. Leaves a trail.*

She huffed out her frustration. Forced to flee again. Forced to pack her few possessions and trawl for another temporary home.

Shouldn't have bothered with him, she thought. *Got soft in my thirties. Felt sorry for him, all alone in New York. I don't do people. I only do me and –*

She slumped on the bed and put her hands over her face. Grief gashed her heart and she wept.

"Oh, Johnny."

She shuddered as the tears poured out of her. She felt cold, lonely.

Where now? How long would this go on for? This running, this hiding?

But she had no choice. She was the last Greenacre. The last werewolf. The authorities would hole her in some laboratory if they got hold of her. They'd put her in a cage and take her blood and her skin and her hair. They'd train cameras on her all day, all night. Wait for her to change. They'd use her DNA. They'd splice it with human genes. They'd try to play God.

Just like Michael did.

He took her bite. Her spit in his blood. His lycanthrope genes fired up again by her DNA. She made him into a monster. Gave him teeth and claws. And then he "made" his cousins werewolves.

Her fault, all her fault.

Her fault that they'd killed those people. Her fault she was known to the world. Her fault she was being hunted.

And now Ruth.

Laura looked up, her eyes burning with tears.

Had Ruth killed those people in Russia, Spain, France, and England?

The scant details made available suggested the victims had been dismembered. It seemed unusual that humans killing in that way would be operating in all those countries. And if it were one murderer, the authorities would have made it difficult for the butcher to travel so quickly from place to place.

Unless that killer was a respectable-looking woman, perhaps.

A chill ran through Laura. If Ruth were a werewolf, how had she done it? The Templetons' lycanthrope gene was dormant. Latent for thousands of years, unused until Michael activated it. But he was only able to do that through Laura's bite. How had Ruth done it?

Panic swam through her.

She looked around the apartment. One room. Her whole life had come down to this. A dust-filled, damp-sodden, mouse-infested hovel. She went to the window. The day broke dull and it hadn't improved. The window showed her the concrete of another apartment block. The alley below was where she'd killed those men three years previously. Back then, police came round. They taped off the building. They took everyone's details. They asked questions. They treated everyone like a suspect. They wanted to know where she was at the time of the killings, where she'd come from, why she was here.

She didn't care about police; she could deal with them.

It was the people who could read between the lines she had to worry about.

And they came too. Men in suits who showed no ID, who asked the same questions that the cops asked but asked them

105

with more steel in their voices. And they asked them harder, too. Not accepting your first answer or your second. They asked hard and they looked hard. Looked hard and long at Laura. But she looked hard and long back. And finally they went away.

And the kill, as always, had been worth it.

It felt good. Flesh in her mouth. Blood in her throat.

Felt like that's what she was made for.

Hardwired by evolution to kill. She was only doing what came naturally.

She went back to the packing. Not much to do. There was never much. Clothes, toiletries, make-up, that was all. No books, no trinkets, no things with a story to tell.

Nothing.

She didn't even have a photo of him. It would hurt too much, looking at him, not being able to touch him. And to have a photo would be dangerous.

She wondered what he was doing. Where he was. How he felt. Did he still love her? She thought about their goodbye in that tunnel, and the pain of running from him.

She'd run for miles. She had no idea for how long. Exhausted, she came to a halt, panting, saliva oozing from her mouth. She'd changed back into human form. Sneaked out of the London Underground station. The Tube had been evacuated. She came across a tramp who saw her bloodied and naked.

"You want my coat, love?" he said.

She took it, and it smelled of rotten vegetables, but it kept her covered. She moved through the street, brushing past people who pinched their noses at her because she stank. But they were too busy to look closely. They were gathered outside Curry's or Argos, any place with a TV, any place to watch the aftermath of Trafalgar Square.

She slept in an alley that night. Cried and slept. The backstreet was dirty and cold and she thought that this would be her life from now on. Alone in alleys, in dirt, in cold. John was gone from her. She lay in the litter-strewn alley and understood that she could never be with him. Grief clawed at her and split her heart and her heart had stayed split all these years.

She slept rough in London for a month. Then she tracked Elena down. Elena wanted her to stay. Elena gave her money, and she found a passport fraudster who gave Laura a new identity.

Rose Blythe.

"Any reason?" said Elena.

"Yes," said Laura, but she didn't explain.

New York was a good place to disappear. She found her way to Brooklyn. An ethnic melting pot, where she got lost. She found work as a waitress. Different places. She never stuck around too long. Everything got OK, bearable. She tried to forget John Thorn, but failed. So she embraced the gloom, accepted it. And she became comfortable with her misery, knowing that this was how she'd feel for the rest of her life.

It was OK.

She made no friends. She spoke to no one, except the occasional call to Elena.

And there was no sign of John. He'd gone to ground. He'd spoken briefly to Elena early in 2000, a few months after Trafalgar Square. Elena told her he'd tried to move on. Even spent some time with a woman.

Jealousy flared in Laura's breast at the time. But she quelled it. *Why shouldn't he move on?* she thought. *We have no life together, no future.*

Still, tears and rage came.

A few years later. He lost his ex-wife and Elena saw him at the funeral. That was the last time. Elena migrated. John disappeared. Laura mourned.

"I'm not like him. We're not made to be together," she told Elena. "And anyway, they'd find us. They'd come for me. Either the authorities or the Templetons. They want me dead. I've seen what they say on the internet. The darkness is livid."

She finished her packing and sat on the bed. The springs creaked under her weight.

Where will I go? she thought. *Stick a pin in a map.*

She pulled on a tattered biker's jacket.

Someone knocked at the door. Her senses sharpened. She sniffed the air. She recognized the scent.

She opened the door and said, "What the hell do you want?"

CHAPTER 24.
DO YOU WANT TO SEE ME NAKED?

ZAK said, "Can I come in, Rosie?"

"What," she said, "do you want?"

"I've... " He didn't finish. He looked her up and down, seeing her jacket. He said, "You off somewhere?"

"Zak. Once more. What do you want?"

"I want to say something. It's important. Not... not about you and me, Rosie, I'm not going to ask you out or, you know, say I love you or anything."

Laura felt her cheeks grow warm.

She said, "I've not got a lot of time."

"So you are going somewhere."

He made a move to come in. Tried to shove past her arm. But her arm stayed where it was. Hand gripping the doorframe.

"Jeez, you're strong, Rose Blythe," he said.

"You try that again and something horrible will happen."

He gulped and his face blanched. "Oh, yes?" he said, a shudder in his voice. "How horrible?"

Laura glared at him. What was he up to? He was fronting her out. She dropped her arm. Gestured with her chin for him to enter. She slammed the door after he'd come in and he flinched.

"Packed already," he said. He grinned. Then he looked around the apartment. He stared at the window for a moment or two.

"Want me to open it?" she said.

"Huh? No. Why? Why would I – "

"I don't know, Zak. You look nervous, that's all. It's not that warm in here, but you've got a sweaty brow."

Her blood quickened. Her senses sharpened. She could smell everything in detail. His odour filled her nostrils. She smelled his fear, smelled his doubt, smelled his weakness, smelled his blood, smelled his meat.

She slavered. She bared her teeth.

Zak took a step back. His eyes were wide and fixed on her.

"Do you want to see me naked, Zak?" she said.

She slipped her jacket off.

She tilted her head to one side, waited for his answer. Her nostrils flared, taking in the smells. Her skin tingled. Her blood pulsed. Her muscles corded. Change began.

Zak gawped. Tried to smile but it didn't work.

"I have to tell you," she said, "that most people who see me naked do regret it."

"Th-they do?"

"Yes, they do." She stalked him. He shuffled away from her.

"I – I hope I wouldn't be 'most people'," he said.

"You are."

"But I – I'm your friend," he said.

"Yes, I'm sure you are. Now, what is it that you want to say?"

He paused for a moment.

Then he said, "I want to help."

She furrowed her brow. "Do I need help?"

"You do, Rose, you really do."

"Do I, Zak? Why's that?"

"Because you're Laura Greenacre."

CHAPTER 25.
NIGHT WORK.

DASAEV looked up and said, "What job?"

"A job, Russki," said Cleaver, "a job Mr Burns wants doing. Now get on your feet and come with me."

Dasaev tossed the magazine aside. He swung his legs off the bed. He slipped his feet into the cowboy boots.

"I like your boots," said Cleaver.

"I like them too."

"You like cowboys?"

"I like cowboy boots."

They walked along the corridor. Dasaev smelled food coming from the kitchen. His stomach rumbled. He'd not eaten. After seeing the trophy room, after speaking to Galina, after being told there'd be a hunt at dawn, he didn't have much of an appetite. He'd come down to his room in the staff quarters: single bed, basin, wardrobe, chest of drawers. Wheeler Burns might have enjoyed luxuries, but his employees had to make do with spartan conditions.

"You like horses?" said Cleaver.

"I don't mind them."

"You like riding?"

"I don't get a lot of opportunities."

"There are plenty of opportunities out here."

Dasaev said nothing. He felt sick by what he'd seen that day. Dread built up him in now.

They hunted humans here.

He felt queasy.

"You OK, Arkov?" said Cleaver.

"Yeah, tired."

They took a Dodge pickup. A 1992 Dakota model, said Cleaver, who drove. They followed the road towards the pines and the spruces. Night was deep. The trees loomed up ahead. Dasaev shuddered. He glanced at Cleaver.

"Where are we going?"

"To a job. I said."

"What job, Cleaver?"

"It's OK. You're not going to get a bullet in the back of the head."

"Why would I get a bullet in the back of the head?"

"Nothing. Just you seem nervous."

"I want to know, that's all."

"Your English is good for a Russian."

"We're intelligent people."

"I could never learn another language. I know a bit of Spanish, is all. But that's like American now, too. Spanish and English. American languages. You got any other tongues, Arkov?"

"No, I've only got the two."

"No special tongues, then? No tongues I'd be interested in."

"No, Cleaver, no tongues you'd be interested in."

They drove on. The track narrowed. Its surface became rougher. The Dodge bounced along.

Cleaver said, "You got queers in Russia?"

Dasaev said they had.

"You like queers?"

"Depends if they ask too many questions."

"I mean, you're not opposed to queers over there."

"No, we're not opposed."

"Mr Burns doesn't like them much. Mr Burns doesn't like much of anybody unless they're white and straight."

Dasaev said nothing. He stared ahead. The headlights illuminated the trees. Cleaver stopped the pickup. Dasaev watched him as he stepped out. They went to the rear of the pickup.

"Help me with this tarpaulin," said Cleaver.

They grabbed the material and whipped it away.

Her eyes were open, and they were glassy and stared up at the dark heavens.

CHAPTER 26.
LIFE AND DEATH.

"DO you have a death wish?" said Laura.

Zak held up his hands and backed away. "Laura, I don't mean you any harm."

"Harm? You can't harm me. I can harm you. I can rip your arms off. That would be harm. That would be a lot of harm. But you can't harm me."

"OK, OK, I'm not here to cause trouble."

"Trouble? You're in trouble. You're in the jaws of trouble, Zak. In the claws of trouble. You want me to get naked?"

"The answer I want to give is the answer I shouldn't give, I guess."

"I should kill you now. It would mean nothing. Leave you here in pieces. I was off, anyway."

"Where to?"

"Fuck off. Don't push your luck. You're grinning. You're giving it all that. But I know you're scared, Zak, I can smell it on you. I can smell your fear."

"I'm scared, all right, I'm scared."

"Why are you here? What do you want?"

"I want to help."

"Help? I don't need help. How did you know it was me?" Laura seethed. The hairs on her nape stood on end. Her fur made waves under her flesh. Her werewolf juices simmered.

Her other self threatened to fold itself out of her and make rags of Zak.

He slumped into a wooden chair. Ran a hand through his hair. He said, "I fell in love."

"Fuck that."

"Eight years ago."

"What?"

"In Trafalgar Square."

"You and your fucking photos."

"I've followed your story ever since, Laura."

"My story?"

"On the web. You know it's alive out there, don't you? Websites, forums, blogs. I followed you. You saved so many people that day."

Laura huffed. "I don't save people."

"But you did, didn't you?"

She glared at him. "I don't save people. Zak... I just *am*. Morality is nothing to me. I am not human. I don't care about good or evil. I don't know love and I don't know hate. I react to the situation at hand, and at hand at the moment, Zak, requires me to take some pretty fucking hostile action."

"There *is* human in you. Everything that humans have. And... and animals are altruistic, aren't they? We know this. What you did that day showed as much."

She shook her head. "Why are you telling me this?"

"Because I want you to know the effect you had on people that day."

Goosepimples raced over her body. Gloom fell on her again.

That day.

That fucking day.

The day she lost him.

Tears welled, but she focused on the now, the moment, and they dried away.

I don't know love.

She didn't. All she knew was that John Thorn jazzed her biology. He made her insides burn and burn in a way. He made her loins purr.

His not being in her life had coarsened her heart. His absence had withered her lust. Without him, there was no spark.

Maybe I do know love.

She cast the hope aside. She had no use for it. All was lost.

Now she said, "I don't care about the effect I had, if I had any. I want to know how you found me and after you tell me, I'll think about letting you live."

Zak told her about Central Park, seeing her sitting there. He said he knew for sure it was she. "But I wasn't, you know, one hundred per cent. Until recently. I got a shot of you. And then I knew."

"Knew how?"

"The birthmark."

Laura scowled. She writhed and the animal in her rose up again. "Birthmark? How do you know about the Greenacre birthmark, Zak?"

He gawped. He flushed. He tried to speak.

She growled.

He gibbered.

She flew at him.

She knocked him back in the chair and straddled him, pinned him to the ground.

Her skin rippled.

Zak yelled, and Laura clamped a hand over his mouth.

Her voice guttural, she said, "No sound. No sound but the truth. You know too much. No one knows about my birthmark. Only those close to me. Only those who hate me. The truth: how do you know?"

She slipped her hand from his mouth.

He shivered under her, and sweat glossed his brow.

He whimpered, trying to find his voice, then found it:

"R-Ruth Templeton – "

Laura tensed.

" – is in America. She's – she's sent men out – "

Dread bloomed in Laura's belly.

" – out to – to kill – J-John Thorn – "

She grabbed him and shook him and he whined. "Where is he? Where is he?" she said, her voice a snarl now, low and animal.

"He's – he's not here – she – she wants – wants to kill you – "

"Where is she?"

"I can – I can take you – show you – don't – don't eat me – "

115

CHAPTER 27.
FOR THE CROWS AND THE WOLVES.

DASAEV'S head spun. He said, "Who – who is she? Child. The poor child."

"She's nothing, no one," said Cleaver and started to drag the girl from the back of the pickup by her feet. "Come on, Arkov, get the shovels – "

Dasaev shoved him away.

Cleaver reeled. Whipped the gun out of the holster strapped to his ribs. Dasaev kicked it out of his hand. The weapon went spinning. Dasaev drove his boot into Cleaver's chest. Cleaver lurched backwards, thumped against a tree.

Dasaev turned to the girl. She'd been shot in the head. Blood curdled behind her right ear, matting her hair. Dasaev sobbed and touched her cold, white face.

Leaves rustled. He wheeled. Cleaver crawled for his gun. Dasaev wiped his tears. He strode over, scooped up the pistol. Aimed it at Cleaver who sat back with his hands in the air.

"Arkov, man, what are you doing?"

"This girl, this child... who is she?"

"Who the fuck are you, man? Are you some kind of fucking saint or something? Some fucking angel of vengeance? It doesn't matter who she is."

Dasaev said, "I will kill you Cleaver. I will kill you and leave you for the crows and the wolves."

116

"Jesus Christ, Arkov." Dasaev crossed himself. Cleaver started to get up. Dasaev nudged him in the chest with his boot. "Don't do that, Arkov. You're crazy. Let me get up, I'll tell you." Cleaver rose. He brushed himself clean. "New jeans, man, new fucking Levis today."

"Give me her name."

"Oh, Christ! She's meat, Arkov. One of Kolodenko's shipments. I don't know. She came from the safe house in Brooklyn. They sent two girls over a couple of days ago. Burns likes to check them out sometimes. I don't know what happened with this one. Something went wrong. Maybe she said no, and these girls, they're not in a position to say no. Maybe that's what she did and then this happened. I don't know, Arkov, OK? Stop pointing that gun at me, man. Look, we don't ask questions."

"The safe house, where is this safe house where they keep them?"

Cleaver sighed.

"The safe house, Cleaver."

"They call the place The Kennel. They cargo them over from Europe and Burns stores them there. He's got guys there, watchdogs. They keep an eye on the stock till they're ready to distribute them to whorehouses in the city. Down to Florida. New Jersey, too. Jesus, man."

"Where is the house?"

"Why the fuck do you want to know?"

"Where?"

"Brooklyn. I don't know. This is what your pal Tomich was involved in over there. Didn't you know that?"

"Did you kill her?"

"No, man, no."

"Who? Burns?"

"Hey, man. I don't know. Stokes, Burns, I don't know."

Dasaev glanced at the girl. "What life did she have?"

"Huh? I don't know. They want to come to America. Someone over there *gets* them to America. It's a service. All round. Women want to come over here, Burns helps them out – "

"With lies."

"What the fuck? They want to come, they come. And here,

117

men want to fuck women. So Burns serves them, too. Service. Grab the shovels. We got to bury her, Arkov."

"For the crows and the wolves."

Silence fell. Dasaev touched the girl's face again. And then he closed her eyes. He said a prayer for her in his head, and it brought tears to him.

Cleaver sighed. "Her name was Panya Belofsky. She was nineteen. From Belarus. Don't know where in Belarus. Don't ask me that. She could play the piano. Really good. I heard her the other day."

Dasaev remembered. The piano tinkling somewhere in the house when Procter and Ruth Templeton had arrived.

Cleaver continued:

"She lived with her mother, but they were poor, you know. Everyone's poor, huh? She wanted to come to America to teach piano. This guy said he could do that for her. For a price, sure. But he could do that. She paid. Every penny she and her mom had."

He fell silent for a few seconds. And then he continued:

"Yeah, they lie to them, Arkov. But everybody lies, huh? You lie."

Dasaev looked him in the eye. He tucked the gun into his belt.

"How do you know all this about her?"

Cleaver shrugged. "Gets tedious in that house. Nice to talk to people sometimes. Nice to get to know them."

"We'll bury her deep. Bury her properly. Not for the crows and the wolves."

Cleaver nodded.

Dasaev carried her in his arms. They found a clearing. They stripped off their shirts and the sweat glistened on their bodies. It took them three hours. And when it was done, Dasaev knelt at the grave and prayed for her.

He laid a hand on the soil and said, "I will always remember where you sleep, Panya Belofsky. I will not let you be forgotten."

CHAPTER 28.
THE DAY OF THE HUNT.

DAWN broke, leaching into the night sky. Two vehicles threaded along a track through the forest. Their headlights showed the path through the gloom. Taking the lead, a white cattle truck driven by Cleaver, Dasaev in the passenger seat. He glanced in his side mirror. The Land Cruiser pickup followed them up the track. Burns drove the pickup. Lawrence Procter sat in the passenger seat. The woman wasn't with them. Maybe she didn't like hunting.

Dasaev looked ahead.

"Will we need to bury another one today?" he said.

Cleaver said nothing. He'd been quiet this morning. Not looking Dasaev in the eye. Dasaev thought the man felt shame for what had happened the previous night.

He asked Cleaver, "How do you live with this?"

Cleaver didn't answer. Stared straight ahead. Jaw clenched. Reminded Dasaev of the "speak no evil" monkey, with his hand clasped over his mouth.

He said, "This is murder."

Still nothing from Cleaver.

With every minute that passed, with every mile travelled, Dasaev's dread grew.

They hunted humans here.

His throat was dry. He lit a cigarette.

Cleaver finally spoke:

"Hey, what the fuck are you doing? You know how Mr Burns – "

"He's going to hunt a human being. I don't give a damn about his distaste for tobacco smoke."

Cleaver said, "OK. I guess it's fine for you to have one... I guess."

"Who is it?"

"Who's what?"

"In the back. The prey."

Cleaver shrugged.

"You know," said Dasaev. "You put them in there, didn't you?"

"I don't know, some girl."

"Is she the one in the photo? The one they say is this monster, this wolf-creature?"

Cleaver shook his head. "Not her, Arkov, OK? She's – she's coming. Being brought here today. But don't ask more, OK? I can't do this, now. Jesus! I can't tell you anything, Arkov, all right. I can't tell you any more."

Dasaev felt queasy. "This has to be stopped."

"You can't stop it. Just go with it. Just today, OK. Jesus, man, you know how tough this is for me?"

"Then why do you let it happen?"

"Fuck, man, who are you? Haven't you seen shit like this in Russia?"

"I have seen a lot of shit, but it does not enable me to endure it, Cleaver."

Cleaver blushed. He was sweating. "Shit, man, we're here. I'm sorry, OK?" He stopped the truck and leaped out. He stared at Dasaev and said, "They'd've killed me, Arkov. Burns would've had me killed." Cleaver strode away towards the rear of the truck. Dasaev glanced in the side mirror. The Toyota came to a halt behind them. Burns, dressed in combat gear, pistol holstered on his thigh: a Colt six-shooter.

A cowboy's gun, thought Dasaev, getting out of the cab.

Something twisted in Dasev's guts. The horror of what was about to happen enveloped him. He tried not to shiver, tried not to be sick.

Burns said, "Dawn's coming." He breathed. "I love that, the

odour of a new day." Procter glared at Dasaev. Dasaev stared right back.

The doctor had stared at him since he'd arrived. Dasaev wondered if he'd recognized him. He couldn't imagine how that was possible. He let it go. Maybe Procter had been told that this Arkov guy was a friend of Tomich. He was maybe trying to remember if he'd seen the Russian somewhere. Seen him with Tomich, with Kolodenko.

"Let's get the truck open," said Burns. "Arkov, do the honours."

Dasaev froze. Looked from Burns to Cleaver. Cleaver lowered his gaze.

"Come on, Arkov," said Burns. "Time you got acquainted with our American hunting customs. Open the fucking truck."

Fear coursed Dasaev's veins. Fear for the victim, the terrified prey he would see once he lowered the door.

He unbolted the door. Took the clips out. Took the weight as it drawbridged down. He said a prayer for whoever was inside. Whoever would be hunted today.

Then a switch clicked in his brain.

The names of the prey and the names of the hunters.

The names of the hunters.

He lowered the door. He saw inside the truck. Something in the gloom.

There are no hunters, he thought.

He steeled himself.

He dropped the door and it clanked on the ground, threw up dust. A shape swelled in the dark interior of the truck. Dasaev retreated.

He glanced over his shoulder. Burns had a look of awe etched on his face. Dasaev told him, "There are no hunters."

Burns, gazing wide-eyed into the truck, said, "There's one. Jesus in heaven, there *is* one."

Dasaev glared into the truck again. His bones turned to ash. His body seemed like water, and he thought he would melt away.

The creature in the truck stepped out of the gloom. Bared its fangs and fixed its yellow eyes on Dasaev.

CHAPTER 29.
NISSAN.

"I HATE them, you know," said Zak. "Hate them. They're
so... dependable. Nothing exciting about them. I hate them
because my dad always said, 'Get a Nissan, son, that's what
you want – never let you down, a Nissan,' that's what he'd say.
And my dad, I didn't like my dad. Slippers and pipe, you know.
In this day and age? Estate agent, see. Family business. Weaver
Properties. His dad's dad, my great-granddad, founded the
firm. Very old fashioned. Believed in customer service. Not in
making money. Not in greed."

He tutted. He left a pause. Laura left it too. He went on:

"That's shit, isn't it? You can't do anything without greed.
Just a little greed, even. Everyone's greedy, aren't they? And
you know, Weaver Properties is struggling, apparently. I don't
speak to him now, my dad. Or my mum. They wanted me to
join the firm, inherit it from him, you see. I'm the only son,
yeah. But I broke their hearts. Came looking for you instead."

Laura said nothing.

"And here we are. Very early morning. Sixty miles from our
destination. In a fucking Nissan. My dad's probably pissing
himself."

She kept quiet, her eyes fixed on the road.

He said, "You're going to have to speak to me at some stage."

She said, "The only thing I'm going to have to do at some stage is eat you."

That shut him up. They drove in silence for a while. Laura smelled his anxiety. The odour of sweat coming off him. His blood quick through his veins.

Zak meant nothing. He was only meat. And when this was done, he'd die. Just an effective, necessary kill.

Her father's voice came to her:

"We can't help it, Laura, we eat flesh and if it's human, so be it. We kill to eat, we kill to protect. That's our instinct. It's how nature made us. You'll understand when you grow up."

And she did understand. She always understood. Even when she didn't know who she was, when she wandered from foster family to foster family, from job to job, from place to place.

And until Elena found her and awakened her memories, Laura had been lost.

But finding herself, discovering who she was, had brought more pain. It fired in her a need for revenge. And the hunt for Sir Adam Templeton, her family's killer, revealed a truth that brought despair and horror.

She was Adam's daughter. Her mother had slept with her family's enemy.

She was half-sister to Michael Templeton, Adam's son.

Better to be lost, she thought.

And if you *can't find yourself, no one else can, either.*

She shut her eyes, thought of John Thorn.

Ruth had sent men out to kill him. The horror of it churned in Laura's belly.

She said, "Ruth Templeton knows we're coming, I guess?"

"Sh-she doesn't," he said.

The lie stank, but she didn't say anything.

He said, "I don't work for her, you know."

"I don't care if you do, I don't care if you don't."

"I'm your trickster, that's all," he said and gave a laugh.

Laura bristled. "I don't care. You have betrayed me, and it makes me sick being close to you."

"Laura, I haven't – "

"I don't know exactly what you've done. But you found me,

and that's scary, that someone as incompetent as you could find me."

"I'm not fucking incompetent, right."

"I said I don't care. You've somehow found out that Ruth Templeton is here. The only way you know she's here is because you have some kind of contact with her, OK?"

"That's not true. I found you, I could find her. I'm fucking good."

"You're taking me to her, Zak, and whether she's waiting for me or not, I don't care. Whether she knows or not, I don't care. If I see her, I'm going to kill her."

He said nothing.

Laura went on: "She underestimates me. I'm much stronger than she is. She doesn't stand a chance. I killed ten of her pups. Ten of them." She glared at him. "You think you're taking me into a trap? You're not. I'll destroy them all, Zak. All of them. Anything that stands in my way. And if I hear John Thorn has died, I'll hunt down his killers and devour them and I'll devour their fucking children and their fucking wives, too."

She breathed deeply and stared ahead.

"And then, Zak... I'm coming for you."

The Nissan smelled of terror.

CHAPTER 30.
MEETING KOLODENKO'S
KILLER.

THE creature skulked out of the truck.

The white-gold fur bristled. The animal looked part-bear, part-wolf, part-human. The lips curled back to bare incisors as long as Dasaev's hand.

The beast snarled at Dasaev, and he moved back.

The animal reared up on its hind legs and stood more than six-and-a-half feet tall. Saliva drooled from the jaws. The yellow eyes narrowed.

Cleaver said, "Jesus holy God!"

Procter said, "Major Lev Dasaev – "

Dasaev heard his name, didn't expect it. He gawped at Procter, and the doctor smirked.

" – meet Vasili Kolodenko's killer – "

And Procter laughed.

Dasaev turned to face the monster. He backed away. Something cold pressed against the back of his head.

"Fucking impressive, isn't it," said Burns, right behind Dasaev, right behind him with the gun. "You want me to do you a favour, Russian, or d'you fancy your chances against this thing, huh? Personally, I want to see you ripped apart, you lying fuck. You fucking, lying, fucking cop. My guess is your death will go unreported. You're not here officially, are you? You're out of your jurisdiction."

"Sure," said Dasaev, "so phone the FBI. Phone the NYPD. Get them out here, we'll talk it through."

"You're a funny guy," said Burns.

"I got better jokes," said Dasaev.

"You think – "

Dasaev spun. Swiped Burns's gun hand away with an elbow. He grabbed Burns's wrist. Twisted, forcing Burns to bend double. Took the gun off him. Kneed Burns in the face. Dragged him back by his hair and got behind him. Jammed the gun in his ear.

Burns moaned.

The creature hunched down on all fours, ready to pounce.

Procter said, "Dasaev, don't be stupid."

Dasaev said, "Call it off, Burns. I only count to two. Two, then I shoot you"

Burns moaned. "You... you broke my jaw... "

The American wilted in Dasaev's grasp. Dasaev said, "One... " as the creature shuffled forward.

Dasaev retreated with Burns in his grasp. He glanced into the Toyota. The keys were in the ignition. He shoved Burns towards the monster and took a wild shot with the Colt.

Cleaver shouted. Procter ducked. Burns tripped into the animal. The creature roared and swatted him away.

Dasaev opened the Land Cruiser's door, leaped into the cab.

The monster lunged. Dasaev started the engine. Slammed the car into reverse, and it swerved and whined its way down the trail. Dasaev looked to the front now. The werewolf bounded after him. The engine revved. The driver's door swung on its hinges.

Dasaev cursed in Russian.

The monster leaped. Dasaev watched, open-mouthed. The monster hovered. Crashed onto the bonnet. Dasaev rammed the accelerator, and the vehicle swerved backwards. The creature clawed at the bonnet. Sparks flew as bone scored metal. Spit sprayed from the animal's jaws, and saliva smeared the windscreen. Dasaev flicked on the wipers. They squealed across the glass, wiped it clean, showed Dasaev a mouthful of teeth six inches from his face. The engine droned. The needle hit 50mph in reverse.

Dasaev yanked on the handbrake.

The tyres screeched.

He twisted the steering wheel.

The car whirled.

Dasaev gritted his teeth. Grasped the steering wheel so hard his knuckles turned white. The werewolf flew off the bonnet and tumbled into the trees.

Dasaev shoved the car into drive – and floored the accelerator.

He switched on the headlights, and they punctured the early-morning gloom. He hammered the Toyota. The vehicle bumped and jerked over the terrain. The impact tossed Dasaev about in the cab. He'd not had time to put his seatbelt on. The door swung. He grabbed it, slammed it shut.

Sighed with relief.

Glanced in his mirror.

And cursed, and this time crossed himself.

The werewolf chased him – gaining on the Land Cruiser.

Dasaev looked at the speedometer. He was doing 60mph on rough roads. Not good for the car. He threw the Toyota around corners. The werewolf came hurtling after him, appearing out of the clouds of dust the vehicle kicked up.

For a moment, he thought he'd shaken off his pursuer, and he slowed.

But then it loomed out of the dust and the darkness at pace. Launched itself again. Landed in the back of the pickup. The vehicle shuddered. Bounced on its suspension.

Dasaev slammed the breaks.

The tyres churned up the earth.

The monster ploughed forward.

The cab buckled.

Dasaev thumped against the steering wheel.

For a second, everything was hazy. He forgot where he was. Then he came to with a start. He looked behind him. The werewolf lay sprawled in the back of the pickup. Dasaev slammed the truck into reverse, then sharply into drive. The creature rolled off the back.

Dasaev kept going, sweat dripping off him, teeth gritted.

The road smoothed out. He saw the house up ahead. He glanced in his mirror. Dawn seeped into the darkness. The forest lay dark miles behind him.

He sped past the house and up the drive – a mile to the front gates. They were shut. He kept his foot on the accelerator. He grimaced. Braced himself for the impact.

The gates rushed towards him.

CHAPTER 31.
HISTORY AND BLOOD.

CLEAVER watched the Toyota's tail-lights dim as the truck got further and further away, heading down towards the house.

Burns, standing next to him, nursing a bloody nose, said, "I hope he doesn't make it out of here with my pickup, I love that pickup. It's the only black thing I like."

Procter said, "He won't. She'll catch him."

"She'd better."

Cleaver watched as the Land Cruiser faded into the early-morning gloom. He hoped the Russian, whatever his name was, got away. Cleaver hadn't known he was a cop. Burns told him the previous night that the Russian would be the prey that morning. Told him after they'd buried the girl, after the Russian showed Cleaver what honour really was. Cleaver had asked Burns why they were killing the Russian, and Burns said, "Because he's a fucking queer, Cleaver. Because he's black. Because he slept with my wife. Because he's got three heads. It doesn't matter why. Don't ask questions. Never ask questions. Just do what you're told."

The men stared after the vehicle now.

Burns paced. He seethed, nursing his injured face. He cursed the Russian. Then he glared at Procter and said, "Where did you find this woman? How does she do that, change into that monster?"

129

"She's from an old family," said the doctor. "Related to the woman you'll be hunting this evening."

"Related? So why does your lady want the other lady dead?"

"They are entwined by history and blood. They trace their ancestry back to two brothers. Etruscans. An ancient tribe that existed before Rome. The brothers, according to legend, were lycanthropes. Werewolves. When Rome arose, one of the brothers wanted to be part of the establishment, wanted power, respectability. He rejected his animal side. He barred his children from using their gift for metamorphosis, you see. He instilled in them human qualities, qualities that position us above the animals. Qualities that have enabled man to progress, to control his destiny – unlike the animal, of course. As the centuries passed, the werewolf gene withered in the Templeton branch. It became vestigial. Unused. A trace of something lost."

Procter leaned on the truck and wiped his brow. The man looked exhausted. He went on:

"The other brother stayed true to his werewolf side. His descendents became the Greenacres. An unruly bunch. Inbreeders. Wanderers. Gypsies."

"And now the Templetons have got their animal side back, huh?" said Burns.

"They have."

"And this Greenacre girl, she's the last of them, the last of her family."

"The last."

Cleaver felt dizzy. This sounded like madness to him. He thought about the Russian. Wondered if he'd got away. He gazed towards the house, but the rise and fall of the land blocked his view. All he saw were shadows.

His phone rang. He fished it out of his coat pocket and looked at the screen. He answered it saying, "What, Stokes?"

Burns looked at him as he listened to Stokes.

He put the phone back in his pocket.

Burns said, "Well?"

"The prey's close, sir."

"She's here?" said Procter.

"Nearby," said Cleaver.

Burns said, "Get yourself set, Cleaver. Don't fuck it up. Has that soldier guy got here yet?"

CHAPTER 32.
GOING BACK.

DASAEV drove north, past gabled cottages with thatched roofs. He drove past mansions and horse farms, past wind turbines and forests and open fields.

He drove twenty miles and then ditched the Toyota off-road in a grove of pines. He tossed the keys out into the trees. The vehicle was wrecked. The engine clanked. Smoke billowed from under the bonnet. The suspension was screwed. He'd lost his hub caps, and he was sure he had a puncture. If he drove any further, he risked getting pulled over by the cops. He rifled through the Land Cruiser before dumping it, seeing if he could find anything useful. He did: a Sig Sauer 9mm pistol, loaded.

He smoked under the canopy of trees.

He watched dawn crawl across the sky.

He trembled, and his heart raced.

What the hell was that creature?

He knew, but didn't dare say its name. It was too impossible.

The animal matched those he'd seen in the video Burgasova had shown him.

Burgasova, he thought.

Dominika.

An urge to hear her voice filled him.

He checked his watch. It would be afternoon. He dug out his phone, scrolled through the address book to the letters "SDB" – Sergeant Dominika Burgasova.

She answered and Dasaev closed his eyes and everything seemed good. He spoke, and she gasped, asking if he was OK. He told her what had happened.

She said, "Are you sure?"

"It was right there in front of me. Its teeth were inches from my face."

"And this is the creature that killed Kolodenko?"

"That's what the English doctor said: *meet Vasili Kolodenko's killer*. I can't say it was an honour."

"A werewolf?"

"I don't know about that word. It sounds like Hollywood, like fables. What I saw was real. What about this English woman? Did you get anything on her?"

Burgasova told him Ruth Templeton had spent time in prison for kidnapping.

Dasaev thought for a moment.

Then he said, "You need to contact the FBI."

"And say what, that one of my superior officers is in their country covertly carrying out a private investigation?"

"Tell them. It doesn't matter what happens to me."

"It matters to me."

Things inside him melted. Things he thought had coarsened over the years. Things that had been encrusted by indifference, by cruelty, by despair.

He embraced the thawing out of his feelings for a moment and then said, "I have to find this woman, the one they are going to hunt."

"Forget it. You have to get out. If I'm contacting the US authorities, they can deal with it."

"I can't do that, Dominika. They'll be too late. Once you contact them, the gears of bureaucracy will crank for hours, perhaps days. This woman doesn't have days. And this Burns, his reach goes high into the establishment. He might be able to delay an investigation. And then she'll be dead. I have to do this now."

"Please… please let the US authorities deal with it; let them stop it, major. You get out. Come home… to me."

He was liquid now, and the feeling of wanting her flowed through him freely.

"I will," he said, "that's what I'll do, Dominika: I'll come home to you."

"Lev…"

"But first I'm going back. I have to. I can't let anyone else die."

CHAPTER 33.
PICKING UP A SCENT.

ZAK said, "What the hell happened to that gate?"

They'd parked opposite the entrance. The gate lay warped on the side of the road. Something had rammed into it, knocking it off its hinges. Chunks of concrete peppered the ground where the pillars had crumbled.

"What is this place?" said Laura.

"This is... this is where Ruth is... supposed to be." He stared at the broken gate. The colour had left his cheeks.

"What's the matter with you? You look like your plan's falling apart."

"Eh? No, no, it's just... " He didn't finish. He looked confused, his Adam's apple bobbing up and down, his eyes wide.

Laura said, "Doesn't look good, does it? You think your friends are in trouble, Zak?"

"F-friends?"

"Yes. Ruth. Whoever lives here. Who *does* live here?"

"I've no idea. Honest."

"Christ, you lie badly."

She got out of the car. She gazed across at the entrance.

A road snaked down through a corridor of pines. In the dim light of dawn, she saw hills and forests and fields. She smelled wilderness. She smelled traffic fumes. She smelled a trap.

She bent and looked through the car window at Zak. "Ruth's here?"

"This is where she's staying. That's what I know. With a friend."

"More friends?"

"Th-they're not friends of mine, Laura. I only brought you here because you want to find her."

Laura straightened. "I didn't want to find her. I didn't want *her* to find me. But anyone comes looking for me, that's their bad luck."

She trotted over the road.

Zak said, "Should I go now?"

"Is that what you've been told to do?"

"No... I – "

"Stay there."

She studied the gate. The bars were bowed. The paint had been scratched away to show steel underneath. The hinges had been torn from the concrete columns. A red light flashed on an intercom pinned to the left-hand pillar.

Laura craned her neck and sniffed. Dozens of odours filled her nostrils. She rifled through them, identifying them one by one.

She froze, only her eyes moving, flitting over the pines that lay ahead of her.

The odour that stopped her was men.

They lurked in there somewhere.

Three of them.

She shivered, her spine rippling.

She turned and said to Zak, "Are you supposed to leave me here?"

"Laura, I – "

"Do what you've been told to do, Zak. If you're going, go. If you're staying, stay."

He glared at her, hate in his eyes.

"You can look at me like that," she said, "but it makes no difference to me. You think it scares me? You think men scare me?"

"You're a bitch."

"I know, but I'm not a coward."

"I'm doing this because it's what you wanted. I'm bringing you to her."

"How much are they paying you, Zak?"

"Nothing, I get nothing."

Laura laughed. "I can smell it on you when you lie. I can smell the blood rising up into your face. I can smell your sweat. I can smell it from here, Zak."

"Fuck you. I wanted you to like me, and I was nice to you. But you're cold. You're a fucking ice queen, you are. Fuck you."

"Your voice, it's trembling. You scared?"

"Fuck you again." He started the car. "Good luck, Laura."

"I'll need it, will I?"

He said nothing. Revved the Nissan.

"One thing," she said.

"What?"

"After I'm done here, I'll find you. I will find you. I want you to know what it's like to be hunted. I want you to know that I'm on your trail, and I have your scent."

He sped away, the tyres screeching. Fumes billowing from the exhaust. The stink of petrol smoke and rubber blanked out the other odours, and Laura winced.

She turned and walked through the entrance and headed down the road. Her head swam, the reek of fuel and rubber heavy in her nose. The odours had doused her sense of smell. The hairs on her nape prickled. Her eyes widened, and she scanned the trees. She couldn't sniff out the men.

CHAPTER 34.
WOUNDS.

RUTH Templeton, clenching and unclenching her fist, blood thundering though her veins, said, "I want him found. I want him brought to me for killing."

She huddled under a blanket on her bed in Burns's house. She shivered, and her body ached. She'd been scarred during the prison raid in England a week earlier. Now the hunt for this Russian had left her with more injuries. Bruises patched her ribs after she was tossed from the vehicle. Pins and needles had spread through her shoulder and neck after she was hurled against the cab when he braked. She'd been knocked out by the impact and had tumbled off the back of the pickup.

Procter offered to look at her wounds again.

"I'm fine, Lawrence. You only want to see my body."

"I am a doctor, Ruth, for God's sake."

"You're also a sex criminal."

"Ruth, please. I'm concerned."

"Get me a gin and tonic, slice of lime in it. I'll be fine."

He stomped out.

"We fucked up," said Burns, sitting on the windowsill. He stared out towards the hills.

"You let your guard down, let him use you as shield."

He turned to glare at Ruth. His nose was red. "He was quick – he was strong."

"I should've gone through you, Mr Burns."

Burns sneered. "Cleaver would've killed you."

"Cleaver, who you treat with such contempt? Your gay cavalier? Ha!"

"He knows who pays his wages, ma'am. He knows who saved him from the lake of fire and all its demons."

"Bad boy, is he?"

"Cleaver was a soldier. They don't like queers in the US Army. He got drummed out. I found him beating up four thugs in an underground, no-holds-barred fighting contest in New Jersey. Four-on-one. Cleaver-the-queer kicking hell and damnation out of them all. He was crazed. Doped up. I rescued him. I am his saviour, and as his saviour, I will treat him in any way I see fit. He knows where salvation lies — it lies here."

"Delightful. Where's the bloody Russian, Mr Burns?"

He licked his lips. "We've not got the manpower to go look for him. Your prey will be here soon. Cleaver and the men are waiting for her. Your soldier's here, too. But the Russian is gone."

"Might he ring the authorities?"

"He might, but he'll have to explain his presence here."

"He might ring them anonymously."

"If so, would you believe him? Would you believe a foreigner babbling about werewolves?"

She looked him in the eye. "I like the way you don't give a damn, Mr Burns."

"I am rich and powerful enough not to, Ms Templeton."

An urge passed through her. He wasn't a handsome man. He wasn't young like she liked them. But men were men when it came to it. And she had an itch.

"Would you like to lick my wounds, Mr Burns?"

"You know, I think I would."

She slid the blanket down over her shoulder.

The door opened, and Procter entered with a gin and tonic.

Ruth bristled.

"There," said Procter.

"Perfect timing," she said.

A phone rang. Burns's mobile. He took it out of his back pocket, answered it. He listened open-mouthed. He shut the phone. Told Ruth, "That was Cleaver. She's here. In his sights. She's ours."

CHAPTER 35.
END OF THE ROAD.

THE first dart struck Laura in the throat. It felt as if her head had been set on fire.

Anger surged through her. She cursed her stupidity, her arrogance. She'd clocked the men. Had them covered. But she lost their scent in the fumes that billowed from Zak's car.

For a few seconds, that's all.

Long enough for them to nail her.

Nissan, she thought, her head swimming, *I hate Nissans...*

Laura yanked the dart out of her neck. Her chest tightened. She stumbled down the road, her vision blurring. Her jaw felt weird. Like the joints were clogged with glue. She opened and closed her mouth. Noises came from her throat. Her eyelids felt heavy. Drowsiness washed over her.

Sleep, she was thinking, *sleep, I need sleep...*

She slipped out of the leather jacket. She tried to kick off her shoes but tripped over her feet. She hit the ground. The asphalt chafed her palms and her knees. The pain crashed through her lethargy. She hissed, and the hurt was good.

She stayed on all fours and stiffened. She looked up. Her head whipped from side to side. Her nostrils flared, trying to pick up the scent again.

She got one. To her right. She snarled. Glimpsed him through the trees. Her flesh rippled. The animal inside her rose and grew. Her shape changed.

The dart pierced her shoulder.

She threw back her head and howled.

She tried to pull the dart out. Lost her balance when she lifted her hand off the ground. Fell on her side. The trees distorted. They swam before her eyes. She felt sick. Tiredness blanketed her again. The desire to curl up and sleep was overwhelming.

No, no, no...

She tried to get up. She couldn't feel her legs. Couldn't feel her arms. Her chin dropped, and she fought to keep it up, snapping her head back.

Stupid, stupid, stupid...

She got into a squat and swayed. Her body swelled. Claws sprang from her knuckles. Her fingers curled inwards and melded into her palms. Her face stretched outwards. Teeth grew from her gums. Fur ruptured through her skin.

But she was too dazed... couldn't make the change... halfway there...

She shook her head. Roared and wailed and tried to stand. Her knees began to bend backwards like the hind legs of a dog, a wolf. But her balance was skewed. The world trembled. The forest swam. The road undulated. She heard crackling. Heard voices and static. Her mind reeled.

She moaned.

A third dart punctured her right eye.

* * * *

Fury charred Zak's insides. He downed the glass of water, but it didn't help. The waitress came with coffee. She smiled, but he didn't give one back. She poured the coffee, and the smell cooled him. He waited until she'd moved to the next table before he took a drink. The caffeine surged through him, and he shuddered.

He'd left Laura standing at the entrance. He came to Pawling, seven miles south of where he'd left her. He found the diner in town. The time was nearly 7.30 a.m. and he thought he could eat. But when the waitress asked if he wanted breakfast, he said no, just coffee and a glass of water.

He wondered who owned the property with the gates torn

off. Cole had phoned him and told him where to take Laura. Told him Ruth would be there. Zak had asked who owned the place, but Cole said it was none of his business.

Cole told him to wait in the diner. "Ruth will meet you there later, bring your fee – and she really is looking forward to meeting you. Likes young men."

Commuters dropped in to the diner for takeaway coffee. They chattered and laughed. Some came to eat in. The odour of bacon wafted through the restaurant. The clank of pots and pans came from the kitchen. Waitresses scurried about, gathering dirty dishes, topping up coffee cups.

He waited, his nerves ragged.

He'd seen the last of Rose Blythe, of Laura Greenacre.

Eight years he'd given this woman. Eight years thinking about her, tracking her down, making contact. Eight years planning her downfall. Eight years dreaming of the future, what he'd do with the money.

He gritted his teeth.

If you'd've been nice to me, I might not've sold you out, he thought.

But it was done now. She hadn't been nice. She hadn't felt for him what he felt for her. The rejection scarred him. He'd come here to find her. To betray her and to make money out of her. And although he still intended to do that, he couldn't quench the lust that welled up in him. He'd given her a chance to like him, but she hadn't taken it.

Stupid cow, he thought. *I gave you eight years of my life, and you gave me nothing back – nothing but contempt.*

But she'd be dead this time tomorrow. He looked at his watch. Coming up to 8 a.m. He'd meet Ruth Templeton. She'd give him his cash, and he'd be gone. Eight years of work done and paid for.

Zak felt empty. Like he'd been bled. Stuff buzzed about in his head and made him dizzy. He thought about what had happened over the years, about Rose/Laura, about the emptiness ahead of him.

How the fuck am I going to fill all that?

He finished his coffee, held up his cup. The waitress, wearing the same smile, strode over.

"More coffee, sir?"
He nodded and she poured.
"Are you having a busy day today, sir?"
He looked her in the eye.
"It's a killer," he said.

CHAPTER 36.
THE BODY.

"IS she dead?" said Stokes.

Cleaver looked at him. Bruises purpled his face. The Russian had given him a real beating. Cleaver fixed on the woman. He crouched and plucked the dart from her eye. Blood trickled from the wound. He checked her pulse.

"She's alive," he said.

He shouldered his Pneu-Dart rifle. They'd used M-99 in the darts. Tranquillizer drugs were never used on people. The narcotics employed could cause breathing difficulties. And a drop of M-99 would kill a human in minutes.

But Laura Greenacre wasn't entirely human.

Cleaver had warned Burns and the Templeton woman of the dangers. They'd dismissed his concerns. And Procter argued that Greenacre's physiology would cope with the drug. The Templeton woman said, "And if she does die, so be it. That's why she's here, isn't it? To die."

Now Stokes said, "The dose we gave her would've knocked out an elephant."

"She's not an elephant," said Cleaver.

The other man said, "We should've used this stuff when I last met this honey."

Cleaver glanced up at him. The guy was called Jerry Bahrman. He was ex-Special Forces. Tanned, scarred, and muscled, Ruth Templeton had brought him in as "a consultant, someone who has confronted the Greenacre werewolf in the past, knows what to expect."

Cleaver asked how they'd fucked it up so badly the last time.

Bahrman smirked. "We fucked up because I wasn't in charge, sweetheart. Ray Craig left some kraut to run the show, guy called Markus."

"I heard she wiped you out," said Cleaver. "Nine of you. Big tough guys. Crying and begging for mercy."

"Seven she killed, pal. She didn't get me, didn't get Stick. We were too cool."

"I heard you ran like chickens."

The tendons in Bahrman's neck flexed. "We retreated in a controlled manner, queer boy."

Cleaver chuckled. Insults didn't bother him. He'd suffered a lifetime of verbal abuse. The most important thing for him was that he was getting to Bahrman. He went on:

"M-99 wouldn't have done you any good back then, Bahrman, because from what I heard you didn't get a shot off. Too scared, huh?"

"You cackle, kid. You ain't seen this bitch when she's furred and clawed."

"I've seen Ruth Templeton furred and clawed. I saw the Russian cop out-run her this morning."

"You should've asked me here a couple of hours earlier. I would've popped the Russian for you. Seeing as you didn't have the balls. And you, Stokes, I heard he spanked you, son."

The giant grimaced. "He caught me off guard."

"He sure did." Bahrman laughed.

"OK, enough," said Cleaver. "Let's get her down to the house before she wakes up. Go get the truck, Stokes."

"She ain't gonna wake up for hours, man," said Bahrman.

"Yeah, well, I guessed one dart would ground her, too. Took three. So I'm not taking any chances. And when she does wake up, I don't want to be around."

CHAPTER 37.
THE DEATH OF AN INSECT.

"AND you'll meet me in New York, Lawrence, in the apartment," she said.

Procter rolled his eyes. "I know, Ruth, but I don't understand why you won't stay to see her being killed. She's the last Greenacre. The last werewolf. Thousands of years of conflict come to an end today, and you won't witness it?"

Ruth reddened. She continued to pack her bag.

Procter tried again:

"See this finished."

She looked at him. "Do you know how I think of her, Lawrence? I think of her as nothing. I think of her as soil. If I think of her in any other way, as a true adversary, as a creature that breathes, that loves, that hates, it gives her, in my mind, a kind of honour, a kind of dignity: we are all God's creatures and other such mumbo jumbo."

She lifted her bag off the bed and put it down at her feet. She continued:

"You see, I don't want her to have dignity. I don't want her to have honour. Staying here to witness her death, however degrading it will be, feels like... a form of respect, somehow. And I don't respect her. I despise her. We thought we'd wiped them out nearly thirty years ago. But eight years ago, she appears from nowhere. Days later, my brother is dead. My nephew is dead. My son is dead. I am imprisoned and humiliated, and my marriage ends. I lose everything."

She looked away from him and gazed out of the window towards the hills, towards the hunting ground. She went on:

"Turning my back on her is a mark of contempt. It's derision. It's disdain. It is an insult, you see. Her death will mean nothing to me. It is like the death of an insect. The combing out of mites. The brushing off of dust. It's meaningless, Lawrence."

Procter sighed. He would've liked her to stay. But he'd see her in a few days. He'd wait here after the Greenacre werewolf had been killed. He'd take the skin and convey it to New York, where Ruth would be waiting.

Ruth faced him and said, "And don't forget the blood, will you."

"I won't forget the blood, Ruth."

He wouldn't forget the blood. Ten minutes later in his room, he had the briefcase open on the bed. Six vials of blood were slotted into the foam inlay. Three contained Laura Greenacre's blood. Samples Procter had stolen from the hospital where he worked, where she was brought for treatment, eight years previously. The other three contained Ruth's blood.

He'd injected Ruth with Laura Greenacre's blood weeks ago and Greenacre DNA meshed with Templeton DNA, giving Ruth the ability to transform her body. To become a werewolf. Now she planned to use the blood to create more monsters.

The Templetons, she said, would be the most powerful family in the land.

They would regain their place in the establishment. They would be in government. They would be in the police, in the Armed Forces. They would be in the church, even. And in all these institutions, the Templetons would hold high office.

Werewolves will rule Britain.

Procter chuckled. The woman was mad. But he didn't care. He felt safe with her, whatever her state of mind. He faced charges in the UK, but he wanted to go home. He missed England. *You would, after living in Moscow*, he thought. Ruth promised to shelter him. His medical skills were useful to her. He'd begun to understand lycanthropes, which would be vital if Ruth's scheme ever came to fruition.

Procter shut the briefcase and locked it. He began to pack his travel bag. He'd have to be ready to leave this evening, after Burns and his friends had hunted and killed Laura Greenacre.

But he had one task after the killing, before he left.

He drew the hunting knife out of its scabbard. The blade glittered. He'd never skinned anything before. It would be an interesting experience.

CHAPTER 38.
HUNTERS.

LEONARD Longman waddled into the library and said, "What the hell happened to your gate? And what the hell happened to your face?"

Burns scowled at the TV producer. "We had an incident here this morning."

"Don't ask him what kind of incident, Lenny," said Lomax Delaney, lounging in a chair, his feet up. "It'll fret you, old fella. You'll sweat and worry yourself."

Longman said, "What kind of incident?"

"Nothing," said Burns. He gestured at the briefcase Longman carried. "Is that your entry fee?"

Longman placed the briefcase on the round oak table. Three briefcases were on the table already. Longman nodded at each man in turn – Delaney, Harris Schumann, and James Wellington – and said, "They all pay the same as me?"

Wellington, parked on a leather couch with Schumann, said, "We've all paid the same, Lenny. Do you want to count it?"

Burns flicked open Longman's briefcase. The dollar bills seemed to glow in the dimly lit library. He liked it gloomy, though. Books lined the shelves, but he never read them. A wall-mounted TV looked over the oak table. Burns liked the odour of leather and brandy that always seemed to hang in the air. Liked to sit at the table and gaze at the portraits and paraphernalia that festooned the walls.

A glass cabinet containing Nazi memorabilia dominated the space above the fireplace. The display included SS armbands, photos of Hitler, a Swastika flag, and an Iron Cross.

A Ku Klux Klan hood and gown hung on a mannequin. Burns's great-great-grandfather, Malcolm Burns, had worn it in Tennessee after the Civil War. "Where's Hurst?" said Longman.

"He was operating this morning," said Delaney. "He should be with us any minute. He had an excuse, you see, Lenny. He saves lives. You make shit TV."

They laughed.

Delaney said to Burns, "This had better be worth it. Better than the last one."

"This'll be worth it, Lomax," said Burns. His eyes raked over the cash.

Half-a-million dollars.

"So," said Schumann, "where did you find this one, Wheeler? Not one of your Russian friend's whores, is she?"

The men chuckled.

"You mean that Kolodenko guy?" said Longman. "Heard he was dead."

They ignored him.

Wellington said, "Hope not. When we last used one of Kolodenko's girls, she didn't last ten minutes. I was having a shit when you nailed her, Lomax, remember?"

"I remember, Jim, because you're always having a shit, or farting."

"Hey, I've not farted in" – he glanced at his watch – "at least, oh – "

He farted.

The men groaned.

Wellington laughed and swigged his brandy.

The fart smell made Burns screw up his face. He could've shot Wellington. He mastered his fury and said, "You need to take this seriously."

The men's laughter and groans trailed off. They gazed at Burns.

"It's OK, Wheeler," said Lomax. "It's a game. This is leisure time."

Burns glared at the councilman. Delaney was the youngest man in the room. Thirty-two, with four children. Envy flared in Burns's belly.

Old money furnished Delaney's lifestyle. He could trace his ancestors back to before Independence. The young man had Irish blood. English too. But more than anything, he was an American. A patriot. And there were only a few of them left these days.

"Lomax," said Burns, "this is not leisure. This is something you've never seen before. This is something that will test our skills. This is something that could be dangerous – "

"Dangerous," said Longman, "I don't do dangerous. The point of hunting is that the hunter kills his prey. At no time should the hunter be endangered, no way."

"What's going on, Wheeler?" said Wellington.

"Yeah, tell us," said Schumann, "or he'll fart again."

Schumann smiled, but no one laughed this time. They stared at Burns. He picked up a TV remote control from the table.

The door opened.

"Am I late?"

"Hurst," said Longman. "You know how to crash a party. Wheeler was about to get serious on us."

Allen Hurst entered. "Money goes here?" he said, placing his briefcase on the table.

"How was the surgery?" said Delaney.

"Excellent. I think she'll survive." He took off his coat. He looked flustered. "OK, gentlemen, what are we watching? Have I missed anything?"

"No," said Burns, "the show's just starting."

He switched on the TV.

* * * *

"Stop the car," Ruth said to Cleaver, rapping on the glass partition.

He pulled over. Lowered the partition and asked her if she was all right. But she ignored him and got out of the car.

"Say that again, Ellis," she said into the phone, "I couldn't make it out. I was in the car, off to meet your young Zachary. Say that again."

Cleaver got out of the car. She waved him away, and he got in again.

Cole said, "Tonight, they're doing it tonight, Ruth."

"What time is it there?"

He told her it was 6.30 p.m.

Ruth said nothing. Her skin itched with excitement.

She could taste the deaths of Laura Greenacre and John Thorn. She could feel a burden lift from her heart. She looked east. The road stretched through fields and forests. *Follow it,* she thought, *and you'll be home.*

She pictured her journey's end, and it was glorious.

CHAPTER 39.
APPETITES.

BURNS and his companions fell silent while the housekeeper and a maid cleared the table. The women stacked the dishes on a trolley. They hurried their task. They were red-faced. Uneasy in the quiet and under the men's gaze.

Procter's eyes followed the maid. She was young, mid-twenties. He'd had his eye on her – but not his hands. Too late now, though. He'd be gone by this evening.

He'd joined the men for lunch, and they looked pale. Burns explained that they'd been shown the footage of Trafalgar Square.

"Now they know what we're hunting," he'd told Procter.

Tension filled the room. The women cleared the plates. Not much food had been eaten. Nerves had doused their appetites.

"Thank Christ for that," said Delaney when the maid and the housekeeper left the dining room, "I thought they were going to take all day."

"She's sweet, that young one," said Longman.

"You're married, Lenny," said Hurst.

Longman shrugged.

"Can we talk about the hunt?" said Schumann. "I'm apprehensive. What are we dealing with?"

Burns said, "We'll be hunting a werewolf. Our job is to kill it."

They gawped at Burns and he looked at each one of them.

"That," said Schumann, "is the craziest thing I have ever heard."

"A werewolf," said Hurst. "What are you talking about?"

"This a joke?" said Delaney.

"What do you mean it's our job to kill it, Wheeler?" said Longman.

"Lawrence, here, and his, uh, companion brought this animal to my attention. They want it dead. It's a long, convoluted story – "

"Maybe I can pare it down, get a three-act structure going," said Longman. He grinned, but got nothing back from the others.

Burns went on:

"We'll never get another chance like this, gentlemen. Next time it'll be back to runaways and drunks. And what kind of fun is that?"

They muttered and nodded.

"Who's hired you?" said Schumann. "Is it this guy?" He stuck a thumb at Procter. "Is he paying you, too?"

"Only you're paying me. It's how we've always done this, Harris. You pay me, I provide the prey and the hunting ground."

"So what does this guy – "

"My name's Procter."

"Yeah whatever. What does this guy and his – what did you say? – companion? – get?"

Procter looked Schumann in the eye and said, "We get what we want, sir. We get this creature dead."

Schumann curled his lip. "I don't like him."

"You don't have to," said Burns.

"I'm still nervous. This... this fucking animal, I don't know. Any of you guys remember this happening in London? Do you remember any of that stuff, Jim?"

Wellington shrugged. "Yes, I remember, but wasn't it explained? The authorities said wild animals, so to me they were wild animals."

"Well," said Procter, "they were werewolves."

"It's too dangerous," said Schumann.

Hurst turned to Procter. "Since you want this thing dead, will you be joining us?"

"Not my thing, I fear," said Procter.

"What do you specialize in?" said Hurst.

"I headed up an accident and emergency department for twenty years. What you'd call ER, I believe."

Hurst nodded. "I'm a paediatric surgeon, you know."

"Yes, I know," said Procter. He bristled. Hurst was twenty-five years his junior. He was handsome, with a full head of black hair flecked with grey. A tan from holidays in Hawaii, no doubt. And the freedom to hand over $500,000 in cash. Procter gnashed his teeth and made a smile. "You're much admired in the UK. I think you operated on a child from our part of the world last year. It was in the papers."

"You didn't have the skill to save her yourself, eh?" said Hurst.

The men laughed.

"All your talent comes over here," said Longman. "I produced a show last year that had three English actors in lead roles. Very able guys. Excellent American accents. But you know, any success over your side of the pond, they're straight over here. Make it big. Big is here. Small is there." He leaned back in his chair. His stomach strained against his shirt.

"You want your children saving, you send them over here," said Hurst, "you want your monsters killing... same thing."

Procter flustered. He sweated and said nothing, no voice in his dry throat.

Schumann continued to gripe. Complained that he didn't feel safe going into the woods with any kind of animal that could eat him on the loose.

"Don't you worry, Harris," said Burns. "I'm not going to put any of us at risk. The hunt always favours the hunter. We'll have an advantage. Now, we're all tense, we're all nervous after what we've seen. I think we need to relax a little." He got out his phone and made a call, saying, "We're ready." He put the phone away and said, "Dessert's coming, gentlemen."

The door opened, and Stokes walked in. He was so large that Procter didn't notice he had someone with him. But when the colossus shoved her forward, Procter saw a redhead. She was

154

young, late teens. Thin and pale, with wide brown eyes. She wore a black, halter-neck dress with a plunging neckline.

Burns said, "This is Inessa, from Belarus. She was one of two. I'm afraid the other one got a bit hotheaded, so we had to, uh, dampen her down. Hope you can make do with just the one, gentlemen."

"We'll do fine," said Longman, moving towards the girl, licking his lips.

Procter quaked with desire as the girl cowered and whimpered when Longman grabbed her arm and tried to kiss her.

Delaney stood and said, "I'm done, gentlemen. This is not my sport, as you know."

Hurst rose also: "You have your fun, guys. I'll go ring my kids, I think."

They left.

"More for us," said Longman.

Procter gawped at Inessa. His mouth grew wet. Longman pulled her over to the couch. Wellington was undoing his shirt. The girl quivered and cried.

She's just excited, that's all, thought Procter, *just excited*.

CHAPTER 40.
LET SLEEPING WEREWOLVES LIE.

CLEAVER checked on her. He crouched next to the cage. The enclosure was six feet high, six feet wide, six feet long. Made of steel. He grabbed a bar, gave it a shake. Solid. Nothing could get out of there.

He looked at the woman. She lay on the cage floor. Her flank rose and fell as she breathed. Gauze patched her injured eye. Cleaver had treated the wound despite Burns telling him to "let her go blind". The dart hadn't penetrated deeply, but anything going into your eye could blind you. Cleaver didn't know if she'd lose her sight or not. Her eye didn't look good, he knew that.

Her survival had stunned him. She'd been shot with three doses of M-99 and it had knocked her out for nearly four hours already. He shook his head.

"Tough lady," he said.

A rusted iron neck brace collared her throat. It was the kind used by slavers. Cleaver had seen pictures in Burns's library: blacks, naked and thin, necklaced together.

A heavy chain led from the collar around the woman's neck to a 300lb cannonball that dated back to the American Revolutionary War. Another of Burns's artefacts.

Cleaver rose and looked around the trophy room. The place stank of death. He screwed up his nose and shivered. The dim light cast shadows that partly hid some of the prizes on show. And that made it worse.

He turned to go but stopped in his tracks.

"Saying your goodbyes, Cleaver? Didn't think she was your type."

Bahrman stepped into the trophy room and kicked the door shut behind him. He was armed, a handgun holstered on his left hip. He scoped the place, and his face paled. He whistled his astonishment. "Now this is what I call a collection."

Cleaver said nothing.

Bahrman said, "I've seen many things in my life, but this – I tip my hat to your boss."

"I'll tell him. He'll appreciate it."

"And this one, she'll be up there soon?"

Cleaver looked at the sleeping woman. "I guess so. If they don't fuck it up."

"Don't worry, Cleaver, I'm here. There won't be any fuck-ups."

"You're not going hunting, Bahrman. You're extra muscle, that's all."

"Ah, come on. I don't want to miss out."

"You had your chance eight years ago. You fucked up back then, pal."

"You know," said Bahrman, "I think I might just shoot her now," and he drew his handgun, a Makarov, and aimed at the woman.

Cleaver stepped in front of the gun.

"You think you'd take a bullet for her?" said Bahrman.

Cleaver licked his lips. He banished the fear from his heart. "She's not yours to kill, Bahrman. She's bought and paid for. You put a bullet in her, and there'll be an empty space up on that wall. And Mr Burns dislikes unused wall space."

They stared at each other for a few seconds.

Bahrman chuckled and held the gun up. "You know what this is?"

Cleaver said he did.

Bahrman went on: "Soviet-made weapon. Used by Arab terrorists in the Seventies and Eighties. I've had this since Eighty-six. Killed a suicide bomber for it in Beirut."

Cleaver nodded. "So you're tough. Big deal."

Bahrman put the gun away.

"She do anything for you, Cleaver?"

"What do you mean?"

"I mean, does she get you hot?"

"She doesn't, no."

"So she's not the one to cure you, then?"

"I don't need curing, Bahrman, I'm not suffering from anything apart from an ailment caused by your presence."

"So what'll happen then?"

"When?"

"Come on, Cleaver, tonight. This hunt. Where does she go?"

"See that wall over there?" He pointed to the pannelled wall at the rear of the trophy room. "That's not a wall. Rolls up like a window blind. There's a door behind it. Size of your garage door. We haul the cage over there and then forklift it onto a truck. Drive it up into the hills."

"Then the guy who draws the short straw, he opens the cage, yeah?"

Cleaver indicated the matchbox-sized unit attached to the front of the cage. "Remote control. Flick a switch, the door slides open. Out she comes."

"And the chain? Round her neck?"

Cleaver stared at the woman. He said, "Evens the odds, so says Mr Burns."

"Good idea. We should've thought of that when we faced her in England all those years ago. Hey" – he moved towards the cage – "why don't we see if she's awake, poke her or kick her or – "

Cleaver said, "Leave her alone."

Bahrman halted. He glared at Cleaver.

Cleaver looked straight at him and said, "Let her sleep, man. She'll be dead in a few hours. Let her dream. Just let her dream."

CHAPTER 41.
AKEL DAMA.

ZAK yawned.

"Put your hand over your mouth," said Ruth Templeton.

"I'm driving," he said.

"One hand will do. Did your mother not teach you any manners?"

He took his eyes off the road to look at her.

"Eyes front, Zachary," she said.

"My mother, quite obviously, didn't teach me anything."

"Eyes front."

He obeyed. The road was clear. He wriggled in the seat. He felt good: money in his pocket, New York getting closer.

"Why didn't you want to stay?" he said.

"I have better things to do."

"But didn't you want to see her get killed? Didn't you want to kill her yourself?"

"She is not worthy of my attention. She doesn't deserve the effort of me becoming an animal." She put a hand to her brow. "You know," she said, "that a man called John Thorn killed my son, Ross."

Zak said nothing.

159

Ruth went on:

"Thorn's going to die tonight. And I'll wash my hands of his death too. I'll not have sour blood on my hands." She looked at him. "You see? You see how I dismiss these people? You see how I can make them worthless? I can make their deaths meaningless, Zachary."

Zak thought, *You're crazy.*

"You think I'm mad, don't you," she said.

Zak shuddered. Could she read his mind?

"I can sense things, Zachary," she said. "I can smell things. I can smell your doubt, read your sweat."

The way she spoke made him hard. It was weird. She was way too old for him, in her sixties. But there was something sexy about her. And the way she'd been touching him, talking to him, over the past few hours had made him hungry for her.

But he wouldn't go there. He'd stay away from her in that way. He wasn't keen on giving her a ride back to New York, but she'd asked him – or ordered him, really.

He'd've been happier travelling alone and leaving this madness behind: leaving Laura and Cole and the Templetons. It was over now. He'd done his Judas bit. He'd pocketed his thirty pieces of silver. He wanted to be far away. On an island somewhere, lapping up the sun, swigging cocktails.

Yes, life would be good from now on. He'd soon purge himself of Laura Greenacre. Any feelings he had for her would dwindle.

Ruth touched his thigh, and a current passed through him. She said, "How about we stop for a while?"

His mind reeled. A sweat broke on his nape.

He was thinking, *No way! Does she want to –*

And she said, "You're young and meaty, and I'd like a little taste before we say farewell."

Zak felt dizzy. He thought, *Helen Mirren's sexy, I'd do her. Joanna Lumley, she's gorgeous. Older women are hot.*

And Ruth Templeton looked forty-five – a delicious forty-five.

His heart raced. He was trying to justify this. He was trying to think if he could deal with it. Really, he didn't want to be involved, wanted to be free of this. But, Christ, what had she just offered him? He decided he *could* deal with it. He knew he could deal with it very well.

He glanced across at Ruth, and she pouted at him, and that gesture made something quiver inside him.

He said, "W-where do you want to – to stop?"

They spotted a sign for a picnicking area. She directed him down the side road. There were no cars, no one about in winter. They got out, and she led him through to the trees, walking ahead of him, not saying anything. The silence making it all the sexier.

He shivered like a kid who was about to do it for the first time.

It felt crazy. He'd never wanted it so badly.

They came to a clearing in the pines. She turned to face him and slid the fur coat off her shoulders. They were ten yards apart. He swallowed.

He said, "You – you want to do it here?"

"Why not?"

"OK, whatever."

Ruth took off her dress. Her skin was smooth and lightly tanned, slightly creased in parts. She stood in her underwear.

She said, "Let me see the flesh I'm going to bite."

"Jesus," he said, and tore off his shirt. Tugged at his jeans. Hopped about, trying to get them down his legs. He looked up at her, hoping she'd help. Wanting her to strip him.

And he saw her smile and her teeth moving in her mouth and her yellow eyes.

CHAPTER 42.
TROPHIES.

LAURA dreamed she was on an island. She prowled the beach, moving back and forth, calling out his name...

Johnny! Johnny! Johnny!

The sea was ablaze. Flames reared up from the waves. His body jerked on top of the fire. She screamed for him, her voice dying in the inferno's crackle.

A clanking noise came from behind her. She wheeled. The forest moved towards the beach. The dark mass of trees ploughed through the sand. They forced her backwards. She felt the heat of the burning sea on her back. The clanking noise grew. The dream slipped away. She opened her eyes, and pain surged through her head. She grimaced. She blinked. Her right eye smarted. She saw shadows.

"Wakey wakey, kitty cat," said a man, as he struck the bars of her cage with a cattle prod.

She wheezed and sat up. Her throat felt hot, and she threw up through the bars.

"Heavy night?" said the man. "Someone's going to have to clean that up. You know what I do with dogs? I rub their faces in it, teach them not to do it again. Should do the same with you."

Laura, rising slowly, said, "Try," her voice a croak. She felt sick, the room swimming in front of her. Her vision started to clear. But only in one eye. The other one throbbed. She touched it and felt gauze. She tore it away and gasped. She couldn't see. She touched her eye again. Caked in blood. She tried to open it but couldn't.

"We think you might lose it," said the man, "but don't worry, kitty cat, you won't be needing it."

She glowered at him through the bars of her cage. She jerked forward, and he flinched. The collar around her throat tightened and chewed into her flesh.

"What — what the fuck's this?" she said. She clutched the brace. The corrosion reddened her hands. She saw the chain and the cannonball. "What's this?"

The man smiled. He was mid-fifties. He wore a Stetson. He had on a green T-shirt with sweat patches under the arms. Combat pants and work boots.

"It's to make sure you haven't got an edge, missy," he said.

"Where's Ruth?"

"She's gone. You weren't worthy of her presence, she said. Last thing she told me was, 'Kill her, Mr Burns.' Oh, Wheeler Burns, by the way. I won't shake your hand. You might bite it off. But nice to meet you. You're a fox, I'll say."

"I'm nastier than a fox, and you'll soon find that out."

He laughed. "You've got backbone. I like that. Most of them piss and shit all over the place. Squeal and scream and beg."

"Most of who?"

"My prey."

"Your prey?" She looked around. The room was dark except for a spotlight on her cage. She sniffed and smelled dried flesh. Her brow creased. "Where's Zak?"

"Gone, I guess."

"You paid him for me?"

"Not me, kitty cat."

"Ruth."

"That's right."

"And what do you get, whoever the fuck you are?"

"I get a good hunt."

She sneered. "A good hunt? Prey? You're going to hunt me?"

Burns nodded.

"I don't think you know what you're doing," she said.

"You think so?"

"I know so. You're going to die."

"No, kitty cat. The odds are in my favour, see. You've got that fine American Revolutionary War cannonball there to slow you down. Heavy old thing. You might be able to drag it along for a while. But you'll tire. Make a decent target. And after I shoot you, I'm going to add a trophy to my collection."

He flicked a switch. The lights blinded her for a moment. She blinked. Her good eye adjusted to the glare. The room became clear.

Dozens of heads were mounted on the wall.

Human heads.

CHAPTER 43.
THE PRIMAL.

ZAK stumbled through the trees, screaming as he went. He was in his underwear. Branches tore at his flesh. His body was slick with sweat and blood. Terror had turned his bowels to water. He'd stained himself, the shit wet down his legs.

He hurtled through the trees.

The werewolf raced after him. He heard the creature crash through the undergrowth. Trees splintered. Branches snapped. Animals scattered.

The strength had drained out of his legs, but he kept running. The flight instinct blazing in him. The need to survive powerful.

Ruth had said, "I'm giving you a most marvellous gift, Zachary. I'm giving you the primal. Hunter and hunted. Nothing more pure than that, darling boy."

And then she'd shown him the animal in her, and it was that animal gaining on him now.

He hurdled a fallen branch. Landed hard and jarred his ankle. He kept going, every step anguish. But the adrenaline blurred out the worst of it. He heard her. Close behind. On his heels. Almost felt her hot breath on his back. Or was that his blood and sweat? He screamed again, the horror of his situation overwhelming.

He dared a glance over his shoulder.

Zak shrieked – short, sharp bursts.

She was ten yards behind, teeth bared, claws gouging the earth, throwing up soil and leaves and twigs.

He looked ahead again. Tears streamed down his face. His strength dwindled. He had nothing left. He felt himself slow and despite his desperate efforts his energy had been sapped.

A car hammered into him – or that's what it felt like.

His neck whiplashed. The breath shot out of his lungs. The world went head-over-heels. The forest blurred. Rough fur frayed his skin. He hit the ground. The impact dazed him for a few seconds, but he came to when he heard growling and tearing and smelled the musty odour of dog.

Or werewolf.

Panic clutched him by the throat, and he couldn't breath.

She was on him. Her claws ripping through his flanks. Pain seared through him. He was being torn apart. He screamed and thrashed. Spit drizzled from her jaws into his mouth. He tasted her, and she was hot and sour.

She roared, her breath fetid. She bit into his head, her teeth sinking into his flesh, tearing skin, cracking bone. He screamed down her throat. He pissed all over her pelt. Her claws dug into his ribs, blood bubbling out of the lesions.

He threw up down the werewolf's throat.

She bit off his face – slowly.

He felt every bone crunch.

* * * *

"What did she make of your little collection, Wheeler?" said Wellington.

"I think she liked it," said Burns. His heart pounded. He had gooseflesh. This was going to be the best hunt ever. The best prey ever.

The men were in the trophy room. The cage was gone. Laura Greenacre had been transported up into the forest. Weapons were laid out on a long table. The hunters checked them – over and over, over and over.

"We've enough ammo?" said Schumann.

"So long as you don't keep missing, Harris," said Hurst.

They laughed, Schumann's face turning red. He said, "I've a problem with my eye."

Burns snorted. "Yeah! It's a roving one – as your wife should've been told before she married you."

"I'll show you," said Schumann, staring down the barrel of a Remington 870 shotgun, "when I nail that bitch of yours today, Burns."

"You'll be too scared, Harris," said Lomax Delaney. "Cowering in some bush."

"Yeah," said Burns, "like you cowered in that girl's bush."

The laughter echoed through the trophy room.

Hurst said, "I don't understand how you can be unfaithful to your wives."

"You've not seen our wives," said Wellington.

"Hey, you don't say anything about Stella," said Burns, flashing a Colt handgun in Wellington's face. "No one says anything about Stella except for me."

"OK, OK, put the gun away, Wheeler," said the banker.

"You all right over there, Lenny?" said Hurst.

Longman stood under a TV screen. The monitor showed an image of the cage in the forest. Laura Greenacre moved back and forth in her prison. She was still in human form. A knot of fear tightened in Burns's stomach.

Hope she fucking changes and makes this worth our while, he thought.

Because if she didn't, if she stayed in human form, these men would mock him.

Then I'm going to have to shoot one of them.

He said to Longman, "She's not going anywhere."

"I'm just fascinated," said the TV producer. "This'll make a great show."

"OK, listen up," said Burns. "Lenny, come over here. I'm going to say something."

They gathered round the table.

Burns continued:

"Gentlemen, you've paid a great deal of money to be here today. Our fees are usually a couple of grand and a beer or two. But today, today we've got something special. You're going to witness something amazing. You are going to be part of something amazing."

He looked each one in the eye.

He went on:

"So it's winner takes all. I've also put half-a-million in, so the pot stands at three million dollars."

Longman said, "Throw in that Russian girl and you've got yourself a deal."

"Yeah, why not," said Burns.

CHAPTER 44.
EASY KILL.

THE man watched from the tree line twenty yards away. Spied Cleaver and Stokes drive up here an hour ago. Watched them lower the cage from the rear of the truck and place it on the track that scythed through the forest. Saw Cleaver kneel at the cage and say something to the girl. Stared at the truck until its rear lights faded into the twilight.

The woman lay down for a long time. He wondered if she'd given up. But she was sleeping. *Maybe storing up her energy*, he thought. He stayed still. His eyes never moved from her.

She stirred. His nerves tightened. He flexed his fingers around the gun's stock.

She rose and looked around. She sniffed the air. She ran a hand through her hair and puffed out her cheeks. Grasping the bars of the cage, she carried out a series of stretches: her legs, her arms, her back, her neck.

And she undressed.

He gawped, couldn't drag his eyes away. It wasn't sexual, his goggling at her: it was astonishment.

Why would she be undressing?

169

But when he did see her body he realized how beautiful she was and something moved in him.

She elongated her body, extending her arms above her head, through the bars above her, making herself long.

And her flesh rippled.

Her limbs grew. Muscles ripened. Fur sprouted.

It was like water, this change in her. An undulation of her body.

He stared and shudders ran through him.

Her face changed. Her muzzle grew. Her ears flared out and became hairy and pointed. Her complexion coarsened. Her jaw expanded. She bared her teeth, her new teeth, incisors and canines that were not human.

He felt small in her presence. He felt like nothing to her.

He felt awe.

And then she was gone, and in her place another species, colossal and powerful, black-furred and white-teethed.

The creature snapped its head round and stared right at him.

And he chilled.

The werewolf thrashed, ramming against the cage. The bars buckled.

The man cursed. The noise of the animal's attempts to escape jarred him. He rose from his hiding place. He strode out into the clearing.

The creature stilled and watched him approach. It hunkered down and growled. Saliva drooled from its jaws.

The man looked the animal in the eye, seeing if he could see human in there. All he saw was monster.

He shuffled forward, gun ready. The creature moved from foot to foot as if ready to pounce. But it was caged. He was safe to approach.

A green light flashed on the cage door. A hum came from the unit attached to the bars. The gate rose with a hum and now the cage was open.

The man froze.

The creature lunged out of the cage and swerved to come for him. The chain became taut and the animal snapped backwards. A growl of pain escaped its throat. The animal yanked, and the cannonball rolled along the floor of the cage.

The man retreated a step. The animal jerked again, baring teeth, clawing at the earth. The cannonball scraped. Slowly, the creature heaved the weight out of the cage. Panted and slathered as it came.

The man thought, *This will be easy. Too easy.*

He moved towards the monster.

The animal looked exhausted and snarled as the man approached.

The man pointed the gun at the creature's head. He stepped towards the monster. The animal lunged, managed to drag the cannonball a yard. The man stepped back, waited. The werewolf howled and the man flinched. The animal cowered, worn out by the effort of hauling the weight.

The man aimed right between the creature's eyes.

The werewolf reared up on its back legs. The man lurched away and tripped and hit the ground. The creature ploughed forward, towing the cannonball, the weight gouging the earth.

The man lifted off the ground and followed the werewolf.

The creature halted again. Gasped for air. Glanced over its shoulder at its pursuer. Moved forward again. Yowling in pain.

It quickened its pace and got into a trot, the cannonball gashing the ground behind it.

The man followed.

The creature hunkered down. The powerful body rising and falling as it gasped for breath.

The man came closer.

He raised the pistol.

Too easy, he thought again, *far too easy.*

PART TWO.

THE DEATH OF
JOHN THORN.

CHAPTER 45.
WHO'D HAVE TEENAGE
DAUGHTERS?

THE BLACK MOUNTAINS, SOUTH-EAST WALES – 8.20
A.M., NOVEMBER 11, 2007

THORN said, "What's his name?"

"Dad," said Sophie.

"I'm only asking his name."

"No you're not, you're demanding his ID, his fingerprints, a DNA sample. You're asking, 'How long before I beat the crap out of him?' That's what you're asking."

Thorn stared at his daughter. "His name."

"Dad, I'm late for school."

"Sophie."

She sighed. "Billy."

"Billy what?"

"Billy... I don't know."

"You don't know?"

"I only met him last week."

"Oh, of course. Sorry. I'm impressed you know his *first* name."

"Don't be sarcastic, Dad."

"I'm not sarcastic, I'm angry."

"Don't be."

"You're fifteen, Sophie."

"Yeah, happy birthday to me. It was a lovely evening. I met Billy."

She opened the front door and stomped out. He followed her into the yard. She went into the Land Rover. Slammed the door and sat there looking fifteen – bottom lip curled out, arms folded.

He got in and said, "Don't look so glum, I'm only looking out for you."

The drive to Abergavenny, seven miles away, was made in silence.

He remembered bringing Sophie here to the Black Mountains. Her mother, Thorn's ex, had died in a hit-and-run five years before. The impact threw Jane thirty yards down the road. The driver raced away. Sophie saw her mum die. Witnesses told Thorn his daughter turned white and never made a sound. Just gaped at her mother's dead body down the road.

Thorn knew the Templetons had killed Jane. Getting back at him for helping Laura. He guessed it was down to Ruth Andersson, who now called herself Templeton again. She ran the family from her prison cell. United them after the Trafalgar Square massacre. United them in hate. They'd lost sons and brothers and cousins to Laura that day. She'd butchered the Templeton werewolves. But they deserved it. They'd killed innocents, and they meant to destroy Laura. Thorn had killed Ruth's son, Ross, on an underground train, after he and one of his cousins had murdered commuters and sparked panic.

"I won't rest until you and your loved ones are dead," Ruth warned him when the jury found her guilty of kidnapping.

Three years later the car ploughed into Jane.

Thorn had been living near Aberdeen at the time of the accident. He picked Sophie up at her grandmother's home. The child didn't speak for weeks, and she didn't really come out of herself, out of the dark place in her mind, for nearly two years. Shock, said the doctors.

Thorn, his nerves shot, knowing Ruth Templeton intended to make good on her promise that day in court, had fled Aberdeen. He'd found a derelict smallholding on the Wales–

England border. Deep in the hills. He could see for miles. Could see them coming.

Thorn and Sophie had made that journey, 510 miles from the north of Scotland to the south-east of Wales, in silence as well.

Now Thorn parked outside the school and said, "You know why I'm like this."

Sophie flung open the door and said, "I want to take the bus from now on." She got out and slammed the door. Thorn flinched. He watched her stride through the gates and greet two girls with a hug.

He drove away, his heart cold.

Twenty minutes later, home. He parked down the road. Walked up to the gate. Checked if the lock had been tampered with.

Once inside the house, he went upstairs and scoped the landscape through his binoculars. He gazed out across the Skirrid, one of the highest peaks in the Black Mountains. He could see the A465 Abergavenny to Hereford road in the distance. A black vein across the green skin of Wales. He followed the narrow roads that snaked up the mountain. They branched off into single lanes that pronged into tracks like the one that led up to the small holding.

It was called "Cors Oer", which meant cold marsh.

"How do you say that?" Thorn had said to an estate agent when he was looking at the property.

The man said, "You say it, 'Cause O-eer'. That's the best I can do. You can always change it, make it English."

Thorn didn't want to. Why should he change its name to make it easier for him to say? He'd changed his own name. His daughter was using her mother's maiden name. Why should this house change?

Thorn went out and fixed a fence. He'd rebuilt the farmhouse and the barns since they'd moved here. The house was small. Two bedrooms, but good enough for them. Damp coursed the walls, and the timber was rotting when he'd arrived. It was only a frame. Now, like Sophie said, it was snug.

But Thorn never felt it was safe.

He wasn't sure he'd ever feel safe again.

He looked out over the fields. They were dotted with sheep. Thorn rented his acres to a local farmer. He thought about this Billy. A shudder travelled through him. He didn't trust anyone. He went inside, made a sandwich. He sat at the living room table and stared out across the fields. His sandwich lay uneaten.

Who the fuck is this Billy? he thought.

He chided himself for being stupid. He couldn't live like this, couldn't make Sophie live like this. He just had to be careful, that was all. He bit into the bread. He salivated, hadn't noticed how hungry he was. He scoffed the sandwich and then took his tea over to the computer.

He checked all the news websites and found something that made his guts grind.

News from Moscow. A known pimp ripped apart. Thorn's nape grew hot. Outside, sheep bleated. He read the story, then Googled the victim's name. He got more hits, more stories about the incident. A senior police officer, Gromeko, said they had a few leads and suspected it may have been drugs related. Thorn found other websites, conspiracy sites, suggesting something more sinister.

Werewolves.

Laura, thought Thorn.

In Moscow?

His heart quickened. He scoured the internet. More stories about this Russian. And one from Barcelona, where a man had been dismembered. Thorn held his breath. She was out there.

But why was she killing these people?

What was she doing in Moscow, in Barcelona?

Was she forced to travel?

He pined for her, and tears welled. Grief tore at his chest – grief for Laura, for his ex-wife, for his daughter and the life she was having to live.

I've got to let her be a teenager, he thought. *I've got to let her have a normal life. I've got to let her see this Billy and have her heart broken – just like any 15-year-old girl.*

He put his head in his hands.

Fall in love, Sophie. Get hurt. Shut yourself in your bedroom. Play sad music. Weep. Mope. Refuse to eat for days.

Be normal.

177

CHAPTER 46.
CHARMER.

SOPHIE said, "What are you doing here?" She blushed and felt hot all over.

Billy flashed her a smile and said, "Came to take my favourite schoolgirl out for lunch."

She wrinkled her brow. "Schoolgirl? Is that what you think I am?"

"That's what you are, whether you like it or not. You're a girl; you're at school."

"Makes me sound young, a kid."

"Come on, Sophie, get in."

She glanced back at the school gates. Kids and teacher milled around in the playground. Other pupils streamed through the gates, headed for town on their lunch break. She got in and he sped off and it made her tummy tingle.

Billy had a flash car. Red, a two-seater. She felt grown-up. Dad wouldn't like it. He'd glower at Billy like he glowered at all the boys she liked.

"Where are we going?" she said. The wheels shrieked as he pulled away from traffic lights. Her heart tripped. She gripped the seat. He glanced at her, down at her legs, and grinned.

"What?" she said, feeling her cheeks flush again.

"Nothing. You look nice."

"Yeah, right?"

"It's a compliment, take it."

"OK, thanks. So where are we going?"

"Where do you want to go?"

Away from here, she wanted to say. From these mountains, this market town. Away from this life. Instead she shrugged and said, "Dunno."

They went to a place called Annette's in Lewis Lane, and Sophie had a jacket potato with tuna. Billy had a burger.

"You like living here?" he said.

She shrugged, shook her head, chewed her food.

He said, "Where you from? There's a bit of a Scottish accent there."

She looked at him. He had green eyes and reddish-brown hair. He was lean, and his skin was pale. She liked him a lot.

"I was born in Newcastle. My mum and dad separated when I was five, and mum and me went to live in Edinburgh. My mum died a few years ago, and I came to live with Dad."

"I'm sorry," he said. "How did she die?"

Her dad's voice in her head now:

Don't give anyone too many details. Keep it vague, don't tell people where we live. Don't use the name Thorn...

She hated the rules, but he'd drilled them into her, and it was instinct to lie – to be vague, like her dad said.

She shrugged. "Car accident."

"Where was that?"

She wriggled in her seat. She mumbled, and he asked her what she said, and she told him, "I just don't like to talk about it, do you mind?"

"Of course not. I'm sorry." He touched her hand, and she shivered.

His eyes were looking straight into hers. His pupils flared. She tensed. That meant a boy liked you. She'd read it in a magazine. Something about body language. Pins and needles tingled in her thighs.

Then he said, "I know how you feel, I understand. I lost three of my brothers."

"Three," she said, "oh my God. How – oh – sorry – you might not – "

"No, it's OK." He squeezed her hand, gave her a grin. "They were murdered, actually."

179

Her chest grew cold. Her mouth made an "O" shape, and then she couldn't close it, her jaw slack.

"London," said Billy, "eight years ago."

A sound went off somewhere in Sophie's brain – an alarm. But it was way off. Hardly worth bothering about. She ignored it, focused on Billy. His green eyes, wide and bright and fixed on her. She wanted to ask, "How?" but then thought she'd not shared, so why should he? Perhaps she should say something. She couldn't keep things bottled up for the rest of her life.

"I think my mother was killed by a hit-and-run driver," she said. She looked at her plate, swallowed, then raised her gaze to his face again. "Do you remember years ago, in Trafalgar Square?"

He shook his head and wrinkled his nose.

She told him about werewolves running wild, killing people. She told him about how her dad was involved, but that's all she said – "involved, he was a policeman." She said some of the people they said were werewolves were from a family, a rich family, and they'd sworn vengeance. "Dad says they killed my mum."

"What do you think?" said Billy.

"I don't know. I think it was an accident. We just – we just have to be careful, that's all, you know?"

"I know."

"So... what about your brothers?"

His face darkened. The smile faded. A scowl etched his brow.

"They were out – young blokes having fun." He paused, stared right at her. The intensity of his stare unsettled her, excited her. "Doing what comes naturally," he said. "Doing what young, virile, strong guys do."

Sophie guessed that meant having fun, drinking, picking up girls, fighting, maybe.

"And they were... " He trailed off. He shut his eyes. Tears came out of them. Sophie's heart hitched. She closed her hands around his. He fought the tears, clenching his jaw. And then he found his voice and said, "They were shot by an armed robber in an off-licence. Some drugged-up loser, desperate for alcohol. Blew them away. It's difficult to be strong."

She brought her chair round the table so she could sit next

to him and threw her arms around him, stroking his hair. His breath seared her neck. He caressed her waist. He kissed her neck and she quivered, and then he brought his lips to hers and her insides burned.

* * * *

"All right, you can go," said Thorn.

Sophie said, "Are you... for real?"

He looked up at her. "I am."

"No gnashing of teeth, no tearing out of hair, no threats?"

He frowned. "I've never threatened you."

"Not me, but you have them – the boys."

"OK. No. No threats."

She cocked her head. "Why, Dad?"

"I've got to trust you. And you know the drill by now."

"I... I do... "

He glared at her. "You do, don't you?"

"Yes, Dad, I do."

She sat on the couch. He was at the table near the window. They'd eaten tea. She'd made fish fingers and beans. He'd told her about his day, fixing the fence, tending the garden, and she'd said, "Billy's a landscape gardener; he'd help you."

He thought he was going to explode to start with, feeling the rage build up in his head. But then he remembered: *I've got to let her have a normal life.*

He said, "OK... maybe," and she gawped.

Then she asked him about going to the cinema and he'd said OK, which made her ask if he was serious.

She asked, "Can Billy come and pick me up? Here?"

Thorn tightened his lips. It would mean a stranger knowing where they lived. Sophie knew she wasn't to tell anyone her address. Only the authorities had her address.

He said, "I'll drive you down to the village. He can meet you outside the Skirrid Inn. Take it or leave it."

"I'll take it."

"I don't like the fact he's seventeen and you're fifteen – no father would."

She blushed.

Thorn continued:

"But I'm going to trust you, Sophie. You're an intelligent girl, you're... you're good. You realize that" – Thorn felt embarrassment burn his cheeks – "if you... if he... it's illegal... you are underage, and I'll... I'll have him prosecuted."

"Oh, Dad, that's so embarrassing," she said, leaping to her feet. She gathered the dishes and took them through to the kitchen. He heard her clunk around in there, washing up, putting things away.

Fear gnawed at his belly. Instinct told him he'd done the wrong thing. He wasn't being over-protective – he was being sensible. They were being hunted, he was sure of it. He'd taken Ruth's threat in that courtroom eight years ago seriously.

And it wasn't paranoia.

A year after the Trafalgar Square massacre, Thorn lived in a caravan on his brother's farm near Alnwick, in Northumberland. He'd quit the police, got his pension, and set about living like a hermit. He yearned for Laura and helped Peter on the farm.

Then a man found him.

He said his name was Keegan, and when Thorn asked what his first name was, the man stared at him through crystal-blue eyes and said nothing.

Thorn's brother, hanging around with a shotgun, said, "Look, mate, you're not welcome here and you come onto my land, I'll shoot your legs off."

"Mr Thorn," said Keegan, glaring at Peter, "you aim that gun at me, and I'll take it off you and shove it up your arse," and then he looked at Thorn and said, "I'm on your side. I'm here to help you. I'm from the government."

Keegan and Thorn leaned on a gate and stared out over a carpet of fields.

"Solitary here," said Keegan.

Thorn said it was.

"No one can find you."

"That's right."

Keegan glanced at him. "I did."

The hairs on Thorn's nape prickled.

"Who are you?"

"I told you, my name's Keegan. I work for government agencies, and I came here to thank you."

"Thank me?"

"For nailing Ray Craig."

"He nearly killed me."

"You nearly killed him."

"I was lucky."

"Lucky's fine. We'd been after him for years. He'd gone AWOL. Became a killer for hire. Sir Adam Templeton hired him in 1981 to kill the Greenacres."

Thorn had a headache. "He's been put away for life. Why are you here? I don't think the government would send someone out all this way just to thank me."

Keegan smiled. He ran a hand through his silver hair. "You're right." He locked his eyes on Thorn again. "I've come to warn you."

Thorn said nothing.

Keegan said, "Ruth Templeton wants you dead. She's not happy you killed her son."

"Self-defence. He was going to eat me."

"Mother love. It's deadly."

"I'm safe here."

"I told you – I found you. She can too."

"She's in jail."

"The Templetons are gathering. Last year's slaughter of their youth has galvanized them. We've been keeping tabs on them. They're angry."

Thorn shuddered. "Can't you arrest them?"

"They've not done anything illegal yet. Being angry is not a crime."

"So you're saying what?"

"I'm saying move. And keep moving if you have to. Change your name."

Thorn's chest tightened. "I have a daughter... "

Keegan nodded. "Tell your ex to be careful."

Terror flooded Thorn's heart. His mind started to fracture. "Can't you... can't you protect them?"

"To a point."

"Do it, then."

"Not up to you, not up to me. Your ex-wife, she'd have to approve it."

"She would. You tell her. I'll tell her. Force her."

Keegan shrugged. "As I said, there's nothing concrete yet."

"What the hell are you saying to me? You're warning me my daughter's in danger and then you say, 'Well, it's not for real.' What are you saying?"

"I'm telling you my hands are tied. I'm telling you I strongly believe there's a threat. I'm telling you that Ray Craig wants to kill you too."

"He's in for life."

Keegan said, "That doesn't mean a thing. He's been in jail before. In Afghanistan. A Russian camp. He broke out. In Zaire. A fucking hell hole you can't imagine. Broke out." He looked out across the fields. "He's monstrous, Thorn."

CHAPTER 47.
SEGREGATED.

RAY Craig's stomach rumbled. He glanced through the bars. The white sun stood high in the grey sky. It was nearly lunchtime.

He rolled off his bunk and onto the floor. He pushed out fifty press-ups. He looked at his forearms cording with each rep. He leaped to his feet and went down again quickly into a press-up position and did a squat thrust. Leaped to his feet again and then down again, another squat thrust. He did this fifty times. Then he squatted down and jumped, squatted, and jumped, repeated this fifty times. He craned his neck. Grabbed the horizontal bar screwed into the ceiling. Performed fifty pull-ups. Sweat poured off him. His heart thumped. He went down on the floor. Did another fifty press-ups. Went through the other exercises again, finishing with pull-ups. And then repeated the circuit twice.

He filled a plastic pint carton with water from the tap and drank it down. He panted but felt good. He could smell his sweat.

He flexed his bicep and it bulged. Veins crisscrossed the muscle. *Not bad for sixty*, he thought and then said, "Not bad at all."

He'd lost more than 40 pounds since being in prison. He was leaner now than he'd been for forty years – and because of his sentence, he was meaner too.

The judge sent him down for life, saying he had to serve a minimum of thirty years.

The judge said, "You're an extremely dangerous human being, Craig."

"Thanks, judge," said Craig.

"And the world is a safer place now that you'll very likely be spending the rest of your days in jail."

"Yeah? Fuck you too. I'll cut your head off, cunt."

The court erupted.

Craig had kicked a security guard in the head, knocking him out. He'd kneed another in the balls. He'd headbutted a third.

He'd leaped from the dock. The judge had scurried off though a door behind his chair.

Craig had raced across the court. Screams and shouts echoed through the building. He smashed through tables, chairs, barging past officials, lawyers.

Police had tackled him to the floor. Manacled his already-handcuffed wrists and his ankles. Strapped him in a strait jacket. He bit off a cop's finger, blood gouting from the stump, the cop shrieking.

"I'll fucking kill you all," said Craig as they dragged him feet first out of the court.

As they hauled him away, his gaze had fixed on a silver-haired man with sharp features. The man smirked at Craig.

"Fuck you, Keegan," said Craig, craning to stare at the man.

Keegan, thought Craig now, his heartbeat dropping. Down to 80 beats per minute. The bastard secret services guy who'd been hunting him for years.

Hatred welled in Craig.

Thorn came to mind. John Thorn, the cop who broke Craig's back. Tossed him over a banister after Craig had beaten him to a pulp in London eight years before.

Lucky fucking bastard.

Craig ground his teeth. How the hell could he get out of here to kill everyone who'd fucked him up?

Jailed for murder – it didn't look likely.

A bell rang, and he got up off his bunk. He towelled sweat off his face. His cell door clanked open. A breeze wafted into the cage, and Craig shuddered.

"Step back," said a voice.

Craig retreated against the far wall.

Two hefty prison guards appeared. They greeted Craig, and he nodded.

The guards parted, and a prisoner in a kitchen tunic rolled in a trolley. Craig smelled food, and he salivated. He stared at the prisoner. The man was called Jolley, and he was known to spit in food.

"Curry and rice today, Mr Craig," said the prisoner. "Followed by mangoes and cream."

Jolley put the covered plate and bowl on the table that was fixed to the floor. He laid out plastic cutlery. He left a can of Coke. Jolley nodded at Craig, reversed out of the cell with his trolley. The guards parted, and he backed up between them and reversed into the corridor. "Hope you puke on it, Craig," he said just before the guards curtained him off.

They slammed shut the door.

Craig sat on the fixed chair and uncovered the food. He licked his lips. He added Jolley's name to the list of those he'd kill when he got out of here.

CHAPTER 48.
MEETING BILLY.

"A WORD," said Thorn, gesturing for Billy to follow him.

"Dad," said Sophie, dressed like no fifteen-year-old should be: skirt too high, top too low.

"It's all right, Sophie," said Billy, "your dad's being sensible, that's all."

They were parked outside the pub. Thorn's Land Rover in front, the lad's MX5 behind.

They went back, towards the Mazda.

"Nice car," said Thorn.

"Thanks."

"It's not cheap, is it."

"Not cheap."

"Sophie says you're a landscape gardener. You do big gardens, eh?"

The youth shrugged. "I do what I can."

Thorn glared at him. "What does that mean?"

"I work. In between my studies."

"A student? Where?"

"Herefordshire College of Technology. I study horticulture."

"So you're not quite a landscape gardener, yet."

"I'm getting there. Quite quickly. You can speak to my tutors."

"Quick enough to buy an MX5?"

"My dad bought it for me."

"Rich dad, eh?"

"Well off, yes."

"Spoils his son."

"He does a bit, I admit that. I'm the only one left."

Thorn stared at him.

Billy said, "My brothers were murdered."

Thorn shot his daughter a look. "Sophie didn't say."

Billy looked straight at him. "No... well... I try not to think about it too much. I was a kid."

Thorn stiffened. That unsettled him. He floundered for something to say and came out with, "I'm sorry." He looked off towards the pub. They said it was haunted. The oldest pub in Wales. It's where Sophie had met this character. She'd wanted to go there on her birthday. A couple of older girls from the village said they'd take her there for a meal.

"You can go," Thorn had told his daughter the previous week, "but don't let me hear anyone's bought you a drink. Just food and soft drinks. The landlord'll tell me if you've been misbehaving."

Did she misbehave? She didn't drink, but this Billy was there and he had chatted her up.

Thorn looked at Billy. "She's fifteen, you know, and only just. Don't you think she's a bit young for you?"

"Two years' difference, Mr... Taylor" – Thorn picked up on the pause between his title and his mother's maiden name – "I'm not going to disrespect her. I don't think I'd like to piss you off."

"Why?"

Billy smiled. "You look mean."

Thorn nodded. "I am, where my daughter's concerned."

"I know. I'd be the same."

"You live here in Wales?"

"No. Hereford."

"Don't take her there. To your place, I mean."

Billy nodded.

"Bring her home by ten. Is that clear?"

Billy nodded again.

"I'll meet you here. Don't make me wait."

"OK, sir, I won't. I promise you."

Thorn turned his back on the youth and headed for the Land Rover. He embraced Sophie, pressing his face into her hair. He smelled her, his child. Tears dampened his eyes. He told her he loved her and got into his vehicle. He drove off without looking back.

CHAPTER 49.
BACK ROW.

THEY went to see an animated film in Hereford, but Sophie didn't remember what it was called or what it was about.

Her stomach cartwheeled. Goosepimples tingled her skin. Billy filled her thoughts. She kept glancing at him. Looking down at his thighs. Wondering if he might hold her hand.

Don't be stupid, she thought, *it's a first date – and Dad probably threatened to cut his hands off if he touched me.*

First date or not, she was going to get a snog out of him.

He'd called her a couple of times after they met at the pub. Saw her in Abergavenny for a chat at the weekend, but he had to be going somewhere. When he picked her up yesterday lunchtime, it was the first time they'd been together on their own.

She glanced at him. He was handsome. Her school friends were delirious. "He's got a sports car," said one, and another said, "He looks like Zac Efron." They squealed when Sophie said he was taking her out.

Her older friends from the village, the ones who'd organized for her to go for the pub meal on her birthday, were less enthusiastic. They scowled and said, "Watch him, Sophie, he's a player," but one of her school friends suggested those girls were jealous, that they just wanted Billy for themselves.

It didn't matter who wanted him now. He was here with her. She put her hand on his, and he glanced at her. His eyes flashed and he smiled. She smiled back. Snuggled up to him. But he returned his gaze to the screen. Sophie's shoulders slumped. She sighed.

"You OK?" he said into her ear, the whisper making her shiver.

His face was there so she went for it. Planted her lips on his. Cupped his face in her hands. He wore aftershave, and the odour swept into her nostrils. She breathed him in. He put his arms around her waist and pressed against her. She gasped. Their tongues rolled. Sophie's heart knocked. She whimpered and writhed and lifted her knee across his –

"There are children here, you know."

Sophie flushed, drew away.

Billy wheeled.

The man in front, sitting with a woman and two kids, had twisted round in his seat.

The man said again, "If you want to misbehave, do it outside. This is a children's – "

He didn't get to finish. Billy punched him in the face. The man sagged. His wife screamed. Billy rose, punched the man again.

Sophie couldn't move. Staring at Billy beating the man.

The wife got up, screeching. Their kids cried. Other cinemagoers got out of their seats. They were shouting.

Billy stopped beating the man. Sophie gawped at the victim. Blood on his face. His wife yelped, and his kids wailed. Sophie felt herself being yanked away. It was Billy, pulling her into the aisle.

The lights came on. The action on screen faded. Cartoon voices filled the auditorium, but the only thing Sophie saw were people crowding the beaten man, helping him, comforting his family.

And then someone pointed at her and said, "It's them, call the police."

* * * *

192

Billy stomped out of the cinema, gripping Sophie's hand. She trotted after him. Cold with shock. Trying to find words but failing. They slipped into a pub. Billy plonked her at a corner table. She shivered and looked around. Customers glanced at her, mumbling, their voices a tirade in her head.

Billy came back and put a drink on the table.

She looked up at him.

"Coke. Drink it," he said.

She grabbed the glass and drank down the coke. It was like acid. She hissed and shuddered, her face screwed up. She came to and said, "What... was that?"

He sat, putting down his pint, leaned on his forearms. "Do not tell your dad." His voice rasped. His green eyes blazed. His forehead was folded into a scowl.

Sophie's guts churned. Bile rose up into her throat, and she retched.

"You drank it too quickly, silly," he said.

"What... what happened?"

"He had a go at you – I was defending you."

"He – he didn't, Billy – "

"He did, he called you a slag."

"He didn't – "

His face darkened, and it gave her gooseflesh. She looked at him and couldn't move.

Then his expression softened and light came into his face again and he said, "I'm really, really sorry, but... but I was so happy with you in there and when... when he said those things, I just lost it."

Sophie narrowed her eyes. Tried to corral her scurrying thoughts.

Had the man said anything, called her names?

She said, "I'm... trying to remember if he called... "

"He did. Hey, we were, you know" – he touched her hand and pouted – "getting carried away. I was hot. Were you hot?"

She was hot now. Shame rising up into her face. She looked away but nodded that, yes, she was.

And she had been.

"I was scared, Billy. I've never seen... I don't like violence, fighting. It was horrible. He had children."

"He shouldn't have put them in danger, should he. Should've kept his opinion to himself."

She furrowed her brow, thinking, trying to remember.

"I've never been called a slag, I'd remember being called a — "

He grabbed her hand. "I wouldn't have done that for anyone else, Sophie. I usually don't care, you know. It came out of me, that's all. It came out of here," and he tapped his chest.

A siren wailed. Blue lights flashed past the window. Billy craned his neck.

"We should leg it to the car," he said.

"Do you think they have CCTV in the cinema?"

"I don't know. Why?"

"If they put it on the news. I'll – we'll be on the news, and Dad'll see and he'll go ballistic."

They went outside. Up the road a police car sat outside the cinema. The vehicle's emergency lights blinked in the darkness.

"I was defending you," said Billy, eyes on the cop car down the road. "Your dad would understand." He turned to look at Sophie, touched her cheek. "But don't say, OK?"

She looked at him, and she felt scared and excited at the same time, and said, "OK."

CHAPTER 50.
LOST, THEN FOUND.

IT had taken two years after her mum died for Sophie to become human again.

During those two years, she was a ghost. Lost to the world. Living inside her head, which cascaded with images and noises to do with the accident:

The car screeching down the road –

Mum shoving her out of the way screaming, "Sophie, Sophie" –

Pain shooting through her leg as she fell –

Mum calling her name, but only half her name coming out: "Soph" –

A thump that made Sophie's bones rattle –

The car whizzing by –

The driver glowering at her –

His mouth moving with angry words –

His face, dark with rage –

Mum windmilling through the air, down the road –

Screams and shouts, people swearing –

Mum thudding to the ground, skull cracking against the pavement –

Sophie's head swimming, everything blurred and spinning –

Sick in her throat –

A sour smell in her nose –

The puke in her lap –

Spit hanging in tendrils from her mouth –

Ice filling her veins, her throat locked, not remembering words –

She didn't remember anything else. Nothing about her life. Nothing except the accident.

But the world slid back into her brain slowly. The man who took her away and brought her to a mountain and a house set in fields said he was Dad, but she didn't recognize him as Dad for months.

She started to come back to life, to her human state.

And grief ploughed into her.

"I was in a state for six months, then," she told Billy as they drove back from Hereford. "Crying every day. Refusing to eat. Before then, they'd been feeding me, and I didn't know anything about it. I was a ghost. A zombie. But when I came to, I went mad. I wanted to die. Everything in my head – what I remembered about the accident – became real. My mum had died."

Billy nodded, eyes on the road.

Sophie went on:

"I went off the rails a bit."

He glanced at her. "Did you?"

"I drank a lot, smoked dope."

"Like most kids do."

"I was awful. It's only in the last year or so that I pulled myself together. My dad" – tears welled but she fended them off – "my dad, he's been... I don't know where I'd be without him."

"That's what dads are for, yeah?"

"I guess, but not all the time. He's been through a lot."

Billy's hands tightened on the steering wheel.

She asked if he was OK, and he said he was fine.

She said, "He'll know something's wrong."

He glanced at her, fire in his eyes again. "There's nothing wrong, is there?"

"There is. You beat that man. It changes things."

"Changes things? What do you mean? He insulted you. I'm telling you not to tell your dad because he'll probably want to find the bloke, won't he. Won't he?"

"Yeah... maybe... I don't know... "

"And *how* will he know?" Billy's voice grew tighter, more high-pitched.

"He'll be able to tell by looking at me. He looked at me for two years, and he learned to read me. Learned to see what was in my head. He told me later, when I got better, he told me he could see everything I could see. He could see my memories. Hear them. Smell them. He looked into my dead eyes for almost two years and saw everything, and he can still see everything."

"No one can see everything," said Billy.

* * * *

Billy parked the car behind Thorn's Land Rover. He felt sick. He'd drunk his pint at that pub in Hereford on an empty stomach – and drunk it too quickly. He'd hoped to eat. Sit down with Sophie somewhere. Have a bite.

But that twat at the cinema, that fucker who should've minded his business, spoiled everything.

The leash restraining Billy's temper had snapped.

White light and hot blood.

And he ploughed into the twat. Wanting to destroy him. Seeing him red through his eyes. Seeing the twat and nothing else.

Thorn stepped out of the Land Rover wearing that scowl, that "don't-mess-with-me-or-my-family" scowl.

Billy's courage withered.

"I won't come out," he said.

"OK," she said.

They looked at each other, and her eyes were wide, waiting.

"I think it'll be all right," she said.

"Yeah," he said, and they leaned into each other and pecked each other on the lips.

She got out of the car and shut the door, and Billy blew air out of his cheeks. Thorn put an arm around her shoulders and glared at Billy.

Billy went cold, but he found the strength to nod.

Thorn nodded back and turned away with Sophie. Went into the darkness. Billy watched his outline get into the Land Rover.

He waited till Thorn had driven away, the taillights dwindling to leave nothing but the night up ahead.

Then he said, "Jesus fucking Christ," and slumped forward, forehead pressing into the steering wheel.

His heart beat like a jackhammer. He steadied his breathing, focusing on his heartbeat, hearing it slow.

After two minutes, he sat up and got his phone out of his pocket.

He dialled. It rang once before it was answered, the voice on the other end saying, "Billy?"

"Dad," he said, "there's been a fuck-up. I think we should kill them now. Can we?"

CHAPTER 51.
FAMILY MATTERS.

NICK Sears slapped his son across the face and then embraced him.

"You fool," he told Billy. "I love you, son." Sears eased his son away. "Sit now."

Billy's cheek stung. He sank into the leather armchair and looked round the apartment. Family photos decorated the walls. There were antiques everywhere from his dad's Mayfair store. The place smelled of tobacco and flowers and leather.

His dad lit a cigar and perched himself on a stool near the sideboard. He puffed smoke into the air. Reached over and took a framed photo from the sideboard. He studied it.

Billy knew it showed his brothers. All the photos here showed his brothers:

Jack, Sam, and their half-brother, Anton.

"Our family," said his dad, "has gone through a great transition. In the past few years, we've had to deconstruct ourselves. We've thrown out everything we believed in. Everything we fought for and against. It has been painful, Billy. Many of us, we didn't really think ourselves as members of the family. We were related, yes – at a distance. But, you know, blood is not always thicker than water."

His dad smoked the cigar and looked at the photograph.

He went on:

"Then your brothers, your darling brothers, were drawn back into the Templeton fold by Michael. Drawn back by the promise of old glories, ancient splendour, and new empires. For thousands of years the Templetons had rejected the animal in us, had hunted and killed the Greenacres and the monsters they were. But then Michael found a way to re-ignite the wolf in us."

His dad sighed and put the photo back.

He took another puff on the cigar and then said, "And it cost me three of my sons." He faced Billy. His face showed rage and he shook with anger. "Murdered by a Greenacre bitch. Slaughtered and left torn in Trafalgar Square. We saw, your mother and I, our children naked and destroyed. Naked and destroyed. Their blood on the street. I wish... I wish I could put my hands around that Greenacre bitch's throat and squeeze, squeeze the poisonous, corrupt life out of her, but we are not completely returned to our primal selves. The Templeton family still has honour – and cunning. Ruth deals with the Greenacre bitch in her way, and we destroy the bitch's mount – this fucking John Thorn and his fucking pup."

Billy flinched, not used to hearing his father curse.

"It was a simple enough scheme, Billy," said his dad, glowering at his son now, "but you conspired to fuck it up. How did you conspire to fuck it up?"

"Dad, I did find them, and I don't think it's fucked up – "

"Don't curse. Your mother's lying down in the bedroom."

Billy shook his head and gawped.

His dad grimaced. "Just do as I say, not as I do."

Billy frowned. "I – I – I don't think I messed up, Dad."

"How haven't you messed up?"

"She's been calling me these past three days."

"And you're ignoring her calls?"

"Of course. Let her dangle. Let her stomach roil. Let her not want to eat. Young love hurts, and I know how to make the pain worse."

His dad nodded. "Why did you attack that man?"

"I lost it, that's all."

"Ruth is not aware yet that we've tracked Thorn down. Mr Cole thought it best not to involve her until we were certain, until we have confirmation – "

"We *have* – "

"Be quiet, Billy. Listen. Ruth will not abide this kind of behaviour. It is best, really, that she doesn't know at this stage. She is utterly ruthless. I never knew her well, only on a nodding basis. But she is pitiless. She's killing already. In Moscow. In Barcelona. The Templeton werewolf is sharpening her claws. Nothing will stop her. And as a family, we are either for her or against her. And against her, I feel, will mean death at some point. She would hunt us down."

"But you wouldn't go against her, would you? You believe in this?"

"Of course. I want to avenge my sons."

"Then let's kill Thorn and Sophie now."

"Why? You say the girl is still calling you."

Billy blushed. "I know, but... "

"But what?"

"She still might've told her dad about what I did to that guy, and there's no way he'd let her see me then."

"Do you think fathers have any say in who their children see?"

"Thorn's different. He's not normal. He's paranoid. Extra careful."

"Then we will be too. We'll not rush in. We'll show patience and cunning. We'll show our hand when we're ready. Ruth will be pleased with us. With you. Then she will tell us what to do. I know she wants Thorn killed in the house. She is very ritualistic about it. If that's what she wants... " He shrugged.

"And what about this maniac, this guy who's helping us?"

"We'll be told about that soon enough. Be patient."

"But isn't he in jail?"

"Be patient."

His dad slid off the stool and held out his arms. Billy rose and went to him, and they hugged.

His dad said, "You were a child when your brothers died, but children sense things. You felt the hate and the anger that we had in our bones, and you fed on it. It gave you a fury,

Billy, there's no doubt. It's good in many ways, makes you uninhibited. Useful, I'm sure, when it will come to killing. But for now, temper it."

His dad drew away, gripped Billy by the arms.

"I tell you, Billy, if you damage this scheme, Ruth will come for you, I am sure of it. And I'll be able to do nothing, *nothing*, to protect you from her savagery."

CHAPTER 52.
HEARTBREAK.

"YOU'LL get over it, I promise you," said Thorn.

"Thanks for hiding your relief, Dad," she said.

He grunted. "I don't want you to be upset, but this happens. It happens all the time."

"Doesn't make it hurt less, does it."

She curled up on the sofa, a box of Kleenex tucked into her lap. She had a tissue in her hand now. Dabbing her tears with it now and again.

"I don't like seeing you like this, Sophie."

"Then leave me alone, go out."

"No. I'll make you tea."

"Tea?"

"Yes, you'll feel better."

"Tea?"

"I'm trying to help."

"No you're not, Dad, you're gloating."

"I am not gloating. Do you think I like seeing my daughter in tears?"

"You like it that he's not called me."

"I didn't like him, Sophie."

"Well that's all right, because he didn't want to go out with you."

He sat next to her, laid a hand on her arm. "This'll pass, sweetheart."

She glared at him. The hairs on the back of his neck stood on end. He could hear her words before she said them, and then she did say them:

"It hasn't passed for you, has it?"

Her voice cut him. He withered, his shoulders sagging. The tear in his heart widened, and an ache spread through his chest. He felt dizzy and put a hand to his brow.

"Dad?" she said, but he barely heard.

His mind filled with Laura, and his heart split. Pins and needles flecked his skin. He rasped, as if he were trying to clear his throat. Heartbreak chafed him, and an ache went through him. The craving made him whine.

"Dad," Sophie said again, put her arm around his neck.

He hugged her and cried into her hair.

"Oh Dad, oh Dad," she was saying, rocking him. "I know it hurts, I know."

He drew away, turned his back on Sophie.

He said, "Christ," and wiped his face. He gritted his teeth. Fastened himself together again. "I'm sorry, sweetheart," he said. "That was ridiculous."

"It wasn't, was it. You know, now."

Anger flashed in him, and he wheeled. "Don't compare, Sophie. It is not the same. It is not nearly the same."

Her face stretched with longing. "It's heartbreak, Dad."

"No – no, not for you. You're – you're young, you're – "

He shook, couldn't get the words out.

"I'm what?" She stood up. Craned her neck towards him. "I'm what? A kid? A child? I know pain; I lost my mum. I lost someone who'd been around me... for always. I know pain, Dad, and this pain's just the same. And it's the same as yours."

"No." He made a slicing motion with his hand. "No. Don't say this. That – that – fuck."

"Fuck?"

"That fuck. That Billy. It's not the same."

Thorn bristled.

Sophie wept again.

She said, "He fought for me. He defended me."

Thorn froze and gawped at his daughter.

Her eyes widened, and her mouth stayed open.

Thorn, voice steady now, said, "What did you say?"

The tension left Sophie's expression. She dropped her shoulders and looked away.

Thorn said it again, firmer this time:

"What did you say?"

"Dad – "

"Don't 'dad' me. What did you say?"

She faced him. "Dad, it was this guy, this man at the cinema, he – he called me – "

"What? Called you what?"

"A slag – "

Thorn felt his rage boil over.

"And Billy protected me from him, gave him a beating."

"Why did he call you a slag?"

Sophie blushed. "We – we were – "

"Sophie?"

"Snogging, Billy and me, we were snogging in the cinema, and he, this man, he turns round and calls me a slag, a whore, and Billy lays into him."

Thorn looked his daughter in the eye and saw things he couldn't figure out yet: he was too angry, too out of control. He took in what she said, and it confused him. He didn't know what to feel for a moment. The boy had come to Sophie's defence.

Thorn calmed. The fire in him dwindled. He took his thoughts to the table near the window and sat there.

Sophie slumped on the sofa, head in hands.

Thorn said, "It's OK."

"It's not, is it."

Her phone rang, some rap tune. Dizzee Rascal, he remembered. Sophie bounded across the room and grabbed her bag and dug out the phone.

She answered it: "Hi, this is Sophie."

Thorn was relieved. The ringtone drove him mad. But the relief was short-lived.

Sophie put her hand to her breast and said, "Billy."

CHAPTER 53.
DELIVER MY ENEMY.

NICK Sears said, "He was up there yesterday, in Thorn's house. And there was even a David and Saul moment."

Ellis Cole curled his lip. "A what?"

"David and Saul. A David and Saul moment. Don't you know the story of David and Saul? From the Bible?"

"The Bible." Cole guffawed. "Why would I know that?"

Sears sighed. He lit a cigar. Puffed on it a couple of times. The tobacco relaxed him. He said, "King Saul went looking for David in the wilderness of Engedi, pledging to hunt him down. Saul and his army rested, and the king fell asleep in a cave. God said to David, 'I will deliver your enemy into your hands,' and David found Saul sleeping in the cave."

Cole yawned, scratched his armpit.

Sears continued:

"His men urged David to kill Saul, but instead, David sliced off a piece of Saul's robe. He could've killed him, you see. Ended the hunt. And when he showed the fragment of robe to Saul, he said this: 'I have spared you'."

They were silent for a few seconds.

Cole said, "Very nice."

"What I mean," said Sears, "is that Billy found Thorn sleeping on the couch."

Cole gawped.

"He could have killed him," said Sears.

"Oh... "

"But spared him."

"Oh... "

"Had you been a brighter man, I wouldn't have had to ramble on so, Mr Cole."

Cole shrugged.

Sears glanced round the bedsit. Junk cluttered the room. The place stank: sweat, stale food, mould. "You live in squalor, Mr Cole."

"No, man, I live in Newcastle." Cole belted out a laugh.

Sears shut his eyes, wondered how his family got involved with this halfwit. "Shall we get to the point?"

"Yes, let's get to the point." Cole shuffled some papers on his untidy desk. "Ruth's coming to England."

Sears sat up. "What? When?"

"Few days."

"Does she know we've found Thorn?"

"Not yet," said Cole.

"She needs to know, Mr Cole."

"She will, she will. We need to be certain."

"We are."

Cole shrugged. "I can't contact her. I don't know where she is at the moment. She rings me, tells me her whereabouts. Then I know for a few days, a few hours. Means I can contact her. But I don't know where she is now, so I can't."

"Why is she coming to England?"

"She's been killing, you see."

"I noticed. That's her, is it? Moscow? Barcelona?"

"That's her."

"So why is she coming to England?"

"Ray Craig."

"Shouldn't we deal with this matter? Keep it in the family?"

Cole smirked. "You couldn't cope with John Thorn on your own, Nicky."

"Nick, it's Nick."

"Thorn's hard. Like flint. And he's a bastard. Wipe his arse with you."

"I won't be alone. I'll have the Strakers with me. My son, too."

Cole flapped a hand. "Do what you're told, Nicky – "

"Nick. Fucking Nick. Or Nicholas. Or Mr Sears."

Cole pulled a face. "If Ruth says Ray Craig is involved, Ray Craig is involved. If Ruth says you dress up as a fairy and sing 'I'm A Little Teapot', you do that."

"Craig's in prison. Allow us to deal with – "

"You want your sons avenged, do as you're told. Follow the plan. Ruth will sort Craig out. We'll be in touch. Then we hit Thorn and his duckling." Cole furrowed his brow and leaned across the desk. "Have you seen his daughter?"

"I haven't, no."

"Tell your son to put her on her back, Nicky. She's a tasty little dish."

"You're disgusting."

"Yes, I know."

CHAPTER 54.
DEAD AND COLD.

HMP REDHILL, CUMBRIA, ENGLAND — 9.30 A.M.,
NOVEMBER 19, 2007

CRAIG, lying on his bunk, said, "Missus what?"

The prison guard in the doorway said, "Missus William Smith."

"William? A woman called William?"

"That's her husband's name, Craig. Don't act the fool. Tradition isn't it: take your husband's name. Husband owns you."

Craig sat up and cricked his neck. His trapezius muscles were stiff. They made his neck look like a tree trunk. "OK, let's meet this Missus Smith."

Two guards led Craig from the segregation block. They walked down a green corridor. Their footsteps echoed off the tiles. Strip lights lit the way. One guard behind, one in front. Craig thought of ways to disarm them, overwhelm them, and came up with plenty.

He whistled as they went.

They passed the recreation area. Craig glanced inside. He locked eyes with another prisoner and bridled.

The prisoner was a loyalist thug from Londonderry who'd tortured a Catholic priest to death three years before.

Craig was born a Catholic, but he was Brit through and through. The loyalist hated him because of religion.

The men had tussled in the canteen. Two bulls locking horns. The loyalist had layers of thick muscle. He was a bodybuilder. He was nasty. But Craig was nastier. He put a fork through the man's cheek – he was off target, aiming for the eye.

The prisoner fought on with cutlery hanging out of his face and blood pouring from the wound. Craig smashed his nose, broke his jaw. Guards dragged them apart.

The loyalist hissed hatred as staff separated them: "I'll fucking kill you, you fucking Papist cunt."

"Yeah? Come on then, Paddy, and I'll stick a knife in your other cheek and a spoon up your fucking nose."

The man growled and thrashed in the prison guards' grip, hating being called Paddy by Craig. "I'm a fucking Brit, a loyal fucking Brit... " and he had carried on complaining as the officers hauled him back to his cell.

They passed the recreation area now and the loyalist slid from view. Craig's hate faded. He focused on this Mrs William Smith.

"This woman, can I take her back to my cell if she's half tasty?" he said.

The guard leading them said, "Think she'll be agreeable, then, Craig?"

He shrugged. "Never thought of that. Does it matter?"

"Does in the real world, son."

"Don't call me son, son."

The guard stopped, wheeled to face Craig. He was heavy, freckle-faced. Ginger goatee. Craig squared up to him and smirked.

The guard said, "You can go right back to your cell if you like, Craig; I don't give a shit sideways."

Craig chuckled. "Yeah, OK... *sir*. I'm going to be good."

Craig stared at the back of the guard's neck as they walked. He saw the rolls of fat. He imagined ramming a knife between the folds. Through the skin. Slicing through the vertebrae. Paralyzing the man.

They walked down a green corridor, their footsteps echoing. They were buzzed through a door. A guard frisked Craig while two others kept watch.

He smelled paint. Peered through the porthole window in the door that led into the visitors' centre.

"Been decorating?" he said.

A guard said, "Nice peach colour. Goes with your skin tones, Craig."

They buzzed him through the door with the porthole window, into the visitors' centre. The smell of paint grew stronger. Craig made a face.

Figures sat at tables: prisoners with wives, girlfriends, mothers. Kids yelped and shouted in the playroom.

Craig shivered.

He saw the woman.

His belly squirmed.

The guard said something, but he didn't hear.

He looked into her eyes as he approached the table where she sat.

She stood up and smiled with her mouth, but her eyes were dead and cold.

"You've lost weight, Ray," she said.

"You bitch, Ruth," he said. "You bitch."

* * * *

"You said you'd come when you were released," said Craig.

"Men are so childish. Does it matter, now?" said Ruth. She fanned a hand in front of her face. She wore a blue dress. Her hair was clipped back from her face. Elegance oozed out of her. Her perfume made him dizzy, and it overwhelmed the odour of paint.

"It matters. It's about respect, honesty, sticking with your mates. That's why women can never be soldiers – you've got no bond, no brotherhood."

"How melodramatic you are, Ray."

"What do you want?"

She sniffed the air. "I still excite you, don't I?"

"What?" He felt his cheeks go red.

"You've got blood racing through your veins. I can smell your excitement."

"You're joking. You leave me cold."

211

She laughed and threw her head back to show her throat, white and graceful. He was tempted to lunge across the table and sink his teeth into her flesh and rip out her arteries.

She said, "You've no idea how I've changed, Ray."

"Prison toughened you up, did it? Thought an old bird like you would've found it hard going."

"It was atrocious, I can't pretend. My anger, I think, became white hot, and it still burns like a furnace now."

Ruth told him about Laura Greenacre and John Thorn, her plans to kill them, to avenge her family. Her eyes flitted around and she spoke quietly.

"And that's why I'm here," she said.

He put his hands on the table. She glanced at the handcuffs and then back up to his face. He said, "Who's *Mister* William Smith?"

She told him. "He's outside, waiting in the car. We needed a pseudonym, you see, because he's still wanted. Fled before he faced the trial."

"So you're not married?"

"To him? Never. He's staff. Now, Ray, your expertise."

He sighed. "What do you want?"

"John Thorn."

"What about him?"

"I want you to" – she glanced around the room, then fixed Craig with eyes full of fire – "kill him."

He stared at her. "How am I supposed to do that? I'm in here."

CHAPTER 55.
THE CREATURE ON THE
SCREEN.

"DAD," said Sophie, her voice a whisper, "is that her?"

Thorn felt a something crawl up from his belly into his chest.

He dragged a chair over and sat next to Sophie. They stared at the computer screen. The creature on the monitor looked like a werewolf.

"But it could be anything," he said.

"And it could be... could be Laura," said Sophie.

She was in her school uniform, ready to head off.

"What are you doing on the computer?" he'd asked her.

"Got to check something with my homework," she'd said.

He knew she was lying. She was on MSN Messenger or Facebook or Bebo, chatting to Billy.

"Switch it off, Sophie," he'd said, and then she'd said, "Oh my God, Dad," and he raced out of the kitchen.

Thorn stared at the image now. He tried to spot any features he remembered. Fear riddled his body. He couldn't tell if it was Laura.

He yelled out and Sophie glanced at him.

"Sorry," he said. "Frustrated, that's all. I should recognize her, shouldn't I. Should be able to tell. But... but it's a... "

"Werewolf?"

"I don't know." He put his head in his hands.

"What if it is her? In New York."

"When was this?"

Sophie checked the details. Someone had emailed it to her. A friend who'd found it and thought it was "cool", forwarded it to her mates.

Everyone knew about werewolves. Who wouldn't, after Trafalgar Square? The authorities were still in denial and claiming the creatures that rampaged that day were wild animals released from a private zoo.

What they wouldn't explain was how, after they died, the animals had changed into men. The authorities had taken the bodies away and said they'd never existed.

But there was footage.

Doctored, said the government.

There were witnesses.

Mistaken, said the politicians.

And there was a girl.

Troublemaker, said the police.

Is that you, Laura? he thought now.

Sophie said, "It was posted a few days ago. On a website called findthebeast.com. But the footage" – she scrawled down the screen, read some info – "shows the killing of a group of drug dealers in Brooklyn three years ago."

The strength drained out of Thorn. The image swam before his eyes. His heart was being shredded now, and he could feel tears fill his eyes.

He rose. "We've got to go."

"Dad, is it her?"

"I don't know." He scurried. Got the car keys. Got his coat. "We've got to go."

"It's not eight yet."

"Sophie."

She tutted and got up. Went to her room to get her things.

The image glared out at him. He moved towards the computer.

214

Her face, a catch of it, a corner. An eye, yellow. Teeth bared white, sharp and lethal.

Her fur, the black satin he'd stroked beneath London years ago.

He pined, recalling the smell of her pelt and the touch of it, and a sound came from him.

The sound of an animal torn from its mate.

The sound of a broken heart.

CHAPTER 56.
JAILHOUSE RAIDER.

HMP REDHILL, CUMBRIA, ENGLAND – 11.30 P.M.,
NOVEMBER 20, 2007

SLIM Williams yawned. His gaze drifted across the bank of monitors in reception. The black and white images were grainy and mostly still. A guard would pass in front of a camera now and again. But it was late. There was nothing. The murderers and rapists and fraudsters were all sleeping.

He put his feet up on the console, careful not to nudge anything with his heel. A Manchester United mug rested on his belly. The coffee had gone cold, the way he liked it. He took a swig, smacking his lips at the sweet taste.

He reached for the copy of FHM and rested it on his lap. He flicked through the magazine. Came to a spread showing a Hollyoaks actress in her underwear. He licked his lips and stirred in his seat. Gawked at the half-naked soap-opera star.

Wish Sally wore things like that, he thought. *Wish Sally looked like that*.

He tutted, turned the page. Glanced up at the screen.

Camera 7 showed the segregation block: quiet and still.

Camera 10 showed the gym: couple of guards in there, working out.

Camera 1 showed the gatehouse: the entrance to the prison.

Where's Euan got to? he wondered. *Should be at the desk*.

Camera 4 showed the chaplaincy: God sleeps too.

Camera 2 showed the corridor between the gatehouse and reception: a creature prowling along the passageway towards him.

Camera 12 showed –

A chill crawled down his spine. He tossed the magazine aside and sat up. Coffee spilled across his shirt. The chair fell backwards. Slim, mouth agape, no scream coming out, retreated from the monitors.

His legs felt weak, and his stomach rolled.

The creature neared the door.

Slim looked towards the door now, the creature outside.

He looked at the monster on screen again: the size of a bear, lean like a wolf.

White-furred.

"Jesus in heaven," he said, finding his voice.

The door buckled.

Slim screamed.

He looked at the screen.

The creature threw itself against the door a second time, and inside the room, it buckled again.

Slim screeched.

Now the door cracked, a slit appearing from top to bottom.

Slim glanced at the screen again. The creature prepared for a fourth charge.

Slim found strength. He lunged at the console. Broke the "Emergency Alarm" glass. Slammed the red button.

Sirens wailed.

The monitors filled with flashing lights as alarms went off throughout the prison.

Guards spilled into shot.

The two in the gym sprang from their machines.

Slim babbled and fled the reception area. He entered healthcare. The smell of disinfectant hit him. Behind him, in reception, the door splintered.

He banged on the office window. Keith in there, with his feet up. Napping as chaos erupted on his bank of monitors.

Keith woke with a jerk.

"Fucking hell," he said, with Slim inside the office, both officers looking up at the screens.

The creature bounded along the corridor from reception towards the housing block, where most of Redhill's 600 inmates lived.

Dogs barked in the distance, the German Shepherds unleashed.

"What is it, Slim?"

"Fuck knows, Keith."

"What do we do?"

"I don't know."

"We've got to get out there."

Slim glared at Keith. "Why, for fuck's sake?"

"To do our job, man."

Keith stormed out.

Slim let him go and turned his attention to the screens again.

He saw Keith enter the corridor, baton in hand.

He scanned the screens.

The creature was on another screen.

In the same corridor.

"Oh God, Keith, get out of there."

The creature – *werewolf*, thought Slim, *it's a werewolf* – glanced over its shoulders. Saliva slavered from its jaws. It looked fierce. It turned, hunkered down.

Keith, on the other screen, retreated, dropped his baton.

The werewolf leaped.

Slim moaned.

The werewolf burst into Keith's screen. Keith fled, but the monster ran him down.

Slim screamed.

Keith writhed and flapped, fought for his life.

But pieces of him were coming off as the werewolf raked him with its claws and bit him. The blood was black, but there was a lot of it, spraying the walls.

The werewolf moved away, back up the corridor.

Keith lay there, a fan of black spreading around him. His eyes were open, fixed on the camera. His white shirt and white skin had been scoured away to show dark blood and dark organs.

Slim stared at his murdered colleague.

The sirens blared. The dogs barked. Screams echoed through Redhill.

Slim staggered out of healthcare and headed towards the gatehouse.

CHAPTER 57.
BREAKOUT.

CRAIG bunched his fists and tightened his muscles.

The alarm was deafening, but he ignored it, gritting his teeth.

He stood back in his cell. Up against the rear wall.

Shouts and screams filtered through his door.

Panic had gripped the staff and inmates.

Something rammed against the cell door, and it buckled.

Craig flinched and said, "Christ," and steeled himself.

The door buckled again, a dent forming halfway down. The hinges creaked.

Craig swallowed, tried to make his throat wet.

The door bowed inwards. A hinge shot off. He ducked. The piece of metal clinked off the wall behind him.

The door swayed and screeched.

Hanging off its hinges now.

Craig could see the lights outside in the corridor.

He wanted to run to the door, rip it away.

But she'd warned him – *stay back*.

Something rammed the door again. Craig jerked. The door toppled into the cell and clanked on the floor.

Craig held his breath and stared into the yellow eyes of the werewolf, a white-blonde creature showing him its teeth.

"R-Ruth?" he said.

The creature snarled and then wheeled round. Looked up and down the corridor. Craig watched the tail whip from side to side.

Shit, he thought, *I've fucked that.*

The werewolf moved out of the cell door and down the corridor.

The alarm yowled.

Men screamed and shouted.

Craig heard voices saying, "What the fuck is that?" and "Let us out! Let us out!"

Craig stepped out of the cell. Blue and red lights flashed in the segregation unit. It was like a nightclub. The twenty-three prisoners held here banged on their cell doors. They couldn't see what was going on. They were panicking. They were yelling.

The werewolf prowled along the corridor. Left a trail of bloody saliva. Pieces of meat fell from between its claws.

Craig followed, avoiding the remains.

Half a dozen guards burst into the corridor. They'd come from the main housing block. They wielded clubs. They baulked when they saw the werewolf skulking towards them.

Craig's heart raced.

The werewolf's muscles shifted beneath its fur.

The guards horseshoed the creature. The men looked terrified. They swung their clubs, lunged forward, made grunting noises – like they were herding something.

The werewolf towered up on its hind legs.

Three of the guards stumbled and fell. One of them scrambled to his feet and ran off. Two men stuttered forward, swinging their clubs, shouting.

Craig ploughed into one of the guards who was getting to his feet. He straddled the writhing man. Grabbed the guard's face and forced his thumbs into the man's eyes and pressed until the man screamed and his eyeballs popped and fluid leaked down the pain-twisted face.

The werewolf grabbed another guard by the arm, jaws clenching around the bicep.

The guard screamed.

The creature whipped its head from side to side, shaking the man like a rag doll.

Craig laid a man out with a punch.

The werewolf tossed the guard aside. Bounded through the door with Craig following close behind.

They raced through the main block.

Barred cells here, the prisoners able to see.

They screamed. They rattled objects across the bars.

More guards came rushing down the aisles. They had German Shepherds straining on leashes. The dogs barked and salivated.

The werewolf halted.

The dogs were released.

Five of them darting towards the beast, barking and snarling.

The werewolf lashed out. The dogs pounced and bit and clung on. The werewolf writhed and wheeled. Killed with claws and teeth. Blood sprayed and flesh flew. Slapping against the walls. Tossed through bars into cells. Steaming in piles. Slithering and smearing everything.

Blood and gore greased the iron walkway.

Five dogs lay dead.

Guards saying, "Fucking hell, have we got guns?"

The werewolf went for the men.

Craig followed.

Guards fled. Others stood their ground, terror bleaching their faces.

The werewolf swiped them aside.

One hit the floor at Craig's feet. He stomped on the guard's head.

CHAPTER 58.
THE FUCKING LUNATICS
TAKING OVER THE ASYLUM.

JOLLEY had been up to give the assistant governor her supper when the sirens went off.

He froze, looked around.

He was headed back towards the kitchens. He'd clear up, then be escorted back to his cell. Sleep, then up again at sparrow's fart to help get breakfast ready.

He liked the kitchens. Made him feel special. Made him feel better than this bunch of murderers and rapists he shared Redhill with. He spat in their food sometimes, and once or twice he'd pissed in it.

Like the other day with Ray Craig.

Not so tough in here are you, Craig?

No. Everyone was equal here. Everyone except Jolley. He was more equal. A first among equals, like that Jeffrey Archer book. Archer – ha! Another jailbird.

He stopped now, and listened.

Screams and shouts. Dogs barking. That fucking siren.

What the fuck was going on?

He thought about going back upstairs to the assistant governor's office. If anything was kicking off, he'd be safe there. He didn't fancy being out in the open if there was a riot or something.

They'd have him, the bastards.

He spat in their food.

He pissed in their curry.

He murdered kids.

It was twenty-five years ago. But if they got half a chance, they'd have him.

Nail you to a table, cunt.

Cut your balls off, nonce.

Fuck you up the arse, see if you like it.

Jolley swallowed. Fear crawled through his belly. He rolled the trolley back up the corridor. He had to get somewhere safe. The prisoners yelled, rattled their bars. He could hear them.

He whimpered.

Here it was – a fucking riot.

The fucking lunatics taking over the asylum.

He cried out and his legs buckled.

They'd have him.

Nailed to a table.

Balls cut off and stuffed in his mouth.

Sodomized.

He clenched his arse cheeks.

"No," he said at the thought, "no, no."

He hurried, wheeling the trolley round.

He'd be safe with the assistant governor. She wouldn't let them hurt him.

The noise grew louder.

A cocktail of sounds.

His skin crawled.

The door behind him crashed open.

The noise spilled through.

He quickened his pace and didn't look back.

He started to cry. Something on his heels.

And then his name: "Jolley. Jolley, you fucking nonce."

He screamed. Tears spilled down his face. He kept going, heading towards the door.

Made the mistake of glancing over his shoulder.

The air froze in his lungs.

He tripped over his own feet.

A monster gained on him.

The trolley overturned, spilling plates, cutlery, food.

Jolley screamed as the huge, dog-bear-thing bared its teeth.

"You tell me to puke on my food, do you?" said a voice.

Craig.

Jolley quavered.

Craig.

The dog-bear-thing leapt over Jolley.

Craig bent, grabbed him by the collar, heaved him up.

Craig's breath stank. He snarled into Jolley's face. "Careful what you say to people, nonce. Never know when it'll come back to bite you."

Craig spun him round, clasped him tight.

"Tear him open," Craig said, speaking to this creature.

Jolley squealed. Tried to struggle. Craig too strong. The monster closed in and showed teeth like blades already glazed with blood.

"Oh, you've shat yourself, Jolley," said Craig.

The werewolf reared up.

Nearly seven feet tall.

And fell on him.

Claws opened his chest, and he was still alive when his guts poured out and the beast ate them.

* * * *

Craig wiped Jolley's blood off his shirt and licked it off his fingers.

Hot and coppery. It had been fun to see the nonce torn apart.

That's what you get for telling me to puke on my dinner.

Craig followed the Ruth-werewolf.

Blood stained her fur. It was mostly her victims' blood, but she'd suffered bites from the dogs. Nothing serious, but they might leave scars.

Craig thought about licking her wounds when she turned human again.

Lick her all over.

Then fuck this woman-animal again.

It made his loins flutter. Made him hard.

Freak, he thought, *you're a fucking freak*, and he laughed.

They were headed towards reception. A body lay in the corridor. A guard she'd killed on her way in.

What a fucking monster you are, he thought.

"Stay where you are," said a voice.

The werewolf slowed, looked over its shoulder.

Craig turned to see.

A woman flanked by a dozen men stood at the far end of the corridor. The men wore riot gear. The woman wore a helmet and a protective vest.

The woman spoke: "I'm the assistant governor. I'm ordering you to... " She trailed off.

Craig smiled. She had no idea how she was going to order a werewolf to do anything.

He said, "Ordering us to do what?"

The werewolf whipped past him and he felt the breeze.

The guards formed a protective circle around the assistant governor.

Shouts of *Stop!* and *Stay where you are!* and *Halt!* from the guards did nothing.

The Ruth-werewolf ploughed into them.

The guards scattered.

Craig blinked. The werewolf a blur of white-gold.

The assistant governor's arm in its jaws. She screamed. Guards battered at the monster with batons and shields.

The werewolf hacked at them with its claws. Back feet and front used as weapons against the assault. Blood sprinkled the green walls. Guards fell away.

The Ruth-werewolf raced back towards Craig, Newell flapping in it jaws.

* * * *

Slim slid the corpse over towards the gatehouse door. Trails of blood smeared the carpet.

Poor Euan, he thought. *His poor wife, his poor kids*.

He lay the body down and draped a blanket over what was left of Euan's head and torso.

Slim grimaced.

Poor bloke looked to have been slashed with shears.

Slim reared up, stared at the monitor that showed the corridor outside the gatehouse.

Slashed by that monster that killed Keith.

The sirens blared. The prison was in lockdown. No one in, no one out. Lucky they were in the middle of nowhere, or the noise would've brought half of Cumbria here.

Christ, he thought, *I'm the gateman, the last man standing*.

That wasn't his intention when he fled to the gatehouse. He meant to stay alive. Meant to appear to be doing something. Not like Keith, though. Not chasing that thing, that... werewolf.

"Oh shit," said Slim as Ray Craig appeared on the screen and behind Craig – "oh shit, oh shit" – the werewolf with the assistant governor in its jaws.

Someone hammered on the door.

Slim cringed with fear. He sensed himself shrivelling. Becoming a wrinkled thing in the face of the horror outside the door.

"Open the fucking door," said Craig on the monitor.

Craig kicked the door again and it clanked.

Craig said, "Open the fucking door, or we kill her."

He kicked it again and it swung off its hinges and Slim, gawping at the golden-furred werewolf, almost fainted.

He backed up.

Craig sneered. "Let us out, Williams, or we'll decorate using the assistant governor's guts."

Slim looked at the woman. Sweat glazed her face. Blood seeped from her arm.

"Ma'am?" said Slim.

Craig stepped forward. "Don't talk to her, Williams. She can't talk. She's badly shaken. Open the gate. Your call."

Slim whimpered.

"Come on, Williams," said Craig. "Make your decision. Open the gate, everyone lives. You've got five seconds. After I get to five, you can put her in a casserole. And you'll be the topping."

CHAPTER 59.
DESPERATION.

THE BLACK MOUNTAINS – 7.50 A.M., NOVEMBER 21, 2007

"I'VE got to get to the States, New York," said Thorn.

"What? You can't," said his brother.

"Pete, she's there, Laura's there."

His brother asked him how he knew, and Thorn told him.

His brother said, "You can't. You don't have a passport. You don't exist any more. Not as John Thorn."

"I can be Thorn again."

"You can, but they'll come for you. You remember what that Templeton woman said?"

"I had this all the time when I was a cop. Low-lives threatening me, telling me they'd have me. It was all bravado. They were just big mouths. Nothing ever happened."

"Wasn't bravado killed Jane, was it?"

Thorn fell silent. He felt empty. Like he had nothing inside any more. He leaned on the gate and stared out across the fields. Rain fell and glistened on the grasslands. Damp sheep trudged towards the shelter of trees and bushes. Thorn was soaked, but he didn't care, didn't sense the chill, the water rolling down his back.

He glanced towards the house.

Sophie sat at the table in the window, on the phone.

That fucking boy, he thought.

Billy-fucking-Liar, I bet.

He still didn't like him, still didn't trust him.

He told his brother, "I'm paranoid, Pete, and I can't help it. Everyone's an enemy. Sophie's got this, I don't know, this lad on the go... don't even trust him. I've made a mistake. I've let him in the house. He knows where we live."

His brother told him it was OK, that it would take time to trust people again.

"It's been eight years," said Thorn. "It won't be all right till I see her, till I know she's OK. I've got to go to the States."

"You can't."

"I'll go illegally. Millions do it, don't they? I'll fucking stow away on a boat."

"Don't do anything."

"I can't *not* do anything. I'm going mad here. Knowing she's out there. If I hadn't seen the pictures, if I didn't know, then... then it might be better, just might."

"So was it better when you didn't know?"

Thorn closed his eyes. "No," he said, "it wasn't. It's never better. It's always the same. What the fuck am I supposed to do?"

"I don't know," said his brother.

"Great help you are."

"What are brothers for, eh?"

"Can I use your passport, Pete?"

"Jesus Christ, John."

"We look alike."

His brother sighed. "I'll think about it. I'm heading towards 'no', if only to make sure you're safe, that nothing happens to you."

Thorn's phone beeped. He told his brother he had a call waiting. The brothers said they loved each other and to keep safe and then said goodbye.

"Hello?" said Thorn, taking the other call.

Silence on the line. A chill leached through his guts.

He was about to say "hello" again when a man spoke:

"It's Keegan."

He's been in jail before. In Afghanistan. A Russian camp. He broke out. In Zaire. A fucking hell hole you can't imagine. Broke out. He's monstrous, Thorn.

Thorn, finding his voice, said, "It's Craig, isn't it."

Keegan told him it was and what had happened at Redhill High Security Prison in Cumbria the previous night.

Thorn held on to the gate. He looked over at the house. Sophie was gone, and cold fear shot through him.

Then she stepped out of the front door, gestured at her watch.

Thorn waved at her and turned away.

He told Keegan, "There's been nothing on the news. Are you sure?"

"There won't be anything. There's been a news blackout. The prison's in lockdown."

"Are they looking for him?"

"We're looking for him, Thorn."

Thorn paused. "We'll be OK," he said, and saying it made him believe it for a second.

Until Keegan said, "No you won't."

CHAPTER 60.
JOB DONE.

"IS that it, then?" said the girl.

Billy, phone in hand, waiting to make a call, sneered at her. "Yeah. What else do you want?"

She was a student. Short blonde hair, tattoo of a lily on her left breast. Billy thought that might be her name, but he didn't remember.

"I don't know?" she said. "A good-bye kiss, perhaps. A 'see-you-later' or a 'can-I-ring-you?' possibly."

"I've got a phone call to make." He sat at the table and poured Tesco's own cornflakes into a bowl.

"Can we have breakfast then?" she said, gesturing at the cornflakes.

"Fuck off," said Billy. "You've had a shag, now fuck off. Count yourself lucky."

She blurted. Started to cry. Her shoulders shook. "I'll get my boyfriend on you, say you attacked me." She flung open the door.

"Yeah, whatever" – she slammed the door behind her, Billy started dialling – "I'll have my aunt eat him – and you too, you fucking cow."

The phone rang three times.

It was answered with, "Ellis Cole speaking."

Billy said, "It's Billy."

"Billy-boy, Billy-lad, Billy-club, how are you doing?"

"Don't call me that."

"Hey, hey, I'm only being friendly, Billy-boy."

"I don't want to be friendly with you, Cole."

"You're a charmer, you are, lad. Just like your aunt. Like your dad."

"Fuck off. You know I've found Thorn."

Cole said, "You've done great. I had your dad in here a few days ago telling me all about it, something about David and Saul. Tell me, have you, um, had your oats with the lass yet?"

"No."

"Ah, well. Not to worry."

"I don't worry. I get them elsewhere."

"She's a pretty thing, though."

"Yeah, she's tasty."

"Fifteen, though. Dangerous."

"Yeah, dangerous."

"Thorn doesn't suspect?"

"I don't know if he does or doesn't. He's going along with his daughter. She likes me, that's it. He looks mean, though. Never smiles. Always scowling at me."

"Ruth will be pleased. I've not told her yet. Wanted to be sure, you know, but now we are. It's Thorn, no mistaking."

"It's Thorn."

"She'll ask me how you found him, Billy. How d'you find him?"

"I didn't find him, I found Sophie. That's the mistake you lot made. You tried to find Thorn. But he's hidden. They've got a different surname now. He uses Taylor. John Taylor. She's still using her mum's maiden name. Burrows."

Billy got up and went to the fridge. He took out a carton of milk from the door and sat at the table again and milked his cornflakes. He spooned some into his mouth. He spoke and crunched at the same time:

"Thorn was always going to be tough to locate, but Sophie... easy... kids, teenagers, they're a doddle to find because they *want* to be found."

"How d'you mean, Billy-boy?"

"Facebook. MSN Messenger. Yahoo! Messenger. Bebo. This is like second nature to our generation, Cole. It's automatic. It's like brushing your teeth. Like breathing. You can sign up to stuff like Facebook and keep your page private. I guess that's what oldies like you would do."

Cole guffawed.

Billy said, "But kids, teenagers, they just want the world to know they're out there. They want to be someone, want to be identified, want to be known. Took me nine months to track Sophie Burrows down on Facebook. Then I messaged her under a few fake IDs."

"Like a paedo, eh? Grooming her?"

Billy's face burned. "That's what you'd do, Cole, yeah. Not me. This is not for my pleasure; it's for the family. I lost my brothers and I want them avenged. I want blood for blood, mate."

"OK, OK, Billy-lad, calm down, now. So after you messaged her – "

"I met her, didn't I. She said, 'I'm having a birthday meal at the Skirrid Inn, *Klan*-wherever... ' Welsh name, can't say it. My various online identities told Sophie that sorry, they couldn't come to her party. But me, me myself, I set up just across the border in Hereford. Enrolled at the local college. Happened to be in the pub that night. Just *happened* to be, you know. Turned on the charm."

"Get her drunk did you?"

"She wasn't on the booze. So can we do this? Can we go ahead?"

"Not yet. Wait for Ruth's says so."

"Why? What's the delay?"

"Why? Because she says so, lad. And the delay? She's not out of the country yet. She needs to be out of the country. She needs clean hands. And we've not got Laura Greenacre yet. No worries, though. Won't be long."

CHAPTER 61.
WAITING.

SOPHIE and the boy walked hand in hand across the field towards the farmhouse.

Thorn watched from the window and seethed. He'd been watching for two hours. Back and forth from this window since his daughter and the boy had strolled off together. Watching and waiting for them, for her, to come back.

Hoping Ray Craig wouldn't be lurking out there. Knowing that Craig would come for him one day. Just not knowing when.

And now there was Laura, too.

The stress made him stay awake all night. Made him sweat and made his heart race. He hadn't eaten properly since seeing the werewolf footage, since Keegan rang to say Craig had escaped. He hadn't done any work around the place.

The door opened and they came in, Sophie saying, "Hi, Dad. God, it's cold out there," and Billy waving at him and saying, "All right again, Mr T," Thorn bristling. And saying, "*Taylor*, it's *Taylor* not *T*."

The boy plonked himself in the armchair. Put his feet up on the coffee table. Thorn glanced at his feet. The boy put them on the floor and said, "Oops, sorry, Mr T... Taylor... heh! heh!"

Christ, I want to smash his face in, thought Thorn.

But he'd protected Sophie, hadn't he? Defended her, she said, after someone insulted her at the cinema. That meant Billy's thrashing was postponed. Thorn let his shoulders drop, and he thought for a second:

The lad might be OK. He might grow on me if I can wrestle with this paranoia.

"I'll go make tea," said Thorn and stalked through to the kitchen.

He leaned on the sink while the kettle boiled and listened to Sophie and Billy giggling in the living room. He looked out of the window at the garden that needed tending. Weeds grew, and he would have to till the earth to prepare it for planting in the spring.

But not now.

Other things now.

He took the tea through, and Billy said, "Here's the waiter. Any biscuits, waiter?" and he laughed.

Thorn glared at Sophie, and she tried to grin but he saw the embarrassment in her expression. She mouthed, Please, Dad, and Thorn backed off from dragging Billy outside and slapping him across the face.

"I'll go outside," he said and went to the door.

"Shut the door after you, waiter," said Billy.

Thorn turned and glared at him and said, "You can come outside with me, if you fancy it."

Billy blanched but held his stare.

Thorn didn't like what he saw in the youth's eyes.

* * * *

He swung the axe and it split the log, and the blade wedged in the stump of the oak tree. He worked the blade out. Picked up the halves of the log and tossed them on the pile he was making in the corner of the shed.

He wiped his brow. Sweat poured from his hair and stained his back. A good sweat that came from work and not from fear. He breathed deeply and smelled his own skin and smelled sawdust.

He took another log and rested it on the stump. Raised the axe.

He heard someone come in to the shed and knew who it was before the boy spoke. He swung the axe and split the log, and the halves parted and fell either side of the stump. The blade wedged in the stump. He put his foot on the stump and began to ease the blade out of the wood.

The boy said, "Mr T – Taylor?"

Thorn yanked the axe from the wood and leaned on it to pick up another log and placed that on the stump. He straightened, rested the axe on his shoulder.

"I – I've come to apologize," said the boy.

"Apologize," said Thorn.

"Yes, apologize for – "

He swung round, the axe resting on his shoulder, fire in his eyes. He said, "I know what for, lad. It wasn't a question. I was inviting you to go ahead."

The boy fidgeted. He paled and his eyes flitted around the shed. "Go... "

"With your apology." Thorn waited.

Billy curled his lip as if he had something that tasted bad in his mouth. He looked down at the sawdust-covered floor and then up again into Thorn's face. He said, "I'm really sorry I was cheeky back there, sir. I – I know I've been a bit, well, arrogant I guess. It's just... I'm... really happy, you know? Sophie makes me happy, and when I'm happy, I can be a bit full of myself. You see?"

Thorn didn't see but didn't say anything.

Billy went on:

"The last thing I should do is disrespect you in your home. That's shameful. And I'm really, really sorry. Is – is that OK?"

"As an apology?"

Billy blushed now. "Uh... well... no... is it, uh, OK that I say sorry."

"Yes, that's OK. That's fine."

He stared at the boy for a few seconds more, just to drill into him a fear that if anything like that happened again, it wouldn't be tolerated.

Thorn took the axe off his shoulder, held the handle in one hand.

"Make yourself useful," he said and lobbed the axe towards Billy.

The boy flinched and caught the handle with two hands, but the weight of the axe still tugged him forward a little. Then he stood there, the axe in his hands. His grip seemed to tighten on the handle. His knuckles showing bone. And something passed across his face that Thorn didn't like. But he let it go and said, "Half-a-dozen more to do, then you can come indoors."

Thorn strode past the boy, and when he got to the door of the shed, he stopped and half-looked over his shoulder.

He could see Billy still standing there with the axe. He said, "Billy," and the boy glanced round, and his eyes were wide. Thorn went on:

"If you behave like that again in my house, I'll take you outside and slap you, is that clear?"

He didn't wait for an answer. As far as he was concerned, it was clear.

* * * *

Newcastle – 3.01 p.m., November 26, 2007

COLE, feet up on the table, said, "They're in the US and Ruth says you should make your move. Go see her and take her to Sorrow Hill. It's an estate near the town of Pawling in the Hudson Valley. You know it?"

Silence came back at him.

"Zak," he said, "did you hear me?"

Zak said, "Yes, I heard you. Who owns this estate?"

"None of your business. Just do what you're told."

Zak said nothing.

"What's the matter?" Cole asked.

"What if she kills me?"

"Who?"

"Laura. What if she just doesn't go for it and kills me?"

"Well," said Cole, swinging his legs off the table, tilting his head to see the image of the couple having sex on his computer screen, "you'll have to make sure she doesn't. Turn on the charm, lad."

"She doesn't fall for charm."

"Just tell her Ruth's in the States and that you know where she is."

"And how would I have known that unless I was in league with Ruth?"

"For God's sake, Zak, make something up. Just tell her Ruth's here. You can take her to Ruth. That'll be enough. She won't be able to resist."

"I thought she was going to kill me when I told her I knew she was Laura Greenacre."

"Yes, well," said Cole, liking the woman he was watching, the way her face contorted and the way her breasts swung when the man drove into her. He wished he could turn up the volume now and hear her voice. "It's the price you pay for getting into bed with werewolves."

"I never got into bed with her."

"That's where you missed out, lad."

"Oh, like you ever did."

Cole sighed and switched off his computer, not able to concentrate on the porn. He spun his chair round and leaned back and stared up at the cobweb up there on the top bookshelf. He said, "You've unsettled her, Zak. Laura Greenacre's probably shitting herself. She might even be packing her bags right now. So you'd better get over there sharpish, I'd say. If she disappears again, Ruth won't be happy. And you don't want that, do you?"

"I suppose not. So what's happening over there?"

"Over here? Over here, lad, John Thorn and his little miss are spending their last couple of days together."

CHAPTER 62.
TONIGHT'S THE NIGHT.

HE made her heart race. He made her tummy wheel. He gave her goosepimples and made sweat break out on her back. He made her skin flush, and she turned red every time she saw him.

He'd say, "You're blushing," and she'd tingle and hide her face and say, "No, I'm not; I'm just warm, that's all."

And they'd laugh and he'd look at her, and the laughter would dwindle and his eyes burn, and she'd melt and they'd snog, and a fire would light in her and she'd whimper and pull him and claw him and want him and...

"Whoa," he said.

She drew away, a cold feeling sweeping through her. "W-what? What did I do? W-what's wrong?"

"Nothing, nothing, it's fine. Feel a bit queasy tonight, that's all."

"Q-queasy? Queasy what?"

"What do you mean 'queasy what'?"

"I mean... I mean – " She was flustered, felt hot again, but not good hot – "I mean queasy with... with... me, because... because... don't you like kissing?"

238

He touched her face. "Oh, Sophie, yes, I love it – I love kissing you."

She squirmed. "Really?"

"Yeah, you're a good kisser."

"Really?"

"Really." He leaned in, kissed her. She kissed him back, hoping to draw him in again. But it was a soft kiss. Platonic almost. *Fucking platonic.* She felt sick in her stomach.

"Billy," she said.

"Yes, babe?"

"Are we... are we, like, boyfriend and girlfriend?"

"You're blushing."

She looked him in the eye. "Are we?"

"Yeah, sure."

"Yeah, sure? What does that mean?"

"I'm about to take you to one of the best restaurants in Britain. I'm seventeen and I take you there. How many seventeen-year-olds do that for their... for girls?"

Sophie glanced in the rear-view mirror. In the distance she saw Skenfrith. A patch of lights in the vast darkness. This was the middle of nowhere. The village had been plonked in the hills, nothing for miles.

When they were ten minutes from the restaurant, he'd stopped. "Why?" she asked, her heart skipping. And he'd said he needed to make a quick call.

"Do you think I'm too young for you, Billy?"

He slapped the steering wheel and sighed. "What's up with you?"

"It's just... it's just... well, boys... boys normally want to... " – she shrugged, not knowing how to say it, not knowing *why* she wanted to say it, because everything was good – "... you know, take things... take things... "

"You want me to fuck you."

She gasped. Her gaze drifted towards the darkness ahead of them.

"Well?" he said.

She turned to look at him, her eyes wide and blazing.

* * * *

239

Nick Sears said, "Two minutes."

He sat in the passenger seat of the black Ford Transit. Next to him, in the driver's seat, Gerry Straker and sat between them, Straker's brother, Brian.

Gerry said, "When my sons died at Trafalgar Square... well, you know how I felt, Nick; you felt the same losing your boys."

Sears said nothing. Half-listening, his gaze fixed on the dark landscape. The red tail-lights in the distance.

Gerry went on:

"I wanted revenge. Anger boiled in me. But I didn't know how. I was a property developer, not a soldier, a fighter."

"But we are fighters," said Brian, "we're warriors – the Templetons are warriors. It's just we lost power. Now, now we've found it again."

"Through Ruth," said Gerry.

Something banged on the partition behind them, and the vehicle shook.

"Jesus," said Brian, "that thing in the back scares the shit out of me."

Sears twisted in his seat and said, "Two minutes," rapping the partition with each word.

The thing in the back slammed back.

"Hope he doesn't turn on us," said Brian.

"It's fine, don't fret," said Sears. He licked his lips and swallowed, trying to wet his throat. His heart raced and his skin crawled. This was terrifying. The Strakers and him. Respectable men. Businessmen behaving tonight like criminals, like gangsters.

And his son in that car.

Playing his part.

And doing it perfectly.

I'm proud of you, Billy, he thought. *We're doing this for the boys: for Jake, and Sam, and Anton, for all of them who died that day.*

"What's the time?" said Gerry. "I'm cold with fear. I could do with a piss."

"This place is the back of beyond," said Brian. "Half way up a mountain. Pitch black. Not used to not seeing anything at night. Living in London, there's never real darkness is there. Not like this."

"Do I have time for a piss, Nick?"

"No, Gerry, you don't. Drive."

The van moved off. Their breath filled the cab. Sears kept his eye on the tail-lights of Billy's MX5. Coming closer.

Gerry slowed the van.

The headlights showed two shadows in the MX5.

The shadows were close to each other. Very close. Locked together.

The van drew up next to the car and Gerry killed the lights.

Sears looked down into the Mazda and Billy looked up at him.

* * * *

"Who's that, Billy, who is it?" said Sophie. She pulled the coat around her, shivering.

"I – I don't know."

"Billy, what – what do they want?"

The van had stopped next to them. Stopped right in the middle of the road. A black van with moonlight splintering off its paintwork.

Sophie cowered. "Let's go, Billy, please."

"No, we'll see what they want."

"What? No. No, Billy, Jesus. Please. Please, let's go." But Billy opened the door. Sophie's skin went clammy with fear. She lunged at him. Tried to tug him back into the car. She hissed his name. But Billy pulled away and opened his door and stepped out and slammed the door shut on her.

The passenger stepped out of the van.

He was mid-forties, same height and build as Billy. Looked like Billy. Sophie stared. Panic made her shiver.

The man said something to Billy, but Sophie couldn't hear. Could only see his mouth moving, and it looked like he'd said something about hell...

"... go to hell... " perhaps.

Sophie didn't know.

The man whacked Billy across the head with a baton.

Sophie screamed.

She grabbed for the door handle, rattled it, yanked it, clawed at it.

241

Fucking locked, fucking locked, why did you lock it, Billy?

Adrenaline rifled through her veins.

Men leaped from the van.

She screamed for her father, and her father's name brought a moment of clarity. She scrabbled through her bag. Got the phone. Whimpered and cried. Trawled for his number in the mobile's phonebook. Fingers shaking so not good for delicate work. She found his number and gasped and –

The windscreen shattered.

Glass sprayed her.

She dropped the phone.

She shrieked and curled up into a ball.

The man battered at the windscreen with a sledgehammer.

Glass sliced her arms, her legs.

Hands grabbed her. She fought, scratching at the hands, but they were gloved. The hands scooped her up. Hauled her through the shattered windscreen. Shards cut her as the man dragged her across the bonnet. She writhed, flailed, clawed at his face.

"Come on, Brian," said a voice.

"I'm trying, I'm trying," said the man pinning her to the bonnet.

She looked him in the eye. He looked scared, his face white. It gave her strength. She kicked, her heels sinking into something. The man groaned, doubled up. Sophie shot to her feet. Stumbled a few yards and screeched for help.

Someone grabbed her from behind, wheeled her round. She saw her victim – Brian, he'd been called – squatting with his arms around his belly and his face stretched in pain.

She kicked now, kicked the man behind her. Kicked and kicked.

Billy lay on the ground. The man who'd spoken to Billy crouched over him. Putting something in Billy's pocket. The man looked up and said, "Get her in the van, Gerry, for God's sake."

The man holding her said, "She's... she's a fucking... wild one."

She thrashed about. Reached back to scratch at his eyes. Tried to stomp on his toes with her heels. Chomped on his arm, but he had on a thick coat.

The man with Billy stood now, snarling, came towards her.

She threw her weight back against her captor. Kicked out her legs. The man with Billy yelled out in pain as Sophie's heels stabbed into his chest. He reeled away.

Sophie said Billy's name, shouting, telling him to help her, to get up.

But Billy lay still.

Dead. They'd killed him.

She screamed.

The first man, the one with the sledgehammer, was up on his feet now, staggering towards her.

She lifted her legs. Slipped free of her captor's grip. Hit the ground. He tripped over her, flat on his face. And the sledgehammer man stumbled over him.

Sophie leaped to her feet.

She screamed for help and made a run for it.

The van's back door opened, and something heavy fell or jumped from the back, the road under Sophie's feet trembling.

A voice said, "Did I *have* to get out? Did I have to get out because you fucking amateurs couldn't fucking manage a teenage girl? Did I?" and the voice made Sophie feel sick.

She ran.

Something on her heels.

Thundering after her.

"Come here, you little bitch," said the man chasing her, "you little Thorn bitch."

Thorn, she thought, *Thorn's not my name. Dad's name.* But not now. Not any more. The Thorn name was hidden. Dad was Taylor to everyone now.

Someone grabbed her hair. Yanked her backwards. Pain shot through her skull, and she yelped.

She was being dragged along the ground. Asphalt scorching her legs. A colossus dragging her by the hair. She looked up and he towered over her, twice her height. He dragged her past the downed men, the men she fought, and past Billy, dead Billy.

The man hoisted her up by her hair. She thought her head would tear off her shoulders. She scratched his hands. He held her high off the ground. She screamed. Her scalp on fire and her neck tearing.

She looked him in the eye.

Cold eyes.

Scars crisscrossed his face.

He grinned at her. The muscles in his face corded. His tree-trunk neck flexed.

"So you're his pup, are you?" he said. "John Thorn's little pup. I'm going to put you down, little pup. You and your cunt father."

Sophie cried out. He slammed her head against the van. Stars burst in her vision, and after a jolt of pain, she fell into a dream of her mother calling her home.

CHAPTER 63.
PHONE CALL.

THORN, sick with worry, paced the yard. He stared down the road that led up here, watching for headlights. Nothing but darkness sprinkled with light coming from solitary farmhouses. He watched as vehicles darted along the A465, but none of them turned to come up the mountain.

Sophie, where the hell are you? Billy Liar, I'm going to fucking kill you.

"Can I stay out a little later tomorrow night, Dad, please?" she'd asked yesterday. "Billy's taking me to a nice restaurant, really nice."

He'd asked which restaurant, but she didn't know, and he made her phone Billy and get him to tell her.

"Half-ten," said Thorn. "That's enough time for you to eat, talk... half-ten, no later, if you ring me at eight, say everything's OK."

"Dad – "

"Half-ten, Sophie, if you ring me at eight and tell me you're OK, right?"

His head throbbed as he was telling her, the panic driving him mad. He was trying his best, trying to let her be normal. But Craig was free. Laura'd been spotted. There were signs, and they weren't good.

Now it was eight-fifteen. A quarter of an hour. Not like her if she'd said she'd ring. Something squirming in his belly.

Billy Liar, I'm going to fucking kill you.

A shiver crept up Thorn's spine. He looked at his watch again. He'd thought about phoning the police, but they'd tell him to give her at least an hour and tell him to try her friends first.

He rang her mobile again. No answer. The back of his neck prickled. His mouth was dry.

Billy, he thought.

Billy Liar's mobile.

Shit, shit, shit –

He didn't have it. He bent double. Cramps in his stomach. He straightened and tried to steady his breathing. He looked down the road. Nothing came. No light from a car. No light at all. He dashed into the house.

Fuck it, I'm phoning the cops.

His phone rang.

He snatched at it, not checking the number that flashed up on screen.

"Sophie?"

A groan came down the line and Thorn stiffened.

He said her name again: "Sophie?"

"Mr... Mr T-Taylor, it's me, it's – "

"Billy. Billy, what the fuck's going on, where's Sophie?"

"Help me... help... "

"Billy, where's Sophie – where's my daughter?" Frantic now: his chest on fire, his heart splitting, head swimming. "Where's my daughter?"

"They've... "

Jesus Christ, thought Thorn, *Jesus Christ.*

"... taken... "

Jesus Christ.

"Billy, who's taken her? Who?"

"Help me... help – "

The line died.

CHAPTER 64.
WHAT'S GOING TO HAPPEN.

"NOW," said the big man with muscles, "let me tell you what's going to happen over the next few hours."

He'd trussed Sophie up in the back of the van. Rope tight around her wrists and her ankles. Cutting into her flesh. She was already bleeding from being showered in glass and getting dragged along the road. And her head throbbed after the giant banged it against the van. He'd taped her mouth too. Told her he didn't want to hear her moan and scream all the way up north. Told her she'd listen, and that this would be a lesson for her "and her fucking father", and the lesson was: "You don't fuck with Ray Craig."

And now he said, "This is what's going to happen."

Sophie stared at him. The van rumbled. They were on a straight road. Sounded like lots of traffic. Some of it whizzing past. A motorway, she thought. Up north, the man had said. She rocked around a little, but not much. Nothing to make her sick or make her vomit into this tape so she'd choke on it.

She tried to concentrate on the road. The turns, the junctions, the roundabouts. Tried to feel them, thinking it might important at some stage.

Ray Craig went on:

"Your old man almost left me a vegetable. Didn't though – more's the pity for him, for you. Because now, sweet pea, I'm going to fucking disable him, see. So he can't move. So he can't piss or shit. And then, then sugar pie, he's going to watch while I go at you."

She screamed into the tape.

Horns blared and a siren screamed. Craig and Sophie stared at each other. The siren faded, and a grin stretched across his face.

"Thought they were coming for you, dolly?" he said. "No. No one's coming for you except your dear old dad, and your dear old dad's walking into a trap."

* * * *

"A... black van... black... van... " said Billy. "I... I tried my... tried my best, Mr... Taylor... but... there were... too many and they... beat me... up... "

Thorn found him on an unclassified road off the B4521. No road markings. No street lights. Hedges and trees lining the narrow route.

Billy lay sprawled on the asphalt, groaning and bleeding from a head wound. He had his mobile phone in his hand after managing a call to Thorn. The MX5 was parked on the side of the road. The windscreen was shattered.

Thorn helped Billy into the Land Rover. He tended to the youth's injury. A swelling the size of a golf ball grew through his hair. His scalp was purple, and there was blood. Thorn asked Billy what had happened, and the youth told him about the black van.

"Where did they take her, Billy, did they say?" he said.

Billy shook his head.

"OK, how many of them were there?"

"Two? Three?" He shook his head again, cried.

"It's all right, lad, it's all right."

But it wasn't. Thorn was twitching with rage and terror. He fought to control his emotions. Tried to wring out as much information from Billy as he could.

"Did they speak?"

No, Billy told him, they didn't.

"What did they do to Sophie?"

248

"They grabbed her, put her in the back of the van, then drove off."

"And you didn't recognize them?"

Billy shook his head.

"Number plate, make?"

"Ford Transit... registration... " He shook his head, said he was sorry.

"How did they know you were here, Billy?"

Billy looked at him. "I... I don't know."

"Who did you tell you were coming here?"

Billy appeared to be thinking. Then he said, "A few mates – "

"Who? Which mates? I want their names, all of them, addresses, everything."

"Uh... I... I don't think they would've... "

"Maybe not, but they might've mentioned it to someone, someone might've heard. My daughter's been taken, lad, and I'm going to scour the earth for her if I need to; I'm going to ask questions of everyone. Your dad, your mum, did you tell them where you were going, tell them about Sophie, about this place?"

"No, I didn't tell them. I was... was going to ask Sophie if she'd like to meet them... next week... we were... " He looked down, shut his eyes, fought the tears.

"Your head's bleeding again. Press that on the wound." Thorn gave him more gauze from the Land Rover's first aid kit.

Thorn tried to calm himself. Tried to focus and achieve clarity. And when clarity came, he was bold enough to identify the people who'd taken her: the Templetons.

And Ray Craig.

Too much of a coincidence: Craig breaks out of jail, and a few days later Sophie's kidnapped.

Thorn leaned his elbows on the Land Rover's steering wheel and put his head in his hands. Days ago he planned to go to the US to find Laura.

A crazy idea.

But how else could he get to her?

Then he'd thought: *Perhaps she doesn't want me to find her.*

Laura could have a new life in the States. A boyfriend. A husband. Children, even. Why should he think she'd want him after all these years?

He felt flattened by that possibility. As if there were a weight on his chest.

Now he asked Billy, "Do you know of anyone called Templeton?"

"Templeton?"

"That's right."

Billy considered this and then shook his head.

"I think they took Sophie," said Thorn.

Billy asked why.

Thorn took a breath and told him.

Billy said, "Crazy. I remember that, though. The Trafalgar Square thing. Vaguely. It was the year I lost my brothers, you see, Mr Taylor. That... you know... that took priority in my family. Trying to find out who killed my brothers."

"Did you?"

"Yeah, we did. Their killers haven't been brought to justice, though."

"I'm sorry about that."

Billy shrugged. "Bit... bit cold... " and he tucked his hands in the pockets of his coat. "Hey, what's this? Something in my – " and he pulled out an envelope. Billy blanched and curled his lip, opening and closing the flap of the envelope.

Thorn didn't think too much about what Billy had found in his pocket. He was thinking he should ring the police. But then Billy said, "It's got a name on it – Thorn, John Thorn."

"What?"

"John Thorn. I wonder who that is?"

Thorn snatched the envelope out of Billy's hands.

"What are you doing, Mr Taylor?"

"Who gave you this?"

"I... I don't know, sir. I... they might've slipped it in my pocket... those men... I... I was out, wasn't I... unconscious... so..."

Thorn opened it.

"Hey, Mr Taylor, what are you doing?"

Thorn ignored him. Yanked out a sheet of paper.

He unfolded the paper and read the letter.

He grew sick. A sour taste rose up into his throat.

Billy said something, but Thorn couldn't make sense of his words.

He just read the letter. It said where to come to find Sophie. It said what would happen to her if he called the police, if he didn't do as he was told. It said what they intended to do.

It said, "Your death, her life."

CHAPTER 65.
DRIVEN.

THE M6, NORTH-BOUND – 10.56 P.M, NOVEMBER 27, 2007

THORN hammered the Land Rover. His grip on the steering wheel was so tight that his hands had gone numb. His eyes were sore. Felt like he hadn't blinked for 300 miles. He glanced behind him. The car was still there.

Billy said, "You should take a break, Mr... Mr Thorn," knowing his real name now, knowing everything after Thorn had told him.

Thorn grunted.

"They... they said not to come straight away, to... to go see this Ellis Cole in Newcastle, then he'd bring you."

"Cole," said Thorn, tasting the poison in the name. "If I saw that bastard, I'd kill him. I'd wring his fat neck. Then that would be that. Do you think I'm going to do what they want me to do?"

"What about, what about Sophie?"

"The man I'm dealing with, he's called Ray Craig," said Thorn and told the boy about Craig. "I'll not pussy-foot around him. Pussy-foot around him, he'll smash you and he'll kill you. He's after me and wants me dead. These Templetons want me dead. I'd die for Sophie, I would. But I'd rather the both of us live. I'd rather the both of us got out of this. And we will, we fucking will."

Billy said nothing.

"I said you didn't have to come," said Thorn.

"I wanted to. Sophie, you know. She's... you know."

"Yeah, I know. Thanks, lad. I never really gave you a fair go. But you've been good to her, and this, well, it might be stupid of you to come along, but I appreciate it."

Billy kept quiet.

They drove on. The M6 emptied as the night wore on. Trucks thundered north-bound and south-bound. Thorn noted lorries from seven European countries. He looked in the rear-view mirror. The car still tailed him. The vehicle sped up when Thorn accelerated and slowed when Thorn took his foot off the gas. Thorn left the M6 at junction 43, joined the A69. So did his tail.

Fifty miles to go – hold on, baby, hold on. I'm coming to get you.

He gritted his teeth.

A coil of red-hot anger simmered in his belly.

He watched for a black Transit van, but he didn't really think he'd catch them. They had a head start. A good hour. They were probably already there.

He thought about Craig. Winced as he recalled the pain he suffered after fighting the bastard eight years ago. Thorn knew he'd been lucky, but you made your own luck. You did anything to survive. You fought dirty. You used teeth and nails. You pulled their hair. Kicked them in the balls. Stamped on their toes. It wasn't about honour or dignity. It was about getting out alive.

He wondered if Craig had hired any muscle this time. Had the Templetons brought in paid-for thugs like they did thirty years ago, to massacre the Greenacres? Like they did eight years ago, to slaughter Laura?

He thought about the letter planted in Billy's pocket.

Your death, her life.

Which one of the family had written that? The note wasn't signed. Told him they had Sophie and ordered him to come to Newcastle, see Ellis Cole, "who will bring you to us."

But Thorn knew where they'd taken Sophie. He knew in his guts. And that's where he was going. This was all about revenge for Ruth and her family. Retribution – for Michael Templeton's death, for Ross Andersson's death, for all the Templeton deaths that day.

The Templetons.

It was all about the Templetons.

He glanced behind him, saw the car's headlights.

And I'm going there without you, whoever you are, he thought.

He accelerated.

CHAPTER 66.
THE FAMILY SEAT.

A CHILL rinsed Sears's veins as he stared at the ruin.

"Did you ever come here?" asked Brian Straker.

Sears said no. "You?"

"Once. Years ago. Katrina Templeton's funeral. Sir Adam's wife."

"It's terrible to see the place like this."

"It is, Nick – it's sad."

The van rolled up the drive after dropping them off and made its way round the back of the house. Sears stared after it as it wound along the driveway. He thought about Billy, lying on that quiet road, blood coming from him. How hard had he struck his son? He had to make it look real, but not real enough so as to kill him. He'd knocked Billy out; he knew that. He just hoped the boy would come round quickly. The horror of what he'd done wriggled in his belly.

"Not having second thoughts?" said Brian.

Sears glared at Brian and shook his head. "Just thinking." He looked towards the house. Ivy crawled up the Palladian frontage. Grass sprouted from the stone steps leading to the front door. Leaves carpeted the path. The windows had all been

255

smashed. Weeds overwhelmed the lawns. The beeches and oaks that skirted the perimeter wall were thick and overgrown, in need of pruning.

When they'd arrived, the van drawing up outside the rusted front gates, Sears couldn't see a way through. Brambles weaved a thick curtain through the bars. They'd forced the gate open. A wall of foliage blocked their way. They hacked their way through.

"It's a disgrace," said Sears now. "It must be rejuvenated, restored."

Gerry Straker joined them after parking the van at the rear of the ruined building. He was pale. He said, "Craig's sorting the girl. She's – she's a fighter, but he's... he's pretty rough with her."

"That's OK," said Sears and headed towards the house. "Just remember who she is. Whose daughter she is. What he did to our family. What his girlfriend did. To your sons, Gerry."

The lobby smelled of damp. Rot and woodworm had destroyed the stairwell. Water had pooled on the floor. Twigs, litter, insects, and dead mice floated there. Busts of Roman emperors perched on pillars. The heads were covered in bird shit and moss. The pillars were cracked and chipped. The ballroom was dark with mould. Weeds grew in here too.

They toured the house. It was a ruin. The odour of decay followed them from room to room.

"This is dreadful," said Gerry.

"It's what we've become," said Sears. "This is the Templetons. This is what Laura Greenacre made us. Her and Thorn."

They made their way back to the lobby.

Something clattered at the far end. A door fell off its hinges. Craig stomped through.

"What the fuck are you doing hanging around here?"

Sears said, "Mourning our family seat, Mr Craig."

"Fuck that – we've got to get sorted."

"Where's the girl?"

"She's all right, Sears. You worry about your job; I worry about mine."

"This is all so elaborate and complicated," said Brian.

"It's what your cousin, or whatever she is, wants, mate,"

said Craig. "Ruth gets what Ruth wants. It's all about ritual, isn't it – that's what I heard. Must've gone all new age and supernatural in jail. Thinks blood must be spilled to cleanse this" – he glanced around and sneered – "shit hole you call home. It's a wonder there's no mistletoe hanging from the rafters. No upside-down crucifixes hanging on the walls." He clapped his hands. "All right, have you got the guns?"

Sears said they were in the van.

"Well what the fuck are they doing there? Go and get them."

The Strakers trundled off.

Craig said, "When Cole brings him here, you scare him a bit if you can, stick a gun to his head, count to three – few head games. But I want him alive, OK? You bring him through to where the pool was, back there, and I'll deal with him."

"What are you going to do?" said Sears.

"I'm going to tie him up, next to his daughter. Then I'm going to break his back, like he broke mine. Then I'm going to break a few other bones, till it really, really hurts. Then... then I'll have a go at the girl, see how Thorn likes to watch."

"You like inflicting pain, Mr Craig?" said Sears.

"I usually get paid to do it, and it's a job. This one I'm doing for free, because this one I'm doing for revenge – just like you lot. So don't you get fucking hoity-toity with me. You're not better than I am. You're driven by the same rage. Now get yourselves sorted. And any fucking hoity-toity bollocks, I'll break your fucking legs."

CHAPTER 67.
SWIMMING POOL.

SOPHIE'S head felt swollen. Like it was full of water. Things sloshed about in her skull. And her brain throbbed with pain. Cold air brushed over her, and she shivered. Her arms and her legs hurt, and it seemed as if there were weights attached to her shoulders, pulling them up or –

She opened her eyes.

The world spun.

– *down!*

She tried to scream, but her cries were muffled by the tape strapped across her mouth. The scream filled her head. Increased the pressure in her skull. Made her throat burn.

Pulled *down!*

Panic streamed through her.

She went spinning. Her head was going to explode. Everything whirled. Bile came into her throat and she feared she'd be sick and throw up and choke to death. She didn't know where she was. She didn't know why she was upside down, high above an empty swimming pool.

She screamed till her throat chafed. Till she could only whimper and cry. Till she stopped spinning and instead swayed, thirty feet above the ground.

While they drove, the man called Ray Craig had gone on for hours about what he was going to do to her dad. It made Sophie sick, made her cry. This man Craig tore her world to pieces. And no matter how much she wept, how much she made muffled pleas through the tape across her mouth, he'd not put it back together again.

"Your dad's dead, sweetheart. Get used to it."

Miles and miles of this. Hours and hours.

Till they slowed down, and Craig took a brown bottle from a rucksack. He opened it, and the chemical odour made her dizzy. He dampened a cloth with the liquid from the bottle. Sophie felt her insides turn cold. She moaned, wriggled to free herself.

Craig smiled and came to her. He ripped off the tape.

Her shriek made his face crease up.

He slapped the cloth across her mouth and nose.

She struggled but grew tired, hazy, her eyelids heavy, her mind like lead, slowing down, drifting away, like seeing a boat sail towards a horizon, shrinking, shrinking, the light going, going, to a dot, and gone...

Until...

Waking up upside down, her ankles trussed, her wrists trussed.

She wailed for her dad. Tried to say the word: *Dad*. The word that gave her hope. But the tape stopped her. Stifled the word. She tried to relax and studied her environment. It made her feel sick, being upside down and so high up.

The room contained a swimming pool that was full of debris: branches, leaves, litter, rainwater, mud, slime, girders from the roof. The pool building looked like it was made of glass once. Glass and steel. The frame remained. Corroded by the elements. A skeleton of something that might have been grand once. But all the windows had been shattered. Shards sprinkled the ground. Filled the pool and glittered like ice. Rust flaked off the roof struts and rained over Sophie. She hoped the girders were strong − because the rope binding her ankles was tied around one of them.

And when she swayed, it creaked.

"Hello, doll, how you doing up there?"

She craned her neck. Saw him as if he were upside down in the corner of the poolroom. She struggled and screamed into the tape again.

Craig laughed. "Feisty, aren't you. Men like that, did you know? And tits. They like tits, too." He dragged a fold-up chair behind him and walked to the far end of the pool. His footsteps echoed, and the chair scraped along the tiles.

Sophie twisted round. The far end was in darkness. Craig disappeared into the shadows.

He said, "I'll see you soon, honey."

And he laughed again, and the laugh echoed.

CHAPTER 68.
NOT GOING TO PLAN.

"WHAT do you mean he's not there?" said Nick Sears.

Ellis Cole said, "I mean exactly that: he's not here."

Sears rubbed the back of his neck. He crouched in the rotted stairwell. His backside was damp, and everything stank here. He could hardly see. The Strakers were lurking in here somewhere as well.

Waiting for Thorn.

The plan was that Cole would lead him here. Sears and the Strakers would step out of the shadows and cover him with their guns. They'd show him he was outnumbered and that he shouldn't try anything funny. They'd bash him around if they fancied it. Four-on-one. Then they'd haul him through to Craig.

And death.

Nothing complicated.

"He should've been there by now," said Sears.

"Yes, well, he's not," said Cole. "Perhaps he's had a breakdown. Perhaps he's a slow driver. Perhaps he just can't be bothered. But he's not here, Nick."

"He wouldn't come here, would he?"

"Well, I don't know. He might. He's a stupid fucker. Think what you'd do in his place, Nick. If it were Billy."

"I'd do as I was told."

"You're not John Thorn, are you."

Sears picked up the shotgun. "You should've warned us he might do this."

"I didn't know. It didn't cross my mind."

"You're a fool, Cole, and Ruth will hear of it."

Cole blustered, saying, "I've helped this family... helped Ruth for... for years... sacrificed a career... a marriage... how dare you, how fucking – "

"I don't care," said Sears. "Not now. What matters is, where's Thorn?"

"This was your stupid scheme. Nothing to do with me."

"It's not stupid."

"It is. Why not just kill him? Kill him where he was."

"Ruth wanted it done this way, Cole. She wanted Craig to be the one to do it."

"Yeah, because he's the only one who could."

Sears said nothing. He wondered if he would be able to murder someone. Decided he could kill Thorn if he had to. Maybe he could kill anyone. He felt like he could just now.

Cole said, "Kill the girl, then."

"No, we'll wait a few more minutes."

"Kill her – that's what we told him we'd do if he didn't do as he was told: we'll kill your daughter."

"We'll wait." Sears looked at his watch. The numbers glowed in the dark. "We'll give him ten minutes to get to you. If he hasn't got to you in ten minutes, ring me back. Then... then I'll go and tell Craig, and he can do what he wants."

"Fine," said Cole. "But you keep an eye out. Thorn might be on his way there."

"He doesn't know we're here, Cole."

"I wouldn't put it past him."

Sears put the phone down. A shudder crept down his spine. *Thorn might be on the way here.*

Sears gripped the shotgun. He looked at it. He'd used one before – to shoot pheasants. Thought about having to fire it at a man – at Thorn.

Something rustled outside the front door.

Sears stiffened. Sweat poured off him now.

He said, "Gerry, Brian," in a whisper and Gerry responded, saying, "What was that? Are you going to see?"

"Me?" said Sears.

The noise came again. Like someone kicking through dead leaves. Sears swallowed. He rose from his position in the stairwell. His legs felt papery.

He stepped out of the stairwell, shotgun in hand, sweat on his palms. Narrowed his eyes and focused on the noises.

"Careful, Nick," said Gerry.

Sears thought, *If you think it's dangerous, come with me, you coward.*

He crept towards the front door. The darkness was at its deepest. Just after midnight. He shuffled forward.

The noise again. Leaves rustling. They wafted through the entrance and plopped into the water covering the lobby floor. Sears stepped forward. Watched the leaves float. He wondered why they'd drifted inside.

He moved into the doorway and looked up from the floating leaves and out into the night.

Something hard and heavy struck him in the chest. The blow knocked the breath out of him. He flew backwards, and as he went, he dropped the gun and scrabbled the air for purchase and saw a dark figure loom in the doorway.

CHAPTER 69.
DEAD SONS.

THORN spotted the other two. They were amateurs. They panicked when he put his boot into the other one's chest. Jerked in their corners, the movement catching his eye.

He went for the nearest one. The man rose from his hiding place. He gawped, raised a shotgun. Thorn darted forward and shoulder-charged the man, sent him reeling.

Thorn spun around. The third one appeared from the doorway that led to the ballroom. He came at Thorn, but Thorn was too quick.

He kicked the gun aside. Decked the man with a right cross.

The men groaned. Thorn grabbed their weapons, put them aside. He hauled the men through the water, one after the other. He shoved them together in the middle of the lobby. Their clothes were soaked through. He got one of the shotguns and aimed it at them. He made them sit up. They cowered and shivered.

"Where's my daughter, you bastards?"

They said nothing.

"Tell me where she is. Is she here? Won't take me long to find her – then I'll be back for you, you hear me? Now, where is she?"

Thorn didn't want to race through the house. Craig was here, he knew it – probably with Sophie.

He heard a noise behind him. He glanced over his shoulder.

"Billy, come in here," he said.

One of the men looked up. Thorn saw something in his face, something he recognized.

The man said, "Billy... "

Thorn's guts grinded. He wheeled as Billy swung a branch, and it clipped Thorn's temple. Stars appeared before his eyes, and he dropped the shotgun.

The men sprang to their feet.

"You bastard," said Billy, and he came at Thorn again, swinging the branch.

Thorn parried the blow with his forearm. Pain fizzed up the limb, into his shoulder.

The men sloshed through the water towards him.

Four against one.

Billy waded in with his fists.

Thorn yelled and lunged and blocked Billy's attack with his forearms and headbutted the youth full in the face. Billy slumped like an empty sack.

The man who'd shouted Billy's name said it again. His face darkened. "That's my son, you bastard. Your girlfriend killed my three boys, murdered them in Trafalgar Square eight years ago. You remember?"

Thorn said nothing. He eyed the men closing in on him. Their faces were etched with hatred.

Templetons, no doubt.

Fathers of dead sons.

The second man said, "She killed my boys. Two of them. My only two."

The third man said, "You know who we are, don't you?"

Thorn said, "I know who you are."

The first man crouched over Billy and rolled him on his back to prevent him from drowning. The man looked up at Thorn. "Those boys were innocent – "

"They weren't fucking innocent," said Thorn. "They were werewolves. They were killing people – "

The man rose. His cheeks purpled. His shoulders shook and his hand were fists.

Thorn narrowed his eyes, winding the man up. " – and they deserved to die. Every one of them. Your sons, too – "

The man yelled and dashed forward. His attack encouraged the others. All three ploughed into Thorn. They drove him backwards. He kept his feet. He whirled, tossed one of his attackers aside. Sent the man crashing into the stairwell. Rotten wood splintered.

The other two threw punches. Thorn covered his head. He spun round, stamping his feet, splashing, stomping on toes. He threw punches, threw elbows. Missing. Hitting. Missing. Fists hammered at his arms. Kicks jarred his legs. He kicked back. He stomped and he punched. Kept spinning, kept lashing out with fists, feet, elbows, rolling his body.

Fighting blind, fighting for his life.

The men yelled, cursed, growled, groaned...

Thorn staggered backwards. His chest burned. He panted. Arms felt like lead weights. The assaults died away. He dropped his guard and looked around.

The men lay sprawled. They writhed and groaned. Their blood spilled into the water covering the lobby floor. Thorn saw teeth float by.

He counted the men: one, two, three, and —

Where was Billy?

Thorn's strength had drained out of him. He was knackered. Could barely lift his arms.

But he wasn't done.

Where the fuck are you? he thought.

He shuffled forward with his eyes wide open, trying to see in the gloom.

One of the men made a grab for his leg. Thorn kicked him in the ribs. The man jerked and rolled over on his back and gasped for breath. He clutched his side and groaned. Thorn stomped on the man's hand. Fingers snapped under his heel. The man screeched.

He checked out the other two. He wanted them out of action while he looked for Billy. While he looked for Sophie.

The second man struggled to his feet. Thorn hobbled over. Drove punches into the back of his head till he slumped on the ground, knocked out. Thorn rolled him on his back so he wouldn't drown.

He glanced at his third attacker. The guy cradled his arm in his lap. It looked broken. Thorn left him alone.

Thorn scrutinized the lobby. He knew this place well. He'd worked here eight years previously as Sir Adam Templeton's police protection officer. Templeton was murdered on Thorn's watch. A thug hired by Sir Adam's son got to him and gutted the former government minister.

On my watch, thought Thorn.

The door to his left led to a ballroom and dining room. Sir Adam entertained guests there. The door on the right took you into a corridor and off that were the lounge, TV room, library, ground-floor bathrooms, and kitchen. The door at the far end of the lobby was the entrance to the swimming pool.

"Come on, Billy, you little bastard – come out," said Thorn.

A sound came from the ballroom, as if someone had tripped over something.

Thorn darted through the door.

"Billy," he said.

His voice echoed. The wind rushed in. Branches rattled against the shattered windows. A pigeon flapped from its perch on a dust-coated chandelier before roosting on a roof joist.

Thorn hissed air out his lungs.

Something cracked behind him. He was about to spin round, but cold steel pressed against the back of his neck. He recognized it as the barrel of a gun.

CHAPTER 70.
RATCATCHER.

COLE knew Thorn had gone to Templeton Hall. He had a bad feeling.

This whole thing had excited him at the start. Being part of Ruth's schemes. Part of Ray Craig's troop. He'd called Ruth in the States earlier. Told her Craig and the others were kidnapping Sophie that night.

Ruth was quiet for a long time. But then she praised him, told him he'd done well, told him he'd be rewarded.

Respect at last. Attention at last. Valued at last.

Should he ring her again and tell her, *I told you so*, and say Thorn hadn't turned up here?

He decided not to. He was in Ruth's good books and liked it that way. Giving her bad news would piss her off. She'd curse him and call him useless again. He'd have to go over to Templeton Hall himself, see if he could sort out this mess. He had to. Thorn couldn't be left alive. Ruth would go mad.

And if I could kill him, if I can sort this out...

Ruth's high opinion meant everything.

He clambered up the stepladder and reached up. He patted the shelf, feeling for something. Something he hid there a year ago. Dust puffed up. Cole stretched. He held his breath, straining.

Where was it?

Had he put it there?

His hand touched steel.

"Yes," he said.

He grabbed the gun and came down the stepladder. He laid the weapon on his desk. It was an American Derringer Model 1. John Wilkes used a Derringer pistol to assassinate Abraham Lincoln in 1865. They were the kind a female spy would whip out of her purse or her stocking in the movies. The gun weighed 15 ounces. The stainless steel barrel was three inches long. The handle was cherry wood.

He picked up the Derringer and checked it over. He opened it.

Two bullets. Two shots.

Two shots to down Thorn if he had to.

If he could.

He dusted the gun down.

His wife had given it to him six years ago. "We need to be armed," she'd said, "we're hunting monsters."

They didn't really hunt monsters. They sat in this bedsit and scoured the internet. The guns weren't necessary. The most dangerous thing Cole had encountered here was a rat. He'd put the gun away by then but was nearly persuaded to retrieve it when he saw the size of his prey. "Fucking thing's as long as my arm," he told his wife. He got some poison in the end, and that did for the rat.

No monsters, then.

Until now.

He got his coat and slipped the pistol into the inside pocket. He zipped up the coat and grabbed his car keys. Fear made him cold inside, it prickled his skin.

Don't give him a chance, he thought.

Shoot first. He'll kill you if you don't.

He got into his car.

Shoot first.

Shoot again.

The car pulled away.

Two shots.

* * * *

The driver let Cole's car go round the corner before he switched on his engine and followed him.

He'd lost Thorn on the A69 but knew he'd been told to come here to Newcastle, to Ellis Cole's home. Cole would then lead him to wherever they held Thorn's daughter.

He'd followed Billy Sears and Sophie earlier that night. They'd driven into the hills. Dark, narrow, winding roads. He lost them in the labyrinth. Wandered down lanes that led to farm tracks that led to dead ends. Three-point-turned in tight corners and reversed up hedge-lined lanes. He cursed himself and consulted his map and kept driving till he saw a car's tail-lights. Billy's MX5. Ditched down an unclassified road. Billy lying there, blood coming from a head wound.

He found a letter in Billy's pocket and opened and read it before putting it back. Billy groaned. The driver shivered. Retreated from the unconscious boy.

Was this all part of the plan? Had Nick Sears beaten up his own son for the sake of their scheme?

He wouldn't put it past Sears. He was ruthless. Losing his sons had turned him into a monster. Murder wasn't beyond him. He'd killed Thorn's ex-wife. Ploughed into her. The driver knew that, but Thorn didn't. Thorn would've gone after Sears. Put himself in danger. Giving his son a whack would've meant nothing to Sears. Not if it was part of their scheme.

After reading the letter, he knew where they were headed.

Billy started coming to. The driver scuttled away. He waited again. Headlights illuminated the gloom. They highlighted Billy's prone form. A Land Rover stopped. Thorn got out and attended to Billy.

The driver watched. His nerves fizzed. He wanted to dart out of his hiding place, tell Thorn what was going on. But he didn't want to jeopardize anything. He needed Thorn to lead him to the Templetons, to Cole. This was war. He had to use all means necessary to protect her.

To protect the werewolf.

Now he followed Cole – and they headed towards Hexham.

CHAPTER 71.
BOY WITH A GUN.

"HANDS up, way up," said Billy.

Thorn raised his arms.

Billy said, "I'm thinking, should I blow your fucking head off now, or do what I'm supposed to do and hand you over to Ray Craig?"

"Put the gun away, Billy; you've no idea what you're doing."

"Ha! Don't patronize me, you bastard." Billy shunted the barrel into Thorn's nape. He jerked forward and hissed out in pain. Billy said, "You broke my nose, you know."

"I shouldn't have trusted you, should I. I didn't like it. But you caught me at a bad time. Just when I decided to lighten up a little and give Sophie some leeway. Trust her fucking boyfriends."

"Teach you, won't it."

"And that's your dad out there, is it? And your uncles, or whatever they are."

"My dad, yeah."

"Planned all this, did he? Bashing you over the head included."

"We all planned it. All of us. Driven by our hatred for you, Thorn."

"Did you kill my wife?"

"Don't know what you're on about."

Thorn grunted. "The letter in your pocket?"

"All planned. Don't know who opened the letter, though. Was it you?"

Thorn said no.

"Maybe Dad did it before he stuck it in my pocket. Don't know why. I was out cold, see. He knocked me out. He really knocked me out. No messing, no pretending. See what we're willing to do? See? We have will, Thorn. We have will."

Thorn flagged. He felt weak. This would go on and on unless he stopped it. "How d'you find us?" he said.

Billy told him.

Thorn cursed himself. Thought he'd been careful. Thought he could protect Sophie.

"How are you related to this pond-life, then?" said Thorn.

Billy told him – something about Michael Templeton's grandfather being Billy's grandfather's cousin.

"Distant cousins," said Thorn.

"It's blood, though."

"Yeah, and my blood's here somewhere. Where is she, son?"

"Don't fucking 'son' me." He jabbed the barrel into Thorn's neck again.

Thorn had to move. He gauged Billy's position. He bunched his fists. Stepped from foot to foot.

"Stand still," said Billy.

"Pins and needles in my feet. It's age, Billy."

"Don't worry, you'll be put out of your misery soon enough."

"Oh yeah – "

"You and your bitches."

Thorn tensed. "What did you say?"

"Bitches, I said, bitches. Right now in New York, that murdering bitch Laura Greenacre's being put down."

Thorn shuddered.

Billy said, "Aunt Ruth's tracked her down, and she's being killed."

Thorn's mouth was dry, and his head swam.

"And then it's you," said Billy, "and that tasty little treat, Sophie. I tell you, she was fucking delicious."

Billy let out a laugh.

The barrel moved away from Thorn's skin.
Thorn spun round and lashed out.
The gun went off.

CHAPTER 72.
DAD.

SOPHIE came to with a jerk. The gunshot deafened her. Made her ears ring. Her eyes were blurred, and everything swam. She panted, panic swarming through her again.

She struggled and the rafter creaked. She shrieked, but the tape muffled her cries. She craned her neck to look down into the debris-strewn pool. Then she lifted her head to see outside, to see if there were any hope there.

Nothing. Pitch black. Deep darkness.

She made the noise of "Dad" in her throat, with her taped-up mouth.

Tears came.

Dad, where are you, Dad? Please, please don't let them hurt me.

She was so scared. Had never been so scared. She thought of Billy and what had happened to him. If they'd killed him, no one would know she'd been taken. That sparked another surge of dread.

Please help me, please help me.

She tried to think, now. Tried to think who these men were. Why would they take her?

They had to be Templetons.

She struggled against the rope. Her wrists were raw. She could feel the skin being chewed away.

Templetons.

And they were going to kill her, like they'd killed Mum.

They were going to kill her and kill –

Dad, she cried, but the word didn't come out. Only a sound: *DNNNNNNND!*

She tried again, this time shutting her eyes, mustering every gram of energy in her body:

DNNNNNNND!

Had he abandoned her?

The thought devastated her. She'd hang here forever. Hang here until her flesh rotted away and the crows came to pick at her eyes. Hang here till she was bone.

Had they killed him already? Waited for him to arrive, shot him in the back. Her belly tightened. Was that the gunshot she'd heard? Dad taking a bullet?

DNNNNNNND!

She whirled around like a spinning top. Rust rained on her from the creaking girder above. Her body shook with grief. Her eyes smarted from all her crying, and her head throbbed from being upside down and full of blood. As she turned and turned, she opened her eyes.

A figure sneaked out of the gloom in the far corner.

A fire lit in her chest.

She tried to shout the word again, and this time he'd hear her for sure.

She tried, but she couldn't.

No name came out. No word. No "Dad" – just a hissing noise that could never be heard from where he was stood.

And he could never know that Craig lurked in the darkness, waiting for him.

CHAPTER 73.
FINDING SOPHIE.

THORN blinked, tried to adjust his vision to the gloom.

He sniffed: the air was dank, but the staleness held a trace of chlorine. He listened: the wind swished through the shattered windows, the rafters creaked. He licked his lips. They were dry, cracked. He tasted blood and spat it out. Wiped the sweat off his face.

He edged towards the swimming pool. Tried to breathe steadily. He scanned the scene. Came to the side of the pool and looked in.

Littered with debris: glass, leaves, branches, beer cans and bottles, mouldy pizza boxes, and dead animals and birds. Kids used the place. Their hideaway. Templeton Hall had lain empty since Michael's death at Trafalgar Square.

An ache of sadness filled in his chest. A memory flared. He saw the place like it was, a grand house. He'd lived here; he'd worked here. This house was where it began. August 1999. The alarms blaring to indicate a trespasser. Bodyguards panicking that someone had come to kill Sir Adam. Thorn hunting down the invader. Dismembered guard dogs strewn among the trees. Laura, naked and bloody in the gloom.

The grief threatened to swamp him.

He parried it away, focused on the now.

He stared across the pool. Towards the far end. He narrowed his eyes, trying to penetrate the darkness. He saw nothing.

The struts creaked above him.

He hopped down into the pool. His feet crunched on glass. He skulked forward and called her name in a whisper:

"Sophie? Sophie, are you here?"

He shuffled forward, his nerves fizzing. He shivered with fear and cold. Moonlight made a pool of light on the tiles. He skirted around the radiance, not wanting to showcase himself. He sensed movement in the glowing circle, a shadow shifting, but thought nothing of it.

The beams above him creaked again.

Something dark passed across the moon's beam.

A cold finger traced a line down Thorn's spine.

He held his breath. The shadow swayed. Particles flaked down. He followed a batch as they fluttered down to the tiles. *Rust*, he thought. *Slivers of rust.*

He craned his neck slowly. The rust drizzled over his face. He brushed it away. The shadow moved across him. Her hair hung down. Her skin was bleached. Her face creased in anguish. Her eyes, glittering in the gloom, fixed on him.

Horror turned him to stone.

She made a noise:

DNNNNNNND!

And he recognized the word, and it pierced his heart and melted him.

He screamed her name and it echoed and carried out across the acres and into the night.

The ground trembled. Thorn came to. Blinked himself into the now. Lowered his gaze and fixed it on the darkness. A figure thundered towards him out of the gloom. Moonlight splintered off the attacker's knife.

PART THREE.

FIGHTING FOR SURVIVAL.

CHAPTER 74.
REST FOR THE WICKED.

RUTH wrapped the fur coat around her and gathered her clothes. She went back to the car. She opened the boot and from a travelling bag took out jeans, a shirt, a pullover, cowboy boots, socks, and new underwear. She scrunched up her dress and underwear and stuffed them into the bag. She got dressed in the car.

It had been 3.15 p.m.

The taste of meat remained in her mouth. Raw and wet. Warm in her throat. Her pulse quickened. She had pieces of Zak Weaver in her teeth.

She'd ripped off his face, biting through bone and muscle and cartilage. He'd screamed down her throat. She'd clawed his flanks away to show ribs and organs.

His death was slow and agonizing.

She imagined his suffering, and it pleased her.

Shock finally killed him. *Being without a face is quite shocking,* thought Ruth.

He had twitched and jerked. Blood spouted from the maw where his good looks had been. Chewed meat looked like coral – pink and wet and frayed.

She ate.

There was not much of him left after she'd finished. Bones with rags of flesh hanging off them. His blood dampening the ground. The flies that gathered while Ruth fed on him had then settled on his remains.

She sat in the Nissan and drank a bottle of Evian, then gargled and opened the door to spit out the water. She applied lipstick, eyeliner, and blusher. She dozed off in the car and slept for an hour. She woke up with his taste still in her mouth.

She fired up the car and headed back towards the parkway.

She came to a travel plaza and stopped. She went into the diner and found a booth. The waitress came over with a smile and asked what could she get her.

Ruth said coffee.

"Anything to eat, ma'am?" said the waitress.

"I've just eaten, thank you."

Ruth had three cups of coffee. By then it was 5.30 p.m. The day had faded. Night had swept in. The hunt would start soon. Laura Greenacre would be dead. In England, John Thorn's offspring would be used as bait to draw him into a trap. He'd be dead too.

Her enemies vanquished. A blood sacrifice to her ancestors. Justice served.

Ruth left ten dollars on the table and walked out of the diner.

She drove south.

Manhattan welcomed her. Early evening in civilization. Behind her and out of sight lay barbarism.

CHAPTER 75.
THE HUMAN INSIDE.

TOO easy, way too easy.

The Sig Sauer 9mm pistol pointed at the werewolf's skull. The creature wheeled and glowered at him. The animal showed its teeth. The one good eye was a yellow slit. The other eye remained shut.

This werewolf was a black-fur. Not the blonde-fur that had chased him earlier that day. Dasaev wondered how many of them there were.

The werewolf lunged. Dasaev recoiled. The animal didn't get far, the chain tightening and tugging it back by the neck. The creature grimaced and groaned.

"Are you Laura Greenacre?" said Dasaev, gun still fixed on the creature. "I – I saw your picture – they are going to kill you."

The werewolf grunted.

Dasaev cocked his head. Did she understand? She was part human, so perhaps the human in her remained after the transformation. He appealed to that human side again:

"I am Lev Dasaev. I'm – I'm going to help you. This is too easy for them, far too easy. I am going to – "

He reached out.

The werewolf snapped.

Saliva sprayed and was hot on his hand.

The werewolf growled at him.

He looked around. Darkness came. Headlights glowed in the distance. They were coming. He had to hurry.

He tucked the gun into his belt and held up his hands in surrender.

He said, "Let me help you, let me even the odds."

He shuffled forward. The werewolf lowered its shoulders. Narrowed its eye. The pupil in that eye flared, and Dasaev's legs weakened. He was being measured for attack, he was sure of it. He held out his hand. He was two yards away from teeth that could rip his arm off with one bite. If the werewolf decided to attack, Dasaev knew he'd be dead.

I hope there's human in you still, he thought.

Was it like the movies? Did the werewolf lose all its humanity? Did it forget who it was, what it was?

To hell with movies, this is real.

And for a second he thought about retreating.

The werewolf snorted. Steam plumed from its nostrils.

Dasaev looked towards the house again. The headlights bloomed. Vehicles approaching.

I'm going – " he said, but the words locked in his throat. The werewolf yelped. Dasaev's neck prickled. Goosepimples covered his body. He was going to have to walk away. He'd have to watch this animal and the woman inside die.

He cursed and crossed himself.

"Why don't you understand?" he said.

The werewolf grumbled and lowered its head.

Dasaev stared.

The werewolf raised its gaze to Dasaev. Made the grumbling noise again and lowered its head once more.

Dasaev moved forward. He touched the animal's neck, and the fur bristled.

Standing as close as this, Dasaev could comprehend the werewolf's size. The animal was on all fours, but at shoulder height, it was level with Dasaev's belly.

"Are you Laura?" he said.

The animal made no noise.

The groan of engines grew louder. Burns and his friends were getting closer.

Dasaev studied the neckbrace that bound the creature to the cannonball. A padlock hung off the collar. Dasaev rattled it. The werewolf stiffened. Dasaev tensed. He quaked and sweated. Thought about what he could do.

He whipped out the Sig Sauer. The creature growled and bridled. Dasaev thought, *She thinks I'm going to shoot her.*

The animal whipped its head round with a snarl.

Dasaev fired.

The bullet sparked off the padlock.

The noise exploded in Dasaev's head.

The cordite filled his nose.

The padlock fell away, and the neckbrace split.

The creature spun towards him, teeth bared.

Dasaev, disorientated by the noise, stumbled away.

His vision swam.

A black blur came from the darkness towards him.

He fell on his backside.

Saw the werewolf coming.

The animal sprang.

Dasaev threw his arms across his face.

CHAPTER 76.
CRAIG VS. THORN, PART II.

THORN threw up his arms. Craig roared and slashed with his knife, and the blade sliced through Thorn's jacket and into his skin. The pain shot up into his shoulder, and pins and needles erupted in his head.

Craig rammed into him. Sixteen stone of thug crushing Thorn against the edge of the swimming pool. The air gushed out of him. Blood ran down his arm.

He threw elbows and stamped his feet. His heel trampled Craig's toes. Craig yelled and hacked at Thorn with his knife.

Thorn kept moving, ducking, dodging, weaving. Adrenaline kept pain at bay. He threw punches. His fists were like pistons, striking and missing, delivering glancing blows. Thorn felt the attack ease. He stole the chance to roll away. Wheeled along the edge of the pool. Blood splashed from his arms. He looked at them. The knife had ribboned his jacket, slashed his skin.

Craig reeled. Pulled himself together. He snarled and came again.

Thorn looked up to the rafters.

Sophie, he thought, and the dread that only a parent feels drenched his heart.

He felt desperate, and he reached deep into himself for the courage he needed.

But courage was useless. What he needed was the will to do anything to survive and save his child. Anything.

Craig stomped over broken glass. Coming again like a bull.

Thorn stumbled away. Sweat coated his body. Fatigue made his limbs heavy. Blood thundered through his veins and pulsed from the wounds in his arms and drizzled down his sleeve and splattered the tiles.

Craig said, "I'll cut you to pieces, Thorn, then start on your girl – but I'll spend some time on her, make her appreciate me."

Thorn bent down. Scooped up a chunk of concrete. The size of a cricket ball. Craig rampaged towards him, brandishing the knife. Thorn chucked the concrete.

The missile struck Craig on the bridge of the nose.

The big man stopped. He stood frozen for a second. His mouth was open and his eyes stared ahead. Blood seeped from the bridge of his nose. The trickle became a torrent. Flooded out of the wound and out of his nostrils.

Craig shook his head and blood squirted over his face. His eyes glared white from the red mask. He screamed with fury and stumbled towards Thorn, who backed away and tripped over a branch.

Craig lunged, blood spraying from the wound in his face.

Thorn kicked out. He caught Craig in the chest. The blood-masked lunatic lurched away. Hit the ground. Glass crunched under his body.

Thorn staggered to his feet and slipped on blood.

He looked up at Sophie. The dread filled his chest again.

Craig was on his feet. Snarling through his blood mask.

The brute's muscles corded. Thorn saw his power. A power fuelled by rage.

And he came again. Lumbered forward. Teeth bared and eyes wide in the scarlet of the blood that soaked his face.

"Jesus," said Thorn.

He picked up a metal girder. Gripped it in both hands, like a baseball bat. Craig rushed forward. Thorn swung. Metal smashed into Craig's ribs. The crack of breaking bones echoed. Craig screamed and keeled over. Fell to one knee.

Exhausted, Thorn dropped the girder. He panted.

Craig, at his feet, drove the knife upwards.

The blade whipped through the air. Headed for Thorn's face.

He saw it coming, flashing in the moonlight.

He reared up.

The point cut his chin. He thought his face was going to be sliced in half. He cried out. Kept leaning away, straining, back bent.

The knife whisked past his face. Blood trailed the blade from the nick in Thorn's chin.

He kicked Craig in the jaw.

Craig toppled face first into broken glass.

Thorn craned his neck. Sophie hung from the rafters. Her eyes glittered in the gloom. Thorn limped out of the pool area, leaving her.

CHAPTER 77.
TABLES TURNED.

"WHERE'S the bitch gone?" said Burns.

The wind whipped across his face. He pressed a hand to his head to keep his cap on. His headset crackled. A growl came through the static.

Burns stiffened.

A "yee-ha!" burst out of the headset. Burns blew air out of his cheeks. One of the others hurtling around the forest on his bike, that's all. Being over-enthusiastic, as usual.

Schumann on the Kawasaki and Wellington in the Spyder sidecar had split off first, hurtling into the trees. Hurst on his Apache quad bike and Delaney riding his Polaris Sportsman quad shot off in different directions. They would corral the werewolf and herd it back towards Burns, Longman, and Cleaver in the Dodge pickup. They'd trap it and kill it and take photos and get drunk.

He switched off that image. No good thinking about the future. *Think about the now, about the hunt*, he told himself.

Burns didn't think the creature would get far. The hunt would be over quickly. Not much of a challenge. Not a fair fight. But who gave a shit? He wasn't about to risk his life. He had to even the odds, and weighing the monster down had seemed like a good idea.

Until someone did this.

He knelt and picked up the padlock. The smell of cordite came off the metal.

He tossed the padlock aside.

"What's happened?" said Longman, loping over.

Burns scanned the darkening forest. He gripped his AR-15 rifle. He said nothing to Longman. Walked past him towards the Dodge and vaulted into the rear of the pickup. He stepped over the sack lying in the trailer and he gripped the roof rack.

Cleaver turned round in the driver's seat and said, "What's going on?"

Longman said, "Oh fuck, what's this?" and he held up the broken neckbrace.

Burns ripped the headset off. His hat flipped back. The wind clutched it and scooped it away. Burns clawed the air after the hat, but it was gone. He slapped the pickup's cab. "Let's go, Cleaver."

"Where to? You want to go back?"

"No, we'll drive on."

Longman lumbered back to the pickup. "We've got to go back, Wheeler. It's got free."

"We can't let it loose here, Lenny. We've got to kill it."

"No way, take me back."

Burns glared at him. "Get in now, or I'll leave you out here as bait."

Longman whined. He got in the passenger seat. "I'll fucking sue you. I'll sue you to death, Burns, you fucking sloppy bastard."

Burns kicked the cab behind Longman.

Cleaver drove on. Headlights and roof lights showed the track ahead. Burns ranged his flashlight across the trees.

Ten minutes later, Burns scratched his head. He wished he still had his baseball cap. His scalp prickled with cold. He was getting scared now. Wished he'd brought the closed-circuit monitor. There were cameras installed throughout the forest, but without a monitor he couldn't see what they showed. He told Cleaver to stop. He picked up the headset. The sack wriggled. He jabbed it with his boot and the thing inside whimpered. He put the headset on.

"Jim... Lomax... Allen... anyone hear me?"

Static crackled in his ears.

Longman said, "I don't like this. My balls are in my throat, man."

Burns scanned the trees. The darkness in there was thick. He shivered and his guts twinged. He didn't know what to do. He wanted to go back. But the werewolf was loose, and he knew the animal would come for him.

I just have to hunt it, he thought. He looked at the sack at his feet, and he looked at Longman and Cleaver.

Hunt it using live bait.

CHAPTER 78.
LIFE AND DEATH.

ALLEN Hurst had saved the life of a three-year-old girl on the operating table that morning. The child's father shook Hurst's hand and cried, saying, "Thank you, thank you." Hurst smiled at the man and said he was welcome.

I'm only doing my job, he thought at the time.

He'd always wanted to be a doctor. He loved kids, had three of his own. So it seemed natural to choose paediatrics. But it was the work that drove him, not the patients. Saving lives thrilled him. It made him feel like God.

The power of life and death.

In the operating threatre and on the hunting ground.

Taking lives thrilled him. Made him feel like God, too.

He weaved his Apache through the pines. He could get places the others couldn't in the pickup.

He stopped in a clearing. He switched off the engine and raised his earmuff so he could listen, and then pushed his goggles up his forehead. He smelled pines and spruces and grass. He looked around. Something glittered in the moonlight. A CCTV camera clung to a tree, the lens catching the moon. Cables snaked down the trunk and into the earth. Burns had this place wired. Cameras everywhere, so he could film the hunt. Edit the footage and put on a show with beers and pizza and girls maybe.

Hurst didn't do the girls. He was happily married, loved his wife, adored his kids. He didn't understand why men wanted to be unfaithful.

He guessed it was a man-thing, just like hunting.

The sex thrilled them. Did it then make them feel like God?

He got off the quad bike and hissed at the pain. His hip had been sore these past few months.

"You're getting old, honey," his wife said.

Old? Jesus, he was in great shape. Not fifty yet, for Christ's sake.

He unstrapped the crossbow from the Apache's flank and loaded a bolt. He eyed the forest. The darkness made him shudder. The depth of it.

A crackle drew his attention. He turned, his neck prickling.

He relaxed. The sound came from the headset he'd tossed into the quad's carrier. He took the headset out. Popped it over his ears after removing his muffs. Burns always insisted on headsets. He wanted this to feel like a military campaign. But it wasn't. They just hunted street life. Hurst sometimes watched his patients, and his mind drifted to thoughts of, *Would they make good prey?*

He'd shake himself out of it. No way he'd regard the children and their parents as fodder. The quarry would always come from the gutter.

A junkie, a drunk, a prostitute. The best ones were ex-Army. They had some survival skills. Drink or drugs had sapped their will and strength, but Hurst and the others could imagine they were hunting someone worthy.

But this was different.

This animal – whatever it was – was like nothing he'd seen. Burns told him he'd have to forget about any rational explanations.

"We know what they're called, Allen," Burns had said. "We have a name for them, and you better accept it and use it. Because when we're out there hunting, that's how I'm going to be identifying this creature. Get used to it."

OK, he thought now, *I'll get used to it:*

Werewolves.

A twig snapped to his left. He wheeled round. Jammed the crossbow's stock into his shoulder. He stared into the gloom. A shadow whipped through the trees.

"Jesus Christ," he said, sweeping the crossbow after the shadow.

He fired. The arrow hissed. Thudded into a tree.

"Shit," said Hurst, re-loading, eyes roving the forest.

So dark, so fucking dark.

He listened to the headset. Static filled his ears.

But then through the interference he heard someone say his name... *Hurst*, they were saying... he was sure of it... and, *Where is he?* They were asking, *Where's Allen? Where's Hurst?*

The trees rustled. Branches cracked. Something colossal charged towards him. Crashed through the undergrowth, destroying everything in its path. A roar filled the air and made Hurst shake right through.

He made a noise he didn't recognize. But then he'd never felt this scared before.

A black shape thundered towards him through the tangle of forest.

He lifted the crossbow. The weapon felt heavy. No strength in his arms.

"Oh lord," he said.

He screamed.

The werewolf tore out of the forest. Teeth bared. One yellow eye fixed on Hurst. The eye glistened.

He fired in panic. The bolt spiralled over the werewolf.

Hurst shrieked. He mounted the Apache. Kickstarted the bike. The werewolf hurtled towards him. Ploughing up the earth, scattering debris.

Hurst got the quad bike going. Panic flooded his heart. He felt weak with terror. His wrists felt like string. Tried to twist the accelerator. The bike jerked and stalled.

The noise of the monster was loud. The ground shook. Hurst trembled. Cowered on the quad bike. Said his children's names. Waited for the monster to plough into him.

He didn't wait long.

CHAPTER 79.
RESCUE ATTEMPT.

THORN stopped climbing. His body ached. His forearms where Craig had sliced them throbbed. He'd taped up the wounds, but blood seeped into the strapping.

He could hardly breathe. Wind lashed him. Rain blinded him. He shivered, his bones cold, his blood frozen.

The ladder creaked in the wind. A few rungs were missing. Rust had eaten them away.

Thorn had known he could get up to Sophie. Known there was an exterior ladder from his days working here. But he hadn't expected the ladder to be in such bad condition.

He was halfway up, twenty feet off the ground. High enough to make his head spin if he looked down. So he looked up. No stars in the sky. Pitch black faced him.

He climbed on, his hands numb on the ladder's corroded rungs.

Thorn got to the roof and slumped forward. He groaned in pain. He got on all fours. Crawled forward along the structure's steel skeleton. Most of the glass had cracked or shattered. He looked down but couldn't see for the gloom. He tried to spot Craig's body. *Shapes down there, but they could be anything*, he thought.

Thorn crawled and yelled out Sophie's name.

He saw her. Hanging like a giant bat from the rafters.

Hate filled him. Hate for the people who put her here, for himself for endangering her. He pushed on with determination. His legs ached. He was parched. The wind howled. Rain soaked him. He tensed his muscles, keeping his balance.

He called her name again, and she wriggled and swayed. He called her once more. His throat burned with the effort.

Thorn was above her now. He looked down. She looked up, and her eyes had hope in them. He eased himself down and rested his feet on the beams below. He crouched, one hand gripping the rafters. Reached down. Gripped the rope tied around Sophie's ankles.

"Don't shake, baby," he said.

Sophie stopped struggling.

She hung in the gloom.

Forty feet below, the wind swept in and tossed leaves around the pool.

Thorn straddled the rafter. He leaned down. Grabbed the rope with both hands. He swayed, and his head swam.

He cursed, his belly lurching. He hauled on the rope. Every muscle hurt. His limbs burned. Shoulders straining out of their sockets, tendons as tight as piano wire.

He pulled on the rope, hand over hand. The rope tore into his palms. Blood ran down the twine and soaked into it. His veins stood out. The wound in his arm pulsed.

He yelled out. Heaved Sophie upwards. Sweat poured down his face, down his back. He had no strength left, but he was desperate to cling to her. Embrace his child. Make her safe.

That desperation drove him. Made him forge strength out of nothing. He pulled her up, roaring with every tug on the rope. Hoisted her out, onto the roof. Tore the tape from her mouth and heard her say, "Dad!" in a voice that broke his heart. She cried as he untied the rope around her wrists and ankles.

She said, "Dad, Dad, oh Dad," and he cried, blubbering, saying her name and thanking God she was alive.

She threw herself into his arms, and they shuddered with emotion and cried into each other's hair. He shut his eyes and said her name over and over. And the wind lashed them and the rain drenched them, but Thorn didn't care.

Sophie was safe.

He opened his eyes.

Craig loomed out of the darkness. Blood and rain poured down his twisted face.

CHAPTER 80.
HUNTERS HUNTED.

BURNS threw the headset aside. The screams and the snarling sent shockwaves through his brain.

"Who's that? Who's that screaming?" said Longman, hearing the same noises in his own headset.

Burns told Cleaver to stop the vehicle. He clambered out of the back. He listened. Wind whispered through the trees. Nothing else.

Longman and Cleaver got out of the Dodge. Cleaver came to stand next to his boss and he tapped his headset.

"Don't tap it, Cleaver. There's nothing wrong with your headset, pal. We all heard it."

"Might've been static."

"Static?" said Longman. "Static doesn't sound like that. Static doesn't say his kids' names and then fucking shriek like a girl."

Cleaver shrugged.

Burns whipped the headset off Cleaver's head and spoke into the mike: "Hurst? You out there? Schumann? Wellington? Where are you guys?"

He got static. Terror chilled his bowels. He looked back towards the ranch. *Long way back*, he thought. They were deep in the forest. The track wound down through a carpet of trees beyond which lay Sorrow Hill.

Longman said, "Oh fuck, oh fuck, we're fucked. We've got to get back. We've got to get back."

"Shut up, Lenny – I'm trying to listen."

"Fuck you, Wheeler, something's got them. She's got free and she's got them."

Burns tried to ignore him. Scanned his surroundings. Thought about what they should do. He asked Cleaver, and Cleaver said, "We should go back."

"Get me out of here, Wheeler," said Longman. "I want to go back, now."

"What about the others?" said Cleaver. "We should go find them."

"The others can take their chances," said Longman. "Wheeler? Do you hear me, Wheeler?"

"Yeah, I hear you, Lenny."

"Then let's go."

"Truth is, Lenny, no matter where we go, she's going to come for us."

"Not if I'm in LA, she's not."

"You're not going to get that far, pal," said Burns.

"Wh-what do you mean?"

"I mean she'll get us before we make our way back to Sorrow Hill. Or she'll get us when we're there."

"No way, Wheeler. When I get back to the house, I'm leaving directly, my friend. Directly. I'm not waiting for some fucking monster to come after me. I tell you, Wheeler, I'm suing the ass off you."

"If you want to go, go. Walk," said Burns. "It doesn't matter to me. What matters now is getting out of here alive. And for that to happen, we've got to kill her – before she kills us first."

Cleaver said, "Sir, Mr Burns, sir, I think – "

"This hunt's gone wrong, Cleaver. We go back, she'll track us. We'll be dead before we see the house. We've got to do what we can."

"Do what we can?" said Longman. "You're crazy. Call this fucking hunt off, Wheeler. Call it off."

"You can only call it off if you're the hunter, Lenny. We're not the hunters any more. We are prey."

* * * *

Schumann said, "What's going on?"

Wellington said, "Don't know. All I can hear is static. Did you hear that scream? Wheeler's fucked-up communications system again. They never work. He only uses them because they make him feel like a general."

Wellington took the headset off and tapped it against a rock.

Schumann straddled the Kawasaki. A Remington 870 shotgun lay across his lap. Wellington's Winchester semiauto .22 was propped up in the Spyder sidecar.

Schumann said, "You hear what's going on? Are we still circling her, or what? Get Wheeler on the line."

"I can't, Harris. I don't know. I heard screams in the headset."

"Get back in the Spyder, Jim. We're going. I knew this was a bad idea."

Wellington stared into the trees, his brow furrowed.

"What's the matter?" said Schumann.

Wellington said nothing. His eyes stayed fixed on a point in the trees. He stepped to the sidecar and picked up his rifle.

Schumann dismounted the motorbike. He raised the Remington to his shoulder. He said, "Jim, what've you seen?"

Wellington paled. He whirled round and hopped into the sidecar. He stared ahead. "I think we should get out of here, Harris," he said.

"Huh?"

"Harris. Get on the bike. Start the engine. Let's go."

Schumann backed up. Eyes fixed on the dense forest where Wellington had been staring. Where he'd seen something that scared him.

"Harris, come on."

But it was too late, and Schumann knew it. Knew it in his guts. He said, "Oh hell," and spun round. Slung the shotgun over his shoulder. He mounted the Kawasaki. Slammed the kickstart. The bike growled.

And something growled right back.

Wellington and Schumann said, "Oh shit," together.

The bike shot off.

Wellington glanced over his shoulder.

Schumann said, "Is it still there?" his voice loud over the engine.

The bike tore through the forest. The tyres rutted the earth. Dust and dirt kicked up.

Wellington said, "Go faster, Harris."

"Is it still there?"

"Fucking go faster!"

Schumann stared ahead. Eyes on the narrow track. The bike whined as it flew along the trail. The wind swept through Schumann's hair and whipped across his face. His knuckles were cold, even with gloves on.

He said, "Shoot it, Jim, shoot it."

"I'm not looking back, Harris. I'm not. I'm staying sat here. Where I won't fall out. Fall into that thing's path."

Schumann dared a glance in his side mirror.

His balls shrivelled.

The werewolf bounded after them.

CHAPTER 81.
ENOUGH ROPE.

CRAIG rumbled towards Thorn and Sophie. Thorn's nerves became taut again. He said to Sophie, "Stay out of the way," and she crawled along the girders, crying as she went.

"She can't run, Thorn. Not from me," said Craig. When he spoke, blood drizzled from his mouth and down his chin. His face was a red mask. His hands were claws.

Thorn braced himself.

Craig charged.

Thorn thought, *If I'm going to die, he's coming with me.* He had to protect Sophie. Couldn't leave her alone with this brute.

They smashed into each other. Craig clawed at Thorn's face. Thorn punched and kicked, but Craig grabbed his head and squeezed and tried to gouge his eyes out. Thorn threw uppercuts into Craig's solar plexus. Hammer blow after hammer blow. Thorn's head spun, and pain shot through him. He kept punching. Kicked out and lost his balance. Windmilled on the rafter. His unsteadiness threw Craig off his attack. The brute's grip loosened. Thorn headbutted him in the nose.

Craig roared and staggered.

Thorn went to kick him off the roof. His boot swung wide.

Craig rushed in, seized Thorn's collar. Thorn's hands clawed at Craig's throat. He growled in Thorn's face. Spat in his eyes. Blood and saliva blinded Thorn. He headbutted again, hoping for the best — and got it. Craig groaned, slackened his grip. Another headbutt, and Craig's nose was mush. Blood and rain streamed down and soaked Craig's shorts and showered into the dark pool below.

He called Thorn a cunt and threw a punch. Clipped Thorn on the temple and sent him reeling. Thorn, gasping, dread freezing his blood, skipping from girder to girder, trying not to fall, while Sophie screamed, "Dad! Dad!"

Craig came again. All blood and rage.

Thorn was dizzy and in pain.

He tried to defend himself, but Craig kneed him in the stomach. The air blew out of him, and he bent double.

Craig kneed him in the head. Everything went spinning. Thorn lurched away. The girders blurred. The pool, forty feet below, hazed. He gasped. Clawed the air. He stumbled. Fell across a girder.

Craig swerved like a drunk towards him, feet landing on the rafters. More luck than judgement, Thorn knew that.

He had no strength left. Didn't know if he could stand. Gave a shout and kicked out. Caught Craig in the shin. Craig tripped. Straddled a girder. Thorn heard the impact — balls on steel. And Craig's face said it all: his mouth an "O", his eyes crossed.

Thorn groaned but got to his knees and threw a punch — a flailing, roundhouse punch driven more by hope than anything else.

His knuckle dented the soft tissue at Craig's temple. Craig's eyes rolled back in his head. He swayed on the girder, and Thorn thought, *He's going*.

Craig whipped out a hand. Grabbed Thorn's sleeve.

Thorn's belly flipped.

Craig toppled. Thorn went with him and yelled out. Scrabbled and clawed for purchase, but found nothing but air. Saw the rope that Sophie had been tied to and made a desperate lunge. His hand closed on the wet cord. Kept falling. Readied his shoulder for the impact when the rope tightened.

The men fell, and the rope unwound while Thorn wrung it around his wrist.

The rope yanked and scored Thorn's skin and nearly pulled his shoulder out of its socket.

Craig grimaced, holding on to Thorn's jacket and shirt. Thorn's head felt like it was about to burst. Blood vessels popped in his face. Trying to hold up an extra sixteen stone. Sixteen stone of brute that was trying to kill him.

They dangled from the rope.

Thorn pummelled Craig with his free hand.

Craig slid down his body. Grasping, clawing.

They spun.

Craig headbutted Thorn in the ribs. Thorn gritted his teeth. Pain seared through him, his body on fire.

Craig held on to Thorn's belt with both hands, causing Thorn's trousers to slip down. Craig started to climb up. Thorn's shoulder began to dislocate. He tried not to scream. Held the pain in.

But Craig bit into his side. He had to scream then. Let it gush out of his throat till he was dizzy. He was sick with pain.

Craig bit again. The fat right under Thorn's ribs. Teeth tearing into his flesh. He writhed and kicked. He punched Craig in the head, but the bastard wouldn't let go.

The rope chewed into his wrist. Blood soaked the cord. He reached up with his free hand and grabbed the rope. He mustered energy from somewhere and pulled. Loosened the bind around his wrist, slid his hand out of the coil of rope and grabbed a hold above his other hand. He gritted his teeth and pulled with both hands. His elbows bent and they went up. Hand over hand. Felt like a mountain to him, but it was only a few inches.

Hanging in the air.

Craig scaled Thorn's body. Coming up for the kill. Thorn had no strength. He had nothing left. He looked up. Saw Sophie's pale face. Saw his beautiful child. Imagined her in Craig's grasp.

Craig sank his teeth into Thorn's shoulder. Thorn screamed. The rope draped down over Craig's back. Thorn clenched his jaw. Tried to bear the agony. Flesh being torn from him. Craig's head shaking like a dog at a bone.

Thorn clutched the loose end of the rope. Coiled the tail around Craig's throat. Craig looked up, eyes wide with shock. Mouth full of Thorn's shirt and Thorn's skin.

Craig said, "What are you – "

Thorn heaved to one side. They twirled in the air. The rope tightened around Craig's throat. Craig gurgled and released Thorn. The brute clawed at the rope. His face reddened. His mouth sagged, and his tongue lolled and his eyes goggled.

Thorn loosened his grip on the rope.

He slid down Craig's body and grasped the man's knees, embracing them. And his weight jerked Craig down.

Craig choked. Thorn looked up. The brute's face had purpled. Blood bubbled out of his mouth. The rope gnawed into his throat, blood thick around the cord.

Craig thrashed about. Thorn held on. Tugged again.

The rope bit through Craig's throat and severed his carotid artery. Blood fountained from his neck, showering Thorn. The fluid was hot on his face, and he shut his eyes.

Craig's body twitched. Thorn held on. Held on until the carcass stilled. Until they dangled there, swaying in the darkness.

Thorn stayed where he was. Hugging the dead man's legs. He didn't know how he would climb up. He had nothing left. He was wrecked.

"Dad?"

He opened his eyes and looked up, and she was there.

He said her name, and the sound of it filled him with hope.

CHAPTER 82.
BAIT.

"SLOWLY, Cleaver," said Burns from the back of the pickup. His gaze roved the gloom. Dense forests and rolling hills. He listened. Motorbikes in the distance. He tightened the AR-15's strap around his forearm and swallowed. He would kill this creature. He'd kill it and mount its head on his wall. He'd use Cleaver and Longman as bait if he had to. Nothing would stand in his way.

Longman continued to moan. Wanting to go back. Threatening to sue Burns. On the phone, trying to ring his lawyer.

Burns ignored him. The pickup slowed. He kept looking, trying not to blink.

Cleaver stopped the truck and got out. Longman stayed in the cab and complained. Burns started dragging the sack out of the back of the pickup. "Help me, Cleaver," he said. Together they heaved it off the trailer. The sack writhed.

"Get her out of there," said Burns.

Cleaver undid the sack. He dragged the girl called Inessa out by the arm. She screamed in her own language. Tears streamed down her face. Her wrists and ankles were bound with tape.

Burns ordered Longman out of the Dodge. Cleaver drove the pickup into the trees. Longman looked at the girl and asked if it was the one he'd fucked earlier. He got no answer. He asked,

305

"Wasn't the winner supposed to be taking her home as part of the prize?"

Burns said, "You're not going to be the winner, Lenny, so why are you worried about it?"

Cleaver came back and asked, "Shall we leave her on the path, sir, or toss her in the trees?"

"Leave her here." Burns watched her wriggling on the trail. "And cut her."

"What?"

"I said cut her, Cleaver."

"Cut her?"

"Yes, fucking cut her. We need blood. Something that bitch animal can smell. A scent."

Cleaver leaned over the girl. He made a movement, and she screeched. Burns felt something wriggle in his belly. Cleaver stepped away from the girl, and Burns saw blood drizzle from a cut on her arm.

Longman wandered off, trying to get a signal on his phone.

Burns looked around. He'd lurk in the trees. The spot would give him a good view of the track. He reckoned the creature would follow the path. Try to make it back towards the house. Then he'd nail the animal.

"Can she smell that blood, boss?" said Cleaver.

"There's wolf in her, Cleaver. She can smell it a mile off."

Longman had drifted off into the trees. Burns heard him jabber. Burns said to Cleaver, "He's getting on my nerves. Do you think we should shoot him?"

"Uh... that's your call, sir."

"I'm asking your opinion, Cleaver."

"I have no opinion on that, Mr Burns."

"Jesus, does no one have a backbone?"

Longman was shouting into the phone. Telling someone that he couldn't hear anything, could they speak up.

Burns looked over his shoulder to tell the TV producer to shut up when Longman fell silent.

Burns stared into the trees where Longman's voice had come from. He waited a few seconds. Longman might be on the phone. Listening to the person on the other end of the line. Not that he ever listened for long. He liked talking too much.

Burns furrowed his brow. He said, "Lenny? Hey, Lenny, you back there?"

Cleaver said, "What's the matter, boss?"

"Oh, shit."

He trotted towards the treeline, and Cleaver followed. They brushed aside branches. Entered the forest and weaved through the trees for a dozen yards.

Longman appeared out of the gloom like a ghost. His white face hovered in the darkness, and his hands were above his head. He came closer, and Burns saw there was someone behind him.

Burns seethed.

The Moscow policeman had a gun pressed into Longman's temple. He told Cleaver and Burns, "Put down your weapons."

The girl on the track wailed.

Cleaver held his hand aloft. Burns didn't move. He said, "Where's my Toyota Land Cruiser, you bastard?"

The Russian said again, "Put down your weapons."

Burns said, "Fuck you," and fired.

* * * *

The Kawasaki hurtled through the trees, kicking up dirt and dust.

Schumann glanced in the side mirror.

He whimpered.

The werewolf gained on them.

A gunshot came from the west. Schumann hoped someone was firing at the creature. He looked in the mirror again. Terror rinsed through him. If the shot was meant for the monster, they'd missed. The creature was still coming. Ripping up the ground between them. Closing on the bike with every bound.

"Shoot it, Jim," he said in a loud voice, "For Christ's sakes, shoot."

Wellington turned in the Spyder to look at their pursuer for the first time. He screamed and looked to the front again and said, "Jesus, go faster, go faster."

"Shoot it," said Schumann again, his throat burning because he had to shout above the roar of the engine.

Wellington twisted round in the sidecar. Schumann glanced at him: the guy quaked. But at least he raised the Winchester now and started taking shots at the werewolf.

Wellington said, "I can't get a clear shot."

"Jesus, get any kind of shot!"

The creature was twenty yards behind.

Schumann had no idea where he was headed. This was only his third hunt with Burns. He didn't have his bearings yet. But he was convinced this route would take him back to the main trail, and then he could head back down to Sorrow Hill and safety.

Gunfire deafened him. Wellington firing. Schumann jerked with every shot. He looked in the side mirror. The creature kept coming, trailed by dust.

"Can't you shoot straight?" he said to Wellington.

"Not if we keep jerking around, Harris, it's – "

Schumann yanked the handlebars to the right to avoid the branch. The bike tipped onto its side. The sidecar lifted. Wellington held on. Schumann held his breath. The Spyder slammed back down. Wellington jolted. The gun flew out of his hands. Schumann looked at him and asked if he was OK, and Wellington nodded, a look of horror on his face.

Schumann took another look in the mirror.

His heart nearly stopped.

The werewolf filled the mirror.

He said, "Hold on, Jim, hold the fuck on – it's right behind us."

Wellington screamed. Leaned forward in the Spyder. Schumann fixed on the path, following the Kawasaki's headlight through the gloom.

Bad idea, he was thinking, *this was a bad idea. I said it was, right from the start, right from the damn start.*

He didn't blink. Scythed through the forest.

Wellington screamed. Bounced up and down in the Spyder when the Kawasaki hit ruts.

Schumann looked over his shoulder.

The werewolf was there.

He leaned over the handlebars. Gritted his teeth. Metal clanked, and the Kawasaki rocked. Schumann jerked, trying to control the machine. He trembled and the engine shuddered and the bike seemed to get sluggish.

What the hell was that noise?

Then the Kawasaki accelerated. Shot off as if fired from a catapult. The ride smoothed out. The bike felt light. Like the Spyder and Wellington weren't there. He looked and was about to tell Wellington they'd got away.

The Spyder and Wellington *weren't* there.

He looked in his side mirror. The red sidecar lay in the dust cloud. Shapes thrashed around in there. He stopped the bike and looked over his shoulder. The werewolf had dragged the Spyder and Wellington free of the Kawasaki.

And now the monster was killing Wellington.

Schumann cried and got off the bike.

He swung the Remington off his shoulder.

The dust and the darkness made it hard to see. He heard growling and ripping sounds, like clothes being torn. But he knew it wasn't clothes. He narrowed his eyes and tried to focus on the shapes in the haze.

If the werewolf were busy with Wellington, he could sneak up and kill it. Claim the cash. Be a hero. First kill – and what a kill.

He shouldered the shotgun. Moved forward.

Silence fell. No growling. No ripping. The bank of dust hid something terrible. Schumann froze. His palms sweated on the stock of the shotgun. He thought, *Fuck this, I'm going back*, and was ready to spin and dart back to the bike when something pitched out of the dust.

Schumann gasped. "Oh, Christ," he said. He looked at the object. Wellington's arm. The fatigues covered in dust. The hand curled into a claw. The stump a mess of blood and meat. "Oh, Christ."

The werewolf exploded from the dust cloud.

Schumann screamed. Wheeled and raced for the bike. The earth shook. He felt hot breath on the back of his neck. He screamed again. And something rammed into him, knocking him through the air.

CHAPTER 83.
CLEANING DUTIES.

PROCTER gawped at the bank of monitors. The camera showed Schumann being butchered by the Greenacre werewolf. Procter had already watched Allen Hurst die. Now he turned his attention to the screen showing Inessa lying on the trail. Burns and Cleaver had gone out of shot.

He sat in the booth just off the trophy room. The room was panelled wood and leather. Burns made his home movies in here.

The door opened, and Procter spun round in the chair.

"What the hell's going on up there?" said Bahrman.

Procter said nothing. He looked at the monitors again.

Bahrman pointed at one of the screens. "Who's that dickhead on the quad bike?"

Procter saw Lomax Delaney shoot across the monitor.

"He's coming back," said Bahrman.

The mercenary was right. The councilman seemed to be heading back to the house.

"Shit," said Bahrman.

"What is it?"

"It's not how it was supposed to be."

"Well, no."

"I mean we have to bring things forward."

"What are you talking about, Bahrman?"

The mercenary cocked his head and sneered. "You know what I'm doing here, doctor?"

"You're waiting for me, aren't you? Waiting for this to be done, then taking me to New York where I can convey the good news of Laura Greenacre's death to Ruth."

"Seems you're not going to be conveying any good news."

Procter glanced at the monitors.

"And," said Bahrman, "I have another task."

"Another task?"

Bahrman drew a handgun out of a holster near his armpit.

"I'm the cleaner, doctor."

Procter tried to speak but failed.

Bahrman went on:

"Ruth brought me in to clean up, see."

Procter found his voice. "C-clean up?"

"Ruth wants a respectable silence from everyone who's connected to this place, everyone who was here today. See, if one of these hunters ever gets arrested, if anyone ever hears what Burns is up to here, there'll be questions. And the cops, the FBI, will ask, 'So who was here? Who visited Sorrow Hill?' Ruth doesn't want that. So I'm cleaning up any mess."

He cocked the weapon.

Procter flinched.

"P-please, I – I'll – "

"Oh, doc," said Bahrman. "I'm not killing you, man. She likes you. OK, not really, but she didn't tell me to shoot you."

The door opened. Lomax Delaney stumbled into the booth. Dust coated his fatigues. Dirt matted his hair and covered his face.

He said, "It's all fucked up, doctor, it's gone wrong – "

Bahrman shot him in the face. Blood splashed on the wall. Delaney wilted and hit the ground. Procter smelled cordite and blood. The top half of Delaney's head was gone. Fluid poured from his skull, and bits of brain dotted the varnished floor.

"You've made a mess, Mr Bahrman."

"I think we should go, doctor. Back to New York. I think this situation is now out of our control."

"Aren't you going to finish cleaning this place?" He looked from Bahrman to the bank of monitors.

"I'm not going up there. Not while she's running around. Are you coming?"

CHAPTER 84.
NO PEACE.

IT took a while for Thorn and Sophie to make their way down off the roof.

When the adrenaline slowed, the pain kicked in, and Thorn had to sit down for a few minutes. Sophie curled up in the crook of his arm. He told her not to look at Craig's dangling body. The blood covering Thorn smeared onto Sophie, but she didn't seem to care. She was quiet. Shivering in his arms.

He'd asked her if she was all right, but she said nothing. Buried her face in his armpit. They didn't say a word while they climbed down the ladder. Every rung was anguish for him. His hands were raw. His legs felt like water. Some ribs broken, his body bruised. Head throbbing.

He'd stopped halfway down and thrown up. He needed a drink. His throat felt like it was full of gravel.

They got down and stopped again. He held her, and she shuddered in his arms.

What have I done to you? he thought.

He hated himself. Cursed his life. Love brought this suffering. Love for Laura. He would abandon it now. Not harbour hopes of finding her. Forget about stowing himself on some boat and heading to America.

Crazy, he thought. *Let it go. Live with the loss and the pain.*

After all, it was only heartbreak, wasn't it? Did people die of a broken heart? Maybe they did. The way he felt now, he'd welcome death. Only Sophie kept him going. Only his responsibility towards her. Perhaps when she got old enough, eighteen or twenty-one, he'd kill himself. End it. He was no good to anyone. He only brought anguish and danger and death.

They hobbled into the pool area. A putrid smell filled the air. Thorn saw blood on the tiles. He glanced towards the roof. Craig's dark shape hung there, rocking from side to side.

Relief washed over him.

Embrace the gloom, he thought. Live with the loss.

That was the way. Life was meaningless, anyway. No point in fighting that.

They shambled towards the exit in the far corner. He'd have to sleep before he could drive back. He stiffened. Sophie stopped and looked up at him. He smiled at her, hugged her. Didn't want to worry her with his fears:

Billy, Sears, and the Strakers.

Were they recovered and waiting for him?

He halted again and said, "We'll go round the outside, sweetheart. Sorry. Go back this way." They turned and hobbled off in the direction they came from.

He heard the footsteps behind him but ignored them, hoping they were in his head. But the voice wasn't:

"You've made a right mess here, Johnny lad."

Sophie gasped and pressed herself against Thorn, and he turned towards the speaker. A figure stepped out of the shadows at the exit and pointed a gun.

CHAPTER 85.
THE HUNT ENDS.

LONGMAN lay dying, with a bullet hole through his gut. He writhed on the ground. Scrabbled leaves and twigs with his feet.

"Cleaver," said Burns, gun trained on Dasaev, "go see what all that firing was about, that screaming."

They'd heard shooting to the east.

"I can guess what that was, boss," said Cleaver. "Let's hope they were on target, huh?"

"See if you can get anyone on the radio. Schumann. Wellington. Anyone."

Cleaver went back towards the main trail.

Dasaev grimaced. The bullet that was killing Longman had penetrated the TV producer, probably slicing his aorta, and lodged in Dasaev's left thigh. His leg simmered with pain.

"Hurts, huh?" said Burns.

Dasaev said nothing.

"You take the collar off that bitch?"

Dasaev looked Burns in the eye. The werewolf had bounded towards him, and he thought she was going to kill him. But she didn't. Hurdled over him and tore into the forest. Stopped in the trees and looked over her shoulder at him. Made a grunting noise that Dasaev liked to think was a "thank you", and then raced away into the darkness.

Burns said, "If you did take the collar off, you murdered my friends. You're a murderer."

Dasaev made a noise. An attempt to laugh but it came out like a grunt.

And then he found words:

"You hunt people to their deaths, and you call me a murderer."

Burns frowned. "The prey I hunt, they're nothing. Society's spillage. The detritus of the streets. They need culling. It's good for the world. These men who come here, they're the elite. Two Wall Street bankers. A doctor who saves children. A TV producer with a raft of Emmys to his name – "

"Who you have just killed."

"He got in the way. He knows the rules."

Longman made a keening sound, like an animal in agony. Blood bubbled from his mouth and stained his clothes.

Burns said, "Cleaver," over his shoulder, "d'you get anywhere?"

Cleaver trundled back into the trees. "Nowhere, boss, I got nowhere." He glanced at Dasaev and then drew his eyes away.

"Hey, Cleaver, how are you?" said Dasaev.

"Don't talk to him, Cleaver," said Burns, and then to Dasaev: "You broke his heart, Russian. He's a queer scorned. Nothing worse than a queer scorned."

Cleaver glowered at Burns, and Dasaev saw an opportunity in that look.

He said, "You don't have to be part of this, Cleaver."

"Shut the fuck up, you commie bastard," said Burns.

"I'm not a communist."

"I don't give a shit what you are. Come on, get out of here," said Burns, gesturing for Dasaev to walk towards him and out of the trees. "Cleaver, put Lenny out of his misery. Knife'll do."

Burns marched Dasaev out of the trees.

Cleaver said, "I'm not doing it."

Burns halted Dasaev with a jab to the back and said, "I'm not sure I heard you there, Cleaver? Did I hear the word 'not' in there? 'Not doing it,' I think you said."

"That's right, Mr Burns. I can't kill him."

"You've killed people before, Cleaver. You've put them down before. Now, put Lenny out of his misery. He's suffering, see. Like an animal."

Longman moaned. Sweat and blood glazed his face.

Cleaver said, "I'll ring 911, get a medic up here – "

Burns said, "Jesus, Cleaver, am I going to have to – "

A growl from the track stopped him.

"What the hell was that?" he said.

"Three guesses," said Dasaev. He hobbled through the undergrowth. He tried to ignore the pain in his leg. It hurt right up into his head. Burns followed him. Calling after him to stop. But Dasaev kept going.

He knew what waited for them on the trail and knew that Burns would die.

Dasaev stopped at the edge of the track. Burns came up behind him said, "Oh Christ," in a gasp.

The werewolf sniffed at the girl on the ground. The animal moved around her. Steam billowed from its nostrils. The girl whimpered and quivered. The werewolf smelled a wound on her arm and licked it with its long, pink tongue.

"Here we go," said Burns and he raised his AR-15.

Dasaev swatted the barrel.

The gun went off. Pain exploded in Dasaev's ears.

The werewolf raised its head and snarled.

Burns darted out, onto the trail. He aimed at the werewolf again and fired. The bullet grazed the animal's cheek. The creature growled.

Burns screamed. He ran across the trail. Disappeared into the forest. Dasaev saw the Dodge's blue paint through the foliage. Bells rang in his ears. An ache pulsed in his skull. Dasaev crawled towards the girl lying on the trail.

The pickup burst out of the trees, bouncing onto the trail. Weaved down the track, tyres blowing up dirt and dust. The werewolf chased. Bounded up on the back of the Dodge. The pickup jounced. Burns lost control. The vehicle swerved.

Head-on into a tree. Burns jerked forward in the cab. The werewolf slid, slammed into the back of the cab. Burns scrabbled to get out, screaming for help, for Cleaver. Cleaver stood there, watching.

The werewolf smashed through the cab's rear window. Glass sprayed. The pickup shook. Springs creaked. The animal's front end was buried in the cab. Burns screamed. The werewolf's hindquarters thrashed from side to side. The long black tail whipped. The pickup jolted and rocked. Dasaev couldn't see Burns, only heard him. He could see a black shape in the cab, that's all. And then tearing sounds and shrieking and blood splashing all over the inside of the Dodge, splattering the windscreen, the side windows.

Dasaev drew his eyes away from the killing and tore the tape from the girl's wrists and ankles. He held a handkerchief to the wound on her arm. Her brown eyes gaped up at him. Tears and dirt streaked her white face. Mud matted her red hair. He was about to tell her everything was going to be OK when she said, "Ne delaitye mnye bol'no, pozhaluista."

Please don't hurt me any more.

Dasaev scooped her up in his arms and said, "Bol'she nikogda. Bol'she nikogda."

Never again. Never again.

* * * *

"This hasn't gone to plan at all, has it," said Ellis Cole, gun pointed at Thorn. "I knew you'd fuck it up, Johnny. Knew you wouldn't lie down and die. You're a real pain in the backside. It wasn't such a big job to kill you. They were really up for it, Sears and them. It should have been a doddle. But no. Here you are. Alive and kicking. You and your lovely lass. Hello, Sophie. You look nice. All covered in blood and shit and smelling of piss."

"Don't talk to her, Cole." Thorn's voice came out guttural.

"Why not, lad? I like talking to girls."

"They don't like talking to you."

"No matter."

"You're not going to use that, are you?"

"This?" said Cole, waving the gun.

"Yeah, that. It's a Derringer. Woman's gun."

"Still kills, though. Want to see?"

He aimed at them. Thorn stepped in front of Sophie.

Cole said, "What a brave daddy you are."

"What do you want?"

"Well, first I wanted you to be dead. That didn't happen. Seems I'm going to have to do it myself. Never done it before, killed a man, but it's exciting, I have to say. Got myself a stiffy here" – he cupped his crotch – "which I might have to put to good use after shooting you, Johnny. Your pretty daughter might enjoy spending time with me, eh?"

Thorn shuddered with anger. "I'll fucking cut it off for you, Cole."

"Calm down, John, calm down. You should be proud. She's a lovely girl. Now, send her over to me."

"You can fuck off."

"Send her to me, or I'll shoot you, then... well, you can only imagine what I'll do to her."

Thorn bridled. Sophie whimpered.

"What do you want, Cole?"

"Your daughter first."

"Never."

"I'll kill you now."

"Cole, I'll – "

"It's OK, Dad." Sophie appeared from behind him. She stood straight. Blood matted her hair. Her skin was streaked with dirt. But she looked Cole in the eye, and Thorn saw the man quake. Sophie kissed Thorn on the cheek. "I'll be fine." And she went to Cole, who stepped back and looked her up and down before grabbing her and snaking his arm around her throat and making her face her dad.

Thorn boiled with rage. He looked at Sophie's face. Her eyes gaped with fear.

"These women of yours, they're tough, aren't they," said Cole.

"What are you going to do?"

"I'm going to have to kill you in self-defence. You're a murderer. I was going to phone the cops. Have you arrested for murder, but you attacked me, so I had to shoot you."

"Murder? Whose murder? Craig?"

Cole glanced up towards the rafters. "Aye, and the Strakers."

"They're not dead."

319

"They are. They've got bullets in them out there in the lobby, and it weren't me, mate. As I said, I've never killed a soul – yet."

"I've not killed them."

"Well, maybe it was Sears and his lad then. They've made a getaway, at any rate. I don't care who killed them. Only who'll get blamed for killing them. And when I do away with you, this pretty little lady will need looking after. And I'm just the fellow."

Sophie squirmed.

"I swear, I'll fucking tear you to pieces, Cole."

"Ha! Ha! Thought it was your girlfriend who did that sort of thing. Not for long, though. It'll all be over. You and her gone."

"You knew she was being hunted. You're in on all this, aren't you, Cole."

"Not all of it. I wish I was, Johnny. It'd be fun seeing her as prey. They're a bunch of Nazis, I believe. Nasty crowd."

"She'll kill them."

"Not this time. It's not a fair fight. They're cheating. She's dead, mate. You'll be dead. Ruth has her vengeance."

"And what do you have?"

"This one here." Cole squeezed Sophie. "And a place at the top table. The Templetons' legal advisor. Rolling in money. She's coming back here, you know. Ruth. Rebuild this old place. Build the family's reputation again. But doing it with a difference. She's part animal, now. Got what Michael had in him. Got the werewolf bug. Bit of a monster."

"You're fucking me about."

"Haven't you been watching the news? Killings across Europe?"

"Ruth?"

"Aye, Ruth. Anyway, enough talk. Me and Sophie, we have to get going."

Sophie squirmed in Cole's grasp.

"Dad," she said, the anguish in that one word devastating him. He wanted to rush Cole. Shove Sophie out of the way and smash into him. He knew Cole couldn't be that good with a gun. And would he really use it if he had to? But all you needed to do, if you had the will, was point and shoot. It was easy. Too easy.

"Let her go," said Thorn.

"Dad," said Sophie again. He looked at her. She made a gesture with her eyes. Bit into Cole's arm. He yelled out and loosened his grip on Sophie, and she lurched away. Thorn sprang, ignoring the pain running through his body.

Cole's face stretched in fury. He screamed. Aimed the Derringer at Thorn and fired. The bullet whizzed past Thorn's head. He kept going. Straight for Cole. Eyes fixed on the bastard.

Cole aimed again. Right at Thorn's head. No way he'd miss. Thorn knew that and drove his legs harder.

"You're fucking dead, Thorn, fucking dead – "

The gunshot exploded in Thorn's ears and blood splashed into his eyes.

CHAPTER 86.
DELIVERANCE.

CLEAVER came into the kitchen and said, "There's no one left. They've all gone. Procter's gone. Stokes. That Bahrman guy. They're gone. I found Lomax Delaney dead in the trophy room, his head blown off. But the rest, they've cleared out."

Dasaev handed Inessa another glass of water. She sat at the counter, eating her way through a second plate of cheese and ham. They'd been back an hour now. Driven down in the blood-stained Dodge. The werewolf had dragged Burns's body into the trees. Dasaev, Cleaver, and Inessa had leaped into the pickup and driven back down to the house.

Dasaev said to Cleaver, "And no staff?"

"Mr Burns, he dismisses everyone before a hunt. Gives them a vacation. Just a few days off." Cleaver's brow wrinkled. He looked at Inessa. "Is the girl all right?"

"She's OK," said Dasaev and watched Cleaver, trying to work out what he was thinking.

And then the man said, "How can I right my wrongs, Dasaev? All the dead who have passed through here. How can I redeem myself?"

"Help her, and you can put it right."

"That doesn't put it right."

"It's a start, Cleaver. You made the right choices today, didn't you."

322

Cleaver went to a cupboard. Opened it and took out a bottle of whisky. He uncorked it. Found a glass and poured himself a drink. He held up the glass to Dasaev, who shook his head.

"We got vodka," said Cleaver. "Doesn't every Russian like vodka?"

"No more than every American likes pizza."

"You know, I think every American *does* like pizza."

"I don't drink," said Dasaev.

"You're a character. Hell of a guy. OK, so how do I help this girl?"

"By telling the US authorities how Burns brought them in. Where he kept them."

"I told you I don't know that."

Dasaev said nothing.

Cleaver said, "See, I can't be saved. There's no salvation for me, man."

"There is always salvation. How long has he hunted people?"

"A few years. Thinks it makes him a man. He had no idea what made a man."

Cleaver finished his drink and smacked his lips.

Dasaev said, "We should bury what remains of them."

"Let me do that. You go. Get out of here. I'll clean up. Let that be my act of deliverance."

"You can't do it all on your own. The authorities will come. These men, they'll be missed. Everyone knows they are friends with Burns. They will come here, Cleaver."

"That's OK. Maybe that's what I want, you know. The chance to do penance. Serve some time. A lot of time. Come on, man, you need to be gone in the next three or four hours. I'm headed back up there. When I get back, I don't want to see you here, OK? Or I'll shoot you."

He smiled, and Dasaev nodded.

* * * *

Laura rode the Kawasaki back down the hill. Her mouth tasted of meat. She wore fatigues torn off one of her victims. The clothes smelled of blood and shit. But the wind was good in her hair and on her face. Her right eye hurt, and she couldn't see through it properly.

She thought about the man who'd shot off the neckbrace. Saved her life. Wondered if she'd see him again. She remembered his eyes: black like coal.

She rode out of the forest and saw headlights in the distance. A pickup wending its way back up the hill. She slowed and stared after the vehicle. Accelerated again and headed down towards Burns's mansion.

She raced past the corral, and the horses bucked and neighed. Dogs barked and whined in the kennels. She got off the bike, letting the machine slide away through the dust and plough into a Mercedes.

She kicked down the back door and entered the lounge. She looked around: plush carpet, leather furniture, Western landscapes hanging on the walls, floor-to-ceiling windows staring out towards the dark hills she'd just left.

Footsteps clumped up a set of stairs. Whoever it was was walking with difficulty. Laura braced herself. A man brandishing a pistol strode through the door.

It was him.

And Laura said, "It's you."

He aimed the gun at her. He said, "Do you remember me?"

"Don't point that gun at me; it pisses me off when people point guns at me."

"You remember me?"

"Put the fucking gun down."

He lowered the pistol.

She said, "You said you were Dasaev."

He gawped at her. His black eyes glittered.

She cocked her head. "Why did you save me?"

He looked her up and down. "Your clothes are shit."

"It's the fashion. Blood and shit chic. Why did you help me?"

Now he looked straight at her. "It was unfair. The hunt."

"You risked your life. Could've got chewed up out there."

"I know that now."

"Your leg, that looks really, really bad." His jeans were dark and wet with blood. "You need that looking at."

324

"Your eye, that looks bad."

She touched her wounded eye. "Let me look at your leg."

"Let me look at your eye."

"Leg first."

"OK."

She moved towards him. She said, "Where's the Dodge going? I saw it heading back up there."

The Russian sat down.

"Cleaver. He's going to bury what's left."

"There won't be much. I tend to clear my plate." She sat next to him. "Shall I help you off with your pants?"

CHAPTER 87.
THE WAY OF ALL FLESH.

WHEELER Burns and Allen Hurst were piled in chunks into the back of the Dodge along with Lomax Delaney's body, and now Cleaver trawled the forest for Schumann and Wellington.

Blood soaked his clothes. Pieces of meat clung to his hands. The odour of decay hung in the air. Flies droned, and all Cleaver had to do was follow the noise. He traipsed through the woods. Flashlight beam spearing the night. Tarpaulin strapped to his back. He followed his nose and his ears.

He came to a clearing. The smell made him retch. The flies buzzed. A cloud of them swirled in the flashlight's glow. The earth had been scoured. Like something had torn through here. A rut gouged in the ground. A motorbike, maybe.

He put on a facemask, went to work.

Schumann's remains were strewn in the undergrowth. Not much left of him. Only from the sternum up. His face pale and his eyes gone. Pecked by crows, Cleaver guessed. Schumann's mouth stood agape, as if astounded by his mutilation. Trails of innards slithered from him. His spine tailed from the remains.

Cleaver found Wellington nearby, with his chest and belly ripped open and his insides scooped out.

Fuck, did that woman do this? It was hideous. *She's a monster*, he thought.

But what was she supposed to do? These men planned to kill her. Shoot her and then laugh at her carcass and tell tales of how they'd brought down a dangerous animal. Then they'd cut her head off. Burn her body. She'd be gone. Never existed.

He laid out the tarpaulin. He gathered up what was left of Schumann and Wellington. More meat and gore on his clothes. His gloves soaked through. Warm blood on his hands. The face mask did little to stave off the smell. He packed the remains in the sheeting. Took them back to the trail. Dumped them in the back with Burns, Hurst, and Delaney. He went back and got the Spyder sidecar.

He sweated and huffed, but this had to be done. It had to be like this. He hoisted the Spyder onto the Dodge. Had to be like nothing ever existed.

He took a minute and stared down towards the house. One light in the dark distance, that was all. A glimmer. So far away from him. He opened the door of the pickup and pulled out the petrol can. He soaked a cloth in petrol and jammed the rag into the Dodge's fuel tank. He poured petrol on the earth, and the fumes made him dizzy. He tossed the can in the back of the Dodge. He looked towards the house again. Tears came to his eyes. He wiped them away and smeared blood on his face.

He said, "Oh, shit," but then laughed, realizing it didn't matter.

All that mattered was absolution.

* * * *

Laura bathed his wounds with iodine. The pain made him woozy. He lay on the couch with a blanket covering his crotch. Only his wounded leg showed. The bullet had lodged in his thigh. A bruise stained the flesh. Blood ran from the hole in his leg. Inessa sat and watched. The gash on her arm had been bandaged. And the Russian girl had washed Laura's eye and taped gauze over the lesion earlier.

Attending to the injured after battle, thought Dasaev.

"You need a hospital, Mr Dasaev," said Laura. She rose from her knees and wiped her hands.

"Lev, call me Lev."

"Well, you still need a hospital."

"Can you take the bullet out?"

"Yes I can take it out. I could chew through your leg. I could bite a chunk off your thigh."

"Put your fingers in the wound. You can do that. You're not squeamish. You eat men."

She looked at him. "It'll hurt like fuck."

"I know it will hurt like fuck, but it hurts like fuck already." He crossed himself. "You are a bad influence."

"Me? Why?"

"Making me curse."

"You don't curse?"

"I try not to, but it is fucking difficult when it fucking hurts so fucking much."

"Why don't you go to a hospital?"

"Why don't you? You might lose your eye."

She shrugged. "OK. What do I care? It's your leg."

"It is your eye."

He gazed at her and thought how lovely she was. How unlike Galina. He understood beauty then. It was deep. It was behind the eyes and in the breast. That's where it lay. Not on the skin.

"Dig it out," he said.

He told her he didn't drink when she offered him a bottle of brandy.

"You might make an exception," she said.

He took the bottle and drank. It was like drinking acid. His screwed up his face and hissed.

"More," she said.

He glugged more, and his eyes swam.

"Pissed already. What a lightweight," she said.

Dasaev groaned. Everything blurred. Two Lauras hovered over his leg. Three Inessa's wavered. Laura sank her fingers into his leg. He felt it and yelled out. Sour liquid filled his throat. He moaned. Thought he would faint. Could hear the mushy sound as she burrowed in his thigh. Blood spouted all over her and over his legs and the carpet and the couch.

Dasaev cursed in Russian, and Laura said, "Would that be something you'd say to your mother?"

"Mother... dead... "

328

"Join the club."

He drank some more brandy. Missed his mouth. Drink dribbled down his chin.

The world reeled, and he saw his father and spoke to him, saying he was sorry he got drunk, and he saw Galina with a group of men, laughing at him, mocking, and Dominika reaching for him as he drowned now, swirling down into a whirlpool, his father tutting and Galina laughing and Dominika stretching.

He screamed. Sat up.

Laura said, "I got it, I got it," and held up the bullet in her bloody hand.

He looked at his leg. Leaned over the edge of the couch. Moaned and threw up. Laura dodged out of the way just in time. He panted, feeling sick, feeling weak.

"I'll never drink again," he said.

* * * *

Cleaver sat in the back of the Dodge with the remains of the hunters. The smell of petrol and meat combined to make him sick. He looked up at the sky and tears ran down his face. He remembered being in these hills and what he did here.

Put him down, Cleaver.

Put her out of her misery, Cleaver.

Cut her throat, Cleaver.

Bring the head, Cleaver.

Burn the bodies, Cleaver.

Wheeler Burns's bagman.

He took a Zippo from his pocket.

He flicked the wheel. The spark became a flame. He leaned over the edge of the Dodge. Lit the rag.

"Bye, Mother. I love you."

The fire ate the rag and went into the tank and the Dodge erupted.

Cleaver was burned alive, but he tried not to scream.

The fire licked the ground and swept towards the trees.

* * * *

329

The flames lit up the forest. The hill turned orange. Fire whipped through the pines and the spruces and the grasses. Smoke rose in thick clouds and swept north.

"Cleaver," said Dasaev, hobbling out of the house.

He could smell the fumes.

"Jesus," said Laura. "Come on, we've got to get out of here. Place'll be crawling with cops."

Laura and Inessa dashed towards the garage. Dasaev limped after them. Laura heaved open the garage door.

"Which one?" she said.

"What is there?" said Dasaev, reaching the women. He saw the cars. He said, "That one."

CHAPTER 88.
911.

A TRUCK driver rang the Dutchess County Sheriff's Office in Poughkeepsie, saying he was just passing Route 22 when he saw an explosion up in the hills. Caused a fireball, he told the deputy. Must be a UFO crash-landing. Tearing through the pines up there. The flames, he said, were spreading. The blaze lit up the hillside like the neon lights of a titty bar, he said.

"Like a titty bar, did he say?" said Sheriff Roy Decker, answering the phone as he was going up to bed.

"That's right," said the deputy.

Twenty minutes later, Decker led a convoy of officers from Poughkeepsie. Included in the entourage were members of the Homeland Security and Detective divisions. A team from the Emergency Services Unit was also headed to the scene, called in to deal with the possibility of a "Marksman Situation".

"In case someone's up there blowing things up and they're armed," said Decker.

The 22-mile journey would take maybe 20 minutes. The roads were empty. The police cars raced along Route 55, sirens wailing, lights flashing. Ten miles out, Decker saw the blaze. Flames veined across the hillside from the fireball. Smoke darkened the sky.

"What do you think caused that, sir?" said the deputy who was driving.

Decker said nothing. He didn't know.

Headlights flared and blinded him. A yellow Ferrari 612 Scaglietti zoomed past them, heading the other way. A guy with two girls. A redhead and a blonde, the blonde driving. *Lucky guy*, thought Decker. *Nice car, two girls.*

He focused on the fire again as it illuminated the night and wondered when he'd be done and when he'd get to bed.

CHAPTER 89.
BAD NEWS.

"IF YOU want something done, you have to do it yourself,"
said Ruth, and she hurled the Georgian chair against the wall.
The antique splintered. Wood showered the carpet and the
wallpaper was gouged.

Ruth paced the living room. Rage purpled her cheeks.
Procter could feel the fire in her, the anger. He glanced at
Bahrman and Stokes. Bahrman looked cool, lounging on the
couch with his arms stretched out across the back of the seat.
Procter wished he could be so calm in the face of this storm.

"Useless," she said, "utterly useless, the lot of you."

Stokes huddled on a stool next to the fireplace. His eyes were
wide, and he rubbed his hands together.

They were holed up in Burns's apartment. A pre-war, three-
bedroom condo. He'd given Ruth the key. They wouldn't be
here long, she'd said – a couple of hours, maybe. Then head
home. But it had already been 24 hours. And now they might
have to lengthen their stay. Ruth wouldn't leave until she knew
Laura Greenacre was already dead or about to be.

She glared at Procter. Her eyes were glassy. He sensed they
might change at any moment – lose their human quality and
become animal.

"I should kill you now. All of you."

Bahrman raised an eyebrow. He drew a Makarov pistol from his belt and laid it on the glass-topped coffee table. "If you're going to eat me, ma'am, you better do it when I'm asleep. I tell you – you get animal on me, and I'll shoot you."

Ruth glared at him. "Thank you for advising me, Mr Bahrman. That's what I'll do, then. Wait till you're sleeping." She turned, went to the drinks cabinet. "But really, you're just not worth it. None of you." She made herself a gin and tonic with a slice of lime in it. She took a gulp and then said, "How? Tell me how this could have happened."

Procter told her what had happened at Burns's place.

"So you're not sure if she's alive?"

"No, Ruth, I'm not sure," said Procter. "She did seem to be having the best of it, though. And when Delaney returned" – he coughed, glanced at Bahrman – "he said they were done, it was over."

"And it's all over the news, is it?"

"Yes. TV stations have got helicopters out there. There's a fireball tearing through Burns's estate. The forests are burning."

"Maybe the fire killed her," said Ruth. "Any idea who started it?"

Procter said he didn't have a clue.

Ruth said, "You're useless, you really are."

"Excuse me, Ruth, but I've brought you the briefcase. Had I stayed there, I might've been arrested or killed. And where would your precious blood be, then?"

She spun round. Her eyes were yellow. She strode towards him. His skin crawled, and he tried to say her name, but his voice died in his throat. She lashed out, and her nails scored his cheek. Blood ran down his face. He lurched away, his flesh stinging.

"Never speak to me like that," she said.

"Christ, Ruth," said Procter. "Christ. I'm – I'm trying to – help you."

"Try harder." She looked at Bahrman. "What about this Russian?"

334

"What about him?"

"Do we know where he's got to?"

Bahrman shrugged.

Ruth tutted and went back to the drinks cabinet. Finished her gin-and-tonic and made herself another.

"No one can be left from Sorrow Hill," she said. "I can't be placed there. I must be whiter than white. I mean to live on in England. I mean to regain my place in society. My honour, my respect. Mr Bahrman, find anyone who was there who might've seen me, and kill them."

"That'll add to the bill, ma'am."

"Add to it, then. I can't believe this went wrong. I should've never listened to you, Lawrence."

"What?" said Procter. His cheek hurt. He felt sick. He'd sat down now and was dripping blood on the carpet.

"You took me to Burns, didn't you? You indicated he could be helpful."

"I didn't suggest he hunt Laura Greenacre."

She said nothing. Her eyes brimmed with rage.

Procter said, "At least Thorn's dead."

She wheeled to glare at him and made a noise that wasn't human.

"No, he's not," she said. Her skin surged, as if there were something crawling beneath it. "Nick Sears rang. Moaning that Thorn fought them off."

"B-but what about Craig? Didn't he – "

"I don't know, Lawrence. Sears and his son fled. They were on a flight to New York this afternoon. Donny and Jason Muir as well. Christ!"

Procter said, "Why are they coming over?"

She said, "Firstly, I'm going to berate them for failing to kill Thorn, and then I'm going to make them werewolves, Lawrence. I want you to inject them with the blood. They'll be strong and powerful. They'll have Greenacre's blood in them. And they'll have my blood in them. They'll be my weapons against her."

"To kill her?"

"To kill her. In the streets."

"But only four of them... She fought off twice that number in Trafalgar Square, Ruth."

"They'll be stronger," she said. "And we'll have some added insurance this time."

She looked at Bahrman.

CHAPTER 90.
LAST STAND.

DASAEV said, "When you need help, you go to your people.
It doesn't matter what you've done; they will shelter you. It
doesn't matter who you are. They used to call this part of town
Little Odessa. So many Ukrainians, you know? Now Russians
too. And they welcome you. They provide refuge."

When they'd arrived the previous evening, they'd stowed the
Ferrari in a garage owned by a Russian mechanic. His wife,
a nurse, had tended to their injuries. She was worried about
Dasaev's leg and Laura's eye. She gave them each a tetanus jab.
She cleaned their wounds and made sure they weren't infected.
She stitched the wound on Dasaev's leg and gave him a bottle
of Novamoxin and an injection of procaine.

The nurse had told Laura, "You might lose eye. You have
injury to the lachrymal gland, here" – and she pointed to the
inside corner of her eye – "where you cry from. Now you cry
blood, not tears. You go to hospital. New York Methodist. On
Ocean Parkway. You go now." Laura didn't. She stayed where
she was. The nurse shook her head and left, saying something
in Russian that Dasaev dismissed with a flap of his hand.

They were brought to this room, an abandoned apartment. The whole floor was abandoned, as far as Laura could see. They'd slept a long time. Until early afternoon. They'd woken stiff and hurting. Laura had gone out to buy food and medicine.

She looked round the room now. Brown paint peeled off the walls. Damp stains in the corners. The ceiling buckled. Newspapers and pieces of carpet covered the floor. The room smelled musty. A single bulb cast its dim glow over the bedsit. Inessa sat on a mattress in the corner. She'd been chattering away for hours. Asking for help to save her friends, who were being held in a house somewhere in Brooklyn. Dasaev and Laura hadn't paid much attention.

Laura focused on the photograph at her feet. The one Zak took of her at the restaurant. Her back to him, her shoulders bare and the birthmark prominent. Dasaev had taken it from Sorrow Hill.

"Treacherous little shit," she said.

"Why have they taken this?" said Dasaev. "It's from the back. You could be anyone."

"No I couldn't," she said. "I could only be me."

She looked at Dasaev. He'd showered after they'd arrived here, and she saw how fine he looked under the dirt and the blood and the sweat that had been on his skin and in his hair. His crewcut was sandy-coloured, and his eyes were obsidian. They brimmed with determination. They were bright and fiery, and she thought this man would be good to have at her shoulder. She trusted his odour. She smelled on him no fear or nervousness or uncertainty.

A ginger cat popped its head round the door and miaowed.

Laura curled her lip at the animal.

The cat came in, rubbed itself against Dasaev's foot.

"She likes me," he said.

"No, she owns you."

Inessa said something in Russian. Dasaev and Laura ignored her.

"Owns me?" he said.

"She's scenting you. She owns you. You're hers, now."

The cat curled up against Dasaev's legs and purred.

He said, "They were going to kill you. Burns. The woman called Ruth Templeton."

"They were going to try. I'm not that easy to kill."

"I have seen this."

"Can she change? Do what I do?"

Dasaev told her a gold-furred werewolf had chased him. "I think it was her."

Laura put her face in her hands.

"Is that bad?" he said.

"That's very bad. You were lucky to get away from her."

"I'm not that easy to kill, either." He looked at her. "You are the one they link to the Trafalgar Square massacre. Dozens dead. The Templeton men."

"I didn't kill men. I killed wolves – werewolves."

"The internet is full of you, you know. Many people looking for you."

"I know," she said, getting to her feet, "and now some of them have found me."

"This Ruth, she is ruthless and cruel. She has no heart. She is dangerous. You must leave here. Leave New York."

"She will keep coming after me. She'll try to find me again and again. No... I have to stand and fight. This has to end."

CHAPTER 91.
WARNINGS.

"LAURA'S out in the open, and she needs looking out for," said the man sitting opposite Thorn at the table. He said his name was Paul French, a former inspector with the Met's armed response unit. "I arrested you, Thorn. In the tunnel. Don't you remember? You said, 'I'm Johnny.'"

Thorn shook his head. All he remembered of that time in the tunnel was his heart being torn out. Laura disappearing into the darkness. Losing her.

French took a sip from his tea and looked out of the window. "Is it always rainy in Wales?"

"Always grey, always rain. I like it," said Thorn. He touched his forehead and felt the bump there. He ached all over. Bruises blotched his face and body. Three of his ribs were broken. His hands were raw, no skin on the palms, and they were swathed in bandages.

"Can't see a thing," said French. "Mist and darkness."

"Good that way. If you can't see, they can't see either."

French looked him in the face. "They tried to kill you both, and they nearly succeeded."

"Is Laura all right?" said Thorn, eyeing the man. He wasn't sure about him. But French had saved his life. Shot Ellis Cole dead at Templeton Hall less than twenty-four hours previously. Killed a man and now he was eating Digestives.

"We think so," said French.

"Who's this 'we'?"

French explained. People who'd witnessed what had happened at Trafalgar Square. A community of souls, he called them, who felt obligated to Laura Greenacre.

Thorn said, "She wouldn't see it like that. She doesn't want anyone to be obligated to her. She wants nothing."

"She wants you."

Thorn felt heat flood his face.

French continued:

"You were in a daze when we arrested you. You seemed to be on drugs, which is why we tested you. You barely answered our questions. Then that guy Keegan turned up. Security services, he claimed. Sinister chap. Shook your hand and said, 'You've done what we've tried to do for twenty years, Mr Thorn – you've nailed Ray Craig.' And you came round. You were OK. No drugs after all. Keegan told us to let you go, and we couldn't really argue."

"Why are you doing this?"

French stared into his tea for a few seconds and then raised his gaze. "When I saw her there on that plinth, I was just awestruck. Like a holy thing, you know. Like a vision. What an amazing creature. They wanted us to kill her, and we should've. We were well within our rights. But it was obvious she was protecting people. Fighting against all those other werewolves."

"She wouldn't see it as protecting, either."

"Doesn't matter so much. People see what they want to see. They read things into everything. We look for meaning, Thorn. We look for patterns. What would we do without them? We'd go mad. We'd realize that we're all just animals. OK, she's a loner and she can take care of herself, but it can't do any harm to look out for her."

Thorn said nothing.

French went on:

"I just kept thinking about what I'd seen. It was a national event, of course. People spoke and wrote about it for months; they still do. But the whole story flourished, became more than it was. People who were never there talking bollocks, analyzing, claiming it for themselves. I was fed up. I'd looked into her eyes, into the eyes of this – remarkable woman, this fabled creature. I felt connected. Not – not in love or anything... "

He furrowed his brow.

He continued:

"I saw... that she was worthy of our respect. Our awe. I went online, came across this forum run by Gala Larsson, a Swedish girl. There are other forums, too. Like Ellis Cole's fucking werewolf porn crap, findthebeast.com. I kept tracking him. I hacked into his accounts. Dirty copper tricks. I found they'd got you and your daughter. Traced you, followed them."

"Why didn't you stop it when you could, when they took Sophie?"

"Craig was there. Too many of them. Look, I did my best."

"I don't know."

There was a silence.

The men gazed out into the night. They saw nothing.

Thorn said, "You killed the Strakers?"

"Yes."

"What happened to their bodies?"

"Keegan's king of the cleaners."

Thorn nodded.

"What about Nick Sears and his little shit of a son?"

French shook his head.

They were quiet again. French drank his tea. He said, "You know Ruth will come for you again."

"I know," said Thorn.

"She's making more Templeton werewolves, Thorn."

Thorn looked at him. His chest tightened. The dread rising again.

French said, "You need to move. Leave here."

"I can't. Sophie needs stability. I'll make a stand."

"You can't. Not against Ruth. Not against monsters."

CHAPTER 92.
THE DAY HAS COME.

Terminal 5, Stockholm-Arlanda Airport, Sweden
– 1.30 a.m., November 29, 2007

GALA Larsson's leg shook. She slapped a hand on her thigh, tried to stop the quivering. Didn't work. Fear rifled through her. So many people here. Racing around. Milling about. Filing through departure gates. Greeting loved ones off incoming flights.

Gala sweated with dread.

Crowds terrified her. Public places shredded her nerves.

Ever since Trafalgar Square.

She was flying Continental Airlines to Newark. The first time she'd flown since she and her church friends, along with Mrs Heg, returned to Sweden from London eight years previously.

The first time.

The worst time.

Her leg wouldn't stop shaking.

But this had to be done. She had to be brave. What was the point in launching a campaign to "protect the werewolf" if she weren't willing to get up off her backside and actually protect it? She always knew this moment would come. Knew Laura would be unmasked again.

Laura's allies and enemies had tracked the recent murders in Europe. They'd seen the footage released on findthebeast.com. They watched the news and saw the fire spread in the Hudson Valley. They heard the crackling message picked up by a radio ham in New York State who then transmitted it on the internet. The message came from the site of the blaze, hours before the fire was reported. One word in that brief transmission got Gala and the others off their backsides.

The word, smeared by interference, was:

"... werewolf... "

Gala immediately blogged on the Protect The Werewolf site:

"The day has come. Now she needs us. We must be brave and stand with her."

Gala hoped the others would respond. She hoped they were as serious as she. She hoped this wasn't a foolish endeavour. A childish adventure best played out in front of computers, in bedrooms.

She took a breath and clenched her jaw. Time to be brave, Gala, she told herself. Time to stop staring at the PC and repay your debt.

CHAPTER 93.
VAUKALAK ... VOURDALAK...

"I DON'T know what you're saying." said Laura.

Inessa babbled again. Dasaev had gone to buy breakfast. Left Laura here with this prattling crybaby. The girl looked at her hands as if she were seeking inspiration there. Her brow was creased in concentration. She looked up and stared at Laura. The girl had chattered since they got here on Tuesday evening. But now that she had Laura on her own, she obviously had something important to say.

Inessa said, "I... little... English... "

"I... fuck all... Russian... " said Laura.

"Girls... " She pointed at herself. "In house... many... " She put her wrists together as if they were handcuffed. "Men... " She squared her shoulders and puffed out her cheeks – pantomiming a muscleman, Laura guessed. The girl went on: "Take girls... houses... to... to fuck... men... " She imitated cash being handed over.

"Yeah, I get it," said Laura.

The girl nodded.

Laura said, "So?"

345

The girl's face wrinkled, and tears glistened in her eyes. She said, "You... " She made claws and snarled. "Vaukalak... vaukalak... vourdalak... "

"I don't understand."

"Vourdalak... " The girl snarled again.

"All right."

"You... save... "

Laura heard footsteps in the corridor. She scuttled to the door and sniffed. Picked up a scent. "What did you bring?" she said.

"Meat," he said .

He limped in carrying a brown paper bag, and Laura smelled the food and salivated at the odour.

"This one," she said, "she's saying stuff to me. What's – "

The girl said, "Vaukalak... vourdalak..." and pointed at Laura.

Dasaev put the bag down.

"Belarusian. And Russian. Same word."

"What's it mean?"

"Werewolf."

* * * *

Laura packed a rucksack with a change of clothes. She slung it on her back and said to Dasaev, "You going back to Russia after this?"

He told her yes.

"How are you going to take Procter and Ruth back with you? Especially if you're here, you know, undercover."

He said he didn't know. He took two penicillin and swallowed them dry. The nurse had come over again the previous night and looked at his wounds. Told him once more to go to hospital before giving him another dose of procaine.

Laura said, "You might not have to worry about it, not if I get to Ruth first."

He narrowed his eyes and his cheeks reddened. "He has something."

"Who has?" she said.

"Procter. He has something."

346

"What does he have?"

"I don't know. Blood, my bosses say. And they want it. I think maybe their bosses want it, too." He told her Procter was injecting Kolodenko with the blood.

Laura creased her brow. She thought about what Procter might have in his possession and then guessed: "It's my blood."

"Your blood?"

"That's how he turned Ruth Templeton into a werewolf. The only way."

She told him about the Greenacres and the Templetons. Told him what happened to her in England.

"But I don't know why he was injecting your Russian guy with it," she said. "Unless he had my genes or the Templeton genes, it would do nothing. Blood poisoning, maybe."

Dasaev shrugged. "Procter's way of making himself special to Kolodenko, perhaps. Lying to him about the special blood. Saying it could make him live forever." He looked at her. "Why would they want your blood? If there is no Greenacre or Templeton, they can't use it to make... another you."

"They can experiment, can't they. They can carry out research. They might find something, I don't know, a component that they can use. Who knows? So you're going to bring them the blood?"

"My job." He shrugged. "I'll see."

"In the car, you told me about your wife. You should go back to her."

"Back?"

"And tell her to fuck off."

"Oh, good advice."

"This other girl likes you. This Dominika. You like her?"

"I'm married, and I promised to be faithful. It's my duty to at least try to salvage my relationship."

"That takes two."

Dasaev looked at his cowboy boots.

Laura breathed out. She said, "You can't compromise on happiness, Lev."

"You do."

She stared into his eyes and said, "If I didn't, we would die. Him and me."

"Looks like someone wanted you dead anyway. Whether you were with him or not. You should've just got together. It makes no sense, this being apart. This would still have happened. They would have come for you still. You shouldn't compromise on happiness."

Laura lowered her gaze. Tears welled. Her bad eye felt sore.

"I am sure he'll be OK, your man," said Dasaev.

Inessa nudged her arm.

Laura snapped out of her gloom. "Yes, OK. I'm coming." She looked up at Dasaev. "You're a good man. Like my man. I see it in your eyes, and I smell it on you. You get home and dump your wife and be with this Dominika. You get home."

He smiled at her and nodded.

She went on tiptoe and kissed his cheek.

CHAPTER 94.
THE MUIRS AND THE SEARS.

"YOU idiots," said Ruth. "You useless idiots."

Nick Sears lowered his gaze. The man looked tired. His eyes were bruised. Scratches peppered his face. Procter smirked. He liked seeing people humiliated. As long as it wasn't him. The men, four of them, sat on the couch: Nick Sears, his son, Billy, and the brothers, Donny and Jason Muir.

Ruth, standing near the fireplace in a red dress, went on:

"Dreadful mess you made of killing John Thorn. A simple task, surely. What happened?"

They said what had happened, and Procter tutted and shook his head.

Ruth glared at him. "I don't know why you're tutting over there, Lawrence. You're no better, are you? I should savage you all, I really should. So you can't even tell me if Thorn *is* actually dead?"

"We don't know, Ruth. We... we were injured. My son was injured. We had to get out of there. We couldn't have fought Thorn again."

"You are cowards," she said, her voice laced with fury. "I've not heard from Cole either. I swear that I will kill you all if you fail me again."

"Give us the strength that you have, Ruth," said Sears, "and we shan't. We need to be more than human. We need to be like you."

"You two," she said, gesturing to the Muirs.

They were in their mid-twenties. Good-looking men. Dark-haired and tall. Had that Templeton swagger about them. Procter hated them immediately.

"You lost your brother at Trafalgar Square," said Ruth.

"His name was Kevin," said Jason. He had a goatee. Procter liked it and scratched his chin, wondering if facial hair would enhance his looks. Jason continued: "We want her dead, Aunt Ruth."

"Yes, darlings, I know. So do I. And she should've been, were it not for Lawrence's useless friends."

"Now hang on – "

"Sit down, Lawrence. I've had enough of you. Get the blood."

Procter seethed. He strode out of the living room. *Bitch*, he thought. *Hate you, you bitch.* But he worshipped her too. That was the trouble. He craved her attention. He lusted for her praise. He couldn't get enough of her. And she despised him.

He went into the bedroom and got the briefcase.

When he returned to the living room, Ruth was saying, "... and I shall have to leave, certainly in the next few hours – ah, Lawrence – "

"Are we leaving?" he said.

She flushed. "Soon, yes. The news is reporting Burns's disappearance. They've discovered charred bodies up in that forest. They'll identify him and his friends. And they'll trawl his properties. I've not been here forty-eight hours, but it's too long."

"I didn't know we'd be going." he said.

"Don't you fret about that, Lawrence. Let's have you, now. Show us what you hide in that old school satchel of yours." She clapped her hands.

Procter opened the briefcase. The six vials of blood sat in the foam inlay. He took a fresh syringe out of his pocket, ripped open the plastic bag with his teeth.

The men stood and stared. They rolled up their sleeves.

Ruth said, "Greenacre's blood and my blood. This will either kill you" – they each shot her a glance – "or make you very, very powerful."

Procter half-filled the syringe with blood from a vial marked with a white sticker. He lifted a vial with a red sticker from the briefcase, then syringed blood out of that so the two fluids were mixed in the hypodermic. "Who's first?" he said.

Billy Sears stepped forward. He glowered and said, "Me."

CHAPTER 95.
THE KENNEL.

MORRELL Danvers, thirty-five, admired the tattoo he'd had done the previous afternoon. The image inked into his left forearm in red with a black outline displayed two "Sig runes" forming the insignia of the Schutzstaffel – Hitler's SS. The tattoo went well with the *Parteiadler* wrapped around his right bicep and the numbers that ran down the inside of his right forearm: 1 4 8 8.

He put his feet up on the table and stared at the portrait of Hitler on the wall. Danvers leaped to his feet and "sieg heiled" the painting. He sat back down and finished his beer. He looked at his watch. Glanced out of the window. The sky was grey overhead. The noise of traffic wafted up from the street.

Shit, I'm bored, he thought. *Where the fuck is Wheeler Burns?*

"And what the hell am I supposed to do with these bitches?" he said to himself.

Last he'd heard from Burns was a week ago. Ordered two Belarusian girls for Sorrow Hill. Had some guests coming, said Burns.

Danvers sent him two girls and heard nothing. Not like Burns at all. The man poked his nose into every corner of the business. Wanted to know daily what was going on here at The Kennel, a four-storey tenement bought by Burns ten years previously. No one else would touch the property. Bad area and bad condition, but great to store meat.

Danvers cared nothing for the neighbourhood's reputation. This place was like a castle. Reinforced door. Windows in the lower floors blocked up and barred. They had men here – Steed and Cooper, two young skinheads who enjoyed inflicting violence – and they had guns.

Danvers scratched his beard and thought about things. He knew one of Burns's contacts in Europe had been killed recently. Didn't know the details, because he never watched the news. Too many blacks and Hispanics on TV. They were everywhere. He bunched his fists. His stomach knotted.

"Fucking America," he said.

He grabbed the phone and called Burns's number again. A dead tone. Where the hell was he? *What do you want me to do with these women, Burns?* A batch was due to be shipped out to New Jersey tomorrow. But only after Burns or his right-hand queer Cleaver had OK'd the goods.

"Steed," he called out, "Steed."

Feet clumped up the stairs. The door opened, and the nineteen year old stomped in. His saucer eyes darted around the room before settling on Danvers, who said, "Don't you knock?"

"I knew you were here. You called me. Why knock?"

Danvers blew through his teeth. "Get the truck ready. We're going to ship the New Jersey load out today."

"Shouldn't we wait for Mr Burns?"

"Mr Burns does not seem to be available."

"What about his queer?"

"Neither does his queer."

"What's going on?"

"I don't know, Steed. Just do as you're told."

Steed shrugged and left the room.

"Shut the door," said Danvers after him, but Steed didn't come back. Danvers listened to the skinhead's feet tramp down the stairs.

And then he heard the sound of metal buckling, and the alarms blared.

His hackles rose. He bolted out of the chair, out of the room. Stared down the stairs. Shouted Steed's name and Cooper's name, and shouted them again when they didn't respond. Tried to listen over the wail of the alarm.

Screams rifled through the house.

Danvers cursed and started down the stairs.

CHAPTER 96.
CHANGES.

DASAEV staked Burns's apartment.

He lounged in the Ferrari. He wore a navy-blue suit bought from a second-hand store in Brighton Beach, along with the cowboy boots. Aviators sat on his nose, hiding his dark eyes. The sun sheltered behind a band of grey clouds, so he didn't really need sunglasses. But it felt cool. They went with the Ferrari.

He'd showered in a Ukrainian hotel porter's bathroom, whose wife also made him sandwiches. The Ukrainians lived in the building across the street. They'd welcomed him the first night. *Good people*, he thought. *His people* – although not any more. Not Soviets now. All different countries.

The Russian nurse washed and dressed his wound again that morning and gave him another shot of procaine and repeated her advice that he go to New York Methodist. She was right. He should've gone to the hospital. His thigh throbbed. He couldn't put any weight on his leg without fire racing through his body. He limped around like an old man. Grimaced every time he pressed the accelerator. The Ukrainian hotel porter gave him a shepherd's staff that he'd made himself. Cherry wood with an ivory handle. The cane perched next to him in the car.

He'd parked down the road and was able to scope the entrance to the building. A doorman stood at the front. Dasaev raised his gaze to the fourth storey. He remembered what Burns told Ruth Templeton.

Keys to my – ha! – crib, as the young and the black say. Use it when you want. Feel free. Make yourselves at home. You're my guests.

Cleaver had told him which apartment it was, where it was. He thought about Cleaver now. He'd set the forest on fire. And he was dead. Dasaev knew it in his guts. The man had sacrificed himself. He went on about salvation, doing penance for what he'd done over the years. He wanted to purify his soul.

And he'd done that with fire.

Dasaev looked at his watch. He'd been here nearly ninety minutes. He'd clocked Ruth and Procter at the window of the apartment earlier. Bahrman and Stokes had left the building an hour ago, and Dasaev was ready to dart inside and smash down the door and do what he came here to do. He still had the Sig Sauer. If Ruth went animal on him, she'd get a bullet between the eyes. But after seven minutes, Bahrman and Stokes returned with four men:

First man: middle-aged, medium build, dark brown hair, walked with a limp.

Second man: late teens, medium build, reddish-brown hair, bruised face.

Third man: mid-twenties, six-two, medium build, jet-black hair, goatee.

Fourth man: ditto, without the goatee.

Three and four were twins, Dasaev guessed. One and two were father and son, maybe.

Templetons? he thought.

Laura had told him Ruth would make more werewolves. He thought about that and then thought about what Laura advised him.

Tell Galina to fuck off.

Be happy with Dominika.

But he rejected her counsel. It was wrong. Had to be. You can't turn your back on your marriage. You had to fight. His head told him so, but his heart beat to a different rhythm. His heart drummed for Dominika. He tried not to think about any of that. Focused on the job. Neck craned and eyes fixed on that large window up there. Thinking about how to deal with Procter and Ruth when the time came.

Up in the apartment, a man pressed his back against the window. Dasaev tensed and sat up. The man whipped across the glass, back and forth. Then curled up and fell to his knees. Reared up and stretched out his arms, grasping at the window frame, thrashing his head from side to side.

Dasaev knew what it meant.

Ruth Templeton was making werewolves.

* * * *

Jason Muir vomited on the carpet. He was stretched out like something crucified against the window.

Procter, empty syringe in hand, watched.

"What did you put in me?" he said.

"Same as what I put in Billy, here. Laura Greenacre's blood, combined with your auntie's blood," said Procter. He sealed the syringe in a plastic bag and dropped it into a litterbin.

Donny Muir huddled on the couch. His face had turned chalk white. His eyes were wide. His sleeve was rolled up, ready for the needle. He gawped at his retching brother. The smell of puke filled the apartment. Procter unwrapped a clean syringe. He smirked at Donny. He filled the hypodermic again. Blood from a white-stickered vial and a red-stickered one.

"Come on then, sunshine," Procter said to Donny.

"I'm dying. I feel like I'm on fire," said Jason.

Billy, rolled up on an armchair and, coated in sweat, said, "Take it, you coward, just take it. The pain's our pain. It's Templeton pain. It's clan pain. It's us changing. Becoming who we really are. Take it."

Nick Sears had been on all fours at the fireplace for ten minutes. He'd thrown up on the slates. He panted like a dog, and sweat poured off him and onto the carpet. Blood dripped from his nose.

Jason collapsed and writhed on the floor. His back arched. His face contorted. His muscles corded. Snot dribbled from his nose and stuck to his moustache.

Procter ignored him and stepped towards Donny. "You now, wolf boy."

Donny blinked. "I – I don't – I don't think – "

Procter frowned. "Do you want me to tell Ruth that you're a coward? Do you know what she'll do? She won't just shout at you, you know? You're family. You've no choice. If you turn away now, you'll die. She'll kill you."

"I'll fucking kill you," said Billy, his brow knitted with rage.

"You're a good one, Billy," said Procter.

Jason threw up again. The smell was awful now.

"Come on, Donny," said Procter. "Give me your arm."

"No, no I don't want to, I – "

"Give him your fucking arm, Donny," said Jason.

Donny turned to stare at his brother.

Puke dribbled from Jason's mouth. His face was dark and his eyes bloodshot.

"Give him your fucking arm," he said again.

Donny kept his eyes on Jason. His mouth stood open. Gave Procter his arm. Procter smiled and grabbed the arm. Stuck the needle into the flesh. Donny didn't flinch. Kept staring at his brother.

"Why – why does it hurt?" said the older Sears.

"You're changing," said Procter. He drew the needle out of Donny's flesh and put a piece of disinfected cotton wool on the pinprick of blood. He made Donny press the cotton wool to the wound. Donny still stared at his brother and rocked back and forth on the couch.

Procter went on:

"Your DNA is melding with Greenacre's DNA and your aunt's. The ancient codes in your genes are switching on again. It's remarkable. It's incredible. It is beyond me, to be honest. I'm only a doctor, not a scientist. Wish I could market it and – "

Procter stopped talking.

Donny had turned to gawp at him. The young man's mouth fell open. His throat went up and down.

Procter smirked and said, "Does it hurt?"

Donny jerked.

Vomit gushed from his mouth and washed away Procter's sneer.

CHAPTER 97.
FREEDOM.

THE women filed out of the room, flooding the corridor. They swept past Laura after she'd gone from room to room, shouldering the doors open.

The women screamed at first, and then Laura said, "Get out, all of you."

One room housed white women and girls. More than thirty, Laura guessed. And when Inessa shouted at them, Laura figured they were Russian or Belarusian or wherever Inessa came from. Inessa ushered the women out. Shoved them, shouted at them. They piled down the corridor.

The second room was full of black women. They squealed and cried as Laura hurried them out. A third room along the same corridor contained Asian women – Chinese, Filipino, and Thai.

As the women crowded the corridor and herded down stairs, Laura studied the third room. It reeked of sweat and damp and rotten food. Plaster peeled, and chunks of it had been gouged out of the wall.

Graffiti smattered everything: the ceiling, the floor, the blacked-out windows. Words in different languages. Chinese characters and Cyrillic script. Drawings of islands and of ships, of lorries packed with stick figures, of manacles and of sex were scrawled everywhere too. Laura traced the women's story from the drawings. The same story every time. Captivity and abuse.

Blankets covered the floor. Laura saw needles too. She saw crushed beer cans. Half-eaten, mouldy loaves of bread. She smelled rats and urine and shit.

Her gaze fell on a Chinese girl, no older than twelve. The child sat on a rotting mattress. Her legs were hidden under a blanket, and her bones showed through paper-thin skin. The girl's face was pale. Her brown eyes were wide. Her dark hair was scraped back over her skull. She looked like a ghost. Something that had died in this room and still lingered here, looking for peace.

"Out," said Laura.

The girl quaked.

Laura said, "Out," again, this time making a gesture with her hand.

The girl didn't move. Started crying. Laura's heart twisted. She went to the girl and said, "Come on, sweetheart," and whipped the blanket away.

Laura gasped.

The girl's legs were gone. Stumps from mid-thigh down. The child shuddered and wept. Rage seared Laura. It felt like fire coursing through her veins.

She scooped the girl up in her arms, and the child felt like a pillow.

She carried her out into the corridor. Inessa was there, scurrying the women out. Laura gestured for Inessa to take the girl. Inessa got two women to help her and they ferried the child down the corridor.

Laura's heart felt heavy, watching as they took the girl away, Inessa looking back with wide, glassy eyes.

Laura and the Belarusian girl had taken the bus from Brighton Beach to Nostrand Avenue in Brooklyn, and then walked. Inessa seemed to know the way, although they got lost a couple of times. Laura became frustrated, unable to understand the Belarusian's rants. Inessa attempted her broken English now and again, but she might as well have stuck to her own language. They finally found the house, Inessa pointing and saying, "Here... here... kennel... dogs... "

Laura had handed Inessa her rucksack and drove her shoulder into the door, and it buckled. Inessa gawped at her strength. Laura shrugged and said, "*Vaukalak*, huh?" and then rammed the door again. The hinges snapped. She kicked down the door, and they stormed through the trash-laden foyer, up the stairs. Inessa knew where she was going. This had been home.

Now Laura told Inessa to get out.

She heard footsteps stomp down from the upper storeys.

A man's voice said, "What the fuck is going on? Cooper, where are you? Danvers. Danvers, they're getting away."

And she wheeled, faced the stairwell at the end of the passage.

A young skinhead leaped into the corridor. Muscles swelled under his tight-fitting Swastika T-shirt.

His face twisted with fury and he said to Laura, "Who the fuck are you, you fucking whore?"

"I'm bad news, that's who I am," she said.

"Get those bitches back," Swastika T-shirt said.

"Make me."

"Make you? I'm going to make you my bitch."

He stalked towards her. His face purple and hardened by hate.

Laura snarled at him.

"Don't you fucking show me your teeth, bitch. I'll knock them out of your bitch head," he said.

She leaped at him and locked her knees under his armpits and pummelled his face and head with her fists. He yelled, reeling away, tripped over his feet and hit the ground.

Laura sprang off him. Raced down to the end of the corridor. Watched the women file down the stairs.

Swastika T-shirt lifted himself off the floor. Cursed Laura again. He reached into his back pocket. Took out a flick knife and snapped open the blade. He charged down towards her.

She tightened her muscles.

And unfolded out of herself.

Her clothes strained and tore as her body transformed. Coarse, black fur sprouted from smooth, white flesh. Claws jutted from her knuckles as her fingers curled into fists and became joined with her palms. Her muzzle stretched, and her teeth lengthened and sharpened.

Swastika T-shirt stopped in his tracks and gawked. He backed up.

His fear filled her nostrils.

He screamed and turned and ran.

As she chased him down, shouts came from the foyer.

A man's voice saying, "Get back, whores, get back up those stairs," and the women screaming.

* * * *

Cooper came back from the store to find the door smashed off its hinges. At first he thought, *Shit, the cops*, but he didn't see any CVPIs with their sirens wailing and their lights flashing in the street.

He barged through the broken door, and the women flooded down the stairs. They screamed and screeched, and their languages crisscrossed each other – it was like the Tower of Babel, and his head throbbed.

He dropped the grocery bag. Food and drink spilled. He got out his ASP baton.

Should've had my gun, he thought.

He whipped the baton, and it extended. He struck the first girl across her face. A welt rose on her cheek. Blood sprayed from her nose. She fell and didn't move. The other women cowered on the stairwell.

"What the fuck's going on?" he said.

His heart hammered.

"Get back, whores, get back up those stairs," he said and laid into them, swinging with the baton, smacking flesh, the women screeching and trying to pile back up stairs.

He couldn't force them back. Too many of them were stacked there in the stairwell. He retreated and called out for Steed and Danvers. He told the women to get back up the stairs again, and they began to go, tripping over each other, shoving, wanting to get away from him and his baton. The woman lying on the floor groaned. A wound scored her face from jaw line to temple. He bent down and grabbed her by the hair, dragging her to the stairs.

Someone screamed and he froze. He let go of the woman and craned his neck. Another scream. And it wasn't a woman's scream, either. He heard a sound: the sound of... what?... material being ripped. He creased his brow.

"Steed, you up there?"

No answer.

"Come on – Steed?"

The women at the top of the stairs screamed now, and they were pushing forward again and coming back down, running into the ones at the front who were stumbling and spilling back into the foyer.

"What the fuck is going on?" he said.

Something dripped on his head. He put a hand in his hair. More drips, the liquid warm and thick. He looked at his hand.

"Jesus," he said.

It was blood.

He looked up.

The ceiling buckled, and blood seeped through the wooden panels.

Whose fucking blood?

The ceiling creaked. The floorboards above him cracked. Blood rained down, and something crashed through.

Cooper yelled out and raised his arms.

A lump of meat landed on him, laying him out.

The women screamed. They dashed past him, out of the door. He watched them bolt into the street, saw them racing away.

He groaned, his head swimming. He looked up and could see through the hole in the ceiling. He rolled the meat off him. Shook his head. Stared with horror at the carcass.

Steed.

Parts of him.

He had half a face, and his belly'd been ripped open. His guts steamed. Blood everywhere. Cooper couldn't breathe. Tried to get up but slid about in Steed's blood. He screamed. Grabbed at the last few women as they spilled out of The Kennel, but couldn't get a hold of them.

He sat in the gore, panting for breath. He looked at Steed and thought, *What the fuck did that to you?*

He heard a noise. A growling or a grunt. Something animal, anyway.

He looked up slowly.

The yellow eye fixed on him from the hole in the ceiling.

CHAPTER 98.
DEAD MEAT.

DANVERS, armed with the AK47, snuck down the stairs. He'd heard the commotion when he was on the way down earlier. Then he'd backed up, got the weapon, and thought about whether to take a look or not. Wondered if there were a way out without having to leap from the fourth-storey window. There wasn't, so he decided to confront whatever was going on down there. Screams had rifled up from down below. Steed shouting, threatening, then Steed going quiet and not responding to Danvers's calls.

Now it was quiet.

No screaming women.

No cops ordering him out with his hands up.

No gang storming through with machetes.

He got to the third-floor corridor. He called for Steed and Cooper but got no response. He checked the rooms on the third floor. Empty, apart from cobwebs, empty pizza boxes, crushed cigarette packets, mattresses.

His legs felt heavy. He couldn't breathe very well, and sweat glued his shirt to his back. The SS tattoo stung.

Second-floor corridor now. Called for Steed and Cooper again, and then said, "Is there anyone here?" but there didn't seem to be. Empty rooms again. The smell of damp and piss. To the end of the corridor. Throat dry. Down the stairs to the first floor, where the women were held.

Fuck, he thought.

They were gone.

The rooms empty.

"Fuck," he said.

How the hell had this happened? Burns would kill him. *But where was Burns?*

His eyes darted around the corridor. His nerves were fried now. He shuffled towards the end of the corridor. The floor over there seemed buckled. Floorboards sticking up. He felt a breeze gush over his face, and it felt good.

He came to a hole in the floor, edged towards it. Something had crashed through, smashing through the floorboards. And there was blood here, too. On the walls. He smelled it. A coppery odour. He'd smelled it before. Many times.

He snuck up to the hole and called Steed and Cooper again, and he peered down through the floor into the foyer and nearly fainted.

Blood and flesh covered the lobby. He saw Cooper's head in the gore and then recognized a part of Steed's face.

He started to shake and say "Jesus, Jesus, Jesus" over and over.

A dark shape moved across Steed's and Cooper's bodies. An animal that Danvers couldn't name. The creature craned its neck and glared up at Danvers through one eye. The beast curled back its top lip to show long teeth smeared with blood

Danvers's hands sweated. He aimed the AK47 at the animal. The creature growled and sprang upwards. Burst through the hole and knocked Danvers back. He reeled, the AK47 slipping from his hands. He crawled away down the corridor, whimpering a prayer, promising God he'd be good.

The floor trembled beneath Danvers as the monster came bounding after him.

CHAPTER 99.
PLAN OF ACTION.

PARK AVENUE, MANHATTAN

"WE draw her out with carnage," said Ruth. They were all in the kitchen. Stokes had been charged with cleaning the vomit and the blood in the living room. Procter had laughed at the big man when Ruth ordered him to wipe the carpet. The giant had got on his knees like a charwoman and washed the sick.

Ruth went on: "She cannot resist a fight. She sees werewolves on the streets, she'll come out to face them. It's the nature of the beast, you see. It's territorial. The need to be the alpha."

Ruth, Procter, and Sears sat at the table. Sears smoked one of his cigars. He was pale and shivered a lot. They had a coffee pot going. Procter had drunk three cups. He buzzed. Injecting the men and watching their spasms excited him. He felt like a god who was making monsters. Billy, Jason, and Donny were perched on stools at the breakfast counter, drinking water. They looked pale and drawn. *Soon be all right*, thought Procter. *They'll get over it quickly enough.*

Jason said, "That's what our brother did. What Michael did in Trafalgar Square. Challenged her to a fight."

"And look what happened to them," said Donny.

"They didn't challenge her," said Ruth. "They went out killing. There was no plan in place. No strategy. This is the only way. She can't resist it. Can't resist getting involved."

"But there are only four of us," said Jason. "There were loads of them."

"You lack confidence, Jason," said Ruth.

"I just don't fancy dying, that's all."

"Think like that, and she's beaten you already," said Billy.

Ruth said, "You'll have insurance."

"Insurance?" said Jason.

She gestured towards Bahrman. He loitered at the door that led to the roof deck, smoking and drinking a beer. He raised his Budweiser in a toast. He strolled over. Slammed his beer down on the table. Stubbed the cigarette out on the tiled floor. He dragged out a chair and sat. He said, "Me and Stokes, we'll be there with you. We'll be armed. Once she's out in the open, she's ours."

"So we're just going to be bait, then," said Billy.

"I don't care how you view yourselves," said Ruth, "the goal is Laura Greenacre's death. She's somehow survived one attempt, but we'll blame that on" – she glowered at Procter – "poor choices, bad planning, amateurs."

Procter blushed and started to say something, but Ruth told him to shut up.

Billy said, "Why can't we kill her? She killed my brothers – I want to kill her."

Ruth looked at him. "It doesn't matter *how* she dies. What matters is that she *does* die."

"How do you get your muscles so big?" said Donny to Bahrman, who grinned and said, "It's all the killing I've done, son. Killing makes everything big on a man."

"I go to the gym, but nothing happens," said Donny. He flexed his arm. Bahrman laughed.

Billy said, "So did it all shrink again when you ran away from her at Templeton Hall, Mr Bahrman?"

Donny Muir sniggered. Bahrman's eyes blazed.

"We retreated, kid," he said.

"You ran away," said Billy.

Bahrman's neck corded.

"Listen, little boy," said Bahrman, "I'm being patient here, so you watch your mouth or – "

"Or what?" said Billy. "Or fucking what?"

Bahrman's brow knitted. He cocked his head. "That kind of mouth usually gets people shot, son."

"You remember who we are, Bahrman," said Billy. "You remember what we can be."

"What did you say?" said Bahrman. They were all looking at him now, and he looked back at them. Each one in turn.

"You heard what I said. We could kill you. Me and my dad and my cousins here, we could kill you before you'd get a chance to fire off a shot."

"Enough, now," said Ruth. "I can't bear this nonsense. This macho folly fogs everything. Keep your rage for Laura Greenacre."

Bahrman relaxed and smiled. He mimicked a gun with his finger and aimed it at Billy.

Ruth said, "All four of you, you don't know how to change yet. Time you learned. Time you got a feel of your new bodies."

"How do we do that?" said Billy.

"Go out," she said. "Do some hunting."

* * * *

Ruth said, "No mistakes this time, Lawrence."

"You can't blame me if it goes wrong," he said.

"Stop whining."

"I'm not whining. But the failure at Burns's place was not my responsibility."

"There you go again: shirking your responsibilities."

"I'm not shirking anything. I've not shirked a thing, Ruth. You've always been able to count on me, and you always will."

She smirked at him. "Of course I will, Lawrence."

The back of his neck flushed, and he was sweating.

She said, "I can smell your anger."

"I *am* angry. I'm frustrated. I'm beginning to think that I am somewhat undervalued here."

"Undervalued? You are a felon, Lawrence. You are wanted for sex crimes. If you were undervalued, I would've dumped

368

you when I was in England, advised the authorities of your whereabouts."

"You needed me. You needed the blood."

"And I still do."

He went to the sink and poured himself a glass of water. Everyone had gone: the Sears and the Muirs, and Bahrman and Stokes. Ruth was leaving too – and leaving without him. He'd travel separately, return to England alone. They'd been travelling as Mr and Mrs Smith for a while now, and Ruth didn't want to raise suspicions, she said. They'd still not heard from Ellis Cole or Ray Craig about Thorn. No one knew if he were alive or dead.

Procter said, "Are you sure these boys and Nick Sears can deal with Greenacre?"

"They have Bahrman and Stokes – and the NYPD, of course."

Procter frowned and asked her what she meant.

"What do you imagine will happen when there are reports of wild animals loose in New York, Lawrence?"

He said nothing.

Ruth continued:

"As they did in London, the authorities will send out their guns. Of course, they all carry guns here. Which is marvellous. And when they hear reports of armed men, also – Bahrman and Stokes – they'll have no misgivings. They will kill."

"But that means... that means Bahrman and Stokes are likely to get shot."

"Of course."

"And... and Nick and Billy Sears... Jason and Donny... "

"A shame, but necessary."

"You're sacrificing them."

"They're sacrificing themselves, Lawrence. For the family. For the good of the Templetons. They'll have given their lives to kill the last Greenacre werewolf. Isn't that something worth dying for?"

CHAPTER 100.
TO YOU ALL FLESH WILL COME.

DASAEV entered the lobby of the building and nodded to the doorman.

He'd watched the four men leave, followed soon after by Bahrman and Stokes. Stokes returned ten minutes later in a Ford Taurus. He parked the car outside the building and spoke to the doorman before going inside. Fifteen minutes later, he came out carrying a suitcase, followed by Ruth Templeton. They got into the Taurus and drove away.

Dasaev had waited another hour. No one else he recognized came out or went in. There was no sign of Bahrman. That left Procter on his own in the apartment.

He waited for the elevator now and stood next to a blonde woman in a fur coat. She looked at him and smiled. She said, "Which floor, honey?" She was in her late twenties. Had skin like porcelain and emerald eyes. She smelled of roses.

He said, "Fourth," and she said, "Hey, me too. Let's go up together."

The elevator arrived, and Dasaev let the woman in first. He looked at her shoes. Red high heels that clicked on the panelled floor as she stepped in.

The elevator hummed upwards.

The woman said, "Have you been in a fight?"

"Car accident," said Dasaev.

"You're foreign. German?"

He nodded.

"I like your stick," she said.

Dasaev looked at his cane and said thank you.

"Not very talkative, are you, mister. You on the fourth as well? Hope we're not seeing the same guy? Maybe he's kinky, huh? Likes to watch." She pouted at him. "If I'm lucky. Or maybe he likes it both ways. You know?"

Dasaev frowned.

"There are only two apartments on every floor, mister. I got called an hour ago. A gentleman wants some company. An English guy. What about you? You don't look like, well, you know... "

He broke into a sweat. He looked straight at her, and her emerald eyes glittered. Her scarlet lips caught the light. She stepped towards him and cocked her head. "Maybe we should practise before we get to him?" she said.

The elevator stopped at the fourth floor.

The woman sighed and stepped back.

The door slid open.

Dasaev turned to step out of the elevator.

Lawrence Procter's smile dwindled.

* * * *

Laura retrieved the rucksack she'd stowed under the stairwell in the foyer. She took wipes and a towel out of the bag and hurriedly cleaned the blood and gore from her face and body, then used the towel to dry her hair. She took a Sesame Street T-shirt, jeans, underwear, and a pair of Chadwicks flat shoes out of the pack and got dressed. She put on sunglasses. She stuffed the towel and wipes back in the rucksack and skipped over the dead bodies in the foyer. She peeked out of the door. No one in the street. Empty buildings boarded up, covered in graffiti. Sirens wailed nearby. She bolted out of the tenement and sprinted away down the road, the wind rushing through her hair, heart pummelling her breast.

371

She ran till she reached Nostrand Avenue. She went into a Golden Krust and sat at a table. Ordered coffee and bulla cakes. Stuffed one in her mouth, crunched and chewed. Crumbs dry on her tongue and her gums, in between her teeth. The ginger flavour got rid of the raw meat taste in her mouth. She washed the cake down with coffee.

Meat was good, but blood and gore made her breath stink and stained her teeth. She didn't want to draw attention to herself.

She sat in the Golden Krust and relaxed. Her body temperature rose when she was in her werewolf form. It always took a while to cool off. She kept her good eye on the door. The other eye hurt. It was sore and kept weeping. She didn't know if she'd lose it or not. Eyes weren't that important. She could always smell. But she wouldn't want to go blind. She thought about not looking into John's eyes again, and it made her heart shrivel.

She wondered where the women had gone. More than a hundred loose in Brooklyn. That wasn't going to go unnoticed. The police would pick up a few, question them, and finally get some sense. And it would lead them to the house where by then those three thugs would be rotting nicely.

A feast for the rats, thought Laura.

She thought about the Russian and if he'd got to Procter. Found what he'd been sent here to find. Her blood. A dull ache gnawed at her belly. There would never be peace for her. Always someone hunting her, seeking her out, delving into her life. If it weren't Ruth or the Templetons, it would be scientists or governments or armies. Everyone trying to harness her powers.

She put ten dollars on the table and left the Golden Krust.

She thought, *Where now?* and felt lost.

She couldn't leave New York. There was a fight to be had.

She could make her way back to her own apartment. It wasn't too far. But she'd just sit there, mulling things over and getting gloomy.

Best to keep moving, she thought. *Sniff things out. Keep my nose to the ground. Walk the streets.*

And wait.

* * * *

Procter wheeled away. He ran up the corridor.

Dasaev stumbled out of the elevator.

The woman yelped.

Dasaev hobbled after Procter. He grimaced against the pain in his leg.

Procter whined as he ran. He wore a red silk dressing gown, and it flapped behind him as he moved. He dived through a doorway, and Dasaev heard the door slam.

He got to the door and pulled the Sig Sauer out of his belt and stepped back and fired three times at the handle.

The woman, who'd stepped out of the elevator, screeched.

Dasaev looked at her and told her to go home.

He kicked open the door and held out the gun. Shuffled forward into the entry foyer. The passageway was dimly lit. Mirrors with gold frames on the walls. The carpet thick under his feet.

"Procter. I'll find you," he said.

He didn't have much time. The gunshots would've alerted someone. They'd call the police. Or the woman in the elevator had already done so.

He stalked forward. A door to his right. He kicked it open and slipped into the room. A bedroom. Double bed. En suite bathroom. Two cupboards. He thought for a minute, then backed out of the bedroom. He moved forward. The living room opened out in front of him, and to his right, the corridor dog-legged into the kitchen. Dasaev pondered. He chose the living room. The smell of disinfectant hung in the air. The floor-to-ceiling window looked down on Park Avenue. The window in which he'd seen the man twitching and thrashing about.

To his left, an open door leading through to the dining room. He headed for it.

A crash came from somewhere, dishes smashing.

The kitchen.

He stiffened.

A flash of red swept into the foyer and raced towards the door.

Dasaev set off after Procter.

Procter made it to the door and was about to open it when Dasaev fired just above his head. The bullet splintered the door. Procter squatted and covered his head with the briefcase he carried. He begged and whined saying, "Please, please don't kill me – it wasn't me, I didn't do anything – it was Ruth, all Ruth..."

Dasaev limped over to the doctor. Grabbed him by the collar of his dressing gown and hauled him to his feet. He slid the gun into Procter's mouth and said, "Any trouble, I put your brains on the wall. OK?"

Procter nodded.

He rammed Procter against the wall, yanked open the door, grabbed the doctor again, and shoved him out into the corridor.

He stepped out into the corridor and looked right and left. Thought about the elevator. Decided to use the stairs. He nudged Procter with the cane, forcing him to move.

"Open the door, down the stairs," he said.

"W-what do you think you're going to do to me?" said the doctor.

Dasaev smacked him on the backside with the cane and Procter yelped.

"Go," said Dasaev, "and don't talk."

They entered the stairwell.

Gunfire erupted. Dasaev ducked. Bullets raked plaster from the wall next to his head. He threw himself at Procter, and they tumbled down the flight of stairs.

CHAPTER 101.
GUNFIGHT ON PARK
AVENUE.

DASAEV dragged Procter down the stairs. The doctor bumped all the way to the bottom. His robe became undone. He wore nothing underneath and tried to cover his crotch.

Bullets pinged off the banister. They thudded into the wall. They zipped past Dasaev's head. He gritted his teeth and kept moving. Braced for the pain of a bullet. His arm was like lead as he hauled Procter. His thighs felt like they had rocks tied to them. The wound in his leg pulsed.

He heard a woman cry up the flight of stairs. More gunshots. Tearing into the wall near his head. Splintering the banister. Procter wailed.

Dasaev grunted through the pain and came to the exit and kicked it open. The fresh air hit him, and he gasped, head spinning, the street swimming.

He pressed the gun into Procter's nape and told him to move. They stumbled down a path. Sweat poured from Dasaev's scalp, down his back. His hands were slick. He gripped Procter's collar tight. Jammed the barrel into the back of the doctor's neck.

Dasaev hobbled down the alley. His heart thundered. His lungs burned. Into the street. Pedestrians seeing him, seeing his gun. They scattered. Dropped their shopping and let go of their dogs. A chihuahua yelped at Dasaev, tried to nip his heels. A woman screamed.

A shot came from behind him.

He ducked and shoved Procter.

Another shot, bullets rutting the bricks.

"Stop, you fucker," said a voice, "I don't want to fucking shoot you."

Dasaev ignored the warning. He said to Procter, "Yellow Ferrari. Get into the back, now," and delved in his pocket for the key, found it, and pressed the button to open the car.

He slammed Procter against the car. Opened the door. Booted the doctor inside, the doctor yelping. Dasaev shut the door. He wheeled round.

His eyes widened and his jaw dropped open.

A muscle-head moved down the pavement towards him. The man held a gun to the head of the woman from the elevator.

Dasaev blanked out the chaos around him. The fleeing pedestrians, the yipping dogs, the blaring horns. He looked the woman in the eye and saw dread in there.

The thug aimed the gun at Dasaev and fired. Dasaev ducked. The Ferrari's rear window shattered.

Sirens wailed in the distance, but they were getting closer. Heading their way.

The gunman glanced up the street. He said to Dasaev, "Time you got us out of here," and shot the woman in the leg.

CHAPTER 102
WARS AND RUMOURS OF WAR.

GRAND STATION TERMINAL

THEY would attack, but where from? And whom would it involve? Would Ruth put herself in harm's way?

Laura had taken the subway from Brooklyn all the way to Grand Central Terminal. Seemed like a good location for her to keep watch on what was going on. Dasaev told her that Burns's apartment was somewhere on Park Avenue, which she could access from the station. Dasaev wasn't sure Ruth and Procter would be at the apartment. Laura could've gone over there, checked it out. But she didn't want Ruth to see her coming. Wouldn't walk right through the front door. If Ruth were a werewolf, she'd have werewolf instincts: she'd smell Laura coming.

No, best lie in wait. Ruth would show her hand, Laura had no doubt. And when she did, there'd be a fight.

Laura loitered in the main concourse. She sat near the information booth, under the four-faced clock. She drank coffee. She had a ham bagel. She wondered if Ruth would move today or leave it till morning. She looked round the concourse. Commuters hurried to meet their trains. Rushed off the platforms to make their meetings. Shopped in the boutiques and stores. Ate and drank in the restaurants and bars. Laura smelled the air and drew in all the scents around her: sweat, perfumes, meat, booze, coffee, petrol fumes, diesel, blood.

She unwrapped her bagel. Went to take a bite when gasps and shrieks swept across the concourse. Anxiety made her skin ripple.

She rose and scooped up her rucksack. Stared towards the eastern end of the main concourse. A crowd had gathered and stared at the huge TV screen above the stationmaster's office. The screen showed a female TV reporter. Behind her, a line of cops guarded a police barrier.

The volume rose, and the TV reporter's voice became clearer.

Laura, gaze fixed on the screen, strode over towards the crowd.

The screen told her the reporter was called Fay Colsano and that she was reporting from Park Avenue, and a ticker running across the bottom of the screen said, "Woman shot in Park Avenue gunfight... police hunt two men... yellow Ferrari sought... "

Laura craned her neck and stayed at the back of the crowd. Gasps and curses swept through the commuters watching the news programme.

The TV reporter was saying, "... we don't know who the woman is, we've not been told if she's linked to the men, but she's been taken to North General Hospital, where she is being treated for gunshot wounds. I understand that she is not seriously injured."

Wind whipped the reporter's chestnut-coloured hair about her face. She had her finger in her ear, keeping her earpiece in, Laura guessed.

The reporter said, "Joining me now is" – the camera panned right to show a bald-headed man in his late forties – "Detective Anthony Ryman from the Midtown South Precinct Detective Division. Detective Ryman, has gang warfare come to the streets of Park Avenue?"

Ryman seemed to bristle. He said, "Fay, this is a solitary incident. We're not linking it to any gangs. We're not linking it to anything at the moment."

"Down in Brooklyn today, dozens of women, thought to be foreign and possibly trafficked into the US, were found wandering the streets. They've been traced to a house in south Brooklyn where your colleagues found three badly mutilated bodies."

Laura sweated. She couldn't move. It was as if her bones had melded together.

"That house, Detective Ryman, appears to be owned by a man called Wheeler Burns, who also owns the apartment outside which the shooting took place."

The detective blushed. "What are you asking me, Fay?"

"I'm asking you if the incidents are linked, detective."

"I don't know. We are in contact with our colleagues in Brooklyn."

"Do you think they're linked?"

"I couldn't tell you at this time."

"There was a fire at Wheeler Burns's Hudson Valley home a few days ago. He's missing. Any comment on that?"

"I couldn't comment on that, Fay. That is a matter for the authorities in Dutchess County, and we will be liaising with them."

"Any trace of the yellow Ferrari yet?"

"No trace yet."

She turned back to camera, ignoring the cop, and said, "The police seem to have few leads at the moment. But we'll be here bringing you the latest. Back to you in the studio."

The screen switched back to an anchor. Laura whirled away from the TV. Her gaze flitted over the concourse. More people had stopped what they were doing to look at the coverage. She felt conspicuous. Her nerves twinged, and she felt her blood quicken. She scanned the terminal.

It's beginning again, she thought.

And she knew, like before, that it would end darkly.

PART FOUR.

WEREWOLVES IN NEW YORK.

CHAPTER 103.
CHASING THE STORY.

FAY Colsano stared at the pint of Guinness on the bar in front of her.

What a bastard, she thought, *what a shitty thing to say*.

"We're sending in Grover Chaney, Fay. This is a big story now, and he wants to cover it."

The editor's voice echoed in her head:

We're sending in Grover Chaney.

Fay had asked, "Are you saying I'm not good enough, that I can't handle this story?"

They *weren't* saying that, the editor had said, what they were saying was that Grover Chaney should anchor all *New York Now!*'s main stories. After all, he was a former CNN and CBS news reporter. He was a name, he had experience. He was *New York Now!*'s chief reporter.

"You'll still be on the story, Fay," said the editor.

She'd retreated to this Irish pub on East 63ʳᵈ Street after the phone call from the editor. The dimly lit bar sported shamrock-patterned wallpaper. Green carpet stained with booze lay underfoot, and green drapes hung on the windows. A signed photo of a man called Jack Charlton was framed on the wall next to photos of the Pope and U2. An Irish tune played on the jukebox. A line of plastic leprechauns stared down from a shelf over the bar. Only half a dozen customers were in at the moment: three old men sipping brandies in a booth and two figures – young men, Fay guessed – playing pool in the back. It was dark, and she couldn't see them clearly.

Fay stared into her drink now and said, "I am good enough. I *am* good enough."

"Pardon me, ma'am?" said the bartender.

She glanced up at him.

He said, "You said something. You OK?"

She nodded and lowered her gaze again.

"You like Guinness, or was this the first place you came across?" said the bartender.

She looked up again. He was smiling. She tried to smile back, but her mouth felt heavy.

"As a matter of interest, not in an arrogant way, do you happen to know who I am?" she said.

"Yeah, I know who you are, Miss Colsano. I seen you on the TV" – he pointed up at the widescreen on the wall – "today, reporting from just down the road."

"Call me Fay, please."

"Fay, cool."

He was standing at the far end of the bar, drying a glass. He was tall. Wore an emerald-coloured,, short-sleeved shirt with the bar's name on the breast pocket. She could see the shape of his shoulders and his arms through the shirt's material. Pool balls clicked.

"Do you think I'm any good?" she said.

"Do I think you're any good? I don't know. Do you think I'm a good bartender?"

"You served me this drink. I guess that's your job, and I've got no complaints."

"You bring me stories on the *New York Now!* news channel. You do that pretty well. I got no complaints."

"Come into the light so I can see you better."

He stepped forward, and she saw he had dark hair with a green tuft on the crown, and when he got closer still she saw his blue eyes. She felt a tingle run through her. It had been a while.

She rested her elbows on the bar, tilted her head. She gave him a pout and narrowed her eyes. He leaned on the bar.

"So," he said, "you like Guinness, or what?"

"My mother was Irish. We went back there a few times when I was young. My grandfather drank this stuff. He got me into it. You know County Wicklow?"

"I'm from right here in New York, ma'am. Never been further east than Queens, never been further west than Ohio. Went to Montreal a couple of times. Been to Miami, too."

"Don't you have an urge?"

"To do what?"

"I don't know. Go further east, maybe. Or south."

"Not really."

"How about getting out of here and being the best you can be?"

"I am the best I can be."

"How do you know that?"

"You just said so. I served you the drink, I did that pretty good, so I must be doing OK."

She chuckled. "But in life. Don't you want to be the best you can be in life?"

He shrugged. He smelled of tobacco and aftershave – a musky, heavy aftershave. "I come into work every day, I get paid, I go home, feed the cat, go out with my friends."

"You got a girlfriend or anything?"

"No, single. You?"

She felt heat come into her face. "No one."

"Why?"

"Why?" she said. "I don't know. No time? I don't know. What about you? Why aren't you... a couple?"

"I like it on my own. I get to do what I want to do."

"Don't you want kids, a family?"

"Why?"

She thought for a moment and then said, "Yeah, why."

"Are you going to drink that? You've been staring at it a while. How about a fresh one?"

She swigged it. The stout was sharp and smooth at the same time. The drink left froth on her upper lip, and she licked it away. "I'm OK with this one."

"You look more like a vodka martini lady," he said.

"We're all full of surprises, aren't we."

"Yes, we are."

She stared at him and thought about things. About the effort she'd put into her career. About the ambitions she harboured of being picked up by a major news provider. About searching for that feeling of contentment her father always told her she should look for. He couldn't tell her what it should feel like: "You'll know, sweetheart," he'd said.

But she didn't. Had no idea. Looked for it the only way she knew how: by working hard, by striving to be a success. Work and career was the way, she'd thought, not love and relationships. So she'd abandoned her heart and trusted her head in the search for this contentment.

She'd not found it yet, so there might be another way.

The words came out of her before she'd thought them:

"Would you like to sleep with me?"

She convulsed, as if jets of electricity were shooting through her.

He raised an eyebrow. "Only if you'd like to sleep with me back."

Her breast warmed, and her belly fluttered. She needed it so badly. She'd ignored her cravings, her desires. He was leaning in and she was leaning in and she smelled his hot breath and her thighs were burning.

"Where?" she said.

"Come behind the bar, in the back."

She got up, barely able to stand, imagining her void full of him. Her nails digging into his flesh. Her teeth gnawing at his shoulders. The throb of him inside her. She put out a hand to balance herself. Hooked her hair behind her ear.

"Two more Magners over here, mate," said a voice.

The bartender – *what was his name? Oh God, what was his name?* – turned and stuttered his words, saying he'd be right over, no problem.

Fay leaned against a bar stool and gasped. She put a hand to her breast. The heat rinsed out of her, and doubts scurried through her mind.

"Bit quiet here today," said the customer, an English accent.

"Yeah... livens up later, you know," said the bartender.

"Looked liked it was about to get lively right now," said the man.

Fay wheeled round. The man who was lean and tall and in his early twenties grinned at Fay. He had a goatee beard, and his eyes glinted in the half-light. His friend loomed out of the darkness. They looked alike. Only the second one didn't have a beard.

"I think I'll go," she said, "thanks for the drink."

"Stay," said the Englishman, "stay and have a drink, come on. We're strangers here in New York. It's OK. It'll be fun."

She looked at the man and then at her bartender. He raised his shoulders as if to say why not.

The Englishman came towards her and smiled, his pale face smooth. Fay quivered. He oozed confidence. He offered his hand and said, "How do you do? I'm Jason and that's my brother Donny."

CHAPTER 104.
SCENT.

LAURA went on all fours and sniffed the pavement.

Her senses fizzed.

Someone said, "What the hell's she doing?"

She didn't care. She continued to smell the urine on the pavement.

Male, she thought. Not Ruth, then. But Ruth's kind. Her own kind, too.

Werewolf.

Geographically, Laura didn't know where she was. She'd picked up the scent a while ago. A hint on the breeze to begin with. Drawing her in. She'd stuck her nose in the air and let it lead her. Blind to everyone and everything in her path. Her blood raced. Her skin rippled, the animal inside her awakening. She'd already called upon her wolf sight. Anyone looking carefully at her would've seen the yellow iris and the black pupil of her good eye.

Another voice said, "Look at that crazy woman."

"Is she sniffing pee?"

"Oh, that's gross."

And then laughter.

Laura looked round and snarled at the group. She sprang to her feet and ran down the street. The scent stations so far had been every 100 yards. Typical of the male werewolf. They urinated to mark their territory and their hunting ground.

She picked up the odour of the next station. Laura's sense of smell enabled her to trace an odour that was more than a mile away. It was more difficult in a city – you had traffic, you had people, you had buildings. But because this werewolf was marking, she was able to track him easily.

Maybe he wanted to be tracked, she thought.

She kept going, dismissing the idea. She didn't care about walking into traps. She'd fight herself out of them.

Laura stopped. The scent was heavy here. Her head spun. She felt dizzy. Her heart pounded. A musky odour wafted on the breeze. She turned slowly towards it. Stared into the entrance of an underground parking lot. Looked into the darkness and growled. She skulked forward and squatted at the entrance. The patch of urine darkened the concrete. She sniffed the piss and the scent was the same. Laura stared into the gloom of the parking lot again and her hackles rose.

Something in there.

She sniffed. The odour of dead meat drifted from the lot.

She listened. She clawed through the noises of New York, hearing something through the forest of sound.

A growl.

A scream.

Adrenaline jetted through her.

Laura shot into the parking lot. She hunkered down and gave a low growl. She sniffed.

They were here.

A scream came from the depths of the lot. Laura went towards the noise, springing off the cars and buckling their roofs as she bounded from one to the other.

Her skin rippled, and her body undid itself. Her muzzle and jaws started to expand. Teeth pressed through her gums. Her breath fogged out of her nostrils.

A woman screamed, and Laura heard the word "camera" in her plea.

Laura squatted on the roof of a car, waited. Saw shapes in the darkness. Smelled male werewolves – two of them. Smelled meat, hot and steaming. The screaming woman stumbled out of the shadows, phone in hand, hair wild, blood streaking her face.

She was the TV reporter from the big screen at Grand Station Terminal.

* * * *

"Get a camera over here now," said Fay Colsano. Panic laced her voice. Growls filled the background.

"What? Fay, what the hell's going on?" said the assistant news editor manning the desk at *New York Now!*'s offices on West 60th Street.

"Do what I say," she said. "Now – Jesus – Jesus, oh God – fucking monsters chasing me – shit – "

"I – I – we've got crews out on Park Lane with Grover – not far from you – "

"I don't care about fucking Grover" – Jesus, she was shrieking, and the assistant news editor held the phone away from his ear – "get someone over here now or you'll never work again! Oh God, there's two of them chasing me – "

The assistant night news editor then heard growls and snarls and another woman, English accent, saying, "Get out of here, you stupid bitch."

The phone went dead.

The assistant night news editor stared at the phone for a few seconds, his mouth open.

He was trying to stop his mind from spinning. This was his second day on the job. He wanted to be eased into it, but this big story broke on his first shift in charge of the desk.

And now he had to make a decision.

He thought about what Fay Colsano had said. She talked about monsters chasing her. He'd never heard fear like that coming from anyone.

He looked around the newsroom. Not many people here. No one to take the responsibility away from him. The widescreen TV showed CNN. The smaller TV screen showed *New York Now!* on cable. Grover Chaney in his camelhair overcoat reporting from Park Avenue, telling viewers that they were safe and that the gunmen would soon be in custody.

CHAPTER 105.
ON THE PROWL.

"IT'S nice to meet you," Fay had said when Jason Muir shook hands with her. She leaned away from him. She felt nervous. Dark bar. Three strangers. One of them a stranger she was going to fuck ten seconds earlier. She glanced at the bartender. He was shooting looks at her, pouring Magners for the brothers.

The brother called Donny smirked.

Fay swallowed. Her throat was dry.

Jason said, "We're not criminals or anything. We're just on holiday."

"Yes, on holiday," said his brother, coming over with the pints.

"Look," Jason had said, and he brought out his wallet and unfolded it, showing Fay an ID that suggested he was a policeman. She creased her brow, looked at the card. He said, "I'm a police constable. Thames Valley Police."

"Scotland Yard?" she said.

"No, not quite that clichéd, I'm afraid."

The brothers laughed. Their laughter made her feel better. It was friendly. Not laced with cruelty.

"So what, you're a detective?" she said.

"No, just a uniform cop. PC Muir, that's me. Lowest rank in the UK. But I'm only twenty-five, still young."

She looked at Donny. "What about you? What do you do?"

"I'm a trainee accountant. I don't have ID. But I am" – he looked over at the bartender – "over twenty-one, though. Can we get you a drink?"

Fay looked at the brothers and looked at the bartender and wanted him. "OK, why not."

Half an hour later, Fay bent over the pool table and lined up a shot. She knew the younger brother was sitting behind her, eyeing her backside. She gave him a wiggle, the booze loosening her.

She was teamed up with the bartender – he was called Ryan – and they were playing the Muirs. The Muirs won the first game, and Fay bought drinks. Fay slugged a Scotch after downing the Guinness. The table swam before her eyes. The white cue ball became two balls and then three, and two again. There were too many balls on the table, as far as she could see. All blurred and spinning.

She took the shot. The cue ball skewed to the left. Jason Muir laughed. The bartender said, "You need another drink, Fay."

"I might need something else," she said.

She was losing herself. The Fay she knew was dwindling, and in her place another Fay rose to the surface. A Fay who'd been missing. She felt loose and dirty. Her imagination reeled with thoughts that had been subdued for a long time. She looked at Ryan and desire sizzled in her belly. She looked at the Muirs, both of them, and trouble pinched her.

"When are you off duty, Ryan?" she said.

He told her he'd been off duty for a couple of hours.

She giggled.

"You know any good bars round here?" said Jason Muir.

"This one, man," said Ryan.

They laughed.

"I'm in the mood to party," said Fay.

They partied.

They moved from bar to bar, and by early evening Fay was weaving along the sidewalk saying, "Don't you know who I am?" to everyone.

Darkness had come by then, and everything became hazy. She did things that didn't seem real. Had she kissed Ryan in the restroom of a bar while the two guys pissing nearby hooted and egged her on? Had his hands been up her skirt, stroking her thighs? Was that Donny Muir grinding against her on that dance floor, letting him cup her breasts, enjoying his hardness against her lower back? Was that Jason Muir who had his tongue down her throat as they waited for drinks at the bar?

Her head throbbed now as they stumbled down a road empty of traffic and people. Their voices echoed off the grey buildings lining the road. She held Ryan's hand. She was a mess. She felt unravelled, but free for the first time.

"I can't have kids," she said to him, "I'm a barren wasteland," and she felt herself cry and her mind spin, "So you can fuck me with impunity, honey. No concerns, no nothing. You'll come in a wasteland. Nothing grows in here." She cackled. "Hey," she said, "where are my boys? Where are the brothers?"

She looked over her shoulder. Donny Muir swaggered along. He'd stopped to urinate again. "I've really got the urge to piss everywhere," he'd said and just went ahead and did so. He said, "Our car's in here," and jutted a thumb towards an underground parking lot. Street lighting made him glow orange. There was something odd about him that she couldn't get. Too drunk. Too confused. Too horny.

But something not right.

She let it go.

"Where's Jason?" she said.

Jason's voice, saying, "Come on, Fay, come on, Ryan", echoed from the parking lot. They walked down the slope. The darkness bewildered Fay. She felt disorientated. She swayed, and Ryan held on to her.

"Back here," said Jason.

And something weird about his voice made Fay stop.

Ryan said, "What's the matter, babe? We're going to a party."

A large shape bounded out of the shadows.

"Oh fuck, what's that?" she said.

Ryan let go of her hand. A bear or wolf or something – huge, furry, all teeth and claws, snarling, spit oozing – charged at them.

Her head ached.

She heard Ryan scream, and then he staggered away.

She looked over her shoulder to where Donny was supposed to be, following them into the parking lot. But Donny was gone. Another monster was there in his place, stalking towards them.

Ryan dashed away into the gloom. Fay looked at him go. He was headed for the neon EXIT sign in the far corner.

Why are you leaving me? she thought. *Don't you want to sleep with me any more?*

And she called his name, raced after him. Her heel snapped. She stumbled. Ankle wrenching. Pain shooting up her leg.

She wailed.

The first creature dashed past her into the darkness, chasing Ryan.

Screams rifled from the gloom. The sound of tearing. She imagined Ryan being ripped into. A guttural noise of anguish echoed. Yellow eyes glistened in the pitch-black, coming towards her. White teeth smeared with blood. A rag-doll Ryan hanging in the creature's jaws. Ryan's head, hanging by ribbons of flesh and arteries. His arms and torso torn to shreds. Bone jutting from his broken body, insides spilling over the concrete, spraying over the cars.

She almost fainted. The stink of death. Shit and blood.

The other monster came now and pounced at the first creature. Snapped its jaws around rag-doll Ryan. Fighting over the bartender's remains. They tore at him, and he came apart. And Fay moaned, remembering him hard against her thigh and... harder in her mouth.

"Oh my God, no!" Her scream echoed through the parking lot.

The recollection of kneeling before him came only now. While he was being shredded by these monsters.

She cried for what was gone. She hobbled away from the feast. Tried to head for the main entrance again. She got her phone out of her pocket, dialled the newsdesk.

"Get a camera over here now," she said. The creatures growled. They were chasing her. The guy manning the newsdesk said something, but it wasn't what Fay wanted to hear, so she blanked it out and said, "Do what I say," she said. "Now –

Jesus – Jesus, oh God – fucking monsters chasing me – shit – "

"I – I – we've got crews out on Park Lane with Grover – not far from you – "

"I don't care about fucking Grover, get someone over here now, or you'll never work again! Oh God, there's two of them chasing me – "

Fay froze and stared at a woman squatting on top of a car.

The woman glared at her, and Fay saw that there was something weird about her eyes. Then Fay saw. One eye was closed and bruised. The other was yellow with a black pupil – like Donny's eyes had been earlier.

She looked behind her. The creatures darted over the cars towards her.

The woman on the car rose and took off her Sesame Street T-shirt. Fay gawped. In an English accent, the woman said, "Get out of here, you stupid bitch," and something happened to her before Fay's eyes.

Something like CGI.

And the woman had gone, and in her place one of those wolf-bear monsters.

Fay dropped her phone and fled the parking lot.

CHAPTER 106.
THE BLOOD AND THE
GUNPOWDER.

BAHRMAN threw a punch. The Russian raised an elbow to protect himself. Bahrman's blow glanced off the Russian's forearm. The Russian hit back. A double-fisted swipe. His wrists cuffed together. Bahrman dodged the attack.

Stokes groaned, nursing his wounds. *Get the fuck up*, thought Bahrman. The Russian was tough. He was cut and beaten and had a bad leg. But he still fought back. He swayed now, though. His eyes were glazed, and blood smeared his face. Bahrman scowled and charged him. Knocked the Russian down. Stamped on the Russian's head, and his skull cracked against concrete. The Russian stilled.

"Jesus, this guy's a maniac," said Bahrman, hands on his knees.

"Kill him, man," said Stokes.

"Not yet."

"Kill him," said Procter.

Bahrman glanced at the doctor. The man looked a mess. In a red robe, hair sticking up, face blotched. He held on to his briefcase.

Bahrman said, "Not yet."

"Why not?" said Procter.

Bahrman had forced the Russian to drive towards the Port Authority Bus Terminal on 42nd Street and Eighth. On their way there, Stokes rang. He'd got back after taking Ruth to the airport. Stokes had panicked: *There are cops everywhere. They've road blocked Park Avenue.*

Bahrman told him where they were headed: a safehouse a few blocks away from the bus terminal.

"How do you know about such places?" Procter had asked.

Bahrman had said, "You do what I do, there are times you need to get out of sight for a while. That can be tough in this day and age, doc. That's why you need places like this."

The street looked grey and grim. A sex shop had "lingerie and DVDs" posters peeling from its window. The smell of meat drifted from a butcher's shop. A five-storey tenement stood next to a grubby restaurant with blacked-out windows. They'd left the Ferrari down the street and hurried to the tenement. Bahrman had keys to the place. He told the Russian to go first and trained the Makarov on the back of the man's head. Procter, moaning and whining, took the rear.

Bahrman guided them down, into the basement.

Empty except for a table covered in dust and two chairs. The place smelled fusty. A single light bulb draped in cobwebs cast its dim light over the cellar.

Bahrman had cuffed the Russian when they arrived. Stokes arrived a while later, white as chalk, raving about "cops everywhere" and "what the hell's going on?" and that's when the Russian attacked, using his head and fists on Stokes.

Now, with the Russian quelled and Stokes and Procter telling him to kill him, Bahrman said, "He might be useful. He's a cop, so a cop as a hostage could be useful."

"I don't want to be involved in hostage taking," said Procter.

"You're involved in worse than that, doc," said Bahrman, and then he looked at Stokes, struggling to get to his feet, and said, "How badly hurt are you, fairycake?"

"Badly," said Stokes.

"How fucking badly?"

"He blindsided me, Bahrman. My neck. The nerves have just clogged up there. Got pins and needles going through my head. Think I've broken a couple of ribs."

"That's the second time this Russian's given you a beating, isn't it, Stokes."

"It's not my fault."

"Who's fucking fault is it, then?"

A phone rang. Bahrman turned towards the noise. Procter fished in the pocket of his robe and took out his mobile. He answered it and listened, his eyes going wide, and his mouth opening and closing. He put the phone away.

He said, "That was Nick Sears."

"Yeah?" said Bahrman.

"He tells me there are werewolves running through the streets of New York."

"Really," said Bahrman.

"The Muirs have changed. They've drawn out Greenacre."

"OK, time we go," said Bahrman. "Can you get up, Stokes, you great fat moron, or are you going to sit there all day?"

"I'm really hurt, Bahrman."

"Sure, pal. But you heard what I said. You're no good to me like this."

Stokes cocked his head and knitted his brow. "What are you — "

Bahrman shot him in the mouth. Stokes's face ruptured. Blood and brains and teeth exploded.

Procter panted. "What the hell did you do that for?"

"He's of no use," said Bahrman, smelling the blood and the gunpowder and liking the odours. To him they were the scents of war. He looked at the doctor. He took the Russian's Sig Sauer from his belt and checked it. He went to Procter and gave him the gun. "You stay here with the Russian. He's cuffed, so he won't cause you any trouble. If he does, shoot him."

"Shoot him? But you said he might be useful."

But Bahrman was leaving.

CHAPTER 107.
CORNERED.

LIEUTENANT Shaun Shortcroft, with a Sig P229 pistol fixed on the terrain ahead, led the way.

Strip lights hummed and cast a weak glow over the parking lot. Shortcroft smelled diesel and blood.

He held point. He gestured to his team of eight. They fanned out. He motioned for them to move forward. They advanced between the vehicles. They scanned the parking lot's ground level with Heckler & Koch MP5 submachine guns. Beams from their headlamps speared the gloom.

Shortcroft felt sweaty under his uniform. He steadied his breathing.

"You watch those things, Shortcroft," the chief said earlier. "Can't tell you what they are. Don't want to venture a guess. But from what we've seen in the past" – he sucked air between his teeth – "they're not to be tussled with. They're to be put down with haste."

Shortcroft scoped the scene. His eyes grew accustomed to the gloom. He shouted across the lot: "We are an ESU team. We are armed, and we will fire. I am asking you to step out where we can see you."

The line moved forward, but no one stepped out where Shortcroft and his team could see them.

He glanced behind him.

Patel and Marinski had the entrance. Two other guys had the pedestrian exit at the rear of the building. The steel gates had been shut. They were locked in now. There was no way out for whatever was in here.

* * * *

The female black-fur hunkered down on the third level of the parking lot and sniffed the air. Breath billowed from her nostrils. She showed her teeth and gave a low snarl. She'd lost the scent of the males. She dropped low and looked under the cars. She saw nothing.

The males had fronted up to her at the beginning.

Three werewolves snarling and growling, rearing up on their hind legs.

She went for them, but they wheeled and darted away. Led her down to the second level, the third level.

Deep underground. Dark and cold here.

And then they were gone.

Now she whipped her head around, trying to pick up their odour again.

She bristled and followed her nose. Back towards the ramp. They'd doubled back on her. She grumbled and trotted up the ramp, her nose to the concrete, tracking the males' scent.

* * * *

Shortcroft moved forward. Headlamp beams sliced the gloom. Motes of dust floated in the light. Something flapped above the team. Shortcroft dropped to one knee. His team did the same.

A dove wheeled in the rafters. The bird landed on one of the beams. Shortcroft stared up at it and relaxed.

The bird shat.

Shortcroft smiled. He followed the shit as it fell and watched it plop on the concrete and splash across the fur of the werewolf staring right at him.

Terror coursed through Shortcroft's veins.

He fired.

The men reacted, started blazing away.

Gunfire barked and lit the gloom. The air filled with the smell of cordite. The werewolf barrelled away, bullets chewing up the concrete behind it.

Shortcroft screamed, "Right, right," and the team obeyed, followed the creature with their weapons, firing in short bursts.

Christ, it's quick, thought Shortcroft.

His stomach lurched. Something wasn't right. He wheeled to the left.

A second werewolf loomed out of the darkness.

Shortcroft shouted, but too late: the monster pounced on Ramirez, jaws locking around his arm.

Ramirez screamed. He writhed and pressed the trigger on his MP5. Sprayed bullets. Tearing into cars. Sparks flying off the metal. Concrete erupting. Flesh bursting and spouting blood. Hutchison went down, shot in the chest. Lacey hit the ground and twitched. The werewolf dragged Ramirez away into the gloom.

And Shortcroft shuddered as Ramirez's screams echoed through the parking lot – and were cut off. Like a switch had been hit. And it became quiet.

Moans broke the silence.

Lacey complained that he was shot.

Two guys attended to Hutchison.

Shortcroft stared, his mouth agape. His mind had stopped, everything moving slowly.

"Lieutenant," said a voice, "lieutenant, come on – "

He wheeled. It was Exeter. Eyes wide with shock. Exeter said, "We've got to move," and then he must've seen Shortcroft's mouth open even wider and his eyes pop in his head, because he said, "What? What, lieutenant?" and turned to see what Shortcroft saw.

Their headlamps framed the werewolf they'd shot at charging towards them.

Shortcroft shoved Exeter out of the way. He aimed the Sig at the monster. Gunfire peppered the ground to the creature's right. The animal veered away. Shortcroft fired again, panic spiking his blood now. The werewolf faded into the gloom again. Shortcroft stopped shooting. The lot smelled of gunfire.

Lacey continued to moan. Shortcroft heard in his earpiece, "Hutchison's dead, he's dead."

"Where did they go?" said someone.

"Exeter, you OK?" said Shortcroft.

Exeter, getting up, brushing himself down, said he was fine and something slammed into him, black and fast, sweeping him away.

Shortcroft gasped.

Exeter screamed in Shortcroft's earpiece. Crunching and squelching came from the gloom. Exeter stopped screaming. Something lobbed out of the darkness and hit the ground at Shortcroft's feet. Exeter's eyes stared up at him, and the dead man's mouth, full of blood, gaped. He'd been torn in half, just under the ribs. Guts and gore spilled from his ripped torso.

Shortcroft couldn't move. He felt his sanity slide away. Clawed it back just in time. He backed away, gun trained on the area where the werewolf had dragged Exeter.

"We're getting out of here," he said.

Screams and shouts, boots clumping on the ground – the sounds of combat came to him now, stirring him from the shock of Exeter's death.

Shortcroft whirled. The men were formed into a circle, back-to-back, guns trained on the gloom, their headlamps sweeping the parking lot.

Shortcroft scanned the area. He felt conspicuous. Pins and needles prickled his neck. He backed away, heading towards his men.

They huddled.

"Lieutenant, what are we going to do?" said Yardley. "Lacey's badly hurt."

Shortcroft listened. Silence. Then a snarl from the darkness to their left. Another from the right.

"We're going to stand our ground," said Shortcroft. "Where are Patel and Marinski? Still at the entrance?"

"Here, sir," said Patel at his shoulder.

"You two get Lacey out of here. The rest of us, we'll finish this job."

Shortcroft watched Patel and Marinski carry Lacey between them, towards the exit. Lacey had a leg wound. A chunk of flesh had been taken out of his thigh. They'd strapped him up. He hobbled, arms over the other men's shoulders.

As he was drawing his gaze away, Shortcroft held his breath.

A dark shape swept along the far wall.

Headed for Patel, Marinski, and Lacey.

Shortcroft couldn't make it out. It was no more than a shadow. His bowels felt icy. He started to shout a warning. The werewolf darted from the gloom. Bowled into the three men. Grabbed the wounded Lacey by the leg.

Shortcroft started shooting. The werewolf dashed between the cars, dragging Lacey along. Panic had taken hold now. Gunfire everywhere. Shortcroft shot at the monster hauling Lacey away, but the creatures were so quick. Smears of black in the dimly lit lot.

The men broke off again, losing the circle.

Shortcroft warned them.

Voices crisscrossed in the chaos.

Another scream.

Shortcroft went weak at the thought of another man going down.

The second werewolf had raced in to snatch the dazed Marinski in its jaws, hauling the ESU man away. Patel stumbled after his buddy, firing with his MP5, hitting Marinski, Marinski screaming as blood spurted from gunshot wounds and bite injuries.

"Patel, over here, get over here," said Shortcroft.

Patel stopped firing. He turned towards Shortcroft. The man's eyes were wide with fear. He ran over. Shortcroft drew the men together. Four of them left.

Jesus, he thought, *how the hell had this happened? This isn't how it goes down.*

Snarls came from the gloom. Ripping noises. The sounds of bones cracking.

"Lieutenant," said Yardley, "they're... they're eating us, sir."

CHAPTER 108.
ONE ALPHA.

DETECTIVE Anthony Ryman arrived at the parking lot and bent double.

"The ESU unit are inside, lieutenant," said a female cop.

Ryman said nothing. Out of shape, out of breath. Chest heaving. Lungs burning. *Too old for this*, he thought.

The female cop said, "I can't get them on the radio."

Ryman straightened. He looked down East 53rd Street both ways. CVPIs blocked off the road, from 3rd Avenue in the west to 1st Avenue in the east. Lights flashed on the CVPIs' roofs. The blinking blue glare hurt Ryman's eyes, and he turned away, still panting for air. Horns blared as drivers caught further back in the gridlock became frustrated. New York sounded pissed off to Ryman – and she'd be pissed off for a while, if this incident got out of hand.

A woman said, "I'm staying, I'm filming this. I almost got killed. This is why you're here. I called you. Keep shooting, Susie, keep shooting."

Ryman looked towards the voice: Fay Colsano, tussling with a uniformed cop. A pink-haired girl with a camera stood nearby, filming it all.

Colsano caught his eye.

"Detective Ryman," she said, her face red, "tell this man, tell him who I am. I was nearly killed in there."

Ryman walked over. The smell of booze came off Colsano. She was unsteady on her feet, hobbling along on a broken heel, and her eyes were glassy.

Ryman said, "Get them out of here, both of them," as a silver-haired man in a camelhair overcoat swaggered down the road with a cameraman in tow.

Grover Chaney.

Chaney smirked at Colsano and said, "Off you go, sweetheart. The pros are here now. The alpha male's come to claim his territory."

Colsano shrieked at him as two cops ushered her away. The pink-haired camerawoman tagged along, trying to film the ejection. A cop swiped at the camera. Colsano shouted warnings, threatened lawsuits.

Ryman said, "If she causes any trouble, arrest her for drunkenness."

"Good evening, Detective Ryman," said Chaney. "Do we have a situation here?"

"Talk to him," said Ryman, pointing at a detective, and walked off towards the parking lot entrance. A pool of light washed over him, and he heard the growl and felt the downdraft.

He craned his neck and put his hand to his brow to protect his eyes from the white light that beamed down from the police helicopter's spotlight. The chopper swept overhead, keeping the press and TV sky teams at bay.

"You tried going in?" said Ryman to the female cop.

"We haven't," she said, glancing at her two colleagues. "Lieutenant Shortcroft told us over the radio we – we should watch the door, not let anyone in – or out."

Gunfire barked from inside the parking lot.

Ryman ducked.

The female cop and her colleagues went for their weapons.

The gunshots came rapidly.

Shouts now too. And screaming. Ryman was at the door. He laid his ear against it. The corrugated steel was cold.

A cacophony of violence drummed against his ear.

He banged the door, and it rippled and rattled.

"Lieutenant, don't – " said the female cop.

She was backing away, her face bleached with fear. Her

colleagues were wide-eyed, licking their lips. Chaney was doing a piece-to-camera with that earnest face of his. The kind of face you wanted to smash.

"Hey," said Ryman to the cops, "are you New York's finest or what? Show some fortitude."

The female cop pulled herself together. Shuffled forward. But the other two hung back.

"How do you open this thing?" said Ryman, kicking the door.

"Attendant says it opens from the inside."

"Only from the inside?"

"No, but he's had to go get the key, sir. And anyway – "

"Anyway what, officer?"

"I'm not sure we'd want to go in."

Screams and gunfire came from within again.

"Christ, what's going on in there?" he said.

He pressed his ear to the door once more.

Something hit the gate from the inside, and the metal bulged. Ryman stumbled away. Stars erupted in front of his eyes. The female cop backed off, gun aimed at the door.

The gate had buckled outwards. The knot in the steel looked like a cyst – a man-sized cyst.

Ryman groaned.

And then something hit the door again and the steel split and a black-furred arm sliced through the metal, the claws slashing at the air.

* * * *

The black-fur watched through her one good eye as the male werewolves savaged the armed men. The smell of blood was heavy and she salivated. Screams sliced the air, and her ears flicked back and forth to pick up all the sounds, where they came from.

She'd made her way up from the lower storeys and now hunkered down on the ramp leading to the ground level of the lot. She lay in shadows, watching the carnage.

Muzzle fire flashed in the gloom as the armed men tried to kill their attackers. But the male werewolves were fast. She studied them. Watched them hunt. Paid attention to the way they dispatched their prey. Gauged their strengths. These two were powerful. More fully formed than some of the hybrids she'd fought at Trafalgar Square.

She noted their scents. They matched the territorial markings she'd followed here. The piss stains on the walls and the pavements.

She growled. Her heart ached.

She'd have to fight them. Nature demanded combat. And she couldn't deny that call. It was instinct. It was how things were. You could have only one pack. Only one alpha. And she was both.

* * * *

Shortcroft stumbled out of the warehouse, saying, "Get out... get... out of here," and blood came from his face.

Ryman got to his feet. The female officer went to help Shortcroft.

"My men... dead," he said.

The female officer struggled to keep him upright. His blood stained her uniform.

A cop helped Ryman to his feet. Ryman's head throbbed. He grimaced, put a hand to his temple.

"What's in there?" he said to Shortcroft.

"Fucking monsters... fucking... tearing my men apart... "

Ryman glanced at the wrecked parking lot door. It had opened like a wound. The monstrous arm had sliced through, then disappeared inside again. And seconds later, Shortcroft spilled out.

Ryman squinted and looked through the gouge in the gate.

He said, "Are they still in there?"

Shortcroft said, "Don't look in there, man, don't look. You don't want to see."

The ESU lieutenant groaned. He sagged in the female officer's arms. She eased him to the floor.

"We need an ambulance," she said, "get an ambulance," and one of the male cops called for one.

"We need to clear this area," said Ryman. "It might still be dangerous."

"I think it is still dangerous, lieutenant," said the female officer.

"Let's move away," said Ryman.

He and the female officer – "What's your name officer?" he said, and she said her name was Kennard – carried Shortcroft away from the entrance.

The two other cops covered the door, standing eight yards away. Guns fixed on the sliced-open steel. The look on their faces saying they were shitting themselves.

"Shoot anything that comes out of there," said Ryman.

Sirens swept across the city. Sounded like World War Three to Ryman. He looked up and down the street. The police cars cordoned off the route. Their flashing lights blinked.

He could hear voices: press and public shouting, demanding access, insisting they were told what was going on.

Damn freedom of information, he thought.

Kennard's radio crackled. She answered the call. She said to Ryman, "They're sending a helicopter, sir. Be here in minutes."

"What about this one?" he said, pointing to the chopper overhead.

"It's one of ours. We need a medic. Hospital's sending one over."

Shortcroft moaned. Blood came from a wound on his face. His thigh was mauled. Clothes and flesh had torn away to reveal a bloody pattern of muscle and bone.

A helicopter roared overhead. Ryman felt the blast from the rotors. Kennard put her hand on her head to keep her cap on. The two cops watching the door scuttled away, and Ryman looked up. The police helicopter lifted away. Another one descended. A red cross on its side. The downblast swirled litter and debris and dust along the street. Ryman put a hand to his brow and narrowed his eyes. The chopper descended. Kennard said something, but Ryman couldn't hear her.

A black shape leaped through the gash in the parking lot's door.

Ryman's blood turned cold.

A second black shape sprang out.

The animals charged the helicopter.

Ryman tried to say "No," but no sound came out – or if it did, it was swallowed up by the noise.

The creatures smashed into the helicopter, one of them diving into the cockpit. The other turned its gaze towards Ryman, Kennard, and Shortcroft.

Ryman's chest tightened. He tried to find a name for the monster and found one but dared not say it. He saw Grover Chaney and his cameraman gawp at the sight. Chaney retreated. The cameraman started filming.

Kennard leaped to her feet and drew her gun and started to fire. The werewolf bolted away.

The helicopter seesawed. The rotors gashed the parking lot's brickwork. Sparks flew. Metal screeched. Ryman knew what was coming.

Chaney stumbled up the street.

Coward, thought Ryman. *Give me Colsano any day*.

Kennard fired after the fleeing werewolf. *Not fleeing though*, thought Ryman. Circling them. Bullets chasing it. Bullets –

He tried to warn Kennard.

Too late.

As she spun and shot after the werewolf, her gunfire hit two cops and the cameraman.

Kennard lowered the weapon. Looked stunned.

The werewolf ran down Chaney. Pounced on him. Tossed him against a wall. Went at him. Ripped off his face and sprang away. The faceless reporter staggered about like he was looking for himself. Blood poured from the mask of meat he wore. He fell to his knees and then toppled over on his missing face.

Kennard fired again. Bullets trailed the werewolf, spitting up concrete.

Ryman hacked at her arm and mouthed for her to stop shooting. Her eyes were wet and wide. Her skin pale.

The roar of blades deafened him, and he ducked down, trying to get away from the noise. He yanked Kennard down with him.

The helicopter whirled. Lights flashed. Sparks flew. The first werewolf rocked the chopper and made blood spray on the windshield. It was in there, thrashing around. Ryman saw nothing of the pilot. Then medics spilled out, trying to flee, stumbling. The rotor hacked one of them, his head spinning off like a football.

Ryman thought about his wife and children, and tears came to him. He and Kennard crouched over Shortcroft.

The creature leaped out of the helicopter. Darted away.

The other one had disappeared too.

The helicopter rolled into the side of the parking lot. A fireball erupted and swallowed the chopper.

The heat seared Ryman's face. He screamed at the pain of his flesh melting. He grabbed Shortcroft and hauled him away. He looked back and saw Kennard. Her face showed madness, her mind gone. The fire engulfed her.

She turned black and red, and the flames lapped towards Ryman and Shortcroft and washed over them, and Ryman screeched as the fire shot down his throat and cooked his lungs.

And a second before he died, he saw another black-fur shooting out of the parking lot and through the flames and east, towards where it was cool and grey.

CHAPTER 109.
BRIMSTONE AND FIRE.

MANHATTAN, NEW YORK

GALA Larsson stared at Paul French across the table in Veniero's Pasticceria and Caffé on East 11th Street. She fidgeted with her coffee cup. Her cannoli was untouched. French coveted the pastry. He'd devoured a slice of cheesecake, but he was still hungry. He'd not eaten properly since arriving in New York earlier in the day. He'd driven to Heathrow from Thorn's place. Got on a plane and had barely slept. Gala looked like she'd been awake for days, too.

"You look very nervous," he said.

"I – I've not been – been out of my home in so many years. Not since – " She bowed her head.

"I know," he said.

"I am so scared, being here. Already there is death. Have you seen the news? There is talk of monsters. Things are happening. Not far from here. I think there are werewolves." She looked out through the window.

Pedestrians choked the sidewalk. Cars crawled bumper to bumper along the street. Two policemen on horseback trotted by.

She turned her gaze back to French.

"London scared me back then," said Gala. "I was ten, never been out of my village. My family was God's people, and they did not want us to come to London. But Alrik and Brit Heg, they said, 'Let them go to see Sodom before God rains brimstone and fire upon it. The Lord will protect us.' But God didn't. *She* had to. Laura Greenacre."

They were quiet for a moment. Sirens blared outside. There was a sense of panic. French felt it, but maybe that was his cop genes. His sixth sense kicking in.

Gala said, "The Templetons are gathering. Ruth's shadow looms over this city. We cannot defeat her. Laura must do that. But we must show Laura we are with her. We owe her our lives." Then she stared straight at him and cocked her head. "But you don't. You owe her nothing. Why are you a follower, Mr French?"

He shook his head. "I don't know. I've thought about it, but I don't know. I was awed, that's all." He looked around. His chest itched. "You can't smoke anywhere these days."

"I smoke. Yes. In my room, I smoke. And I open the window and" – she made a fanning gesture with her hand – "to make the smoke go out, or my mother and father, they would go" – she twirled her index fingers at her temples to indicate madness – "you know?"

French laughed and said he did know.

He told her he'd met Thorn the previous day and she sat up, her eyes widening. French told her most of it, but not him killing Cole and the Strakers. Not what happened in Hexham.

Gala went on:

"If God existed, He would let them be together." She paused, poked the cannoli with a knife. French's stomach rumbled. "You want it?" she asked.

"Do you mind?"

She smiled and shook her head. Nudged the plate across the table. He thanked her and forked a piece into his mouth: the crisp shell cracked and the vanilla-flavoured ricotta cheese melted on his tongue.

She said, "My family, they are still religious, but I'm not, not now. After Trafalgar Square, God went from me, for sure."

"Yes. I understand that."

"God would not have let Alrik die. Or all those other people."
Her eyes glazed over. "Do you believe in God, Mr French?"

"I've seen too much to believe in God."

She shrugged.

French looked at her. She was pale. Her short-cropped hair lacked style. She wore no make-up. This was a young woman who had no idea how the world worked.

He said, "Have you stayed in your room for eight years?"

"Almost."

"Looking for Laura?"

"Looking. Talking to other people. There were many of us."

He agreed.

She said, "In that crowd, on that day, saved by her. And many have said they would be here. I think that they come, Mr French. We are like an army."

He paused and then said, "But what can we do?"

She said, "Stand with her."

CHAPTER 110.
MAD RUSSIAN.

DASAEV came to. His head ached and pain throbbed in his side and his leg. He groaned and sat up. His vision blurred, and for a moment he thought he'd faint. He braced himself, and the nausea passed. He looked round and saw Stokes lying five yards away, his face a mess of bone and blood.

Dasaev gritted his teeth and got up. He cursed as the pain swept through him, and then he crossed himself. His leg pulsed. He tried to find his Novamoxin and some painkillers he'd bought, but they weren't in his pocket. Then he remembered Bahrman frisking him and finding the drugs. The American had tossed them away saying, "You won't be needing these, boy. No pills'll ease the pain you're going to be in."

He hobbled over to Stokes. The man had been shot through the mouth. Dasaev crouched over the body. He smelled the gunpowder coming off Stokes's face. Blood pooled on the floor behind the dead man's head. Dasaev rifled through Stokes's pockets. He found coins and he found a flick knife. He opened the knife and used it to awkwardly pick the lock on the handcuffs.

He heard someone speaking in a panicked, high-pitched voice and froze.

The noise came from the stairs. The door leading to the stairs was shut, muffling the voice. But Dasaev recognized it:

Lawrence Procter.

He rose and shuffled over to his shepherd's staff lying on the floor. He bent and picked it up, and it was like lifting a ton of bricks. The pain caused a sweat to break out over his body.

The voice came closer. Footsteps coming down the stairs.

Procter was saying, "... and he's left me here with a gun, with that bloody mad Russian – I'm half-naked... "

Dasaev stood like a baseball batter three steps from the door, gripping the cane in both hands.

The door opened and Procter stepped out. He carried his briefcase. He was saying, "... and you must, absolutely must, send someone over here to get me, Ruth, this is terrible – " before he saw Dasaev standing there and gawked at him.

Dasaev nodded and then swung the crook. The cherry wood handle cracked Procter on the jaw. The doctor slackened and hit the ground. The phone and the briefcase fell out of his grasp. The Sig Sauer tumbled from the pocket of his robe.

Ruth Templeton's tinny voice was saying, "Hello? Lawrence?" on the phone. Dasaev ignored it. He picked up the gun and checked it. He tucked the weapon into his belt. He retrieved the briefcase and lifted it onto a dusty box and opened it.

He studied the vials of blood.

Gromeko's words came to him: *He has something, a substance... It's blood, but we don't know what kind...*

Why? He wondered. What were they going to do with Laura's blood?

Maybe they would do nothing with it. Maybe it was just to stop anyone else from having it. He shut the briefcase.

Ten minutes later, Dasaev stood in the street.

Helicopters hovered in the distance. Smoke rose from between the skyscrapers and billowed into the darkening sky.

Dasaev, using his cane, limped towards the chaos.

CHAPTER 111.
EAT UP.

BILLY said, "Why are you looking so nervous, Dad? Eat your sandwich, drink your beer."

His dad glowered at him and said nothing and then turned his attention back to the restaurant's TV screen. The news showed chaos in New York. Fire blazed somewhere nearby. Smoke blackened the sky. Monsters prowled the subways and the parking lots. A reporter with blood on her face spoke to a witness, asking what the witness had seen: "I saw two, three, yeah, three... monsters, beasts – "

"Werewolves," said the reporter.

"Yeah, werewolves – "

Behind the reporter and the witness, Billy saw people running and screaming. He saw police cars and flashing lights.

He could smell the chaos. It was nearly there.

They were at Virgil's Real Barbeque on West 44th Street. It smelled great in here. Sounded great, too: the sizzling of meat on the grill. He'd eaten his sliced Texas beef brisket barbeque sandwich and drank a couple of beers. His dad hadn't touched his pulled Carolina pork sandwich, hadn't drunk his beer either.

"I'm just saying, that's all. You're fidgeting with your cutlery."

"Shut up, Billy. This is serious."

"I know it's serious. I'm taking it seriously. That's why I'm not letting nerves get in the – " He broke off and tilted his chair back towards the table behind them. Billy said to the woman at the table, a redhead in her fifties, "Will you keep your fucking voice down, you fat cow – you're making me ashamed to be English."

The woman gawped at him and said, "Excuse me, how dare you speak to me like that," and she turned to her table, two men there: "How dare he speak to me like that, Charles. Did you hear what this vile young thug said to me?"

Billy had straightened his chair by then and had his elbows on the table.

"You didn't need to do that," said his dad.

"Yes I did, everyone's watching TV. She's noisy."

The woman prodded him saying, "You, young thug," and Billy wheeled round, curling his lip and frowning at her. She paled and recoiled and muttered something before turning back to her table. The men there, her husband maybe, and a skinny, bald-headed creep whose eyes raked every waitress that came to their table, had said nothing.

His dad said, "Do you feel anything? I mean, do you think you can change?"

"One way to find out." He rose from the chair. "Are you coming? Looks like Jason and Donny are on their way – "

The reporter was saying that two werewolves had dashed out of the 42nd Street–Bryant Park subway.

"And it seems they're headed straight for Times Square," she told viewers.

A gasp went through the patrons at Virgil's. They ignored their meals, more interested in the news this evening. Someone said, "They're coming this way," and people started to get up.

"Oh my God," said a woman, "those monsters, they're coming."

They're already here, thought Billy, leading his father towards the toilets.

CHAPTER 112.
FAY COLSANO – LIVE FROM
TIMES SQUARE.

"I DON'T know if you could see," said Fay to the camera, "but two of them, two werewolves – I think we have to use that word – two werewolves have just bounded out of 42nd Street–Bryant Park and – "

Shrieks coming from the subway made her cower. She turned to look and then looked back at the camera:

"We had reports of three werewolves rampaging through the subway – on the V line from 53rd Street Station – a few injuries reported among passengers – "

The shrieks grew louder, and Fay glanced again at the subway. People spilled up the stairs, out into the street.

"Oh – " Fay nearly cursed on live TV.

The crowds kept flooding out of the subway.

Just ahead of a third werewolf.

"Another one," said Fay, looking into camera, thinking, *Pulitzer Prize, the Peabody Award... and the winner is, Fay Colsano... this courageous reporter almost died in pursuit of the story of the century...*

The third werewolf, a one-eyed monster, raced up the stairs out of the subway. Stopped and sniffed the air. Fay stared at it, her mouth open. She thought about the woman in the parking lot. Stripping off her Sesame Street T-shirt. Becoming something else – becoming this creature.

The werewolf caught the scent and headed up 42nd Street, towards Times Square. Intense white light blinded Fay as she stared down the block towards the intersection. It would be a great spot to film the werewolves, thanks to the glare from the signs and advertisements.

The "spectaculars" would perfectly light Fay Colsano's production.

She and the camerawoman made their way down the block, Fay talking to her audience all the time. She was going out live. Chaney was missing after the explosion at the parking lot. Fay was anchoring the show, now.

Live from the streets of New York City.

The werewolves bounded towards the lights of Times Square.

Crowds of people flooded towards Fay. The screaming that filled the air made it difficult to hear, and Fay had to shout into the camera.

Three police cars screeched across the road, blocking the way. Officers spilled out. One had a megaphone. He was telling people to move back. Fay told the viewers, "Were going to see if they'll let us through. We are your eyes and ears, ladies and gentlemen, so they should allow us to pass."

"No way," said a female cop, hand out to stop Fay.

Fay said, "We're from *New York Now!*"

"I don't care which New York you're from. No one's going through."

"But ABC have got a studio on Times Square – it's not fair. What about our viewers?"

"They can watch ABC, can't they – now get back."

Fay, shouting over the noise, said to her viewers, "Ladies and gentlemen, the New York Police Department do not want you to know the truth of what's going on here tonight – "

The camerawoman made a cutthroat sign.

"What?" said Fay.

"They've gone back to the studio," said the pink-haired girl. "We're off air."

A roar deafened Fay. A tornado whipped her hair. She couldn't breathe. She ducked and looked up towards the storm. A helicopter descended. Its rotors whisked up litter and leaves and newspapers. Pedestrians fled the downblast. The chopper hovered near the ground. *New York Now!*'s logo adorned its flanks. Fay's heart skipped. A producer from the station beckoned her into the helicopter.

Pulitzer Prize, she thought again, *it's back on…*

CHAPTER 113.
ONE-EYE.

THE werewolf stopped and moved her head from side to side.

She'd lost the scent again. Lost sight of the two males. Too many people. Spilling down the boulevard. The screams made her ears hurt, She flattened them against her head, ignoring her sense of hearing.

Who needed hearing when you had sight, even in one eye? Who needed hearing when you had smell?

But she still couldn't pick up their trail.

Odours cascaded: sweat, blood, shit, piss, diesel, paint, deodorant, perfume, aftershave, dogs, cats, rats, birds, rubber, plastic...

The one-eye growled. She drooled. Looked around. People stared at her as they ran past, stared and screamed. Pointed and said, "Oh my God," and pulled their children away. She skulked forward and sniffed the air.

She pricked up her ears just in case.

People screaming, engines growling, horns blaring, alarms yowling – she shook her head, deafened by it all.

And then, through the cacophony, a voice:

"Shoot them, shoot to kill!"

She snarled and bristled.

Bolted towards the great lights and the heavy crowds.

Gunfire erupted.

CHAPTER 114.
THE VISITOR.

BLACK MOUNTAINS, SOUTH-EAST WALES

"HE'S dead, now. It's over," said the man with silver hair.

"It's not over," said Thorn.

"Craig's dead – that's good enough for me."

Thorn glared at the man and said, "My daughter's pain goes on. My pain goes on, Keegan – or whatever you're called."

"I am called Keegan."

"Who do you really work for?"

"Can't tell you."

"Can't or won't?"

"Won't, Thorn. You know better."

"*Do* I know better?"

"You're a policeman."

"Was a policeman."

"You've still got the genes." He paused and looked at Thorn with ice-cold eyes. He spoke again: "Everything's done. Craig's dead. I came to say there'll be nothing for you to worry about, with regards to his death. Don't worry about the Strakers either. Let the families wail."

"Sweep it all under the carpet."

Keegan cast his eyes over the land. There was nothing but darkness. They were standing outside in the yard. Thorn didn't want him in the house. He didn't know why, he just didn't.

I don't know where you've been, he thought.

And there was something cold about him. Thorn imagined if he let him in, he would drain off all the warmth and goodness that was there.

Keegan had called and said, "I'm on my way up to you, now," and when Thorn complained that it was too late, the middle of the night, Keegan had cut him off.

Now Keegan said, "If you'd prefer, we'll go through the proper procedures, involve the Northumbria Police force. There are detectives up there still wondering what happened to you. How you let slip a potentially successful career. You lost your head, some say. Over a woman. Or something approaching a woman."

Thorn's hackles rose, and he flushed with rage.

"Don't think about it, Thorn," said Keegan. "I'll put you down. You're a tough guy, but I'm tougher." He looked off towards the dark hills. He said, "I'm glad Craig's dead. It's justice, as far as I'm concerned. Let things be, Thorn. I like you. You're a good man, and you were a good cop – you still could be, as I said, but I'm a sentimental sod. But that's for you, not for me. What matters truly is that Ray Craig will trouble you no more."

"What about Ruth Templeton? She still troubles me, and she still troubles Laura. And there are unsolved murders in which she is clearly a suspect. What about that killing in Carlisle?"

Keegan shrugged. "Now Craig's dead, our interest in the Templetons has dwindled. But off the record, I know there are werewolves in this world, and I just accept that now. I've seen evidence. But it doesn't involve me. Like Pilate, I wash my hands of it."

He turned and walked away, out of the yard and into the lane, where a black Vauxhall waited by the gate.

Keegan got in the back and threw Thorn a salute before shutting the door. The car drove away down the mountain. Thorn watched it descend and kept watching, until the headlights and the tail-lights faded, and there was nothing to see but the dark.

* * * *

422

Thorn sat at the table near the window and thought about things. His injuries prevented him from doing anything much. And it wasn't good for him. Too much time to dwell on what had happened.

He thought about Laura and wondered if she'd survived.

If anyone could, she would.

But how far would Ruth go for vengeance?

He shuddered and looked out across the dark mountains.

He didn't hear her come down stairs.

"Dad."

He flinched and turned and saw her at the bottom of the stairs in her dressing gown. Her hair draped over her face. Her skin looked bleached. Her eyes were red-rimmed. He smelled tobacco on her. She'd smoked after her mother died and yesterday started smoking again. He understood why she needed to and let her do it for now.

Watching her, an ache swelled in his heart, and he scratched his chest.

"Sweetheart," he said, but he almost couldn't get the word out, and then: "Can't you sleep?"

She came into the room and sat at the table opposite him. "I've made a decision."

"OK." A chill raced up from his guts into his chest.

"I want to be Sophie Thorn now."

He started to sob.

CHAPTER 115.
THE SCAM.

KARL Corman was glad the kid on the next table had gone. Mrs Dampier nearly got into a fight with him, and that would've drawn attention to Corman. And he didn't want that. He did his best work in the shadows.

Mind you, he thought, looking around Virgil's, *no one would've taken much notice.*

The customers were all transfixed by the TV coverage. And some people were leaving. Corman squirmed in his seat and wondered if he should be making a run for it, too. Something bad was on the way, that's the sense he got from the panic creeping through the restauarant.

He thought for a moment and went to stand up.

"We've come for the ballet," said Mrs Dampier, interrupting Corman's thoughts. She went on: "We love the New York City Ballet."

Corman relaxed again and smiled at the Englishwoman and said, "It's a wonderful company," not ever having seen a ballet in his life, not ever wanting to.

"But one has to be careful where one lives."

"One must, Mrs Dampier," said Corman.

"You see," said Mr Dampier now, "England's a shit-hole – "

"Charles," said his wife.

Mr Dampier flapped his hand and said, "Well, you know, it's awful, awful."

Corman held his grin. His face hurt. But it'd be worth it. He'd skin these two. Leave them without a cent. Then they'd *have* to stay in New York. And not in the plush, Manhattan properties, "ideal for mature people seeking an idyll," that he was selling.

OK, he wasn't really selling them – they didn't exist.

He had photos, but they were apartments neither he nor his made-up firm owned. He showed rich foreigners like the Dampiers the images. Told them, "We don't waste time. We don't arrange viewing appointments with any old John Doe. Prospective clients must prove they have the means to purchase our properties."

That got the dopes excited: exclusivity made them wet and hard.

Even if they didn't have a cent, they'd scrape cash together for the fee. Just to feel special. Ten thousand dollars.

Two of them worked the scam. A one-week-only offer. Corman had nine clients, including the Dampiers. He didn't know how many his brother had. But once the money was paid, by midday tomorrow, they'd scram. Leave fools like the Dampiers in the gutter.

A waitress came to their table and asked if they wanted coffee. Corman said yes, black for him, and had a look at the girl from head to toe. The English couple said they'd have their coffee with cream.

"I thought English people liked tea," said Corman, still wearing his grin.

"That's just a stereotype now, isn't it, Mr Corman," said Mrs Dampier. She was a redhead. Mid-fifties, carrying a few extra pounds. Her husband had rosy cheeks and a drinker's nose and rat eyes that kept blinking.

"Tell me about these wonderful gated communities again, Mr Corman," said Mrs Dampier, wafting her hand in front of her face, fanning her perfume towards Corman. She smelled of fruit. His defences slipped for a moment. Women always did that to him. He had to stay sharp. He shook his head and took a breath. The coffee arrived, and he looked at the waitress's breasts. He looked up into her face, and she seemed scared. Corman shivered and gazed around Virgil's. Customers were spilling out of the door now. There seemed to be a commotion out in the street. Lots of noise out there, too: helicopters, sirens, horns.

He tried to ignore things. *They'll blow over*, he thought. *Focus on the money*.

"England has gone to pot," said the husband.

Corman looked at the man. Dampier's eyes flitted around the restaurant.

Dampier said, "It's all hoodies and chavs and New-fucking-Labour. Tories are no better. Gordon Brown and David-fucking-Cameron. Poncey, fucking do-gooders who've let the country go to ruin."

"Charles," said Mrs Dampier, giving her husband a look.

"Fucking human rights," said the husband. "You know" – and he looked at Corman, leaned in – "friends of ours – the Beades, Malcolm and Rose – some pikey fucks broke into their home – they've got a lovely place, seven-bedroomed, pride and joy. The – what do we call them to be PC? – the *travellers* broke in one night. Malcolm came down, armed with his cricket bat, confronted the little fuckers."

Mrs Dampier had turned away, nose in the air.

Dampier went on:

"Thumped them both, you know. Cowardly little shits, screaming, begging for mercy, Malcolm saying, 'You shouldn't have broken into my home, you pikey bastards,' thumping them, battering them, giving the scum a hiding."

Dampier took a sip of his coffee, face red, into his story now. Corman had the grin on again, showing his white teeth, thinking, *Get on with it*.

Dampier said, "Malcolm, well, he called the police, you know. Three hours later – three fucking hours later, mind you – officers arrive and" – he straightened in his chair, widened his eyes and shrugged – "bloody well arrested Malcolm for assault and wielding a dangerous weapon – and for racially abusing these – these – cunts."

Mrs Dampier whipped her head round and said her husband's name in a voice that sounded like acid burning through something.

But he ignored her and said, "It's disgraceful. Not going to happen in the States is it, Mr Corman?"

"No sir. An Englishman's home is his castle here in New York. Your friend, he'd've been hailed a hero over here. Which is why — "

Screams filtered through the restaurant.

People seemed to be running out. Tables overturned. Chairs flew. Plates and bowls and glasses shattered, spilling food and drink.

Corman turned slowly, his eyes narrowed.

A russet-coloured wolf-monster rampaged through the restaurant.

Sweat broke on Corman's nape, and his insides became waxy.

The creature growled, butting people away with its wolf-head, slashing at them with its wolf-claws.

Mrs Dampier screamed.

Another creature, brown-furred, shot from the restrooms.

The russet-fur charged directly at Corman.

Mrs Dampier was screaming, "Charles! Charles!"

Corman grabbed Mr Dampier by the arm and dragged him forward and used him as a shield against the monster.

CHAPTER 116.
COPS AND ROBBERS.

OFFICER Will Wentworth raced down 44th towards the restaurant.

The screams carried down the street. People flooded his way, panic in their eyes. Sirens wailed. Voices cascaded over his radio. Colleagues were racing to incidents and alerting units to the chaos breaking out in Midtown.

He'd been winding down, his shift coming to an end. He'd bought his daughter a fifth-birthday present. The gift was in the car, and he'd kept thinking, *Will she like it? Will her mother like it? Will it be good enough, this time?*

"Police, let me through," he said. Shrieks came from the crowd in front of him. He heard a roar that made him falter.

Those animals are here, he thought. The ones causing chaos. The ones killing cops. He swallowed, and fear crawled down his spine.

He drew out his gun, hand sweaty on the stock. He barged through, saying, "Please, please let me pass," and the crowd parted for him, pushed away from him, crammed the sidewalks.

Horns blared. Tyres screeched. Wentworth heard a thud and a shout:

"Oh God, you've knocked her down."

A cab had run into a woman. She was sprawled on the street. The cab driver leaped out of his vehicle. He gesticulated, said he didn't see her. A man, the woman's husband or boyfriend, raged. Lunged at the cab driver. Punched and slapped and spat and kicked the cab driver. The driver wailed, saying, "It was an accident, an accident."

Wentworth, torn between what to do, shouted for them to "cut it out". And then other people tried to pull the man away from the driver, and then those people got hot and more fights broke out. Two medics were crouched over the woman. Wentworth sweated and panted for breath. Pressed forward and reached for his radio and called for back-up.

He got to the restaurant. He stood wavering on the pavement. The world swimming. Sweat in his eyes. He blinked and looked at the yellow eyes of a huge, reddish-coloured werewolf standing in the restaurant's shattered window.

Wentworth gaped.

Someone shouted for him to "shoot the fucking thing".

The werewolf glared at him from the shattered window.

Blood dripped from the creature's mouth and from the severed arms in its jaws.

The restaurant was ransacked.

Screams and moans came from the plundered interior. Chairs and tables were overturned. The smell of food wafted through the broken window.

Wentworth thought about the gift he'd bought his daughter.

He aimed his gun and shouted a warning.

The werewolf dropped the arm and sprang at Wentworth.

* * * *

Mrs Dampier screamed and shook her husband, trying to wake him up maybe. Blood pulsed from his severed arm. His chest had been gouged open. Meat clung to his ribs, and his heart glistened and throbbed.

She told everyone that her husband was all right and to please help them. Blood came from his mouth. His face was white and his blue eyes open. She looked into them and cried. No one helped. They were too busy running away or hiding.

Like Corman was hiding behind their overturned table.

He'd managed to shield himself using Dampier. The werewolf barged into them, jaws snapping around the Englishman's arm, hauling him away and shaking him. Corman got knocked to the ground, and he quickly rolled behind the table, crouching there, listening to Dampier's screams while the werewolf mutilated him, listening to Mrs Dampier's shrieks at seeing her husband being ripped up.

Corman peered over the table now.

Saw the werewolf on the sidewalk, mounted on someone, that someone screaming. *Christ*, thought Corman, recognizing the uniform, *a cop*.

The other werewolf was somewhere around. Corman heard noises of panic coming from the kitchen, so he guessed the animal was going berserk in there, making a meal of the chefs.

His eyes fixed on the piece of paper on the floor next to Dampier's twitching body. Corman crawled, whimpering as he went. He had to scuttle past a dead body. The face was missing, a maw of flesh and bone and a pair of eyes staring up at the ceiling.

The stink coming off the cadaver was dreadful. Corman puked. Screams came from the street outside. He chanced a look. Smoke swirled. Some people stood and stared, others were running in all directions. Sirens yowled, and he heard the growl of a helicopter and wished he could be in one.

He steeled himself. Crabbed through blood and gore. Made a face as he felt it, slick and hot on his hands and legs.

Mrs Dampier was shaking her dead husband, shouting at him.

She even nags him in death, thought Corman.

He got to them. He reached for the paper. Blood stained it. He picked it up, gritting his teeth, hoping Mrs Dampier's attention wouldn't be drawn from the carcass of her husband. He unfolded the paper.

Corman's sneer became a smile. The signature on the cheque was fine. The paper would dry out easily on a radiator. He'd take Dampier's cash after all. If he only made ten grand out of the whole scam, it would be ten grand more than he had that morning.

"What do you think you're doing?"

He froze.

Mrs Dampier fixed him with red-rimmed eyes. Tears and mascara drew dark lines down her face. Her lipstick was smeared. Hair tousled and wild. All her elegance gone.

Corman's mouth opened and closed.

He scrunched up the cheque and leaped to his feet. He almost slipped in the blood and the food and the drink spreading across the floor.

Mrs Dampier shouted "thief" at him and made a grab for his legs. But he swerved out of her reach and smiled and backed away, out of the restaurant.

He'd slip into the crowd and escape.

Ten grand the richer.

Ten grand the richer, and alive to spend it.

He retreated, gave Mrs Dampier a wave. She lay sprawled across her husband now, her face screwed up with rage.

Corman chuckled. Then backed into something solid.

He stumbled and wheeled. The werewolf glared down at him. Corman screamed. The werewolf snapped its jaws around his head and swung him around, and Corman kept on screaming.

CHAPTER 117.
THE INSURANCE.

JERRY Bahrman, Makarov in his right hand, an Ithaca Mag-10 Roadblocker shotgun tucked under his left arm, strode down Broadway towards Times Square.

He's seen the werewolf Billy Sears attack customers at the restaurant and kill a cop outside on the pavement. Now the creature snarled at passers-by, its head whipping from side to side as it made its way down Broadway. Blood dripped from its teeth. Pieces of meat clung to the gums. Bahrman sweated. He didn't know how safe this animal was. Laura Greenacre had nearly got him eight years ago in that fuck-up led by Ray Craig and Klaus Markus.

The werewolf loped down the street.

The crowd surged away. A helicopter hovered overhead. Bahrman glanced up. A man with a camera poked out of the copter's door. Bahrman followed the werewolf. He looked over his shoulder. Another werewolf lumbered down Broadway.

Nick Sears, he thought.

Father and son on the hunt.

The Muir brothers should be in Times Square now. The news said they'd been chased by another werewolf – the Greenacre bitch.

They were cornering her there. This time there'd be no mistake. This time *he* was there.

The insurance.

The werewolves could go at each other's throats, he'd hang back and pick his moment. Blow Laura Greenacre away like he'd been paid to do. Blow the others away too, if they got in the way.

That's what Ruth Templeton had told him.

"Kill them all, if you have to," she'd said.

They didn't know that, of course.

He thought about getting out of here now. He'd have to go back to that basement for Procter and the Russian. Use the Russian to barter, if he needed to. The guy was a cop. He was worth something.

A police car sped down the street. Lights flashing and siren wailing. The CVPI skidded around the russet-fur, trying to herd it. The car screeched to a halt. Two cops leaped out, guns brandished. The werewolf lunged at one of them. The other cop aimed at the creature. Bahrman cursed and shot the cop with his Makarov, and the cop fell back against the CVPI.

The crowd swept away from him. He heard voices saying, "He shot a cop," and, "He's got guns." People were running everywhere now. Police officers were trying to maintain order. A riot was kicking off.

After butchering the cop, the russet-furred werewolf moved on. Bahrman followed. Checked the one behind him was still coming. There it was. Chasing into the crowd. Bringing down victims. Killing or maiming. Moving on to the next target. Spreading terror.

Bahrman felt a hurricane lash at him from above. The noise shook the buildings. Made the ground tremble.

He looked up at the helicopter again. The camerman pointed his lens at Bahrman. He raised the Makarov. He never heard the shot; it was too loud here. But he felt the recoil. The camera shattered. The chopper wheeled. The man tumbled out. His arms windmilled as he fell. He thumped the ground and his body bent and bones jutted out of him and blood spouted from his mouth.

Bahrman smiled and moved on.

* * * *

The maître d' said, "Table for one, sir?"

And Dasaev brushed past him, saying, "Do you have anything in the kitchens?"

The restaurant was on West 41st Street. He couldn't get through the crowds crammed down 42nd Street, so he had to think.

Most of the customers were spilling out of the restaurant now. Panic swept Manhattan. Everywhere he looked, there were crowds and there were police cars. It sounded like war.

He hobbled through the restaurant. The maître d' trotted after him, saying he couldn't go into the kitchens – they were private. But Dasaev rammed through the swing doors and walked into a room of smoke. Food sizzled and boiled, the odours making him salivate.

A chef said, "Hey," and made to stop him, but Dasaev showed him the Sig Sauer tucked into the waistband of his trousers, and the chef moved away.

"Way out," he said, hobbling on, "way out," and the kitchen staff pointed.

He stopped at a deep-fat fryer. Fries bubbled and browned in the oil. He laid the briefcase on the side and opened it. He took out the six vials of blood.

Someone said, "Don't put that in there," but Dasaev told him he'd shoot him if he came any closer.

Dasaev took the plug out of the vial and dropped it in the oil. The blood coiled out and sizzled and browned in the frier. Dasaev did the same with all the vials. He watched the blood fry, and then he limped away, down the kitchen.

He came to a door and shoved it open with his cane and stepped out into an alley filled with trash. The noise from 42nd Street flooded down the alley. He followed the sounds and the lights and stepped out into Times Square and was blinded by the glare.

People crowded the pavements. They flooded down the street. Cars bumper to bumper, not moving. Police vehicles crisscrossing the avenue. Armed cops trying to clear the road.

A dark blue van screeched to a halt, and an ESU team spilled out.

Dasaev cursed. They'd shoot her. He quickened his pace. His

leg ached. Blood came from the wound now, seeping between the stitches. He knew he should be lying down somewhere. A hospital, most likely. But he pushed on, shoving aside loiterers, swiping at them with his shepherd's staff.

A megaphoned voice warned the crowd to move slowly, not to run.

The crowd ran.

A wave of people surged towards him. Dasaev gasped, swept off his feet by the throng. He tried to elbow his way through, going against the tide.

A man in a New York Jets shirt threw punches at him. Dasaev protected himself. Took the blows on his forearms. He groaned as more pain piled up in his broken body. He barged past the Jets fan, the man pounding someone else now. Dasaev swam through a torrent of people.

The crowd surged again and then seemed to disperse and fan out around him, leaving him staggering in the road. He turned round and round. The Coca-Cola sign blurred. The Chevrolet clock told him the time. Newstickers warned him monsters were running around Midtown.

The glare was overwhelming. He blinked and put a hand to his brow.

He shook his head, his vision growing accustomed to the dazzling night.

He steadied himself and looked directly at two werewolves.

Black-furs, with their teeth dripping blood and saliva.

They hunched down and stalked towards him.

Dasaev gasped, staggered back. Saw the carnage in Times Square. Bodies lay strewn in the street. Blood pooled on the road. Limbs were scattered around the intersection.

The werewolves growled.

A helicopter swooped overhead.

The werewolves' coats rippled under the rotor's power.

The creatures drew their eyes away from Dasaev for a second.

He brought out the gun and fired at the werewolves. The downblast from the helicopter put him off and the bullet clanked into a police car.

The animals fixed on him and bolted in his direction.

Dasaev yelled out against the pain in his body. He turned

and hobbled away. Not quick enough. Not far enough ahead of his pursuers.

He felt the ground shake as the werewolves bolted after him.

A voice through a megaphone said, "Sir, sir, run, they're after you, sir – oh my God – sir, they're gaining – Jesus, what's that?"

CHAPTER 118.
MAN IN FATIGUES.

A BLACK blur flashed from Dasaev's right and thudded into the werewolf's flank. The impact made Dasaev shudder. The creature yelped and flew across the street. Slammed into a sign and shattered it. Sparks showered from the sign, and glass and plastic sprayed, scattering over the street.

Dasaev backed away.

The other werewolf, ten yards away now, stopped and sought out the attacker.

The black blur took on a shape.

A werewolf, powerful and menacing, ready for another attack.

It had one eye.

Laura, thought Dasaev.

Helicopters roared overhead. Megaphoned voices warned people to keep away. "Move slowly away from the intersection," said the warnings. But they weren't being heeded. This was a show no one wanted to miss – even if it meant putting their lives at risk.

The two werewolves fronted up. The black-fur retreated towards its stunned companion. The one-eye stalked.

Shouts came from the crowd, a cacophony of voices crisscrossing.

Helicopters swooped. The creatures' pelts bristled.

The black-fur that had slammed into the sign rose on unsteady legs and shook itself down like a dog that had been swimming. Glass showered from its fur. Flames spat from the mutilated sign. The animal snarled and charged at the one-eye, sweeping past its companion.

The werewolves clashed.

The earth seemed to shake.

A gasp went through the crowd.

The werewolves tumbled. Dust rose from their coats. They became black blurs, wheeling around the intersection. Ramming into cars. Bowling over people careless enough to get too close.

The other black-fur fixed on Dasaev.

Not again, he thought.

He aimed the Sig Sauer at the werewolf.

A voice said, "Sir, put down your gun," and Dasaev looked.

A police officer had him in his sights.

Dasaev said, "What are you doing?"

The officer, gun hand shaking, said, "Gun down, sir."

From the corner of his eye, Dasaev saw the werewolf dash towards him.

He wheeled to face the creature.

The nervy cop shouted:

"Sir, the gun, drop it or I'll – "

Dasaev fired at the werewolf. The animal veered to the left. The bullet missed. Pinged into a black van. ESU men flooded out of the vehicle. Clad in balaclavas. Armed with submachine guns.

Dasaev said, "Shit."

He turned. The werewolf he'd shot at steered into the path of the nervy cop – and kept going. Dasaev screwed up his face. The werewolf bowled into the cop and ripped him open, clawed out the man's insides.

Dasaev shot at the werewolf. Blood sprayed from its spine. The monster reared up and howled. Dropped down on four legs again and snarled at Dasaev.

The other two werewolves still fought frantically.

Two ESU teams now fanned out around Times Square. They ushered people out of the way. But the crowds were still thick.

New Yorkers hanging around to see what was going on. Dasaev knew the presence of civilians would make the police think carefully before shooting.

He hoped so, anyway.

Because the ESU team were now dropping to their knees and directing their MP5s towards the one-eye and the black-fur.

A throng swept down Broadway, towards him, and Dasaev frowned. Gunfire barked, and he saw muzzle flashes amid the stampeding crowd. And hurtling through the sea of bodies came a russet-coloured werewolf.

Dasaev held his breath.

The crowd parted, spilling into the masses already packed into Seventh Avenue and West 42nd Street.

Following the werewolf came a man in fatigues. He carried a pistol and a shotgun. He kept firing behind him. Didn't seem to care where he was shooting.

Dasaev recognized him.

Jerry Bahrman.

The russet-coloured werewolf ploughed into half a dozen ESU men and they were scattered like ten-pins.

The battling werewolves parted. Each one panted, tongues lolling. Drooling with exhaustion.

The russet-fur slashed and tore at the ESU. The armed men retreated, firing as they went. A section of crowd dropped to the ground. Dasaev heard a "hold your fire" command.

The crowd scattered again. Escaping bullets and werewolves.

The black-fur Dasaev had shot came for him.

ESU guys started firing. Bullets chewed up the road. People dived for cover, screaming. The werewolf dodged a hail of gunfire.

Dasaev hobbled away from its path.

The creature turned, joined the other black-fur and the russet-fur as they stalked the one-eye.

Now she had three of the werewolves closing in on her.

Bahrman fired at the ESU guys and said over the noise, "Kill her, fucking kill her," and the werewolves closed on the one-eye.

CHAPTER 119.
BLOODSPORT.

FAY Colsano said, "Are you getting this? Are you getting this?" her voice a squeal.

The cameraman aimed his lens at the war zone below. He said, "I'm getting it, Fay, I'm getting it." She looked over her shoulder. The pink-haired girl trained her camera over the city. Watched the crowds spill away from Times Square.

An exodus.

Fay's heart raced. She'd never felt this excited. She gripped the back of the pilot's seat. The ground swirled and swerved beneath her. She felt sick and fought the nausea. Couldn't throw up on camera, though. She knew she looked a mess. Her face was smeared with make-up, dust, and blood. But that was OK. Those were war wounds. But not vomit. Especially not her own.

Despite the evacuation, hundreds still crammed Times Square. They blocked 42nd Street both ways, and thronged up Broadway and 7th Avenue.

They were like a crowd at a gladiatorial event. Come to watch a bloodsport. And the advertisers were there too: Budweiser, Coca-Cola, McDonald's, Toshiba, the curved NASDAQ screen. News crawlers giving the latest headlines. The Chevrolet clock telling the time. The glare from the hundreds of signs lit the arena. One of the signs spat out flames after a werewolf had ploughed into it.

Fay looked down, and her head swam.

Three werewolves stalked the black-fur – the woman who told Fay to get out of the parking lot and then changed into this animal.

"When do they want me?" Fay asked the producer over the roar of the rotors.

"We're going live in sixty seconds," he said in her headset. "How are you going to go?"

"I'm going to ask how this happened. Question the morality of stem cell research, cloning. That's got to be something to do with this."

"Fay, this has got nothing to do with that."

"How the hell do you know? How do any of us know? I looked those things in the eye, and they're freaks. They're not normal. Something must've made them, must've created them – and it wasn't God, was it."

"He's not that good; he created you," said the producer.

"I heard that."

The helicopter swooped again. Fay's stomach lurched. She put a hand to her mouth. The cameraman swayed in the door. The producer grabbed the strap that attached the cameraman to the pilot's seat.

The producer said, "Look at this footage," and Fay glanced over at the monitor.

Three werewolves circled the one-eye.

"Don't take your eyes off that," she told the cameraman.

"Don't tell me my fucking job, Fay," he said.

"Ten," said the producer, "nine, eight... "

Fay swallowed. Hand-combed her hair. Fixed on the camera held by the pink-haired girl.

"Live," said the producer.

"We're a hundred feet above Times Square and witnessing an astonishing battle between animals modern science has dismissed as fake, a myth. But they are here in New York City, today, and I've seen them face-to-face. I almost lost my life to them."

The producer rolled his eyes. Fay bristled, and her nape flushed. But she didn't miss a beat.

She went on:

"The authorities are trying their best to evacuate the Times Square area." She glanced down. "New York has learned, it seems, from the experience of London, eight years ago, when a similar incident took place that resulted in the death of dozens of innocent people."

Her hair whipped about. The helicopter veered. The pilot said, "Cops, we need to go," and then she heard a voice over a loudspeaker saying, "This is the New York City Police Department. All unofficial traffic must depart this airspace immediately. Immediately."

"Fuck them," said Fay.

The producer hissed.

Fay gasped. Realized what she'd done.

Said fuck live on air.

She stared into the camera and her mouth opened and closed, but no words came.

The producer mouthed the word "apologize" over and over.

"I am desperately sorry – "

"They've cut you off," said the producer.

"What?"

"Just after you told the NYPD to fuck off."

The roar of the helicopter thundered in her head. She said, "Keep shooting," to the cameraman aiming his lens on Times Square.

The pilot said, "We're being told to leave."

Helicopters filled the sky above the intersection, all the channels vying for airspace. The NYPD chopper hovered overhead.

"CNN isn't leaving. Fox isn't leaving. I'm not leaving," said Fay.

"I am," said the pilot.

Fay fumed. She rose out of her seat. "No you're fucking not – this is my show."

The copter skewed left. Fay gasped, felt gravity pull her. She fell into the cameraman. The producer reached out. Grabbed her clawing hand. Tugged her towards him.

"Careful," he said.

She felt sick.

"Shit, look at this," said the cameraman.

Fay yanked her hand from the producer's grasp and sat next to the cameraman, looking. Two of the werewolves fought. Two others circled the fight. The russet-coloured one stared up.

And a man with a gun stared up at them too. And aimed his weapon right at the helicopter.

Fay's chest turned cold.

He started to fire.

The pilot screamed, and everyone winced at the assault on their ears.

The helicopter swerved. Fay rocked. Her legs turned to water. She knew she was going and couldn't stop it. Head first. Out of the pitching helicopter.

She found her voice and screamed.

The producer called her name.

The air rushed past her. She stared up into the camera as she fell, her face stretched in a scream.

She was being filmed. She was the story.

She hit the ground. Pain exploded through her body. She moaned. Couldn't move. Couldn't breathe. Everything on fire. Her head throbbed, and blood filled her nose and mouth. Her leg was trapped behind her, and her foot was tangled in her hair. The impossibility of it sent her mind reeling, and she realized she'd been unmade and would never be made back again.

She wailed at the realization that she was doomed.

She moved her eyes, and they rested on the russet-coloured werewolf.

Skulking towards her.

Fay blubbered.

Tried to move again, but nothing worked, and the pain was awful.

The werewolf darted forward.

She screamed.

Terror turned her insides to liquid.

She looked up to heaven and saw only a camera staring down at her from the helicopter.

The werewolf went at her with fury.

CHAPTER 120.
FRIENDS AND FOES.

SAFIA'S hand tightened around the blonde's girl's fingers. The blonde girl stared straight ahead. Her face looked calm. Unlike all the other people who were watching what was going on.

They were heaving on the pavement. Pressed together and not moving. The police tried to steer everyone away. But now people had slowed their evacuation. They wanted to stay. Wanted to watch. No matter what the cops said or how much they harried.

Safia didn't want to leave, although she'd seen these creatures before. Seen a black-fur kill her father and his gang, and that killing had made her free.

It was the same black-fur they were here to protect. The one with one eye, fighting with another dark-furred werewolf. The battle was frantic. Safia could hardly keep up. The creatures flashed across the intersection.

At the same time, the russet-coloured werewolf was tearing at the woman who'd fallen from the sky. Another black-fur stalked a hobbling man. And now a brown-fur ploughed into the crowd across the street, grabbing people and tossing them about like they were bones or sticks.

Armed police skirted the area where the werewolves were fighting.

Safia looked up at the blonde girl again and said her name: "Gala?"

It was such a beautiful name for the girl with golden hair and chalk-white skin.

"Gala?" said Safia again, and Gala glanced at her. Safia said, "Will they kill her?"

Gala's gaze returned to the combat. She swallowed, her throat bobbing. She said, "No, they won't. She's Laura. And we are here."

It sounded vague to Safia. That's what they'd been saying on the internet for days, for weeks – for years:

We'll protect her.

They hadn't said how they planned to do that, and Safia was worried that they might not have thought about it too carefully.

She wanted to ask how. But she was the youngest, and they were mostly all grown-up. Gala was nineteen or twenty. The man called Paul French was at least forty. Safia didn't know how many there were of them. She'd come when the text arrived:

The day is here, it said, and explained where everything was happening. Gala had sent it hours ago. She said they should gather in New York.

"Come on," said Gala, and she moved through the crowd.

Safia held her hand tightly. She didn't want to let go. Didn't want to get lost.

They pressed through the throng and out into the street. The glare of the lights beaming from the signs blinded her. She blinked and tried to watch the battle.

The one-eye had the black-fur by the throat.

"Gala – wait," said Safia.

Gala stopped.

They watched. The one-eye forced the black-fur back, teeth sunk into its neck. One-eye shook her head rapidly from side to side. Blood sprayed from black-fur's throat.

The other black-fur yelped and turned away from the hobbling man it stalked and darted towards the fighting werewolves. One-eye tossed the dead black-fur aside and prepared to face a second attack.

Safia's eyes widened as the dead werewolf melted back into a man. She stared at the naked body, blood and dirt smearing his skin. His throat had been torn open. The crowd gasped and screamed. Police hurried towards the body. They dragged the carcass away. They hoisted it up on a stretcher and slid it into the back of a black van, which sped off down Broadway.

"Where are they taking it?" she asked Gala.

"To find out how they change, to experiment on it. They would do the same to Laura if they caught her. That's why she hides."

Gala pulled Safia along again.

Safia watched the werewolves fight.

She said a prayer for Laura.

The noise was loud. Helicopters swooped overhead. Lots of shouting. Sirens screaming, sounding like wailing babies. A man who'd shot at the helicopters was now shooting at the police.

And then the brown-coloured werewolf charged across the street towards them.

* * * *

SHERATON JFK AIRPORT HOTEL, SOUTH CONDUIT AVENUE, NEW YORK

Ruth stared at the TV screen in her hotel room. She put a hand to her chest. Grabbed the collar of her dressing gown.

Interference marred the footage. The cameras shook and the voiceovers broke up. Most of the shots came from the helicopters above Times Square. But now and again, the studio would say they'd had mobile phone footage from witnesses. They cut to that. Blurred and grainy images of werewolves fighting. You couldn't make them out, they moved so quickly.

And then they'd shown Bahrman shooting at police officers, the news programme cutting back to the chalk-faced studio presenter when they realized what was happening.

They cut back to another angle.

The brown-fur – Nick Sears – rampaging through the crowd, causing panic and a stampede.

The ESU teams raced towards the Sears werewolf, drawing their guns away from Greenacre and the Muir boy.

Ruth grimaced. *Shoot them*, she urged the police, *shoot them. Kill them all.*

Kill them all, every one of them.

Her skin prickled. She was on edge. Laura Greenacre would be dead in a few moments. And then she could return to England, revive the Templeton dynasty. She cursed one thing, though: she should've brought the briefcase with her.

The new blood. The blood that would make monsters.

But Procter had to hold on to it. They hadn't known if a single dose would work. Procter would then have had to administer a second one.

But from the footage Ruth was watching, there was little doubt that one measure of Greenacre/Templeton blood had been enough.

Earlier, she'd had a frantic call from Procter, rambling on about being left half-naked with the Russian in a basement and that she *must* send someone *now* to pick him up.

Then the line went dead.

She fretted about the briefcase and the blood. Worried that Procter had made a mess of it all.

She chewed her nails. Watched the TV. Her skin rippled.

A rap at the door snapped her out of the trance.

She told whoever was there to come in.

A young man with olive skin and dark eyes entered the room, carrying a cocktail on a tray.

"Mrs Smith," he said. "Your margarita."

The waiter smiled at her, and she tilted her head.

"That's kind," she said. "What's your name?"

He said he was called Freddy.

"You're delicious, Freddy," she said.

He blushed and dipped his chin. "Thank you, ma'am."

She turned her back on him and waved him out. "You can go now, but come back in two hours, and if I'm awake, you can come into my bed."

She fixed on the TV and heard the door shut behind her.

She watched the battle.

Die, all of you, she thought, *die and leave me to reign.*

She sipped her cocktail.

CHAPTER 121.
LINE OF FIRE.

DASAEV crouched behind an overturned bus.

Bullets pinged into the vehicle. A window shattered. Glass sprayed the road. The helicopter that moments ago had spilled out the woman careered away down Seventh Avenue, towards Carnegie Hall. Two police choppers herded the other TV helicopters away, but some of them climbed to avoid the official cordon. They played chase in the sky.

Dasaev peered around the bus. Bahrman knelt behind a Ford that was raked by bullets. He fired with a pistol and a shotgun. The shotgun took chunks out of the street, out of buildings, out of cars.

People cowered and threw themselves to the ground as the firefight went on around them. The cops seemed unwilling to fire back. They'd not succeeded in evacuating the area and were probably reluctant to shoot with civilians around.

Dasaev didn't want to risk a shot either.

But Bahrman had no misgivings.

Dasaev gritted his teeth against the pain and hobbled as quickly as he could towards Bahrman. The mercenary saw him coming. He wheeled, shock on his face to start with, but a grin spreading when he recognized Dasaev.

Bahrman swung the shotgun round, but he was too slow. Dasaev yelled out. Threw himself forward. Barged into

Bahrman. Slashed with his cane. Bahrman grunted and dropped his weapons. They hit the ground. Dasaev's Sig Sauer slipped from his fingers. A gun went off. Bahrman groaned. Dasaev looked up, thinking the thug had been shot. Bahrman elbowed him in the face.

Dasaev saw stars.

Another blow to the head made Dasaev almost black out.

Bahrman straddled him. Dasaev came to and bucked. Bahrman jerked forward, hands out for protection. Dasaev rammed his knee up between Bahrman's legs, knocking him off. Bahrman rolled away.

Dasaev crawled.

The gun lay two yards away.

He stretched for it.

Bahrman was up, sliding feet first like a baseball player towards base. He booted Dasaev's hand away from the gun. Dasaev punched Bahrman in the face, and his knuckles cracked.

Bahrman's nose bled. He got to his feet and staggered about. He said, "I should've killed you, shouldn't I, Boris."

"You should have," said Dasaev.

Bahrman looked down. Dasaev saw what he saw.

The shotgun at his feet.

Too far for Dasaev.

Bahrman spit blood and smirked, his teeth stained red.

"I'll do it now," said Bahrman. He leaned to pick up the gun.

Mustering all his energy, Dasaev sprang, panther-like, and tackled Bahrman around the waist. They flew out across the street, Dasaev pumping his legs, forcing Bahrman backwards.

Gunfire rattled. Bullets riddled Bahrman. Blood spurted from his body. He jigged in Dasaev's grasp, and Dasaev huddled behind the man, using him as a shield.

Bahrman danced as the gunfire raked him. Dasaev threw himself aside. They shot at him. Bullets hacked into the asphalt. He rolled and rolled till he was dizzy.

Bahrman wilted and flopped to the ground, soaked in blood.

Dasaev took cover under a truck.

He watched one-eye and black-fur do battle. Blood stained the ground. Dasaev went cold with fear. Had Laura been shot? The rain of bullets must have been hard to avoid. He heard screams. The ESU guys shouted, "That one's attacking civilians."

Dasaev saw a brown-fur tear through the crowd. Where the cops couldn't fire.

* * * *

"Run," said Gala, shoving Safia. Safia screamed. The crowd carried her. She didn't want to let go of Gala's hand. She glanced over her shoulder. The brown-fur was ten yards away. Shaking a boy, aged nine or ten, maybe, in its jaws. A woman clung to the beast's flank, her face etched with terror. Her screams coming out as: "My baby, my baby."

Safia's throat tightened. She looked away. Her stomach churned. She felt sick.

"Over here." It was Mr French. He waved at them to hurry.

"We have to be quicker, Safia," said Gala, puffing as she ran.

The brown-fur was close now, clawing, slashing, biting. People fell under its feet, dragged down, trampled by the monster. They were snatched up in the werewolf's jaws and shaken and tossed away. Most survived, picking themselves up, bloodied and quivering with terror. But it was no comfort.

Safia's legs were weak.

"Why – why don't they shoot it?" she said.

"The police can't shoot it, Safia," said Gala. "The bullets might miss, might kill us."

CHAPTER 122.
LAST STAND.

DASAEV watched two ESU men drag Bahrman's remains away, leaving a trail of blood. Then he rolled from his hiding place. Crawled along the road using his elbows to haul himself along. Got to the shotgun. Got to the cane.

He scanned the intersection.

Carnage.

The russet-fur and the black-fur were battling one-eye.

Laura, thought Dasaev.

He rose and cursed at the pain in his body. Crossed himself. Raised the weapon. A Mag-10 Roadblocker. A monster shotgun, weighing more than ten pounds and sporting a 22-inch barrel. A werewolf killer.

He loped forward, towards the fighting werewolves.

He would save her. He would do some good. Even if it meant his death.

But if I do *get through this*, he thought, *Galina is gone. My marriage is over.*

He thought of Dominika. When he got home, he would ask her if there were hope for them. But that was for when he got home. Not now. He cast the future aside. He cocked the Mag-10.

From the corner of his eye, he saw figures flying through the air.

He turned away from the fight. Saw the brown-fur chasing down fleeing people. Hunting them, maiming them. Hurtling back and forth, herding the crowd, picking off the weakest. Dasaev looked around. Found what he wanted. Picked up the chunk of asphalt churned up by gunfire. Hurled it at the werewolf and clipped the creature on the head. Concrete dust puffed up and the monster reeled. Then turned to face Dasaev.

The werewolf snarled, came racing towards him.

Dasaev braced himself, Mag-10 jammed into his shoulder. Eyes fixed on the charging monster. Focusing on what was behind the beast. Waiting for a clear shot.

Ten yards away now. Dasaev smelled the creature's breath, the steam billowing from its snout.

Dasaev fired. The recoil knocked him back. The werewolf's head disappeared in a cloud of blood. The body kept coming, but five yards from Dasaev it just slumped on the road.

For a few seconds, Dasaev couldn't hear anything. He saw a headless human corpse lie where the werewolf had fallen.

The growl of helicopters became louder and louder, and he looked up.

A balaclava-clad man aimed an MP5 at him.

He saw the muzzle flash

Bullets raked the street next to him. He stumbled away. He looked up. The ESU man fired again. Dasaev's instinct was to shoot back. But the guy was a cop.

The balaclava man fired again, hitting the road next to Dasaev. He dived for cover behind a burning car. Felt the heat sear his skin. Were they trying to kill him or get him out of the way?

The helicopter swooped, trying to pinpoint him, spotlight sweeping over the car. He peered towards the werewolves. One-eye had killed the other black-fur and was now going claw-to-claw, teeth-to-teeth, with the russet-fur.

A voice came through the cacophony:

"Shoot the animals, shoot to kill!"

Dasaev's nape prickled.

"No," he said.

Russet-fur and black-fur reared up. They went at each other furiously.

Dasaev shot up at the helicopter and peppered the underside. The chopper swerved away. The shooter rocked in his seat and grabbed at the door.

Dasaev darted from his hiding place.

ESU men raced forward.

They were going to kill Laura.

Dasaev hobbled towards the werewolves. Fear swarmed through him. He knew how this would end. He aimed and shouted for the ESU team to stay back. The armed unit fanned out. Shouldered their weapons. Guns trained on the haze of fur sweeping across Time Square.

Dasaev got within ten feet of the battle. He could smell the musk coming off the animals. He glanced at them once and then held the Mag-10 above his head.

"Don't shoot," he said, his words dying in the sounds of violence filling the air.

"Put down your weapon," said an ESU man.

"Don't kill her," said Dasaev.

The roar of rotor blades made him wince.

He looked at the one-eye. She was mounted on russet-fur's back. Her teeth buried in its nape. Her flanks rising and falling. Blood oozed from her jaws. She issued the killing bite. Snapped her head back and brought out the russet-fur's spine in an explosion of blood.

Dasaev recoiled.

She flung the backbone away and reared up and howled.

She'd killed them all.

And now, unless he'd do something, she would die.

"Kill that animal," said the ESU man.

Dasaev yelled and blasted the air with the monster shotgun.

CHAPTER 123.
THE LAST GREENACRE
WEREWOLF.

KILL her, thought Ruth, watching in her hotel room, *kill her, you idiots.*

"They have the creature surrounded," said the news presenter on the TV, "but – oh my God, the – the guy with the shotgun he's – "

Ruth went cold.

It was the Russian. Wavering there like a drunk. Covered in blood and dust. Swinging a shepherd's crook. Brandishing that shotgun and blasting the air with it. Not even shooting *at* the police.

Weak fool, thought Ruth.

The Greenacre werewolf reared up on its hind legs and howled. The noise set Ruth's teeth on edge, and her insides went cold. Billy Sears lay naked and dead at the werewolf's feet.

The news presenter was saying something about the events, the metamorphoses, what kind of medical experimentation gone wrong was this? "Science gone awry," he said, "like our late, great colleague, Fay Colsano, who died to bring you this story, had feared: stem cell research, cloning, playing God – this is what we have here."

Ruth held her breath.

Dasaev wheeled around.

Three gunshots.

Ruth covered her ears.

Dasaev jerked three times.

The shotgun fell from his hand.

Ruth let out a laugh.

Dasaev dropped to his knees.

He leaned on the staff.

The news anchor's voiceover said, "They've shot him, oh my God, they've killed him, ladies and gentlemen."

The camera zoomed in. Dasaev crumpled to the ground. He stared up at the skies. Blood made a dark halo around his head.

He was dead.

Ruth roared with laughter and then said, "End it, end it – kill the bitch."

The ESU team trained their weapons on Laura Greenacre.

"They're going to shoot it, now," said the commentator.

The last Greenacre werewolf hunched. The creature panted. Blood matted its fur. Saliva draped from its jaws. The animal had no fight left, exhausted after warring with four of Ruth's creations.

"Kill her," said Ruth, and then louder: "Kill her, kill the bitch."

She jumped to her feet. Elation filled her. It felt like a drug.

She wanted to applaud as the ESU team corralled the werewolf, corralled it so they could put it down.

Ruth said, "Now. Kill it now" and the ESU man raised his hand, preparing to give the order to shoot.

And then, in the corner of the screen, something was happening.

* * * *

"Sir," said one of the guys in the ESU lieutenant's earpiece, "sir, look, look at this."

The lieutenant glanced over his shoulder, not wanting to take his eyes off the werewolf too long. Knowing that this kind of creature had wiped out Shaun Shortcroft's ESU team earlier in the day.

What he saw made him freeze.

"What the hell are they doing?" he said, more to himself than anyone else.

"More of them," said another ESU member.

A voice boomed from the helicopter: "Step away from the intersection. Step away from the intersection. Please leave the area immediately. This is an order – "

But they weren't listening.

Dozens of them. The lieutenant's gaze flitted around doing a quick count. Seventy, eighty, ninety, more... they kept spilling forward.

"Who are they?" someone asked.

The civilians filed forward. They looked like they were in a trance. The lieutenant turned back to the creature. The animal shuffled over to the dead man, the guy who had the shotgun. The creature sniffed the man's face and licked it. A whine came from the animal's throat. It nuzzled the dead man's throat, nudging the carcass as if trying to revive it.

The lieutenant was entranced.

The animal whimpered and whined. Craned its neck and howled. The noise made the lieutenant shudder. He raised his weapon.

"Ready, boys," he said.

The werewolf lay down next to the dead man.

The lieutenant aimed his MP5 at the animal.

"No, no, stay where you are," came shouts over his earpiece. He looked up. The civilians were crowding in. Ring-fencing the werewolf and the dead man. Spooling around them. Forcing the ESU team backwards.

The lieutenant shuffled back and said, "Move away, move away," to the civilians herding forward.

A blonde woman with snow-white skin said, "You are not killing her," her accent foreign. "You have no right. We stand with her."

The lieutenant's adrenaline raced. He glanced at his colleagues. They were being forced back. He looked at these people flocking into Times Square. Men, women, old, young. They circled the werewolf and the dead man. The circle growing deeper. Pushing outwards. Coiling like a snake. Compelling the ESU men to retreat.

"She is not yours to kill," said the woman.

"I – I'm ordering you, move away," said the lieutenant, fixing on the blonde who'd just spoken. He wasn't going to fire. No way he'd fire on an unarmed civilian. But he had to threaten her. He said, "We're ordering you to move and if you don't move, I will tell my men to open fire – "

"Oh God," came a voice over his earpiece.

He looked up. The ESU man in the chopper stared down into the circle and said it again: "Oh God." The lieutenant waved the chopper away and it swooped off.

Someone said, "Sir, sir – look at this – "

He wheeled towards the voice. He gasped at the sight. His legs buckled.

Another team member said, "What do we do, lieutenant?"

He said nothing. Watched the crowds pour from the stores and the restaurants and the sidewalk, from Seventh Avenue and from Broadway and from the west and the east along 42nd Street. A sea of people washing towards them.

The crowd swamped the ESU team. Not hurting them. Not laying a hand on them. Just making them part of the throng. The armed officers couldn't fire. Couldn't do anything. The lieutenant heaved, but it was useless. In his earpiece, he heard his men issuing warnings that no one heeded, and he finally relaxed. Allowed the crowd to carry him. Became one with the horde.

Times Square choked with people.

The lieutenant, calm now, asked, "Can, you see anything from up there?"

The ESU guy in the chopper said, "She's gone, lieutenant. She's gone."

"Who's gone?"

"The werewolf... the woman... she's gone."

"Gone?"

"She must've slipped into the crowd. There's only the dead man."

PART FIVE.

THE WINTER IS PAST.

CHAPTER 124.
GOODBYE, LEV.

NOVODEVICHY CEMETERY, MOSCOW – JANUARY 7, 2008

DOMINIKA Burgasova shivered. She'd never known a harder cold than this. It was a cold that went deep into her and froze her heart.

Or maybe that was grief.

She should've known, because she'd felt it before, the grief you feel when love is torn from you. Like love, she thought you only experienced such grief once. But like love, she'd experienced it twice.

After her husband had died, she never imagined another man who could make her heart swell so much would come into her life. But one had, and now he was gone too. Lying cold in that mahogany coffin. The gravedigger chucking ice-laced soil over the wood.

Lev, she thought, and anguish swarmed through her.

She mourned his death and mourned never touching him, never kissing him, never making love with him.

She sobbed and thought of his wife and wondered what madness had taken hold of her to treat him like she did. He was the best man Dominika had ever known, and she couldn't understand why Galina regarded him with such contempt.

She'd been here, of course, Galina. Playing the dutiful wife. Putting on a show for the photographers she'd invited. Not many of them came. Not as many as Galina had hoped for, Dominika was sure. The papers weren't interested these days. She was growing old. There were other starlets ahead of her. But she tried to use Lev's death to generate publicity for herself.

Her time had passed, though. She was not a story any more. She was not the philandering wife of Moscow's most promising police officer now. She was the widow of a rogue cop.

A cop best forgotten.

Dominika cried as the dirt covered the casket. She felt pain for him in her breast. Abandoned by his wife and by his employers. Buried here like a difficult truth.

She'd fought for him. Demanded he be recognized for his courage, for his service. The scenes from Times Square riveted viewers across Russia. And when it was discovered that the man who died trying to protect the werewolf was a Russian cop, the scandal sheets raged and ranted. The American authorities seethed. Held Lev's body for a long while. Carried out post-mortem examinations. Tested him for infection. Considered destroying the carcass if it carried a disease.

The bosses hauled Colonel Gromeko to the sixth floor and savaged him. He came back down and savaged his underlings:

"Dasaev is disgraced," he said. "He is to be forgotten. He brought shame on this uniform, this department. He went rogue."

Dominika went up to Gromeko after his outburst and said, "Do you believe that, or did they tell you what to say?"

He scowled at her and said, "What do you think, sergeant?"

She asked him if he wanted her to go look for this woman, Ruth Templeton. "And if I do, will you throw me to the lions as well?" she said.

Gromeko's face locked in a scowl.

The Templeton woman had disappeared. She'd travelled before under the name Mrs William Smith. A woman of that name had left New York's JFK Airport for Frankfurt the morning after the Times Square tragedy. After that, nothing.

NYPD officers discovered Lawrence Procter in a basement a few blocks from New York's Port Authority Bus Terminal.

He'd babbled and frothed at the mouth, they said. The UK authorities extradited him to England, where he would soon face trial for sexual assault. The Crown Prosecution Service in Britain had charged him eight years previously, but he'd fled before his court appearance. Now they could put him in the dock. The English tabloids salivated. Dominika thought they were worse than the Moscow red tops.

Gromeko told her she would not be sent out to look for Ruth Templeton, but the investigation into Vasili Koldenko's murder did remain open. "And if you do come across new information or evidence," he said, "you should pursue it in the manner one expects from an officer of the MVD."

"As Major Dasaev would have done."

Gromeko leaned in and said, "Precisely as Major Dasaev would have done," and then he spun on his heel and strode away.

Gromeko came to the funeral. The whole department had been there. And they all went to Dasaev's father and shook his hand before they filed away. And when it was Gromeko's turn, he embraced the old priest and kissed him on both cheeks, and when they came apart, Dominika saw that both men were crying.

She shivered now, the cold biting. Everyone had left. Only she and the gravediggers remained.

Six inches of snow carpeted the ground, and it kept falling, making it hard to see. The sky had been grey like lead for days. Gloom had settled over Moscow, and there was no sign of it lifting.

Dominika's hackles rose. A feeling that she was being watched. She shuddered and looked over her shoulder.

A woman stood on the path that led towards the main gate. She was about fifty yards away from Dominika. A dark figure on the pale landscape. She wore an ankle-length black coat. A navy blue *shapka* covered her head, the muffs drawn down over her ears. She also had on a pair of sunglasses. *Not an item you need in Moscow at the moment*, thought Dominika. The woman leaned on a shepherd's staff that was taller than her, and she looked towards Dominika and gave a little bow of her head.

Dominika turned away and hurried over to the graveside. Bent down and handed one of the gravediggers a few roubles. Wheeled round and prepared to stride down the path towards the woman.

But she stopped in her tracks.

The woman had vanished.

The snow fell on her tracks.

The shepherd's staff rested on a gravestone.

CHAPTER 125.
STILL RUNNING.

BLACK MOUNTAINS, SOUTH-EAST WALES – 3.33 P.M., MARCH 7, 2008

SOPHIE'S lungs burned. Her heart thundered, and she thought it would burst. She could barely lift her legs now, and her ankle throbbed. She ran on adrenaline.

She looked behind her.

The gold-fur bounded across the mountains. Thirty yards between them.

Sophie cried. Cried because she was going to die so young and after a horrible, horrible life. Her dad always forgetting her birthday, Her mum and him rowing. Her parents finally splitting. Never seeing Dad. Her mum dying. Billy betraying her. Those men taking her. Doing terrible things to her.

She knew the world must hate her.

She knew she must've done something wrong.

Her stars told her every day.

She screamed, wished she were closer to home, wished Dad could come and rescue her again.

She kept running. She thought she would faint. Came to a footpath cutting through the fields. A path that wound uphill. Her body ached with the effort. Her chest burned – *no more fags*, she thought, *no more fags*. She ran through bracken. Thorns and nettles tore and stung at her legs.

She glanced again.

The werewolf gained on her.

She could see its teeth. She felt queasy at the thought of those incisors tearing into her.

She pumped her legs, eyes fixed on the crest of the hill. Tears burning her eyes.

A dark-haired woman appeared at the ridge. She had a patch over her right eye and looked like a pirate with that and her long coat.

Sophie screamed.

"Help," she said, "please help me."

The woman stood straight and stared out. She beckoned for Sophie to hurry, and Sophie did, finding energy somewhere to clamber up the slope.

"There's a monster – it's coming – we've got to go – it's a werewolf," said Sophie as she came up to the woman.

The woman's good eye flickered, and for a second it didn't look human to Sophie.

The woman said, "It's all right. Stand behind me."

Sophie cowered behind the woman.

The werewolf came, and Sophie felt dread growing in her. The beast snarled and snapped its jaws. Breath billowed from its nostrils. Claws churned up the earth.

Sophie's legs buckled, and she fell to the ground.

The werewolf skidded to a halt ten yards from the woman, gouging the ground, soil and dirt slicing up.

The creature reared up on its hind legs and howled.

The sound blistered Sophie's hearing, and she put her hands over her ears.

The werewolf dropped back on all fours and hunkered down. Swayed as if ready to pounce. Snarled and showed its teeth.

"You expect me to fight you, Ruth?" said the woman with one eye.

Sophie looked at the werewolf.

Ruth Templeton.

Oh my God, she thought. "Oh my God," she said.

Sophie stared up at the woman. Her dark hair flapped in the wind. Sophie knew everything now. Knew who was here on the mountain with her. Knew who stood with her. Who protected her. Knew for the first time that everything could be all right after all.

The werewolf growled.

"I'm not going to fight you," said the woman.

"Please fight her," said Sophie.

"You're not worthy of seeing the animal in me," the woman told the werewolf.

The werewolf bristled. Ready to pounce. Muscles flexing under its damp, golden pelt.

"You are not an animal, Ruth. You are not a Greenacre. You are something to put down."

The werewolf sprang.

Sophie screamed.

The woman flicked back her coat. A gun in her belt. Whipped it out.

The werewolf reared up.

The woman fired.

Sophie flinched.

The werewolf jerked, and blood spouted from its head. The animal staggered away, blood pouring from the scalp wound. The creature whirled around and came again.

The woman fired once more. The werewolf yelped as the bullet slammed into its chest. The monster reared up and reeled. The werewolf coughed and spluttered, and blood came up from its throat and spilled from the jaws.

The creature keeled over and hit the ground and became still.

Sophie goggled as the creature dwindled.

And in its place, a naked woman.

Golden-haired and white-fleshed. Blood in her hair and on her breast.

The dark-haired woman lowered the gun and turned to face Sophie.

Sophie smelled cordite. A plume of smoke billowed from the barrel of the pistol.

Sophie looked up at her and into the eye of an animal.

The woman said, "I'm Laura, and I love your father."

CHAPTER 126.
THE GLADNESS OF HIS HEART.

THORN heard the gunshots. He looked up from his shovel and out across the fields. His heart fluttered and he didn't know why. A knot tightened in his belly.

Shooting wasn't unusual here. Farmers culling fox and rabbits. The Army training in the distance. But these shots sounded different.

A shiver ran down his spine.

Sophie. Where's Sophie?

She'd been spending more time wandering the mountains lately. Maybe she was trying to "find herself" or something. Some new age, self-help crap that didn't or wouldn't work. But if it made her feel better, he was OK with it.

She was scarred, his child.

His child.

It felt more real, somehow, after she'd told him she wanted to be Sophie Thorn.

More real and more terrifying.

He wanted to heal her but didn't know how. Psychiatrists said she needed time.

We have that, he'd told them.

And they did, and he would wait and wait and wait for her to be better again. He would do everything.

They didn't talk much, but she held his hand across the table sometimes and that made his heart swell and the tears come.

Their love had grown these past months. But it was a love forged of anguish and grief.

He looked out across the Black Mountains.

Where was she?

He'd been digging over the vegetable patch. Intended to grow potatoes, carrots, swedes, parsnips. Good, old-fashioned root vegetables ready for the autumn, stockpiled for winter. He stared towards the hills now. Sheep dotted the field. The sky glowered. Rains coming in the heavy, bruised clouds rolling in from the west. They said the winter had passed, but spring hadn't ventured here yet.

He took his phone out of his pocket and called Sophie's number. She didn't answer. He gritted his teeth and his blood quickened.

New York drilled into his mind. The battle of Times Square. The footage had been dreadful to watch, but Laura survived and then disappeared.

Slipped away.

But so had Ruth Templeton.

There'd been no sign of her, but Thorn knew she'd come. He waited every day for her. Braced himself for another attack. It was a way of life that would eventually drive a person mad, but he had to deal with it.

"Sophie." The back of his neck flushed. He shivered, adrenaline flooding his heart. "Sophie." But she'd not hear over these hills. It was desperation. He'd try the phone once more and then go look for her. He sensed something. A scent on the breeze – a danger. Only his instinct, of course. Only his mind: fraught by fear, fractured by suffering. But he didn't like to ignore gut feelings.

He dialled and waited.

The phone rang.

He heard something. A song on the wind. He narrowed his eyes. The phone rang in his ear, and from over the ridge the sound came back.

Dizzee Rascal.

The ringtone from Sophie's phone.

He gasped. Dropped the mobile. Eyes fixed on the ridge.

Two figures appeared over the crest of the hill, and his heart volcanoed.

He made a noise in his throat that was the embryo of a name.

Sophie waved at him.

He raised his arm, and it weighed a ton. His legs buckled. No strength in there to run. He leaned on the wall.

The other figure, the woman, dropped her coat. She started running towards him from the ridge. Half a mile away. Her pace quickened. Her long, dark hair fanned out. Her shape grew, and her clothes shred and rained like confetti, and she became something else in only a few steps.

Thorn dropped to his knees, sobbing, his mouth making a shape – that name again, but no real form to it.

The great wolf bounded across the fields towards him.

It – *she* – howled.

Her call swept over the land.

Sheep scattered. Birds rose from the trees in swarms.

Thorn clambered over the wall, stumbled forward a few yards. Dropped to his knees, the ground damp through his jeans. Held out his arms, and on the air he smelled her pelt and her flesh and remembered her skin on his skin and her name came loudly, like something born:

"*Laura!*"

The name carried across the landscape and she howled in reply and the distance between them shrank into nothing and they came to each other and melded into one.

And again the name, this time as a breath in her ear, his hands in her fur:

"*Laura.*"

THE END.

EXTRAS

THE MAKING OF . . .

MANEATER was never meant to have a sequel. Some reviewers and readers suggested the novel's "open ending" set up a follow-up. But it wasn't my intention. I just like that kind of ending. I had nothing more to say about Laura Greenacre, John Thorn, or the Templeton family.

When Snowbooks asked if I'd be writing a "part two", I said that although I'd never say "never", I wasn't planning to. I was into Skarlet by then – the first part of a trilogy, a long book, so I wasn't really thinking about Maneater. It had been published, I was overjoyed, and I'd moved on to the next project.

But Snowbooks' query planted a seed in my imagination. While writing Skarlet I did start to think about Laura, and Thorn, and Ruth, and Procter – the characters that still seemed to have something to say after Maneater.

And by the time I'd completed Skarlet in September 2008, I'd decided to seriously think about Maneater Part 2.

I like to have a good setting for a novel. Characters and story are the most important factors, but setting's up there, too. I like to use real places most of the time. I think it's useful to do that when you're writing in a fantastical genre such as horror. Seeing werewolves run amok in Trafalgar Square is more authentic than having them run around a made-up square in a made-up city, I think. Watching a vampire hang off Big Ben is more real than if the landmark is fictional.

So I chose New York. Not for any reason other than it was a great city with lots of wonderful landmarks that I could use.

Maneater ended with Ruth Andersson/Templeton finding Lawrence Procter in Moscow. She gets injected with Laura Greenacre's blood and is likely to become a werewolf.

I had to start the sequel there, really.

My Russian hero, Lev Dasaev, is named for two great Soviet-era goalkeepers. Lev Yashin was the intimidating "man in black", a powerful figure between the posts for the Soviet Union side of the 1950s and 1960s. Renat Dasaev was one of the world's great goalkeepers – the best at the time, I think. But he is best remembered for a goal he let in – Marco Van Basten's astonishing volley for Holland in the final of the 1988 European Championships.

The plot of Prey came quite easily. It stemmed from Ruth's lust for vengeance. I did find it difficult to bring John Thorn into the story at the beginning. During much of the first draft, he was sat in his smallholding in the Welsh mountains waiting for something to happen – and nothing much did. It was only when I put him and his daughter, Sophie, in peril that his story started to develop.

I started writing Prey on January 12, 2009 and completed the first draft ten weeks later, on March 20.

My first drafts are always rough. I usually take my outline and write and write, ploughing on, not stopping for mistakes, not stopping to check facts – I just fly through. When the first draft was done, the real work started. It's like chiselling at a piece of concrete, hoping you'll get a nice shape out of it at the end.

Well, it took nearly three months of chiselling until I had something that I could think of sending to Snowbooks. And now, you're holding it in your hands. A book, really, that was never meant to be.

I think the story of Laura and Thorn is at an end now. There's nothing more to say. I can't see another sequel. But, like I said, "Never say never."

DELETED SCENES

This scene was part of the chapter in which Dasaev escapes the safe house near the Port Authority Bus Terminal. He beats up Procter and then intends to make his way towards the trouble that seems to be brewing in Times Square. The roads are clogged and there are police everywhere, but a couple of film buffs come to our hero's aid. The scene was deleted in the third draft. It was just padding and served no purpose. You have to be ruthless when you're editing, and I mulled over this for a while before unleashing my editing pen – T.E.

TEN minutes later, Dasaev stood in the street.

Helicopters hovered in the distance. Smoke rose from between the skyscrapers and billowed into the night sky. Sirens wailed and horns blared.

A passer-by said, "It's like that movie Cloverfield, you know," and his companion said, "More like The Wolfman, I heard."

Dasaev limped towards the smoke.

"You headed back there?" said the film buff.

Dasaev nodded.

"Give you a ride? Looks like something we shouldn't be missing."

They were called Wiseman and Tucker. They took Dasaev to their car, illegally parked on the pavement. It was a yellow Honda. They headed across town in it, Dasaev in the back.

They babbled:

Wiseman: "Independence Day, The Day The Earth Stood Still, they just didn't cut it for me, man."

Tucker: "You still got your video camera, get our own 'day the earth stoodstill' here."

Wiseman: "You seen American Werewolf In London?"

"They had it for real eight years ago, man."

"Hey, might be we're having one today."

They whooped and cheered, and Dasaev's headache worsened.

"What happened to you, fella?" said the one called Wiseman.

"Had a fight with Predator," said Dasaev.

There was a second of silence. Then the guys burst out laughing.

They tried to turn left off East 42nd Street and onto Lexington Avenue, but police barriers blocked the way. Car horns blared. Smoke fogged the buildings. They crawled along. A cop stood by the window. Dasaev hid his face. Wiseman, driving, rolled down his window. He said, "What's up, officer?"

"What's up? Time's up, son, that's what's up."

"That's deep, officer. What's really up? We want to go down Lexington."

The officer took offence. He scowled. His eyes raked over the driver and the passengers. "What's up with the guy in the back?"

"We're making a movie. It's make-up," said Wiseman.

"Where you making a movie?"

"We're runners. This guy's the star. We're taking him to the set."

"And where's that, Mr Movie Man?" said the cop.

Wiseman said, "Where that smoke is."

"Oh yeah? Where all hell's breaking loose?"

"Hey, that's the name of the movie we're making."

"No movie there, son. You're not going anywhere. No one is. Road's closed."

"But what'll Mr Spielberg say?"

"He can say whatever he wants; no one's going through. Now, cut the crap and switch off your engine. This is where you're staying for the foreseeable."

Dasaev got out of the car.

The cop said, "Hey, mister, where are you going?"

Dasaev limped up the road, Wiseman behind him saying, "He's the star: big ego, big noise, does what he wants," while the cop came after him.

Dasaev picked up his pace.

The cop shouted for him to stop.

Drivers got out of their gridlocked cars. Some of them were angry. They tussled with other drivers and with pedestrians. Police on horses tried to separate the troublemakers.

Dasaev weaved through a group of drivers facing up to each other. He glanced over his shoulder. The cop followed him through the standoff. But then the officer halted. Glanced at Dasaev, then back at the worsening confrontation. Dasaev read the confusion in the cop's eyes — not sure whether to follow the lame stranger or do his civic duty and prevent trouble. He chose the latter.

Dasaev sighed. He hobbled on, following the noise, following the smoke.

* * * *

This scene was meant to show how ruthless Wheeler Burns could be. But we knew that anyway: the man hunts humans. The more I read this scene, the more it became obvious to me that it was violence for violence's sake. I think every scene has to be justified, and violent scenes are perfectly acceptable (and necessary in horror fiction) — but only if they serve a purpose. Panya's death is meaningless, but it is given meaning by Dasaev later. I felt it was important Panya was given that "meaning" after the cruel way in which she'd been dispatched in this scene. Of course, her burial scene, which remains in the novel, still serves a purpose. It gives us an insight into Dasaev's character and also hints at what Cleaver's really like — T.E.

THE girls shuffled in, and Procter licked his lips.

"Meet Panya and Inessa," said Burns. "From the country of Belarus."

"How... how do you get away with it, Wheeler?"

"Lawrence, I get away with it because of greed. Greed drives everything. Men are hungry for money, they are hungry for sex, they are hungry for power. If you can give them these things, then you have them by the balls. Corruption, you see, doctor, is a beautiful thing. You can always depend on its existence. You can find it if you look hard enough. Even in the purest of places. It will live. Corruption will find a way. And you can harness it. My grandfather recognized this. My father recognized this. I recognize this. There are too few good men in the world to prevent the spread of corruption. Too few good men who have the steel to deny their lusts. For money. For sex. For power."

Procter stared at the girls.

"How old are they?" he said.

"How the hell should I know?" said Burns. "Who gives a shit?"

Procter hummed. "Only asking." They looked young, late teens maybe. They shivered and gawped. Fear paled their faces. They were thin. Panya had short brown hair. The other one was a redhead. They wore vest-tops and mini skirts.

Burns put his arms around them and said, "We fuck, yes," in a loud, speaking-to-foreigners voice, and then to Procter he said: "They don't understand English, doctor."

"I'm not intending to have a conversation with them, Wheeler."

Burns nudged the girls forward. They stumbled towards Procter. He licked his lips and smiled.

The girl called Inessa, the redhead, said something in Russian. The words spilled out. The tendons in her thin neck were taut. Her eyes goggled.

Burns shoved her in the back and she lurched.

"Shut up," said Burns.

Procter's gaze flitted over the redhead. He loved to touch them, to move his hands over them. Loved to grasp at them and press against them.

And they loved it back. They just didn't know it. And only decided they didn't when bastards like John Thorn dripped poison into their ears. Procter gritted his teeth.

The anger rose in him at the thought of what had happened in England: Thorn encouraging that bloody nurse to go to the police, others coming out of the cracks then, to spread more lies about him. And the humiliation of being arrested, of being charged. He could feel the heat on his skin. He was dizzy, looking at Inessa, thinking about his hell.

The papers had camped outside his house, gone to his two ex-wives, tried to get dirt. The bitches gave them dirt. The tabloids couldn't print anything at the time. Not before a trial. But Procter heard that Harriet and Gwen had made allegations against him – that he treated women like slaves, that he hated them.

His desires boiled over now. He would unleash them on this young thing. He reached out for her, and she recoiled. "Hey," he said, "don't you move from me, it'll be nice. You'll like it," and he stepped towards her.

The girl called Inessa lashed out. She clipped him across the cheek. He whelped, and his skin felt on fire.

His fury erupted. He roared and went for her. Grabbed her by the hair. She shrieked, clawed at his arm. He raised his fist.

"Doctor!"

Burns's voice halted him. Procter froze. He stared over at the American.

Procter said, "W-what are you doing?"

"I am going to show you how strong I am. I am going to show you that I am king here. I am going to show you what I am able to do to people who piss me off."

Procter's grip on the girl loosened, and she wheeled away. He looked at Burns and said, "What are you going to do?"

Burns had his arm tight around the girl called Panya's throat. He had a gun pressed to her temple. She was limp in his grasp, and Procter saw the hope had gone from her eyes. He said, "There's no need – "

"I am going to show you how angry I am, Lawrence. I feel you have misled me. I feel you've not been honest about your reasons for being here. I thought you wanted in on the hunt, that you might even be ready to claim Kolodenko's business, ensuring that we both continue to make money. Instead, you bring me a woman. You bring Ruth."

"And... and she brings you something, Wheeler, doesn't she. She brings you prey. The most remarkable prey you've ever hunted."

"Why does she bring me this prey?"

"She brings it so that you can kill it."

"Why does she want it dead?"

Procter looked at him. "Look, Wheeler, I don't care if you kill that girl, of course I don't. But please don't be angry with me, with us. We can give you a remarkable animal to hunt.

And we have also – I have also – revealed that you have a spy in your midst."

"You may have. But I'm still pissed. I'm pissed that I didn't know the truth. I don't like not knowing the truth. And I want to show you how angry I am, how ruthless I can be."

"I know how ruthless you can be, Wheeler; I've been downstairs to your trophy room, if you recall."

"Yeah, but I want to show you. So that you know."

Procter nodded. His heart raced, and he felt sick. The man was crazy. "Of course, my friend, of course, you want to show me. Go ahead. Show me."

Burns narrowed his eyes. "Why does Ruth want this Greenacre girl dead?"

Procter took a deep breath. "Wheeler, when your Russian dies tomorrow, you'll see exactly why Ruth wants this girl dead."

He aimed the gun at Procter. "Why, Lawrence."

Procter nearly wet himself. He retreated, tried to speak. He babbled, then found his voice: "She... she... wants to be the only one, Wheeler – put the gun down, my friend, put it – Ruth, Ruth wants to be the alpha female – Wheeler, please, put – "

Burns shot the girl in the head.

FIND MORE EXTRAS AT WWW.SNOWBOOKS.COM

ABOUT THE AUTHOR.

Thomas Emson is the pen-name of a writer whose first novel Maneater was published in April 2008. His second, Skarlet, the first part of The Vampire Trinity, followed in 2009. He is contracted to write eight books for Snowbooks over the next four years.

He is also an award-winning playwright and used to be a singer-songwriter. He is a member of the Horror Writers Association and the Society of Authors. Welsh-born, he now lives in Kent with his wife. Visit his website at thomasemson. net or read his blog at thomasemson.com.

ACKNOWLEDGMENTS.

Thank you to Emma Barnes and Anna Torborg at Snowbooks. Wonderful people at a wonderful publisher. Thanks to Emma Yates, Aeron Haworth, Dr Lifon Edwards, Professor Stephen Hutchings. Thanks to everyone who has bought, borrowed, and read my novels. Thank you to Marnie, my spectacular and supportive wife.